To Ma

ASHES ON FALLEN SNOW

by Annie Ireson

Best Wishes

Annie Ireson

www.fast-print.net/store.php

ASHES ON FALLEN SNOW
Copyright © Annie Ireson 2017

A catalogue record for this book is available from the British Library

ISBN 978-178456-451-3

First published 2017 by
FASTPRINT PUBLISHING
Peterborough, England.

Other books by Annie Ireson

THE WHITE CUCKOO

SUNLIGHT ON BROKEN GLASS
(Jeffson Family Trilogy Book 1)

MELODY OF RAINDROPS
(Jeffson Family Trilogy Book 2)

For Barbara Harris
(1933-2016)

ACKNOWLEDGEMENTS

This final book in the Jeffson Family Trilogy has, without any doubt, been the hardest for me to write. It hasn't been easy for the family's descendants, either, even though the majority of the characters are fictitious.

Although I would like, once again, to point out that *Ashes on Fallen Snow* is a work of fiction, the characters' emotions are very real and have come straight from the heart of the family's storytellers. I would like to thank everyone for their support since this trilogy was conceived way back in 2002, and most of all my readers for their patience and forbearance because I have written and re-written this last part of the story so many times.

This book contains additional material in the form of an Epilogue, which, although it tells the story of the writing of the trilogy, is not part of the novel and therefore an optional part of the book.

I am indebted to my four main readers: Lorraine Hogg, Heather Jackson, Amy Nimmo and David Pope who have, once again, done a fantastic job. Special thanks also go to Andy Sipple, who for the last fourteen years has answered lots of difficult philosophical and theological questions for me (as well as some silly ones), and my friend Pam Warren who came up with the book's title. Thanks also go to Mirren Hogg, for being the very professional-looking model for the book cover, and Jamie Rae of RedScar for the cover design.

I'd also like to say a big thank you to Kevin Crick and his wife, Chris, who have always been very supportive throughout the long process of getting this story written and published, along with the late Barbara Harris, who sadly passed away in November 2016.

Finally, special thanks go to my immediate family – my husband, Rob, my children and in-law children (Emily, Garry, Nicky, Lee, Kelly and Christie) and my five - soon to be seven – grandchildren. Despite their constant teasing about my many eccentricities, they are brilliantly supportive and I love them all very much.

AUGURIES OF INNOCENCE

To see a World in a Grain of Sand
And a Heaven in a Wild Flower,
Hold Infinity in the palm of your hand
And Eternity in an hour.

William Blake (1757-1827

Chapter One

Sunday, 23rd December 1962

'Hello, George.'

The woman swayed over the threshold, stiletto heels clicking delicately on the polished mosaic floor. An aura of arrogance surrounded her as she tucked a stray strand of heavily lacquered, blonde hair behind her ear and stepped to one side to allow two nervous children to squeeze past her.

George Foster's jaw dropped in shock. He pulled the pipe from his mouth and squinted at the uninvited visitors, taking in the features of the woman's once beautiful face, sharpened and chiselled by the passing of the years into a self-protective mask. Tiny, vertical lines bled from her red lips, unconcealed despite heavy make-up. A sharp scent of perfume wafted through the air as she shrugged off a beige cashmere coat with a real fur collar that looked expensive.

Her cold hand, bony and as veined as fissured marble, brushed against his when he took her coat. Despite her immaculately manicured fingernails, the papery skin on her fingers was stained with nicotine.

George turned to hang the coat on a hook on the wall, questions crumbling on his lips before they could be asked. His voice was unsteady as he finally spoke to the unexpected visitors. He ran a shaky hand over his bald head.

'Well, this is a bit of a turn up, Violet. You might have let us know you were coming. No one's clapped eyes on you since the end of the war.'

He glanced towards the closed living room door, where

seasonal jollity and high spirits were being played out as eloquently as the ominous opening bars of an old, silent film.

'Are you my father?' one of the children whispered, her eyes wide with a reverence that was almost deifying.

George hesitated, reluctant to let the visitors into his welcoming, happy home – a house filled with the clean smell of crisp, white washing and the aroma of lavender and beeswax polish. It was a place where the teapot was always freshly brewed and the cake tin full of delicious, home-made cakes. He wasn't sure he wanted to welcome this woman into his home, especially at Christmas time. Her jagged perfume and heavy make-up would cleave through the wholesome stratosphere as surely as a fiery meteorite. She would be bound to ruin everyone's Christmas – churning up the past into a steaming pile of bad feelings.

George shuddered. He tried to force a sympathetic smile at the boy as he turned around. 'Whatever gave you that idea? I'm sorry, lass, but I haven't a clue who your father is.'

He turned to question the woman, running a nervy hand over his shiny, bald head, brushing back non-existent hair. 'I take it these are your children?'

Violet peered into the hall mirror and patted her hairdo into place with both hands. 'They most certainly are,' she replied without looking at George's reflection.

George narrowed his eyes and frowned. 'Well, we've obviously got a lot of catching up to do. We didn't even know whether you were alive or dead, let alone that you had some children. Where the heck have you been for the last eighteen years?'

The girl who looked to be in her mid-teens, placed a hand on her brother's shoulder and turned to her mother.

'So why have you dragged us all this way, just two days before Christmas if our father's not even here? You've forced me to walk out of my job on a flimsy promise and it's obvious no one's expecting us. The least you could have done was let this gentleman know we were coming.'

Regaining his composure and good manners, George noticed the girl was carrying a small cardboard suitcase. He held out his hand to take it from her. It was surprisingly weighty.

'I'm pleased to meet you both. I'm sorry, but I don't know your names. I'm George. George Foster.'

'I'm Lydia,' the girl replied, shaking George's free hand, 'and this is my brother, Tim.'

'Timothy,' Violet corrected.

'You'd better all come through,' George said, trying his best to be jovial, despite the awful sense of foreboding that was thumping its way through his temples. 'It's lovely to see you after all this time, Violet, but I wish you had let us know you were planning to visit. And it wouldn't have hurt you to write once in a while, just to let us know you were all right.'

George opened the door from the hallway to the living room, taking in the fine, delicate features of the boy's face and his mop of red hair. There was an aura of mild neglect about both Violet's children. Although the boy's clothes were clean, they were shabby, and the sleeves on his navy blue anorak were too short to cover the unravelling sleeves of his grey woollen jumper and his thin wrists. His faded trousers skimmed the tops of his ankles, making the new, shiny black shoes on his feet look far too big for him.

In contrast, Violet was smartly dressed, her brocade skirt and baby blue twinset complementing her fair hair, which was piled high on her head. She patted the string of pearls around her neck. 'Take your coats off, then,' she said in an unnaturally high-pitched voice as she pushed past them into the living room.

She stopped on the threshold, puzzled, unexpectedly finding herself being surveyed from head to foot by a room crammed full of children, all staring at her with curiosity. A white-whiskered elderly man leaned unsteadily on his walking stick beside an impressive Christmas tree, sparkling all the colours of the rainbow in the light from a crackling coal fire. Christmas cards strung along the wall and tinsel around photo frames fluttered as Violet pushed the door open wider. Above the hearth, a mirror decorated with holly, fat red berries, and a few sprigs of mistletoe framed her reflection.

Tom Jeffson squinted, and then lifted his reading glasses over spidery, white eyebrows, unconvinced of the identity of the woman under her enormous beehive hairdo.

'Is that you, our Violet?' he said, his voice croaky and unsure.

Violet stood still, twisting the pearl necklace around her forefinger. Behind her, George called out his to wife and mother-in-law, who were in the kitchen.

'Rose, Liz. You'll never guess who's here.'

A bent, elderly lady shuffled into the living room from the kitchen, using two walking sticks. Taken by surprise, she was unable to conceal her deep-rooted bitterness.

'Hello, Auntie Liz. It's lovely to see you,' Violet said, stepping into the room and holding out her arms in a theatrical pose.

Liz nodded a curt acknowledgement.

George's wife, Rose, appeared in the doorway behind her mother wiping her hands on a tea towel, a big, friendly smile beaming under shiny, apple cheeks.

'Violet! Oh my word, is it really you? What a lovely surprise.'

Feigning embarrassment, Violet drew the back of her hand delicately over her brow, her palm hanging in front of her face like a wilting leaf. 'I'm so sorry, I didn't realise you'd have a houseful. With everything that's happened to me over the past few days I forgot it was so close to Christmas.'

She shot a look of false humility at the assembled children. 'Are you having a party? I'm sorry to turn up out of the blue in the middle of your games and spoil everything.' She turned to address Tom. 'It's just that I have nowhere to go and I don't have any other family, do I?'

Lydia squeezed past her mother with an audible gasp of astonishment.

'What? Family? You told us we don't have a family. And where's our father? You said he would be here.'

Violet's lips narrowed and she frowned at her daughter. 'Just shut up, Lydia, and give me a chance to –'

'But where is he?' Lydia interrupted, her voice high and anxious. 'You said we were coming here to stay with him for Christmas. Now it's obvious no one even knows him. What's going on, Mother? If these people are our relatives, we have a right to know.'

Violet looked down at the floor. 'It was obviously a mistake to come here,' she muttered. 'Perhaps I should just go.'

Tom Jeffson shuffled forwards and grabbed her arm with a knobbly, arthritic hand. 'No, don't go, Vi ... please? Are these two lovely children really yours?'

Violet gave a forced, shrill laugh. 'Yes, they are – and I must apologise for my daughter's rudeness just now.'

'How old are they?'

Lydia slid her arm protectively around her brother's shoulders, glaring at her mother through narrowed eyes. She answered quickly before her mother could reply. 'I'm fifteen and my brother is eleven.'

Violet swept her hand in the general direction of her children without looking at them. 'Their father buggered off years ago, the bastard. I've worked my fingers to the bone to feed and clothe them. We've just been evicted from our flat in London, so we've got nowhere else to go. And so I thought –'

Tom put up his hand to silence her. 'I'd be grateful if you would moderate your language. This is my house and there are children present. We won't turn you out if you've nowhere else to go, but it's not on, Violet. Just not on. Your children are almost grown-up and have never known us. Had we known you were in trouble, we could have helped you.'

Violet leaned forwards so her face was just inches from Tom's. Defiant and angry, she interrupted him. 'Well, do you blame me for not telling you about my kids? You stole my first baby away from me. So I wasn't about to let you know I had two others, was I?'

Lydia grimaced at her mother's outburst, unable to take in everything she was hearing. If these people really were relatives, it was crucial they made a good first impression and she made them realise that she and her brother were nothing like their embarrassing mother. After all, if they were about to thrust themselves upon people they didn't know, who quite probably didn't want them in their house at any time of the year, let alone at Christmas, they would need to show them they were not likely to cause any trouble.

She pulled down her faded cotton dress in an effort to conceal her knees, which were scarlet red with cold. It was a dress more appropriate for a summer's day rather than a chilly, late-December afternoon, but she hadn't been able to find anything else to wear that morning when her mother, in the midst of a frenzy of chain-smoking, desperate head clutching and frequent outbursts of expletives, had announced there was nothing for it but to stay with their father for Christmas.

At first her heart had soared at the thought she was about to see her father again. He had disappeared without a trace when she was eight years-old and there wasn't a day went by that she didn't think of him and wonder what had happened to make him go away and never come back.

Her dark hair flopped over the frames of her black-framed National Health glasses and she pushed it back. The word *family* echoed and swirled around inside her head and made her heart beat with unexpected excitement. Her mother had just said she had once given birth to another baby – stolen away from her by the old man. What did that mean? Could they have an older brother or sister they had never known about? Were they just about to meet him or her, too, as well as their father?

A small boy wriggled out of an armchair, where he was wedged beside a little girl of about six years-old. Remembering his manners, he grabbed her hand and pulled his cousin out of the chair and said politely to Violet: 'would you like to sit down?'

Violet ignored the boy, and glared in defiance at Tom.

6

'I've put my name down for a Council house here, in Kettering. So you'll probably be seeing a lot more of us in future.'

She sniffed and her face broke out into a decadent, thin-lipped smile. She stretched out a slender leg and pulled her skirt up to her thigh. 'I flashed these at the doddery old git down at the Council offices. Hopefully he'll put us at the top of the list.'

Lydia hung her head, embarrassed beyond words. It was a complete lie – the decision to come here had been made hastily. They had only arrived on the train from London an hour or so ago and her mother had made them walk straight to this house, telling them that this was where their father lived. She hadn't even mentioned moving to this town permanently. Her heart thumped. Something bad was going on. Something she was powerless to prevent, but she had no idea what it could be.

A small girl stepped over a tangle of arms and legs towards Tim, who had retreated behind his sister's back, acutely shy and nervous. Lydia could tell she felt sorry for him as she pointed out all the children in the room, whispering their names to him. The contrast between the shabby clothes Tim was wearing and the smart tartan dress and hand-knitted cardigan worn by the girl was so sharp it made her scalp prickle with embarrassment.

Having introduced all the children, the girl threw a respectful glance towards the white-haired man. 'That's Gramp. He's very old.' She then pointed towards the bent old lady with the walking sticks. 'That's Grandma Jeffson.'

When no one moved or spoke, the girl pulled herself up tall with pride and then threw her arms around George's waist. 'And this is *my* grandad and that's *my* grandma over there.' She pointed at Rose.

Tom Jeffson shuffled over to a cupboard in the corner of the room and pulled out an old tea tin. He extracted some coins and then took a pocket watch from his waistcoat pocket and flicked it open.

'Now,' he said. 'How about all you youngsters go off to

the outdoor beer 'ouse and fetch some bottles o' pop and some crisps to take home with you while we have a little chat with Lydia and Tim's mum.'

'Yeaaahhh,' yelled the children, jumping up in excitement.

The girl grabbed Tim's hand in a friendly gesture. 'Come on. You can come as well. It's not far, I'll show you the way.'

After pulling on their coats, six children tumbled out of the front door, one of the older girls dragging Tim by the hand, each of them clutching some money from the tin. Uncertain as to whether she would be classified as a grown-up or a child, Lydia held back.

Tom extracted a half-crown from the tin and pressed it into her palm, folding her fingers around the coin as he patted her hand with gnarled fingertips.

'You go with them, lass,' he said with kindness in his eyes. 'Treat yerself to some nice chocolates or summat – and you can keep the change.'

'Thank you,' Lydia said, relieved to have an excuse to escape the awkward atmosphere and stunned to have received a half-crown all to herself.

'I can't believe she's just turned up after all these years,' Liz said, shaking her head at the closed kitchen door. 'Those poor children – they look perished – and their clothes ...'

Rose banged the kettle onto the stove and lit the gas with a match. 'She's got a cheek. What's she come back for? She's bound to want money.' She blew out the match and leaned back onto the kitchen table folding her arms over her ample chest. 'But I can't see how we can turn them all out onto the streets at Christmas. Not only that, the weather forecast is –'

'Sssh,' Liz hissed, cupping her hand behind her ear. 'Let's listen!'

The two women bent their heads towards the closed door.

In the living room, Tom and Violet squared up to each

other.

'You nearly sent me mad with worry,' Tom said in a loud whisper. 'You could have at least let me know you were all right instead of sending my unopened letters back marked *"not known at this address"*, or *"return to sender."* '

'Oh, come off it Uncle Tom! Do you blame me?' Violet gave a cold sneer and pushed out her chest, her hands on her hips. 'Since when did *you* ever think of anyone else?'

Tom bowed his head as the scathing remark hit him as painfully as if it had rubbed on an exposed nerve.

'Almost twenty years' worth of water has gone under the bridge since then,' Tom said calmly. 'I'm an old man now. I told you how sorry I was about your little Oliver, and I'm still sorry for what I did to this day.'

Violet flashed an angry, accusatory look at Tom. 'All you're bothered about is controlling people to get what you want. At least I've always been honest, Uncle Tom, and admit that I don't care about anyone else but myself.'

'Not even your own children?'

Violet looked at her watch and then picked up her bag. Tom, having worked all his life in the boot and shoe trade, noticed that it was made of expensive leather, despite Violet's earlier tale of a poverty stricken existence. When she didn't answer, Tom grabbed her arm and forced her to look at him.

'I know you were only young when you had little Oliver, but it was you who signed the adoption papers and gave him away to your mother.'

'Yes, but I wanted him back, Uncle Tom. And you wouldn't let me have him.'

'You buggered off to Scotland ...'

'I was coming back to fetch him,' Violet interrupted indignantly. 'My mother shouldn't have been allowed to look after him. She'd gone completely mad by then – you said so yourself in the letter you sent.'

Tom gulped and slumped back down into his armchair, rubbing his forehead as the memory of the most horrific event of his life came back to haunt him. He momentarily shut his eyes.

'If I could turn back the clock and do things differently, Violet, believe me I would. I loved that little lad.'

Violet sighed. She hadn't come back to her home town to rake over the dying embers of the past and she certainly hadn't meant to argue with Uncle Tom, who she was surprised was still alive after all these years. She had returned for a purpose – a carefully laid plan – and she needed to stick to it and not become distracted. She stared at the ceiling, gathering her thoughts. More importantly, she couldn't allow herself to be drawn back into her family.

'I have to go out for a while Uncle Tom. To see about getting some lodgings over Christmas.'

Tom's eyebrows twitched with alarm. 'What about your children? They'll be back soon. They're only along the outdoor beer house. You should wait until they get back.'

'I'll only be an hour at the most, and I need to go before it gets dark.' Violet opened the door into the hallway and grabbed her coat without looking back. 'I know where I'll get a room to rent for a week or so until I can sort myself out.'

'Where? For goodness sake, Violet. It's Sunday today and it's Christmas Eve tomorrow. I should think even the hotels in town are full. We'll just have to make do over Christmas now you're here. We've got a spare room. We'll manage. You know you're welcome to stay here.'

Violet didn't answer. She turned and left the room, unable to look at Tom.

'Violet. Please come back – you can all stay here – there's no need to find lodgings.'

Chapter Two

The finality of the resounding clunk of the front door drew a thick, black line under her past.

Violet hesitated on the pavement for a moment as she pulled on her coat and then leaned back on the wall of the house, resting her head on the cold red bricks, staring at the sky. She supposed she should feel guilty about abandoning her children, but all she could feel was a permanent numbness. She felt sick. What sort of mother would allow a promise of an exciting new start in life to seduce her sense of self-preservation until it overwhelmed any spark of maternal instinct?

Surely no-one would blame her for leaving Lydia and Timothy with her family in Kettering if they knew she was such a bad mother? After all, they were almost grown-up now and wouldn't be any trouble. She closed her eyes. Her new life enticed her towards it: clean, white, billowing in a cloudless, blue sky, the dirt of her old life having been washed away by unexpected good fortune.

She glanced along the street towards her childhood home. An eerie sense of déjà vu started somewhere in the pit of her stomach and rose in a bubble of bitterness into her throat as she remembered the first time she had abandoned a child. It seemed almost an entire lifetime ago since, persuaded by Uncle Tom, she had handed over her unwanted baby son to her deranged mother.

She stemmed a solitary tear with a manicured forefinger as she walked briskly away, but she couldn't help slowing and then stopping opposite her old home, allowing herself a fleeting moment of regret for her troubled upbringing and the terrible things she had endured in the house as a child.

She swallowed hard, trying to dissolve the lump that had formed in her throat. She was a bad, bad woman, she thought. Three children – her own flesh and blood – each and every one of them given away: abandoned and uncared for like the three symbolic pots of unwatered, dead plants that sat forlornly under the bay window of her former home.

She had been shocked when she had come face-to-face with Uncle Tom after years of self-enforced absence. The overbearing, manipulative man she remembered had changed beyond recognition. Of course, it was to be expected that he'd be very old by now but something else about him had changed. He had developed a warmth – a compassion and empathy which was something that had been completely missing when she had ran away from her family at the end of the war to start her new life in London.

Still, she thought, he always was a sucker for children, inventing her mother's farcical, contrived pregnancy and birth just so that he could get his hands on her baby. Well – let him have two more, she thought to herself. Two more secret grandchildren to feather his nest with adoration.

'I was never meant to be a mother,' she said out loud in a desperate clutch at justification for what she was about to do. She reached inside her handbag and plucked out a lacy handkerchief. She dabbed at the tears welling in her eyes, careful not to disturb the heavy black mascara on her eyelashes. After tucking the handkerchief back into her bag, she extracted a pack of cigarettes and lit one with a shaky hand. 'Another thing,' she muttered. 'I'm no match for Uncle Tom. He'll never forgive me this time.'

She took a deep breath to compose herself, turned and set off at a determined pace, her stiletto heels echoing around the deserted street. She glanced at the expensive watch on her wrist as she pushed her handbag into the crook of her arm, her cashmere coat swinging around her. Everything was going to plan. She had plenty of time. The cold air hit her in the face as she rounded a corner, making her nose prickle and her eyes water. Snow was on the way, according to the news, and it certainly seemed cold enough for it.

Her stomach churned with hunger as she tossed the half-smoked cigarette into the gutter, suddenly remembering that neither she nor her children had eaten anything that day.

As she walked along she fumbled in her handbag for her make-up compact and lipstick, suddenly desperate to fortify the mask that shielded her from the world. It had been almost too easy to walk away, but now the enormity of the abandonment of her children tugged at her conscience and she felt a brief aftershock of shame.

She stopped for a while to reapply make-up. Satisfied with the result, she tucked the compact mirror and lipstick back into her bag. As an afterthought she extracted another cigarette and lit it with a gold lighter, turning her back on the wind.

She glanced back down the road, inhaling deeply. Holding her breath in surprise, she saw that the children had rounded a corner on their way back to Uncle Tom's house. Her son was hanging back from the rest of the crowd, his hair glinting in the watery sunlight in a beacon of burnt orange. Lydia walked beside him, her thin coat blowing open, head down against the wind, bare knees bright red with cold.

Looking around for an escape, she noticed the entrance to an alleyway right beside her. She stepped into the darkening passageway, relieved to have found a place to hide from her children. Tim needed new trousers. How on earth had she failed to see how much he had grown recently? Ashamed, she closed her eyes briefly – her children looked miserable and poverty-stricken in their inadequate, shoddy clothes, unlike the other children who were well-fed, well-clothed and happy. She shook her head. She'd had enough money to buy them new clothes, so why had she completely failed to notice they needed them until now? Could it be that she had always believed herself to be a bad mother, so she hadn't even bothered to prove herself wrong?

Tomorrow, Christmas Eve, would be her fortieth birthday, which was far too old to make amends for being such a terrible mother to her children. She took a deep breath as the pull of a new, clean life shredded her apart from any remaining maternal instinct. Tomorrow, she would be middle-aged, with nothing to show for her pathetic life so far if she didn't grasp the golden opportunity before her. She just had to make things happen – to find the bedrock on which to build the foundations of her future – a future that wouldn't include her children because they were better off without her.

The sound of voices grew louder as the group of children approached the alleyway. She held her breath and closed her eyes, pressing herself into the cold bricks, willing Lydia and Tim to pass by without seeing her. When the gabble of voices began to fade, she breathed out in relief. She edged her way back to the street and tentatively peeped out of the alleyway entrance to make sure the coast was clear.

Startled, her hand flew up to her mouth. Just a few feet away, Tim had stopped, having sensed that someone was hiding in the alleyway as he passed by. He was staring straight at her, his huge blue eyes unblinking, tugging on heartstrings she'd never known she even possessed. The other children, realising their new playmate had been left behind, stopped chattering and turned around too.

'Mum?' Tim wailed, the rising anxiety in his thin voice unmistakable, despite the eerie whistling of cold wind through draughty eaves.

Lydia's eyes locked with her mother's in a glare of disdain. She stepped forwards to stand behind her brother and placed her hands on his shoulders, pulling him into her.

Violet watched, silent, as a hasty explanation dried up and shrivelled in her throat. She took another drag on the cigarette in her hand and blew out the smoke high into the air through pursed lips as if it was the most normal thing in the world to have been hiding in dingy alleyway. A gust of wind blew across Lydia's face and she raised her hand to brush a strand of long, dark brown hair out of her eyes. With a painful pang of regret, Violet realised that, at fifteen, Lydia was the only mother Timothy had ever known, and probably always would be.

She extended her hand towards her son, but Lydia pulled him back, her voice slicing loud and clear through the wind.

'Where are you going, Mum? Why were you hiding from us?'

Violet's hand trembled as she put the cigarette to her lips. Her voice quivered as she lied. 'I'm just going out to find us somewhere to stay.'

'How long will you be?'

Violet looked at her watch. 'Not long. I'll be back soon.'

Lydia sneered in disbelief. 'You're lying. You're going to clear off somewhere posh for Christmas and leave us here on our own, aren't you?'

Violet put her head down, unable to look her daughter in the eye. 'Of course not. I'll be back in a little while.'

A solitary tear slid over Tim's cheek.

Lydia hugged him closer to her, protecting him. 'I think you were planning all along to leave us here with people we don't know without even saying goodbye. Just so *you* can have a nice Christmas without having to be bothered about us. You really couldn't sink any lower than this, could you, Mother?'

'I'm sorry,' Violet said as she turned away from her daughter's accusing stare. 'I haven't any other choice.'

'Your mother's just popped out to find you somewhere to stay,' Rose said cheerfully as Lydia and Tim shrugged off their coats. 'She'll be back soon.'

Lydia blinked back tears of humiliation. Their mother had been lurking in an alleyway, hiding from them and all the other children had seen and heard what she had said. No one had spoken as they returned, subdued, after the confrontation. The embarrassment she felt over her mother's behaviour was beyond description.

The nice lady, Rose, smiled at her, her eyes oozing kindness. Lydia tried to smile back, but instead her mouth quivered and her eyes prickled with tears of humiliation. She hoped Rose hadn't noticed. She supposed she should say something, but knew her voice would betray her worst fears.

Tim sat down on the bottom step of the stairs, tears streaking his cheeks.

'What on earth's the matter?' Rose asked him.

'She's not going to come back for us,' he wailed. 'She's going away. We saw her.'

'Oh no, you've got it wrong, m'duck. She's only gone out for a little while. She'll be back before you know it.'

Lydia's shoulders dropped in despair. 'It's been a really long day,' she said to Rose. 'And we don't know anyone here. We were supposed to be staying with our father, but I don't know where he lives.'

George organised a game of bingo for the children, but Lydia couldn't concentrate on joining in, instead opting to call out the numbers.

The next hour passed interminably slowly, until darkness fell over Kettering in the purple and orange slabs of an angry sky. Eventually, the rest of the children were collected by their respective parents to urgent, hushed explanations in the kitchen about the events of that afternoon and the presence of two children no one in the family had known existed. When everyone had gone home, Lydia and Tim sat side by side on the sofa, frightened and worried.

'Have you any idea where your mother is planning to stay?' Rose asked. 'Did she mention an address where your father was living?'

Although she was more scared and worried than she had ever been before in her life, Lydia spoke with a clear, polite voice. 'No. We've never been here before and don't know this town. We didn't know our father lived here until yesterday and Mum brought us to this house.'

Aghast, Rose's usually cheerful face fell.

'Did you bring anything with you?'

'Not really – just the brown suitcase in the hallway with a change of clothes,' Lydia replied. 'And I brought our library books so we had something to read on the train, and there's some Christmas presents, too.'

'You've *really* been evicted?'

'I think so. We had to hide last week when the rent man came, and then there was a letter pushed through the door which Mum said was an eviction notice. She said we had to be out by Christmas.'

'And it's going to snow,' Tim said to Rose with a hint of drama in his voice. 'So we might be stranded here.'

He brushed the tears from his face with the back of his hand and then stretched out a foot to show Rose his shoes. 'When we heard on the weather forecast there was going to be snow at Christmas, Lydia bought me these new shoes because my old ones had holes in them.'

Lydia hugged Tim to her. 'I try my best to look after him,' she explained. 'Because if I don't, no one else would. I've got a job in Woolworths ...'

Her words ran out as she realised the enormity of their predicament. What if their mother never came back? Would they have to go to live in a children's home? Did their father really live in Kettering, or was it just another lie made up by their mother? Overwhelmed and unable to keep up her confident, sensible image any longer she buried her face in her hands.

Rose patted her shoulder in comfort. 'Don't worry, m'duck,' she said. 'I can't believe that your mother would just go off and leave you both here for Christmas. After all, you don't even know us.'

Rose whispered to George and gestured with her head for him to join her in the hallway. Dragging him by the arm, she hurried into the front room to use the heavy, black phone that had only been installed a few weeks ago. She dialled carefully from memory and tried to remember not to shout into the receiver.

'Margaret – is that you?'

'Yes, Mum. It's me. Is she back yet?'

'No, she's still missing. And the boy said he thought she was going away and wouldn't come back for them.'

'No! What, not ever? Or just until after Christmas?'

'I don't know,' Rose wailed into the receiver. 'Those poor children – they've barely got the clothes they're standing up in. I don't know what we are going to do if she doesn't come back.'

Tom pushed opened the door to the front room with his walking stick.

'Rose? You'd better come off that contraption. Young Lydia has something to tell us about Violet.'

Rose quickly rang off, promising to telephone Margaret to bring her up to date on the emerging events later in the evening. She joined George, Liz and Tom in the living room, perching on the arm of the two seater sofa with the children. Lydia clasped her hands together, biting her lip.

'I should try to explain to you all about Mum – '

She paused to wipe her eyes with Tom's handkerchief and then took a deep breath.

'My first memory is of being hungry. I think I was about three years-old. This particular day, a man came and I can remember asking for a biscuit. Mum put me into my bedroom and told me that if I was quiet, and didn't cry, she would go out to the shops and buy some food later. I was so hungry I sneaked downstairs into the kitchen and climbed up onto a chair to look for something to eat, but there was nothing.'

George raised his eyebrows at Rose. 'Did your father live with you?'

'No, not then. We lived in a house with some other women. It was about a year later when we moved to Croydon with the man Mum told me was my father. Things became a lot better then and I remember being quite happy. Tim was born and we just seemed like a normal family until one day, when I was about eight and Tim was four, two strange men arrived at our house. We were sent upstairs out of the way. Then there was an argument and I saw Dad go out somewhere with the men in their car.

'We never saw him again, although Mum told us that she had met up with him and pleaded with him to come back, but he wouldn't. She said he didn't want to see us, which upset me. I couldn't understand it because we hadn't done anything wrong. After a few weeks, Mum began drinking and crying a lot. That was when things turned really bad. The house was in a right old state. I was only eight years-old, but I tried my best to keep things clean and tidy up for us. Sometimes, I even had to take money out of Mum's purse to buy food for us all. Looking back, I think she probably had a nervous breakdown after Dad left.

'When I was eleven, Mum started bringing lots of different men back to the house. I was frightened, but I knew I had to look after my little brother.'

Tim leaned into his sister and grabbed her arm as Lydia continued.

'I just did it. I *had* to. I began to feel terrified by the men Mum brought back. I kept us both well out of their sight when they were in the house and luckily there was a lock on our bedroom door, so I used to lock us in when there were men in the house. I continually asked when we could see our father again, but Mum always said he had gone up north with his new family. All she was bothered about was the men she brought back, and I was so scared of ... well, you know. I was scared that –'

Lydia grimaced and shot a glance at Liz and Rose who nodded in shocked understanding.

'It was horrible. All the time I tried to talk to Mum and tell her how I felt. One day when I was nearly thirteen, one of the men grabbed at me. I wriggled away and ran upstairs and locked myself in our bedroom just in time. After that happened, Mum was shocked, and stopped inviting men back to the house. Eventually, we moved out of the house in Croydon into the centre of London, but she could only afford a horrible run-down bedsit. She said that because she would be working long hours to pay the rent, I needed to help out by keeping our room clean and tidy and look after Tim.

'Sometimes she would be gone for days on end. If anyone asked where our mother was, I just said she worked nights in a factory and was in another room, asleep in the daytime. Mum did always leave money for us when she came home, but we never knew how long it would have to last and sometimes it ran out before she came back. I knew we needed to keep up with our school work, so I forged Mum's signature on the application forms and joined us both in the local library so we could get ahead at school.'

She turned to look at her brother, pride shining bright in her eyes. 'Tim's very clever and there's no way I'm going to allow him to grow up in a slum. I want to build a good future for us both, but especially for Tim.'

'Do you have any friends?' George asked. 'Or is there a neighbour or anyone else who looks out for you?'

'We don't have friends,' Lydia replied with a sad shake of her head. 'No one wants to know us because ... because ... well ... because I think people know what mum *really* does when she goes out to work. Before I started work in the summer, we used to spend nearly all morning at the library on Saturdays and the rest of the week just reading. We don't often go out anywhere because other kids poke fun at us.

'I always make sure Tim gets to school on time. I wash and iron his uniform twice a week, but we can't risk spending money on new clothes. When we were younger, the worst thing by far, though, was our plastic shoes. I couldn't afford to buy us proper shoes, because we never knew when she would come home to leave us some more money.'

Tom threw up his hands in horror and then leaned forwards, holding them out to show Lydia, palms upturned.

'Plastic shoes!' he shouted, his eyes blazing in anger. 'My whole working life I was a shoemaker, using these hands to craft the best quality shoes money could buy. I can't believe that children belonging to this family have been sent to school in cheap *plastic* shoes.'

'I make sure Tim always does his homework,' Lydia went on, feeling guilty about the shoes and taken aback by Tom's outburst. 'All the studying over the years must have paid off, because I passed my eleven-plus and so did Tim.'

Rose interrupted.

'You said *you* passed your eleven-plus, too. Did you go to a Grammar School in London? Did you manage to take any exams?'

'Yes. I went to the same school as Tim goes to. I took four 'O' levels a year early, last summer. The Head Teacher wrote to Mum a couple of months ago, saying that if money was a problem, he was sure I could apply for a scholarship and stay on for the fifth form, but Mum wouldn't hear of it. She said it was a waste of time girls staying on at school and I ought to concentrate on my new job in Woolworths and finding a decent husband to keep me.'

Rose tutted and shook her head in disdain whilst staring intently at Tom. She might have now been in her fifties, but she still resented being forced by Tom to leave school to work in a factory when she turned fourteen.

'I knew deep down I could never stay on at school,' Lydia went on. 'I had to get a job to try and earn enough money to look after us both. You see, it's *really* important to me that Tim gets a good education. He's so clever. I want him to have a successful life.'

Her face fell apart in panic. 'I can't lose my job now! I absolutely *have* to get back to London to sort things out. I really must be back at work the day after Boxing Day for the sales.'

Her brother gulped nervously. 'Lydia, I saw Mum talking to a man in the street last week. I crept up to them and hid behind a bush so they couldn't see me. She told the man she had made up her mind and that she was going to go off with him. I was really scared because when the man asked what would happen to us, she said not to worry because she had something in mind. At first, I thought we were going to be killed and our bodies dumped in the River Thames.'

Lydia grimaced and nudged her brother with her elbow, glancing up at Tom apologetically. 'Don't worry. He's been reading the papers again and he's got a vivid imagination,' she explained. 'I confronted her about it when she came back to the flat and asked her what was going on. She said we had to move out, because the bailiffs were coming to evict us. She told us that our father had said we could stay with him.'

Liz leaned forward in her chair and interrupted, directing her question at Tim. 'Do you *really* think your mother won't come back for you?'

Tim answered in almost a whisper. 'I heard her say to someone on the telephone at the railway station this morning that she doesn't want us messing up the rest of her life. Then she wouldn't answer Lydia when she was hiding in the alley this afternoon.'

Lydia squeezed his hand, close to tears herself. There was no point in trying to conceal anything. Deep down inside her, she knew their mother wouldn't come back for them.

'We ... we don't want to be any trouble,' Tim added.

Rose pulled Tim close to her comforting him as tears rolled down his face. George pulled a clean handkerchief from his trouser pocket and leaned forwards to give it to him.

'Here, lad, don't cry. We'll sort summat out. You're safe here.'

Lydia took her purse out of a handbag by her feet. She rootled around noisily and then emptied some change into her lap. 'I was wondering if you could you lend me some money, please, so that we can get back to London? We can try to get a train tomorrow. I don't think I have enough here. I promise I'll pay you back. Every single penny. We'll be just fine.'

George interrupted. 'No – don't be silly. You've got nowhere to go if you've been evicted from your flat. You can stay here until after Christmas if you have to. Your mother saying that she doesn't want you to mess up the rest of her life doesn't mean she's never coming back for you.'

'Oh, this is just ridiculous,' Tom said with a dismissive wave of his hand. 'Violet's not going to abandon you. Especially not at Christmas. But I'm buggered if I know what the devil she's playing at, clearing off like this. She'll walk in that door soon and wonder what all the fuss is about.'

Chapter Three

Shame and guilt weighed heavily on Sergio De Luca's shoulders as he prepared for his death. Soon, every man, woman and child in England would know what he had done and the dark underbelly of his star-studded life would be exposed on every news-stand in the country. National newspapers would bear an unflattering photograph of him and cleverly worded headlines proclaim his guilt to the nation. He closed his eyes and shuddered. The problem with being popular, successful and rich was that when you fell from grace, the descent to solid ground was so much further and the damage to your private life and livelihood a complete catastrophe, from which there was little chance of recovery.

He gazed out over the gravel pits – soon to become the place where his young and not-so-young fans would flock to lay flowers and cry hysterically in a synchronised choir of ghostly banshees, their wails drifting across the dank, still water. Just over twenty miles from his countryside mansion, the gravel pits had always been a place where he could slip the straight-jacket of celebrity from his shoulders, pull on a peaked cap and slide on a pair of sunglasses before throwing his fishing kit over his shoulders, and walk free, unrecognised and unremarkable. Just a regular type of bloke enjoying an ordinary few hours of relaxation.

He allowed himself a fleeting, wry smile – his fans would never recognise him now. With his dyed black wavy hair cut into a working man's short back and sides and his famous black moustache shaved off, he was just a local chap indulging in a spot of Sunday afternoon relaxation. The transformation had spectacularly aged him and exposed the greying hair around his temples, but he didn't mind. The unfamiliar maturity contributed to his disguise.

He pulled on a black donkey jacket over his casual clothes and gave a confident, Elvis-like shrug of his shoulders. He lit himself a final cigarette from the half-empty packet and placed it reverently on the dashboard of his car, along with his gold lighter inscribed with an elaborate, intertwined AS, which were the initials of his real name. Blowing the cigarette smoke high into the chilly air, he shut the door with a satisfying clunk and briefly leaned back on it, furtively glancing along the hedgerow and water's edge, making sure there were no stray dog walkers or anglers in the vicinity who might have been watching his actions with curiosity. Through narrowed eyes, he noticed an elderly lady with a small boy in the distance, poking around in the reeds with a fishing net on a stick. All was well; she was obviously unconcerned about the black car and its lone occupant. Content there was no one in the immediate vicinity, he began the walk back to the town, pulling up the collar of his jacket against the cold wind that whipped across the dark, rippling water, tinged red and yellow under a sun that was rapidly sinking into the horizon.

Everything, so far, was going to plan.

He'd met Violet Grey earlier in the year, when he'd been introduced to her by Stephen Ward, whose fashionable osteopathy clinic served well as a cover for less salubrious activities. Violet was different to the other women who supplied young girls to the rich and famous, such as he, as she was far more intelligent than the other madams who worked the London scene. Once he had inched his way under her bitter and cynical veneer, she was more than capable of holding an intelligent conversation on any topic under the sun, and he was fascinated by the other, lighter, side to her complex character. She operated out of a high class house in the heart of fashionable London, where models and show-girls rented expensively decorated and furnished rooms and discretion was absolutely guaranteed. The premises were frequented by well-known figures from the political spectrum, show business and even the House of Lords. As he was a well-known pop star, Sergio was soon invited into Stephen Ward's private home in Wimpole Mews, where, seduced by outrageous displays of extravagance and the secret lives of the socialites who frequented the premises, he had somehow found himself drawn into the murky depths of an emerging political scandal.

Having reached the far end of the secluded track, Sergio glanced back for the last time at his car, parked in a well-concealed spot by the side of the gravel pits in the distance. The elderly lady and the little boy had disappeared. No-one had even passed by him in the five minutes or so it had taken him to walk along the track. He remembered his polished black leather shoes, left conspicuously on the passenger seat, and felt a tiny tug of regret as he imagined his wife's innocent tears sliding down porcelain smooth cheeks as she explained to sympathetic police officers and said: *"yes, Sergio is a keen angler and often visits the gravel pits at Thrapston. He keeps a pair of wellington boots, a basket and fishing rod in the boot of his car."*

Then, a little while later, concealed in a small thicket of trees and bushes, they would discover his fishing basket, tin of maggots and rod placed carefully on its rod rests, the line snaking its way out into the depths of the gravel pits as far as the red-tipped float bobbing in the rippling, murky water. They would search for his body, rubber-clad police frogmen diving down endlessly but finding nothing, and local folk would line the fields in the distance as the emerging story of the mysterious disappearance of Sergio de Luca at the gravel pits in Thrapston shocked the nation.

The pits were notoriously dangerous. Deadly currents flowed through the deep cut channels and he'd done his homework before he'd picked his location, knowing that the bodies of people who had stumbled into the beckoning, deadly fingers of weeds that bordered the most dangerous part of the pits had never been found.

He'd left an empty bottle of whisky in the glove compartment of his car; fuelling the obvious conclusion that he had most likely fallen, inebriated, into the freezing cold water and drowned.

Sergio felt strangely light and airy as he approached allotments that bordered the town. As if his involvement with Member of Parliament, John Profumo, and Stephen Ward wasn't enough to ruin him when news of the emerging political outrage broke, his affair with the Bishop of Ashburton's youngest daughter, leaving her scandalously gravid with his child most certainly would. He couldn't even deny it, as there had been lots of witnesses to their affair.

She'd told him she was nineteen, conveniently changing her name so that he wouldn't suspect her true identity. Back in the summer, he had suspected that she may have added a year or so to her age to appear more sophisticated, but even so, he'd had no idea that she was really only fifteen. Had he not faked his own death, he'd surely be prosecuted for having an intimate relationship with a child, as well as his dirty fingers being yanked unceremoniously from the rapidly decomposing pie of a far bigger national scandal. Profumo's affair with one of Violet's *showgirls* and suspicions about the girl's subsequent liaisons with a Russian spy was something he knew was being investigated at the highest level. It was only a matter of time before the scandal broke, and if he wasn't already ruined before it hit the newspapers, he most certainly would be then.

Faking your own death wasn't an option when you were being held in custody. *"Disappeared, presumed dead"* was by far the most dignified exit from the ostentatious life of Sergio de Luca, the pop star adored by young girls and their mothers all over the nation.

Sergio paused at the top of the track that led through the allotments, tucked in his shirt, readjusted his trousers and tightened his belt. He shivered as he lit a cigarette – the weather was turning colder by the hour. He reached into his pocket for his penknife to cut a winter cabbage, just for show, because that way no-one would ever suspect that he wasn't really just a regular local chap. He would dispose of it in a litter bin before catching the last Sunday evening bus to Kettering. On arrival, he'd stroll down to the railway station, change into the smart suit he'd left in an overnight bag in a locker and join Violet in their hotel room at the Royal Hotel, just a short walk away. The passports were ready. The suitcases were packed. Money was deposited in several secret bank accounts. What could possibly go wrong?

He'd known Violet for only a few months, but he had confided in her, explaining how the Bishop's daughter had pursued him relentlessly, turning up at the stage door at concerts, hanging around him, watching his every move. Afterwards, he had been amazed at the lax parenting regime adopted by the Bishop and his wife. Surely they realised that sending their child to live in London to attend a finishing school of dubious repute was just asking for trouble when it involved such a headstrong, wayward girl? Violet was also fully aware of the drunken orgy that had followed at the country mansion of a friend, because she was there. Violet's colony of glamorous showgirls had clearly set out to seduce him, as they'd emerged, naked and synchronised from the steamy, heated swimming pool filled with successful and beautiful people – film stars, government ministers, Harley Street doctors and gentry.

He hadn't known the girl was the Bishop of Ashburton's daughter. How could he have done? He'd done nothing worse than the other party goers that night. They'd all had girls. The owner of the country mansion, a flamboyant, well-known host of a popular television show, had made sure there were enough for everyone.

A few weeks later the girl had contacted his manager, saying she needed to speak to him urgently. When, accompanied by a friend, she had tearfully told him she was pregnant and revealed that she was really only fifteen and her father was the Bishop of Ashburton, Sergio had fled to London, numb with shock. After a day of wandering around the streets in a daze, he had made an appointment with Violet, and turned up, dishevelled and unshaven. He'd paid her for sex with one of her girls, but somehow, five hours later, all he'd done was talked to Violet, pouring out his troubles, asking her advice on what he should do about the most awful fix he had now found himself in. He'd told her what he knew about Profumo, which had obviously worried her as she could be implicated in the emerging scandal, too.

He liked Violet. She was undoubtedly a hard woman, but he needed her resilience and strength right now. But the thing he needed the most was her dead husband's passport, especially since the dead husband was at the bottom of the North Sea, his body tied to a lump of concrete, leaving his national insurance number and social security benefits intact.

Richard Carl Smith. Occupation: Ground Worker. Date of Birth 11th August 1923 – only a few months different to his own date of birth. It was surely a heavenly sign. The real Richard Carl Smith had, Violet said, been murdered in cold blood in 1955 when he had become involved with some London gangsters in a high profile robbery. His body had been disposed of, with Violet being threatened and beaten into agreeing to keep her mouth shut, forever fearful that if she ever broke the pact with her husband's murderers, the lives of her children would be at risk.

Violet's turbulent past had prepared her well and she was a tough, astute woman. She had explained to him she always used her married name of Smith in her private life and had created another, professional, life as Violet Grey, which was her maiden name. The two personas were very different. In fact, very few people knew that the glamorous and elegant Madam, Violet Grey, even had another home in the form a shabby flat in a dingy street on the outskirts of the capital, where she became plain Mrs Violet Smith, her dyed blonde hair concealed under a tightly knotted headscarf, her expensive clothes hidden by a grubby gabardine mac, living on the edge of poverty, working the night shift in a fictitious factory to make ends meet and bring up her two children.

Sergio could hardly believe his good fortune. There must be hundreds, if not thousands, of Richard Smiths all over the country. It was going to be so easy to assume the identity of just one of them. Violet had shown him a photograph of her late husband, pictured leaning casually on the bonnet of a Ford Zephyr, a cigarette hanging from his lower lip, his shirt open down to his navel. They were not dissimilar in looks, either, which was a huge bonus.

He'd opened a bank account in the name of Richard Carl Smith, depositing just fifty pounds. Then, once the bank account was set up, he transferred a few hundred pounds into it and applied for a passport. It had all been easy – all he had to do was make an appointment at the doctor's surgery where Richard Carl Smith had been registered and ask the doctor for his counter-signature on the application form. After all, Richard Carl Smith had been a registered patient there for the last thirteen years. Sergio had merely sauntered into the surgery, dressed in a pair of grubby overalls, and passed himself off as a hard-working, healthy sort of chap who had rarely needed to visit the doctor.

That evening he had kissed her, properly, on the mouth, which had made her eyes sparkle, instantly melting away the hard shell-like, artificial mask she always wore. She had thrown back her head and giggled like a young girl. He had asked her what it was like to be kissed by a pop star. She had replied that it was very difficult to remember what it was like to be kissed by anyone, and anyway, he wasn't a pop star, was he? He was now just plain old Richard Carl Smith, her husband.

Violet wasn't a bad sort underneath: he was sure they could rub along together quite easily in Spain, where they could rent a villa while looking for somewhere to settle permanently and live out their lives on the proceeds of Richard Carl Smith's Spanish bank accounts, into which he had transferred a large chunk of a secret fortune he had squirreled away over the years to avoid paying tax. He had even ventured to suggest that Violet could introduce him to her children as their long-lost father, and he was more than ready to assume the role. It would strengthen their story, he had reasoned, especially if they went to Spain as a family. Neither of Violet's children would reliably remember what their real father had looked like as they had been so young when he had disappeared from their lives.

Violet had shaken her head and wouldn't be budged, though. *"No"*, she had said. *"Lydia is one of your fans and will surely recognise you even without your moustache and quiff. Anyway, my children are not part of my future. I will take them to Northamptonshire. I have family there who will take care of them."*

He had been more than a little shocked that Violet could give up her children so easily and was prepared to disappear from their lives without trace, especially as, in their eyes, their father had done the same thing to them. Some things about Violet just didn't add up. She had been almost tearful when she had told him about her daughter when she was growing up, and her decision to lead a double life to make sure Lydia never again came into contact with her clients. She had moved from a comfortable house in Croydon, she had told him, and rented a dingy bedsit in a run-down building on the outskirts of London where she could protect them. That wasn't the action of an uncaring, cold mother who cared nothing for her children.

Lost in his thoughts, and seduced by the sound of wind whispering through leaves on nearby trees, Sergio hadn't heard the rhythmic squeak of leather boots approaching him from behind.

'Excuse me, sir?'

Sergio turned around in surprise.

Standing behind him, clutching the shiny handlebars of a bicycle from which he had just alighted, was a policeman, keen to ask him some questions about the black Humber parked at the edge of the gravel pits.

Chapter Four

Violet's room at the Royal Hotel looked out over the town's market place. As the sky turned from a deep blue to rich hues of red, purple and gold, and the brisk wind northerly wind strengthened, creating a spectacular sunset, most Kettering folk who might have been milling around had gone home, hunkering down in front of warm coal fires, looking forward to the Christmas festivities.

The market place was now completely deserted; eerie in the strange, murky light of approaching darkness. Tomorrow, on Christmas Eve, it would be swarming with early morning shoppers, keen to buy their Christmas fruit and vegetables, their wicker shopping baskets laden with Brussels sprouts, carrots and celery, freshly pulled from sooty earth.

The strengthening wind whistled through the eaves of the hotel, adding to the sense of desolation. Violet leaned on the windowsill, suddenly overcome with loneliness. She'd had no time to prepare for Christmas. She'd bought no presents, no decorations and, despite the double celebration brought about by her birthday being on Christmas Eve, she could feel no joy. Even the exciting prospect of Christmas Day and Boxing Day spent in The Savoy Hotel in London before flying out to Spain on Thursday could not erase the strange feelings that were swirling around inside her stomach, causing her to feel sick with trepidation.

Agitated, she looked at her wristwatch. She had been waiting for Sergio for the last half an hour and he was late.

She pulled a chair up to the window and sat down to ease

her aching back, but the windowsill was too high for her to keep watch for the arrival of the Thrapston bus from her vantage point, and so she stood up again, massaging her aching temples with her forefingers, wishing she had brought some Aspirin tablets and a hot water bottle with her, because despite the heavy, old-fashioned radiator, the hotel room was so cold she could see her breath.

Soon, the street below the hotel gradually began to come alive as a string of Christmas lights lit up the road. Men, women and children dressed in their best clothes began to drift past and their laughter and excited voices permeated through the glass, making her feel even more alone. She craned her neck, pressing her cheek up to the window pane to see where everyone was heading and was surprised to see that it was to the town's Parish Church, a hundred yards or so up the street.

Violet's face lit up in a smile at a distant memory of going to church as a child on the Sunday evening before Christmas, holding her Auntie Liz's or her mother's hand as her cousins, Daisy and Rose, walked in front.

Her eyes watered with a deep sadness. The children's party she had walked into earlier that afternoon was a family tradition, held on the Sunday afternoon before Christmas – an afternoon tea consisting of salmon sandwiches with the crusts cut off; trifle made with red jelly and sprinkled with coloured candy strands; followed by a delicious home-made chocolate log cake, topped with an ancient red robin decoration and icing sugar. Although many years had passed by since she, herself, was a child, the tradition in the Jeffson family had obviously survived the passage of time. When she was a child, the Christmas tea party would be followed by board games, concluding with a small present for each child to take home – a book usually. Then, it being a Sunday evening, her mother and Auntie Liz, Rose and Daisy would go to church for the candle-lit evening service and she would go with them. All the children would hold a flickering candle, while the congregation sang Christmas carols and the church choir sang a special song they had been learning for weeks. Afterwards, there would be mulled wine and mince pies in the church rooms, with orange juice and biscuits for the children.

Violet blinked back tears. Although lots of her childhood memories were unhappy ones, she had always enjoyed Christmas, and more than anything she wished she could be magically transported back to one of her childhood Christmases in the midst of the Jeffson family, where she would be the centre of attention on Christmas Eve, it being her birthday, followed by the excitement of Christmas Day itself.

On impulse, Violet decided to attend the Church service – it might help to stir up some Christmas spirit in her heart. She grabbed a pen and a sheet of hotel notepaper and scribbled a hasty note for Sergio to let him know where she had gone when he arrived.

The police car glided to a halt outside the Royal Hotel. The passenger door opened and Sergio climbed out, just at the precise moment Violet stepped out of the front entrance, pulling the fur collar of her coat up over her ears against the cold wind.

'Ah, here she is,' Sergio said cheerfully to the policeman through the open door. 'This is my wife, Officer – Mrs Violet Smith.'

'Evenin' ma'am,' the policeman said, lowering his head to look at Violet as he sat in the driver's seat. He touched his forehead. 'I'm so sorry to have delayed your husband, but he has been helping us with our enquiries. There has been a bit of an incident in Thrapston.'

Sergio placed an arm around Violet's shoulders. 'We both wish you a very happy Christmas, Officer, and thank you again for giving me a lift.'

'There's no problem,' the policeman said. 'It was the least I could do, seeing as you missed the last bus. We couldn't have your good lady wife worrying where you've got to.'

Violet smiled through quivering lips, despite the whirlwind of panic that made her stumble slightly and her hands shake as she pulled on a pair of leather gloves. 'I was just going to church,' she said to the policeman. Turning to Sergio, she added: 'you can quickly get changed and join me now, dear, can't you? What on earth happened to make you so late?'

The policeman leaned over to shut the car's passenger door. 'I do hope you both enjoy the service. Happy Christmas.'

They watched as the police car disappeared from view, waving to the police officer for effect.

'Right,' Sergio said taking Violet by the elbow. 'From now on you must remember to call me Richard. We've just told that copper we are going to church, so we ought to go. If our story is investigated further, then it will all add up. We need to pay meticulous attention to detail from now on. Did everything go all right at your end?'

He led Violet by the arm to walk the short distance to the church, ignoring her request for him to change his clothes.

'Yes, it all went like clockwork,' she said. 'Leaving Lydia and Tim was harder than I thought it would be, but I know they will be looked after by my family.'

'Good,' Sergio replied, pulling her arm through his. 'But I wouldn't have minded them coming to Spain with us. I've never once asked you to abandon them and I want to make that clear. I don't want you to blame me when you have regrets about it.'

Violet shook her head. 'I know. I won't. Trust me, they'll be much better off living here. I was never cut out to be a mother. It's for their own good.'

They walked a few steps in silence, slowing down to allow some people pass by.

'What on earth happened to delay you,' Violet whispered. 'I nearly died a thousand deaths when you pulled up in that police car. I was so worried when you were late.'

'Well, I had the most unbelievable stroke of luck,' Sergio explained with a grin. 'When I left the car, I set up my fishing kit a couple of hundred yards away, as planned. I sat for a while, fishing. There were a few people around – some young lads and an old woman with a little boy – so I reckoned I ought to hang around until they'd gone before leaving my kit. When the coast was clear, I walked back into Thrapston. I was just strolling along, minding my own business, when this copper stopped me to ask if I had seen a black Humber drive down the track to the gravel pits. Apparently, after I left the car, the lads I had spotted earlier had obviously thought it was a bit of a joke to let the tyres down, and the old woman and her grandson had caught them in the act. She had reported it to a policeman on her way home and so he went out on his bicycle to investigate.

'At first, I thought the game was up, but then I realised that the copper actually thought I was a local chap who just happened to be passing by. Well, what an opportunity? It couldn't have worked out better. As Richard Smith I am now a perfectly legitimate witness in my own disappearance. How fortunate is that? I told the policeman I had been visiting an elderly aunt in Thrapston and was on my way to catch the last bus back to Kettering to join my wife at the Royal Hotel.'

They turned to walk up the driveway to the church. 'Do you think that was wise?' Violet whispered, her brow creased in a worried frown at the unexpected turn of events.

'It was a case of snooze or you lose,' Sergio replied. 'It was a golden opportunity. I could either come up with some cock-and-bull story that wouldn't check out, or I could give the copper a description of the old me. I told him that the man driving the car had black wavy hair and a thick black moustache. I said I thought I recognised him from somewhere, but couldn't recall where, and I thought he resembled a film star or something like that.'

'Oh hells bells. I can't believe you said that!'

'It's fine, Violet. Don't worry. Tomorrow it will be on the news and after Christmas it will be all over the papers. It was going to happen, anyway, and there will be no reason for the police to interview me as Richard Smith again – even if they could find me – because I've already given a statement. There's loads of other witnesses who saw my car: the old woman with a little boy and obviously the young lads who let my tyres down.'

They fell quiet as they entered the church. Sergio made sure he made polite conversation with a church warden, who was handing out service sheets.

'Are you from Kettering?' the church warden asked.

'No,' Sergio said. 'We are just visiting family for Christmas and heard about the service here tonight. We'll be returning to London on Thursday.'

'Don't you think you are saying too much,' hissed Violet once they were seated inside the church. 'We need to be lying low, not flaunting our presence.'

'Just trust me,' Sergio whispered. 'It's all working out much better than I expected. Don't worry. Just remember you need to start acting as if we are just a regular married couple and never, ever call me anything other than Richard.'

'What if Uncle Tom reports me to the authorities tomorrow for leaving Lydia and Tim? They'll come looking for us, for sure.'

'He won't do that,' Sergio kissed her on the cheek and then whispered in her ear. 'That's the last thing your family would do on Christmas Eve. They'll wait until after Christmas before reporting anything to the authorities and by that time, we'll be long gone. There will be no way the police force in Thrapston will link the disappearance of Sergio de Luca with the abandonment of two children in Kettering. The two cases just won't be connected – they are totally separate. Even if the Richard Smith connection *is* eventually made, it will all check out, but we'll be long gone. Tracing us will be like finding a needle in a haystack.'

Violet smiled with relief. She could see he was right. And even if the police wanted to trace the witness again, the trail would lead to the Royal Hotel, where they were registered only as Mr and Mrs R Smith and the permanent address in London they had given was just an empty flat close to St Pancras Station.

When the children had gone to bed, a weary Liz struggled into the kitchen to wash up, leaning on her walking stick. Tom hauled himself up on a pair of crutches and followed her out.

'We're much too old for all this trouble, Liz.'

'What on earth are we going to do if she doesn't come back?' Liz said. 'We're in our eighties; we can't look after those children.'

'I know, but how can we turn them away?'

Liz rested her walking stick against the edge of the sink, and squirted some Fairy Liquid into the washing up bowl. 'I like them, Tom. Despite having Violet for a mother, they seem to be very nicely brought up. Poor Lydia. It's such a shame. It sounds as if she's had no proper childhood at all.'

Tom smiled. 'You know, Liz, she reminds me ever so much of you when you were a lass. Sensible and clever, with her head screwed on.'

Liz smiled at him. As he grew older, his heart had softened until it was mere putty in her hands. He could still be abrupt at times, but his family was his whole life. It was all he thought about, and he was so generous with his pension money, she sometimes had to bite her lip.

'I was really hurt by what Violet said this afternoon,' Tom said. 'Did you hear her? She yelled at me, saying the reason she kept her children from us for all these years was because I stole baby Oliver from her and she thought I'd steal those two away from her, too.'

Tears welled in his eyes and he rubbed them away with his forefinger. 'The nightmares never go away, Liz. I find myself back in the nineteen forties, planning it all, and all the time knowing it is complete madness and it's going to end in tragedy. Then my mind just relives the whole episode and I wake up in a panic.'

'I know.' Liz picked up a tea towel and began to dry the cups and saucers. She sighed. 'And Violet turning up out of the blue isn't going to help at all. Don't rake it all over, Tom. We've been over it a thousand times. It will make you ill again, if you're not careful.'

Tom rubbed at his stubbly chin. 'No, you're right. It's no good crying over milk that was spilt eighteen years ago. What matters now is those poor children and what we are going to do about them.'

Liz nodded. 'Violet might be back tomorrow,' she said trying to inject optimism into her voice, but deep down she knew there was little chance of that happening.

Rose Foster woke early on Christmas Eve. Pulling on her pink candlewick dressing gown and shoving her feet into tartan slippers, she shivered and crept downstairs to light a fire, her hair in curlers under a hairnet. When she was satisfied that the fire was lit, she went into the kitchen. She was sitting in welcome solitude at the kitchen table trying to complete the previous day's crossword in the newspaper when the living room door opened. She looked up to see Lydia, dressed in a faded nightdress and a cardigan she had loaned her to keep her warm. Her thick, long dark hair was tousled and, without her ill-fitting, heavy-rimmed National Health glasses, Rose was surprised at how pretty she was. Lydia pulled the cardigan around her and smiled tentatively.

They spoke in whispers so as not to wake anyone else in the household.

'Can I call you Auntie Rose?'

'Of course you can.' Rose pulled out a chair and motioned to Lydia to sit down with her. 'I'll pour you a cup of tea. I'm just having a few minutes of peace and quiet before the mayhem starts. I've got such a lot to do before the big day tomorrow.'

'I just wanted to say how grateful I am that you let us stay last night, Auntie Rose.'

Rose smiled. She sensed the poor girl was so unused to calling anyone *Auntie* that she was revelling in actually having one, and needed to keep repeating it. She covered Lydia's hand with her own and gave it a reassuring squeeze.

'Were you comfortable on the put-u-up in the front

room?'

'Oh, yes. I slept all through the night and I've just crept upstairs to check on Tim, and he must be really cosy in your spare bedroom because he hasn't stirred all night – he's still in the same position he was in when I tucked him in with his hot water bottle.'

Rose felt a sudden rush of admiration for the strange girl-mother who sat before her. It was as if Lydia had somehow inherited a double dose of maternal instinct, unlike Violet, who appeared to have had none whatsoever.

Rose realised she was still holding Lydia's hand and patted it before letting go. 'Whatever happens now, I want you to promise me you'll stay in touch with us now we've found you both.'

Lydia sighed. 'We didn't know we had any family at all until yesterday. It's something I always dreamed of – having aunts and uncles and cousins. Because Mum's parents are both dead, and because she is an only child herself we thought we had nobody in the world. I'm so excited that we actually have some relatives besides our father. But I think Mum has lied about him living in Kettering, and he probably doesn't even want to see us again, wherever he is.'

Rose took another sip of tea. 'What happened to your grandad, Walter Grey? I didn't realise he was dead, I thought he was still living somewhere in Scotland.'

Lydia's eyes widened. 'We've got a grandfather living in Scotland? I didn't know.'

'Yes. After the breakdown of your grandparent's marriage, he went to live in Scotland with his – er – his brother.' Rose hesitated. She didn't think it appropriate to mention to a fifteen year-old girl that her grandfather had been a homosexual and had left her grandmother to live with his lover.

'So their marriage broke down? And we have a great uncle, too? Mum never told me any of this.'

Rose didn't know what to say. Embarrassed, she subconsciously fingered her curlers under her hairnet, checking they hadn't come loose.

Lydia leaned forwards in her seat, curious to know everything about her new-found family. 'Is my grandfather Uncle Tom's brother?'

Rose shook her head. 'No, your grandmother, Doris, was my mother's sister – my aunt. She was quite a few years younger than my mother. I'm afraid she was quite poorly and had a nervous breakdown. She died tragically at the end of the war, so your mother is telling you the truth on that score.'

'How did she die?'

Rose couldn't lie. It was obvious Lydia had been told many lies in the past and there was no point in dressing up the truth.

'She drowned in a tragic accident when she fell into Wicksteed Park Lake. She had this problem with the old mother's ruin, you see. She was addicted to it.'

Lydia fell quiet, absent-mindedly tracing the grain of the wood of the kitchen table with her forefinger.

'Auntie Rose, when we arrived last night, Mum said something about Uncle Tom stealing her first baby away from her. What did she mean? Do we have an older brother or sister we've never known about?'

Rose sighed. Explaining exactly what happened would not be easy. 'No, Lydia, I'm afraid you don't. Your brother, Oliver, was born during the war when your mother was just a young girl. He drowned in the lake, along with your grandmother. It was in all the papers when the truth came out – a dreadful scandal at the time. It nearly killed your Uncle Tom and he always blamed himself for the tragedy. Poor Violet found it all very difficult, and that's why she cut herself out of our lives. I can completely understand why she didn't tell you – it must still be very painful for her, even after all these years.'

'So how come Uncle Tom was involved?'

'It was his idea that your grandparents adopt your mother's baby. He couldn't bear the thought of never seeing the baby again, and so he persuaded your grandmother and grandfather to adopt him instead, so that he could stay in the family. But it was all a big secret and doomed from the start.'

Lydia cupped her chin in her hands, deep in thought. 'I suppose it does explain why my mother holds back from allowing herself to love us and constantly shoves us away. But I don't know why she ever had us if she feels like that.'

Rose nodded. 'I think you're perhaps right, Lydia. It's all very sad. Perhaps when Violet comes back, you can try and talk to her about it. It might even help her to finally talk to you about everything she's kept bottled up all these years.'

Lydia shook her head slowly. 'She won't come back, Auntie Rose. I just know. I think she had it all planned. I've suspected something's been going on for weeks.'

Rose rubbed her forehead and changed the subject. She couldn't worry about the consequences of Violet not coming back. Not on Christmas Eve, when there was still so much to do before tomorrow. The child needed some reassurance, though, that the pair of them weren't about to be thrown out on the streets, should the unthinkable happen.

She leaned forwards, perching her reading glasses on the end of her nose so she could look at Lydia in the eye. 'If your mother doesn't come back for you, I don't want you to worry that you might be turned out on the streets. We wouldn't ever do that. But you can see how old my parents are, and George and I are no spring chickens, either.'

'Oh, we won't need looking after,' Lydia said with a confident toss of her head. 'All Mum ever did for us was give us money now and again. I'll just have to try and find us a room to rent somewhere in London. I might even be able to speak to our landlord and he'll let us stay on in our flat if I offer to pay the rent Mum owes, bit by bit. I can carry on looking after Tim. It's not a problem.'

Rose frowned and shook her head slightly. 'I somehow don't think you'll earn enough to pay rent and other bills and keep the pair of you, Lydia. I don't think you realise how expensive renting can be, especially in London. Anyway, let's look on the bright side. Your mother might come back for you today. We don't know for definite that she won't. After all, it *is* Christmas Eve and a mother would have to be completely heartless to abandon her children at Christmas.'

Lydia looked into her teacup, cradling it in her hands, swirling the tea leaves around and around. She looked up and met Rose's gaze. 'She *is* completely heartless, Auntie Rose. We mean nothing to her. Once, a man said to me that she was *dead behind the eyes.* And that describes her exactly. She's soulless, heartless and, somehow, she seems completely disconnected from us. Did you notice her expensive leather shoes and handbag? Her new cashmere winter coat with a real fur collar? Well, she has a whole wardrobe of smart clothes, while us – her own children – have to beg her for money to buy clothes. Mostly, now I'm working, I use my own wages to buy us food. We have nothing. We've never had anything. We will probably be better off on our own anyway, and I am perfectly able to look after Tim. If I look for another better paid job in a factory then I'm sure I can manage.'

Rose chose her words carefully. She didn't want to belittle Lydia's independence. 'I know you are, and you've done a grand job up until now. It's just that you are obviously a very clever young lady and it's such a waste that you weren't able to stay on at school and take your exams. I'd like to see you go back to school. You've only missed a few months and could soon catch up. Life is not all about working in a shop or a factory, finding a husband and having babies. Don't give in, Lydia, and sell yourself short. You could be a teacher, a doctor – anything you want.'

Lydia's eyes widened and her mouth fell open. 'How would I do that?' she said. 'I have to work to support us both.'

'You could go back to school here in Kettering if you wanted to. I'm sure it's not too late for you to go back. Would you like to take your exams?'

Lydia's jaw dropped in surprise. 'You'd really support us both, and let me go back to school?'

Rose didn't quite know how to take Lydia's reaction. 'Of

course, if you'd rather go out to work, that would be all right too.'

'So, if our mother doesn't come back, we can stay here? I haven't even dared to dream about going back to school.'

Lydia drew herself up straight on the kitchen chair. 'I'd get a Saturday job so that I could give you money for our keep.'

Rose nodded in understanding. She shrugged, her palms upturned. 'That seems perfectly fair to me, but let's just see what happens, shall we? We'll keep all this to ourselves for now. After all, your mother may come back with a good reason for going off yesterday, and it will all be hypothetical anyway. Let's just enjoy our Christmas, whether she comes back today or not, and then we can talk about all this again afterwards if we have to.'

Rose finished her tea and put the cup back on the saucer. 'I like to have things sorted out in my head at times of crisis. I've always been the same, Lydia. I have to know what I'm faced with. What I'm doing. Be organised and prepared, that's my motto.'

She stood up, placing a comforting hand on Lydia's shoulder. 'And there's no point getting Mam and Dad all worked up at their age: we'll just wait and see and take it day by day for now.'

Chapter Five

Later that morning, her carefully curled hair falling in lank rats' tails around her forehead and her face shiny with perspiration, Rose rammed her fist into the turkey's cavity, a mouth-watering aroma of sage and onion filling the kitchen. She lowered her voice as she growled at George.

'You'll have to get some money out of the front of my purse and go and get some presents for those poor children.'

'Violet will be back for them today,' George said. 'Can't we just get them some chocolates from the corner shop?'

Rose wiped her hands on a teacloth before picking up a ball of string and cutting off a good length with the kitchen scissors. 'We can't see them with no Christmas presents to open even if she does come back. They ought to have a few bits and bobs. I haven't got time, so you'll have to go. I've got too much to do before tomorrow.'

'How about our Margaret?' George suggested as Rose tied one end of the string firmly around one of the turkey legs. 'She could pop out – go to Curry's and Berwick's and get some toys and a model aeroplane kit for young Tim. She'll have more idea of what to buy than I shall.'

Rose tutted as she expertly trussed up the turkey with the string. 'And you think our Margaret won't be busy herself? She's so disorganised, she won't be anywhere near ready for tomorrow. And our Daisy has her work cut out with those boys of hers. All this trouble couldn't have come at a worse time. Anyway, Lydia's far too old for toys. How about a nice scarf or some gloves? The poor girl's hands were like blocks of ice when they arrived yesterday. And I noticed the poor child's underwear was full of holes when she unpacked her case yesterday afternoon.'

George rubbed his chin with his hand. 'I know. I noticed, too. I won't have a clue what to buy, though. I'll get all the wrong things. Can't you just find a spare hour and go yourself?'

Rose brought a heavy meat cleaver down on the turkey's neck, severing it neatly, and shot George a menacing look. 'Everyone's running around like headless chickens today. No one's got any time to spare, but someone's just *got* to make time. We can't have children in the house with nothing to open tomorrow morning.'

George took a step backwards, grinning as he killed a chuckle at Rose's choice of words. He scratched the back of his neck. He'd planned an easy day, keeping out of the women's way while they prepared food for Christmas day, then just after lunch he'd help Tom along on his crutches as they made their way to the Windmill Working Men's Club. He'd fancied he might even have a seasonal tot of brandy, too. He and Tom would then have a nice afternoon's snooze in front of the television while the women sat at the kitchen table preparing Brussels sprouts and carrots and peeled enough potatoes to feed what seemed like the entire street.

'I suppose I'll have to go,' he said with a sigh. 'But I'll not really have time to go to the Windmill if I do, will I?'

'No, you won't,' Rose snapped. 'And I won't be able to sit down until God knows what time, especially with two more mouths to feed. Don't you realise I've got eleven people to cater for with our Daisy, Bill and the boys coming for dinner? Mam's a big help, but she's not getting any younger. Roll on Boxing Day. At least it will only be cold meats and pickles – not that I mind doing everything, but ...'

George put his fingers in his ears to shut out the sound of his wife's nagging voice, shaking his head slightly before winking and grinning at Lydia as she appeared at the kitchen door.

Lydia didn't return his smile and George noticed her eyes were too large and too bright. In her hand she held a length of grubby string with which she had been playing cat's cradle with Tim, the sight of which made him feel sadder than he had felt for a very long time.

The weather had turned bitterly cold and the wind was so icy, George felt the skin on his face prickle as he set off into town with a pocket full of money to buy last-minute presents for Lydia and Tim. He had telephoned his daughter, Margaret, and his sister-in-law, Daisy, to see if either of them would go into town and buy the children some presents, but he wasn't surprised when they both swore at him, declaring that they, too, didn't have time on Christmas Eve to go shopping. He extracted Rose's list from his pocket. He had also been instructed to call in the bakery on the way to buy extra bread and some shop-bought mince pies in case they had more unexpected visitors and ran out of home-made ones.

His day was just going from bad to worse.

As he approached the bakery he groaned out loud: there was a queue. It didn't bode well. If there were queues everywhere in town, he wouldn't have time to sneak to the Windmill Club for a swift half on the way back.

Ten minutes later, when George made it to the front of the queue, Sarah Haywood of Haywood's Bakery grimaced as she held her aching back with one hand and pushed a strand of escaping grey hair under a white headscarf, tied up in a knot over her forehead, with the other.

'Hello George,' she said with a weary smile. 'Has someone forgotten something?'

'You could say that,' George said. 'You wouldn't believe what happened yesterday. Our Violet turned up out of the blue with two children we didn't even know existed, and now she's buggered off. Our Rose reckons she's not coming back for them.'

Sarah's daughter, Millie, appeared from the room at the back of the shop having heard the scandalous revelation about Violet.

'Oh my word. Violet's come back? After all these years? I tell you what, George, you go and have a bit of a sit down with Mum in the back and tell her all about it over a cuppa. She's been on her feet for hours. We've never known anything like it on Christmas Eve. I think the weather forecast has made everyone want to stock up: it's supposed to be really bad and we might even be snowed in come Boxing Day, according to the news. I've baked four more batches of bread today already.'

As Sarah gratefully removed her white apron, George rubbed his hands together and stepped behind the counter to join her in the small room at the back of the shop. He might even get a tot or two of something seasonal in his tea. He knew Sarah kept her *little bottle of medicinal fortification* hidden in a cupboard in the back room, and if he wasn't going to make it to the club for a seasonal pint of ale, a few minutes more wouldn't hurt.

Sarah gave him a conspiratorial wink. 'Would you like a little something in your tea? You look perished,'

George took off his peaked cap and grinned. 'Don't mind if I do,' he said, abandoning all thoughts of a quick shopping trip. After all, the ladies who owned the bakery were old friends. They had been invited for tea with the Jeffson family on Boxing Day and needed to know what was going on so there were no surprises in the form of two stray children.

Half an hour and two large glasses of port and brandy later (the first one to toast the compliments of the season and the second, much larger, one to warm the cockles of his heart while he did his shopping), George looked at his watch, having given Sarah an account of the unexpected turn of events.

'So – as well as the bread and mince pies, I have to find another jar of cranberry sauce, presents for those poor children, more wrapping paper – you name it, it's on Rose's list.' He waved a piece of paper under Sarah's nose.

Sarah opened her purse and gave him two half-crowns. 'Can you get those poor children something from me and our Millie? We can't turn up on Boxing Day empty-handed.

You can drop their presents off when you come back from town and pick up your bread and mince pies. I'll put you a couple of loves under the counter because at this rate we shall run out.'

George set off on his quest, feeling the pleasant warm glow from the port and brandy flood into his arms and legs. He actually felt quite cheerful, despite having wasted half an hour chatting to Sarah and finding himself with two more presents to buy for the children.

As he reached the town, he spotted his son-in-law's father coming out of The Swan. He shouted out to attract his attention.

'Noah!'

The tall, thin man pulled his peaked cap down over his ears and walked off in the opposite direction, not having heard him. George broke out into a run and caught him up. 'Hey, Noah, Happy Christmas, mate!'

They stood talking for a few minutes, George explaining why he was shopping in town at two o'clock on Christmas Eve when he should have been in the Windmill Club.

'I tell you what, George,' Noah said. 'Why don't we pop back into The Swan for a swift half? No point in chin-wagging out here in the cold, is there?'

An hour later George and Noah spilled out of the pub, full of goodwill and Christmas spirit. Noah thumped him on the back. 'Well, I hope you and Rose have a happy Christmas, despite all your troubles. And if you need anything – anything at all – you know where we are. You only have to give us a shout.'

After much back slapping and sentimental declarations of family solidarity, George set off on his quest to buy presents. It was now gone three o'clock and all he had bought from Rose's list was bread and mince pies. Never mind. He still had an hour to finish his shopping and get back to the bakery to collect his shopping before the shop shut for Christmas. There was plenty of time.

He belched and thumped his chest, his eyes unexpectedly filling with sentimental moisture at the good fortune of meeting Noah. He was a good bloke, offering to help his family like that. He didn't know why their Margaret didn't get on with him. He'd have to have words with her and tell her to make a bit more of an effort with her father-in-law because she'd got him all wrong. He wasn't a *miserable tight-fisted so-and-so*. After all, he'd just put his hand in his pocket four times in the pub, insisting that he buy George yet another drink because he was such a good chap to be giving up his Christmas Eve at The Windmill to buy presents for the poor, abandoned children.

A couple of minutes later, he reached Cobley's grocery shop. Ah yes – cranberry sauce. He grinned crookedly, and waggled a forefinger in the air as he staggered slightly on the pavement, pausing to regain his balance. There were no flies on him: he'd remembered what was on Rose's shopping list without even looking at it.

George's old friend, Wilf Cobley, greeted him with a red cheeks and an unnaturally wide, seasonal grin. 'Mister George Foster,' he proclaimed at the top of his voice as if George was royalty. 'Just the chap. Here, come and try some of my mulled wine. It's only one-and-six a bottle, and the finest money can buy. Guaranteed to warm the cockles of your heart.'

George almost forgot to buy the cranberry sauce when he left the shop twenty minutes later, but remembered just in time and went back for it. He was quite enjoying this shopping lark. It made a nice change from the Windmill. In fact he might even volunteer to do it again next year, so pleasant was it to bump into old friends in town and exchange Christmas cheer. Not only that, after sampling a couple of glasses of the delicious mulled wine, he'd bought a couple of bottles for Rose and Liz. They'd enjoy it on boxing night when they were warming their toes in front of the fire beside the twinkling Christmas tree, watching television with Sarah and Millie. Rose was such good fun when she had a drink inside her. It reminded him of the early days of their marriage, when they'd sneak up to bed with a little drink or two – or three – and snuggle up together. Those were the days. He chuckled to himself as he waited for Wilf Cobley to fetch his jar of cranberry sauce.

'Happy Christmas, mate.' he said, downing another sample of mulled wine before teetering out of the door. He looked at his pocket watch and squinted. He tapped it with his index finger. It must be going wrong in the cold air. It couldn't possibly be four o'clock already. The shops would shut for Christmas soon, if he didn't get a wiggle on.

Back in Cornwall Road, frightened and forlorn, Lydia and Tim sat on the rug by the coal fire, alone in the front room of the house.

Tim turned his head towards the window and the darkening sky outside. 'She's not coming, is she? She's just thrown us away and ground us into the dirt under her shoe like one of her fag ends.'

Lydia shook her head. She couldn't answer. She felt so low, she couldn't even speak. She took off her black-framed glasses and inspected them. They were far too small for her now, and meant for boys. One side was taped with yellowing Sellotape that was coming undone. The only other option when she had chosen them four years ago had been pink-framed, piggy-like girls' glasses and, with her thick dark hair and brown eyes she had looked ridiculous in them.

She blinked back tears of despair. They had no home, very little money, hardly any clothes and now they had no mother. She stared into the fireplace, trying her hardest to draw some comfort from the warmth and glow of the coals. She would never hate her mother more than she did now. Since the conversation with Auntie Rose early that morning, for the first time in her life she had allowed herself the luxury of feeling bitterness for the missed opportunity of a decent education and ending up selling stationery in Woolworths instead. She knew she was capable of much more. Had she been born to someone else and had a normal upbringing, she had enough fire inside her to make it to university. Now, it seemed like the whole world was crushing the spirit out of her. It was far too much responsibility to have to go to out to work to earn enough money to care for her younger brother. She should not have to be thinking about putting a roof over their heads, clothes on their backs and food on their table at the age of fifteen. She should be whirling and twirling around in a new pair of black slacks and yellow and green pop-over top she had seen in *Top Pop Fashion Shop,* over the road from where she worked, its windows full of the exciting things she should be buying at her age.

It was Christmas Eve, for goodness sake. What sort of mother abandoned her children at Christmas?

The radio in the living room was playing Elvis Presley's *Return to Sender* and she could hear Auntie Rose singing along tunelessly. Would they end up being returned to sender, despite Auntie Rose's assurances this morning? Was this family they'd never known being nice to them just because it was Christmas, and then on Thursday they would be trussed up like unwanted parcels and dispatched off to the Council, where a nasal-voiced pompous Children's Officer would interview them before tearing them apart from each other – sent to different foster homes where they'd never see each other again?

Auntie Rose had told her this morning that they once had a brother who had died when he was a baby. There was so much they didn't know about this family, and yet their mother had just dumped them here in a strange town, where no one knew them.

The radio began blaring out *Rocking around the Christmas Tree.*

Lydia sniffed back tears. This was just the worst Christmas ever. She wished she was back in their flat in London, preparing vegetables for Christmas dinner for the three of them and trying to make the yellow Formica-topped table look nice for Christmas day. She had bought a plastic printed tablecloth decorated with festive sprigs of holly and "*Merry Christmas*" and "*Season's Greetings*", scrawled all over it in gold copperplate writing.

She had bought and wrapped all her presents, too. Tim had a jigsaw puzzle, a Cadbury's selection box and a fancy drawing pad with a special pen. You could use it again and again by just pulling up the cellophane, which erased the drawing underneath. It wasn't much for an eleven year-old, though. There was a present for her, too, from Tim, and a bottle of 4711 scent for their mother, wrapped up neatly and labelled: *"To Mum, Happy Christmas from Lydia and Timothy"*. It was a good job she'd grabbed the presents before they'd left the flat, otherwise Tim would have nothing to open tomorrow.

On the way to the station she had stopped at a newsagent's shop, insisting she bought their elusive father something for Christmas. She could only afford a packet of ten Park Drive cigarettes, but it was better than nothing. Violet had tutted, telling her not to bother, because their father wouldn't be expecting them to bring anything.

Perhaps, with hindsight, instead of filling the suitcase with Christmas presents, she ought to have brought some more clothes and underwear for them both.

She buried her face in her knees and began to cry. They didn't even have any clean underpants to put on after tomorrow. She would have to ask Auntie Rose if she could do some hand washing in the kitchen sink later, when they had changed into their night clothes.

'Don't cry,' Tim said. 'At least there's two of us. It would be horrible if we didn't have each other.'

In the living room, Lydia heard Uncle Tom singing along to *Rocking around the Christmas Tree.* Then her Auntie Liz said: 'Ooooh. Stop it Tom. Leave me alone. You're worse than a teenager.'

It wasn't fair. Old people in their eighties shouldn't be singing and messing about, most probably slapping each other playfully on their backsides. Did they not realise how awful it made her feel, hearing them laughing?

'Look,' Tim went on, jolting her out of her thoughts. 'We've got beds and even hot water bottles, and there's proper curtains and wallpaper on the wall. We are spending

Christmas in this nice house with warm fires and everything. And we are going to have turkey and Christmas pudding tomorrow. Things aren't that bad.'

Lydia buried her head further in between her knees, sniffing back the tears that were filling her nose. Her heart thumped painfully in her chest. The authorities would definitely send them to live with foster carers. Auntie Rose and Uncle George were too old to look after children, and Uncle Tom and Auntie Liz were probably the oldest people she had ever met in her life. If only she was already sixteen, things wouldn't look so bleak.

Tim burbled on desperate to cheer her up. 'We've even had breakfast today. We didn't have any yesterday.'

Lydia forced herself to look up and rubbed at her eyes. Despite how awful she felt, she had to carry on for Tim's sake. He was her brother and she loved him so much, it made her heart ache in a funny, but nice sort of way. He was her world and she would rather die than give up on her quest to make sure he was happy and made something of himself when he grew up.

'... and there will be mince pies and they might even set fire to the Christmas pudding ...'

Tim stood up and carefully lifted two family photographs from the top of the polished mahogany bureau in the corner of the room. He sat down again beside his sister. 'Look, Lydia – I think these are the children that are coming for dinner tomorrow. Auntie Liz pointed them out to me this morning.'

'Who are they?'

Lydia stroked one of the photographs with her thumb. It was of three little boys, the oldest looked about seven and the youngest just a baby.

'They are our Aunt Daisy's children, and I think that might mean they are our cousins,' Tim continued. 'You know they keep talking about someone called Daisy? Well, she is Auntie Rose's sister so she must be our aunt, too. Uncle George told me last night when he popped in to tuck me up in bed and make sure I was all right. He said that if we were still here on Christmas Day, it would be great fun because she was coming for dinner with her three boys. But I don't think they were here at the party yesterday.'

Lydia took the other photograph from Tim's hand, it was of a very jolly-looking man, standing with one hand on a chair on which sat a lady with the kindest eyes Lydia had ever seen.

'Is this our Aunt Daisy, do you think?' she said, pointing to the woman in the photograph.

Tim shook his head. 'I don't know, but Uncle George told me that Mum lived with her for a while when she was a little girl and that she can't wait to meet us.'

Tim scrunched up his face and put his hand on Lydia's arm. '*Please* cheer up, Lyd. Let's just enjoy Christmas and pretend we are on some great Famous Five adventure, where everything turns out fine in the end.'

Rose's head snapped upwards from the depths of the steamy kitchen sink, where she was hand-washing a plastic bowl full of tea-towels in hot soapy water. 'Where on earth have you been?' she squawked in a voice that reminded George of an angry hen. 'You'd better not have been in The Windmill – and for goodness sake shut that door before we all get frozen to death.'

George teetered over the threshold, killing a hiccup before it could rise from his chest and erupt from his mouth. He glanced at the kitchen clock – it was half past six. He bent down to put down several bags of shopping on the kitchen floor and groaned as he straightened up, holding his aching back. 'It's all there,' he said with a triumphant wave of his hand. 'Except the bread. The bakery had shut by the time I got there to pick it up.'

Rose expertly wrung out a tea towel. George grimaced, glad it wasn't his neck.

'Millie dropped it off – and the mince pies – and you'd better thank your lucky stars she did, because we would never have had enough to last until Thursday with two extra mouths to feed.'

George flinched as Rose pressed her lips together and frowned, narrowing her eyes. She was rattled because he'd been out all afternoon while she'd tackled all the Christmas preparations single-handedly. There was no point in denying he'd been to the Windmill Club, because she would never believe him anyway.

He rustled about in one of the bags and extracted two bottles of mulled wine. 'Happy Christmas, love,' he said with a grin. 'This'll be just the job on Boxing night, when you've excelled yourself in giving everyone a grand Christmas and finally got time put your feet up with Sarah and Millie.'

'Never mind about that,' Rose snapped. 'Did you get those children some decent presents?'

'Oh yes,' George said, pulling himself up with pride. 'It was all a bit last minute and there wasn't a lot of choice left, but I've got some right nice stuff for them to open tomorrow.'

'Well – we'd better shove those bags in the pantry for now. I haven't got time to look. You'll have to wrap it all up when they've gone to bed. Now – did you remember my cranberry sauce?'

George grinned and winked at Lydia, who had appeared at the living room door. 'Sauce? What sauce?'

'Oh George! I can't trust you to do anything, can I? There won't be enough to go round. Now I'll just have to make do and ration out what I've already got or mix it with some stewed apple.'

George put his hand in his coat pocket and extracted the jar of cranberry sauce, holding it up in front of Rose's face, grinning broadly.

'Only joking,' he said.

Lydia stepped into the kitchen, trying to inject some cheerfulness into her voice. 'Uncle George – Tim and I have been listening to the news on the wireless. Where's Thrapston?'

'About eight miles or so from here. Why?'

'You know the famous pop star, Sergio de Luca. Well, according to the news he's gone missing in Thrapston. They found his car by some gravel pits yesterday afternoon.'

'Missing?' Rose said. 'At Christmas? In Thrapston?'

'Apparently. The Police think he went fishing and might have fallen in. They found his fishing basket and rod. The line and float was still in the water, but there was no sign of him. He's just disappeared. And there was an empty bottle of whisky in his car.'

'Oh dear,' Rose said. 'Those pop star types are all the same. I bet he was blind drunk. Those pits can be really dangerous. Lots of currents and weeds. There was a woman drowned there only last summer. And what was Sergio de Luca doing in Thrapston, anyway? He's supposed to be on *Christmas with the Stars* tomorrow night. I'd have thought he'd been in London, rehearsing or something.'

'It will have been recorded,' George said. 'He wouldn't actually be singing on Christmas Day. And I think I read in the papers once that he's a keen angler and doesn't live very far away from here.'

Rose turned away, emptying the plastic bowl of soapy water down the sink before drying her hands. 'What a terrible thing to happen at Christmas,' she said. 'His poor mother and family.'

'Oh, by the way,' George said to Lydia. 'I called in Learner and Woodward's on the way back from town and got you and young Timothy some bits and bobs to keep you going if you are going to be staying over Christmas.'

He rifled through the bags at his feet and handed a brown paper package over to her.

'I hope these are all right,' he said. 'I can't say I've ever been shopping for this sort of thing before.'

Chapter Six

Despite her exhaustion, Rose had slept badly, her brain jerking itself into a hyperactive repetitive cycle of worry about a situation over which she had no control. After a seemingly interminable night, she counted chimes from the clock downstairs. It was now six o'clock – she should get up now, or else she would risk falling asleep when there was still so much to do to make sure the family had a good Christmas day.

She heaved herself out of bed feeling as groggy as if she had just been administered an anaesthetic. Pulling back the curtain slightly, she peered out of the window. It was so cold in the room, the inside of the windowpane had frozen into a delicate seasonal wonderland of wispy ferns. Grimacing, she rubbed at the frost with her forefinger to clear a small peephole. Yesterday's ashes would need raking out and today's fire wouldn't light itself. It would take at least half an hour to get it going and warm the room for when the rest of the household woke up.

Standing in the open doorway to the living room in her candlewick dressing gown, she switched on the light. Sighing wearily, she clutched her forehead in the palm of her hand, shaking her head in disbelief at the scene before her. There were empty, unwashed cups on the mantelpiece containing the dregs of Horlicks and hot chocolate and George had left a pair of scissors, a pen and scraps of wrapping paper on the floor.

In two years' time she would be sixty years old. How much longer would she be able to keep going? Her mother was so frail, and the arthritis in Liz's hands so bad she could hardly hold the knife yesterday when she'd offered to help prepare vegetables for Christmas dinner. At a time when she, herself was struggling to cope with day-to-day housework as well as working almost full-time at the shoe factory, her mother was slowing down, unable to do anything more than the odd batch of baking or tackle a small pile of ironing.

Now, on top of everything else, she had two children to think about. She was determined to give them a good Christmas, but she was almost at the end of her tether. Her back ached, her legs felt as if they were about to give way beneath her and there was so much to think about she felt as if her brain was bubbling away like a sheep's head in a pan of collards and onions from George's allotment.

She had fully intended to help George wrap the children's presents, and had wanted to see what he had bought on his last-minute shopping excursion, but he had been most insistent. At half past ten he'd made her a cup of Horlicks, filled two hot water bottles and put them in the bed and then, as an afterthought, folded an extra blanket over her side, because it was so cold.

'You go up, love,' he'd said, putting an arm around her shoulders as she took two aspirins to ease her thumping head. 'You've done a grand job today – the house is absolutely spotless and the Christmas tree and decorations are just the job. Everything looks lovely for tomorrow, and I know you'll put on a spread fit for the Queen of England. Don't you worry about a thing, I'll wrap everything.'

She had been shattered. Although she loved Christmas, and having the family around, she felt trapped in the house in Cornwall Road that belonged to her parents. Each year since her grandchildren had been born, she'd shed a few tears of regret over Christmas Day. Their only daughter, Margaret, lived nearby, just a few streets away in Regent Street, but her son-in-law always put his foot down, insistent his family would spend Christmas in their own home and their children would absolutely not be dragged all over the town visiting elderly relatives when all they wanted to do was play with their new toys. Usually easy-going and amiable, Brian had steadfastly refused when she had begged him to spend just one Christmas Day in Cornwall Road while her grandchildren were small. He had shook his head and said he was sorry. They didn't mind how many people come round to their house on Christmas Day, but they were not budging from their own fireside.

The very first Christmas she was a grandmother had sealed future Christmases in all its disastrous glory. That year, Margaret had walked over on Christmas afternoon with her baby granddaughter, Anne, in her pram and stayed for an hour. Brian hadn't come, though. He hadn't wanted to go out in the cold, drizzly rain. It had been lovely to spend some time with Margaret and her new granddaughter, but George had been uneasy all the time she was there. He had said to her later: *"You shouldn't have put our Margaret under pressure to turn out, Rose. They're a family now. You're pulling them apart. It's not as if you don't see them all the time, is it, love?"*

George had then told her that Margaret had been in tears, sobbing on his shoulder in the kitchen because she and Brian had argued on Christmas morning about the visit to Cornwall Road. It just wasn't right that her granddaughter's first Christmas had been spoiled by her parents arguing and all that had been achieved was Margaret in tears on Christmas Day, a soaked pram and a fretful baby that had cried its head off, irritating Tom and Liz so badly that Margaret had felt compelled to leave after only an hour.

Pulled almost to breaking point, Rose was always at her lowest point at Christmas and this year was no exception, despite the unexpected turn of events.

Last night, she had trudged wearily up the stairs, wishing she could just walk away from everything and everyone in the morning and relax with her daughter and family in the cosy terraced house in Regent Street. She had been too exhausted to help George wrap the presents he had bought, but now she wished she had stayed up just a little while longer to oversee the process. He'd made a real mess of them, and not only that, he'd placed them all higgledy-piggledy and hadn't even put them into piles.

She opened a cupboard door in the recess beside the fireplace and took out two spare Christmas cards and a pen. The children must have a card each on Christmas morning. It was a good job she had remembered. It would have ruined their day not to have even a single Christmas card. As an afterthought, she wrote out one for Violet, too. After all, she might just turn up, despite having been missing since Sunday afternoon.

When she had written the cards, Rose turned her attention to the fire grate. She shut her eyes momentarily and audibly exhaled in relief: the fire had already been laid, firewood laid neatly under the coals, ready for the match to alight twists of old newspaper stuffed between the kindling.

George was forgiven in an instant for his slip-shod wrapping and leaving a mess in the living room. She really must stop nagging him. What did it matter that he'd had a few drinks yesterday? After all, it was Christmas. She was so lucky to have such a caring and thoughtful husband.

She leaned back on her heels, watching the flames lick around the coals, making sure it was going to take hold. After a while she stood up, satisfied, and placed the fireguard around the fireplace. Now she would have time for a quiet cup of tea before everyone else got up.

Rose busied herself for a while, trying not to make too much noise, fretting that she had forgotten to do something. She checked the prepared turkey, and worked out the cooking time again – just to be absolutely sure it would be perfect by two o'clock, ready to serve up the dinner so that they would be finished by three, ready to watch the Queen on the television. She rearranged the holly and mistletoe around the mirror above the fireplace; she rehung all the Christmas cards on the wall, putting the largest in the middle of the string, graduating to the smallest at the edges; she fetched a duster from the kitchen and dusted each decoration on the Christmas tree in turn; and then, noticing how many pine needles had dropped, she swept them up quickly with a dustpan and brush. Finally, she sorted out the presents on the sofa, arranging them into neat little piles.

When she was satisfied everything was perfect, she went into the kitchen to make a cup of tea and wait for the rest of the family to appear, wondering if, in Regent Street, her grandchildren were up yet, excited because Father Christmas had been, ripping wrapping paper off their presents and whooping and shouting in delight.

She had just sat down at the kitchen table when she heard footsteps running down the stairs. The muffled, excited voices of Lydia and Tim in the front room made her chuckle out loud. Tim had obviously woken up and gone to wake his sister. It was grand to have children in the house on Christmas morning. She couldn't wait to see their faces when they saw their presents, even if everything had been bought hastily. Soon, she heard more movements above her head, and the creak of the stair rods as everyone made their way downstairs. Obviously no one was thinking of having a lie-in.

She patted the curlers under her hairnet, checking that none had fallen out in the night. She supposed she ought to go and get dressed, but she wanted to have a bath first. After all, what was the point of having a brand new bathroom installed earlier that year if you weren't going to use it for a bit of self-indulgent luxury on Christmas morning?

Soon, everyone was assembled in the living room. No one had dressed, but it didn't matter because the room was filled with Tim's incessant chatter, interspersed with George's witty comments and Liz ordering that the children should open a present in turn rather than just ripping off paper willy-nilly, which would cause no end of mess.

She heard herself giggle and then speak, tossing away Liz's comment with a dismissive wave of her hand. 'It doesn't matter, Mam. We can pick it up later. Let's just enjoy the day and not worry about housework for a change.

Folks will just have to take us as they find us.'

"Christmas Day 1962

Hello new diary! Today is the best day of my life because we are spending Christmas with our new family.

Tim got a super-duper penknife. He is so pleased with it he can't stop turning it over and over in his hand. Uncle George said it even has a little gadget for getting stones out of horses' hooves. Auntie Rose said if the horse saw her in her curlers it would bolt with fright and wouldn't stop to get a stone hooked out of its hoof. Tim also got a gyroscope which came with a little book to explain why it stays upright when it's spinning. Uncle Tom and Uncle George played with it all morning – poor Tim didn't get a look in, but he did learn all about centrifugal forces. He also got selection boxes, some really nice marbles, a balsa wood aeroplane kit, some Meccano and a box of Matey bubble bath with lanolin and hexachlorophene which Auntie Rose said sounded like it would explode and blast him out of the bath into outer space like a Sputnik.

I had some fab presents too. I got a real leather, cream handbag with a gold clasp and when I opened it there was a Panstick, a block of mascara with its own tiny brush, some lipstick, a blue eye shadow and some black and white Mary Quant nail transfers, which are the grooviest thing I have ever seen in my life. I can't imagine when I shall ever wear them, though! I also got a Dancing to the Loco-motion record and this diary, which even has a lock and key.

There was a new purse in the handbag made of real leather and when I opened it THERE WAS A FIVE POUND NOTE INSIDE, I was about to take it out to say thank you, but Uncle George tapped his nose, shook his head and winked at me. He says not to tell Auntie Rose about the money because she might moan at him. Five pounds – all for me! I can't believe it. I'M RICH. I also got some chocolate liqueurs, but Auntie Rose has eaten nearly all of them. She says Uncle George shouldn't have bought me such grown-up presents and didn't approve of the make-up and absolutely hated the nail transfers, but she did like my new bag and purse. She says she will replace the liqueurs with a nice bar of Cadbury's Dairy Milk, which is much more appropriate, considering I am only fifteen. She also said that Tim would slice all his fingers to the bone with his penknife, but he's been using it to cut up different things all day and he's only had to have two plasters put on his fingers so far.

Uncle George is the best uncle in the world. I love him already, but I'm not so sure about Auntie Rose. She was a bit of a tartar all day yesterday and was horrible to Uncle George. He says she's always like this at Christmas and on Sundays and not to take any notice.

It turned out the photograph we found of the children in the front room is quite old. Stuart is now nearly eighteen and WOW he's such a dish! We had a real fab time. I was squashed up against him for dinner which was an unbelievable thrill, and I absolutely LOVE Aunt Daisy. She seems so young compared to Auntie Rose. There are two other boys as well as Stuart. Trevor is about the same age as me and really annoying and Neil is the same age as Tim. It's nice for Tim to have found a friend, who is also our second cousin!

After a yummy Christmas dinner, when the table had been cleared and all the furniture put back, Uncle Tom made all of us children do the washing up to give Auntie Rose a bit of a rest. It was so funny. She had eaten so many chocolate liqueurs and drunk so much sherry she was really squiffy and laughing her head off all the time. Uncle George made her go upstairs for a lie down. When we were washing up, Tim and Neil were singing Christmas songs and Trevor kept rubbing soap suds all over my face singing: "for hands that do dishes can feel soft as your face."

Tomorrow, some friends of the family called Sarah and Millie are coming for tea, and Auntie Rose and Uncle George's daughter and their grandchildren are coming round as well. Auntie Rose said that all the men go to the working men's club at dinner time and then we have cold meat and pickles *for dinner when they get back. It sounds like so much fun. Oh, and it's going to SNOW according to the weather forecast. We might even be able to build a snowman in the back garden!*

I am running out of space for 25th December, so goodbye for now, new diary. I shall write in you again tomorrow."

Lydia put the top back on the pen Uncle Tom had given her and placed it carefully in her new handbag.

'Have you finished?' Liz said, while Lydia was quietly re-reading her account of the day.

Lydia nodded. 'Yes, that's the very first entry. I shall write another one tomorrow.'

'Can I see?' George asked.

Lydia's face fell, but she reluctantly handed over her diary. It seemed rude not to let Uncle George have a look at what she had written, but she wished she hadn't written the bit about Auntie Rose being a tartar and a bit squiffy and Stuart being a dish.

'Only joking!' George chuckled as he handed it back to her. 'You lock it up and go and hide that key where no one can find it. Perhaps one day, when you're all grown up, you can let me read it.'

Lydia grinned as she stood up to take her diary and new handbag into the front room to put with their other belongings. It was a quarter to nine. They really should go to bed now to give the grown-ups some time to themselves.

If Christmas Day had been exciting, Christmas night watching the television had been truly magical. Neither of them were used to having a television and Tim had been spellbound. He'd not moved from the fireside rug all night, laying on his tummy dressed in an over-sized old tartan dressing-gown loaned to him by Uncle George, his chin cupped in his hands, mesmerised by *Christmas Night with the Stars,* featuring Billy Cotton and the Band Show, Arthur Askey and Russ Conway. He had rolled around laughing at a Steptoe and Son sketch and then sat, sombre and cross-legged at Dixon of Dock Green.

Then, there was an announcement when missing pop star, Sergio de Luca, had been scheduled to sing and they had put Andy Williams singing *Moon River* on instead.

'There,' Auntie Rose had said smugly to her Uncle George. 'I told you Sergio de Luca wouldn't be on the television if he has disappeared into thin air. It was nice of Andy Williams to step in at the last minute though.'

George had chuckled and tossed Lydia a conspiratorial wink. 'All of it is just filmed beforehand, Rose,' he had said to her. 'But it wouldn't be right to put Sergio de Luca on the telly when he's missing, presumed drowned. Folks would be ringing up police stations all over the country to say they'd seen him crooning *Forget Me Not* on the telly!'

Rose had sniffed into air, not wanting to admit defeat. 'Well, filmed or not, it was all very nice. Now, who would like some cocoa? *The African Queen* will be on in a minute, and I've been looking forward to a bit of Humphrey Bogart all week.'

Now, the perfect day was almost at an end. Lydia wanted to hold on tightly to every moment. 'Uncle George, you are so funny,' she said giggling at the latest of his many jokes. 'I'll make the cocoa and then Tim and I will go to bed, won't we Tim?'

'No,' Tim complained. 'Not yet. I want to watch the film, too, and I *never, ever* want this day to end.'

Billowing clouds of heavy snow enveloped Kettering on Boxing Day, flakes settling easily on the frozen ground in an icy blast of cold air from the north. While adults kept an eye on dismal weather forecasts and frequent news reports, children all over the town whooped and danced in excitement at the prospect of a few days of tobogganing, snowman-building and epic snowball fights before going back to school after the Christmas holiday.

Lydia sat alone by the window in the front room, her new diary open on her lap, pen poised but unable to write anything. She watched the snow for a while, marvelling at the mystery of the intricacy of snowflakes. The intermittent patter on the windowpane should have soothed her troubled thoughts, but in the same way as the cold weather front turned tiny drops of moisture into thick clumps of snow, the nugget of worry that had formed inside her since they had arrived on Sunday afternoon began to swell and grow until it made her gasp with its enormity.

She stared at the blank page before her and for a moment wondered why the pen in her hand was shaking. She wasn't cold: she could feel the warmth from the fire on her legs and Auntie Rose's hand-knitted cardigan was cosy and comforting. It smelled of lavender and honeysuckle and the sweet aroma of vanilla essence, captured in every fibre of the soft wool during a cake-baking session. She wished she could somehow preserve the fragrance of Auntie Rose's cardigan, together with the Christmassy smells of pine needles and mulled wine, and take them with her in a bottle when they left this house, because they would forever remind her of the lovely day they'd had yesterday.

Tim's voice drifted through from the living room again. He was laughing, whooping with delight and singing *Frosty the Snowman*, while Uncle George said something about finding Margaret's old sledge in the barn and borrowing a pair of wellington boots for him so that he could play in the snow when they went to Aunt Daisy's house tomorrow.

It wasn't fair – while Tim was obviously living in the moment, without a care in the world other than playing in the snow, she was having to worry about where they were going to live, how she could earn enough money to put food on the table and most of all, whether they would ever see their mother again. She wrote a few words in her diary: *"Today is Boxing Day ..."*

She couldn't continue. It was as if the falling snow was freezing out the words in her head and making her hands shiver. There was an unnatural, hushed silence in the street outside, dampening and dulling the happy chatter, the drone of the television in the background and Tim giggling in the living room.

The snow should be bringing grandeur and enchantment to the festive season, like a Fairy Godmother sprinkling diamond dust over multi-coloured Christmas tree lights and sparkling tinsel. The distinctive smell in the air outside – wood smoke and burning coal absorbed in each and every flake from the chimneys of happy households – should have infused her with joy and excitement. Everyone knew snow at Christmas-time was a miracle.

But the snow was not a miracle. Not this year. Not when tomorrow, Christmas would be over and the peculiar metamorphosis of Tim would be complete. Somehow, over the space of just two days, Tim had pulled all the confidence and sense of self-worth out of her and transferred it into himself, leaving her feeling empty, quiet and tearful in a crash to earth after the magical day they'd had yesterday.

There was no doubt about it: their mother had known they would have a happy Christmas here – much better than the Christmas she could have given them – but like so many decisions in her life she had made the wrong choice. From the moment she had walked away from them on Sunday, she and Tim had begun to be pulled apart, like two pieces of a jigsaw puzzle spilt into the innocent optimism of a child and the quiet pessimistic worries of an adult, because that was now what she must become. On some primal level, she knew she had always been more than a sister to Tim, but now their mother had left them she knew that no matter what the future held, she and Tim would never be the same again.

The arrival of the snow somehow completed the change. It had smothered their past, covering and imprisoning reality. It had muffled the harshness of poverty, hunger, cold and fear, blurring the distinction between the time that had gone and the time that was to come. Everything was now fresh, clean and sterile, but it was also uncertain – the future illuminated from below; their world turned upside down by a reversal of light. But Lydia knew the snow would eventually melt, and when it did it would reveal a vicious underworld of truth for her brother, forcing him to grow up when he was still a child, and she would need to become a proper mother to him, instead of an older sister.

Tim burst into the front room, his cheeks glowing. 'It's getting deeper, Lydia. Isn't it exciting? It's so *white!* Uncle George says that when we go to Aunt Daisy's tomorrow, she will let us have a snowball fight, so you'd better ask if you can borrow a pair of gloves.'

Lydia smiled at her brother, determined to overcome the gloominess that had engulfed her. It was so good to see him confident, talkative and happy for once, even if his cheerfulness did seem to be at her expense.

It was almost dark now. She stood up and pulled back the curtain so she could see just how deep the snow was. Just for a while, she allowed it to blank out her worries and fears for the future.

Snow is like cotton wool for a troubled mind, she thought as she walked out of the room to join the rest of the family. She made a bargain with herself. *While the snow is on the ground I won't let myself worry about what is going to happen to us.*

Chapter Seven

The hiatus caused by the arrival of the snow was finely balanced, with the scales tipping first one way, then the other, weighted with a series of dichotomies for both Lydia in Kettering and her exasperated mother stranded in a London hotel.

While Violet paced up and down in frustration as flight after flight to Barcelona was cancelled because of the treacherous weather conditions, each news report of Sergio de Luca's sensational disappearance provided a welcome distraction for the Jeffson family and gave them something to talk about. As each day rolled and tumbled into another in a snow globe of enforced togetherness, Lydia grew closer to her new family, her old life in London receding further into the distance and she found herself hardly thinking of her mother at all. But for Violet, it was as if she was outside the glass, drawn constantly to peer inside, each trip down memory lane bringing painful reminders of the children she had left behind. *"Go back for them,"* Sergio had said to her. *"I honestly don't mind if they come to Spain with us."* Violet had shaken her head, turning away from him so he couldn't see her tears.

Immediately after the Christmas holiday, the family had alerted the council to the children's predicament and reported Violet as a missing person at Kettering Police Station because, George had reasoned, she might have just had a terrible accident or been taken ill and not abandoned her children after all. Two days later an officious-looking Child Care Officer had, in his own words, taken his life in his hands to battle through an arctic blizzard to satisfy himself that Lydia and Tim were being looked after by their family. After two cups of tea laced with brandy, two mince pies and almost half a Victoria sandwich cake, he had once again braved the whiteout with a promise to a hysterical Lydia and a subdued Tim that: *"no, they wouldn't be sent to a children's home while Mr and Mrs Foster and Mr and Mrs Jeffson were willing to look after them and give them somewhere to live."*

Following George's report of Violet's disappearance, a police constable had marched, Gestapo-like, through the snow in oversized wellington boots to confirm to the family in a stilted, monochrome voice that a Mr and Mrs Richard Smith had stayed at the Royal Hotel before checking out at 12.05 hrs on 27th December: destination unknown. Lydia had cried when the policeman, eyes cast upwards so that he didn't have to look at her, confirmed that her description of her mother matched that given by the hotel. The family had shaken their heads in shocked disbelief at the news. Not only had the children been abandoned by their mother, but it appeared that everything had been planned with meticulous detail and that their long-time absent father had not even wanted to see them when they had arrived in Kettering.

Finally, on Thursday, 3rd January, the first hint of an end to the whiteout came with a good weather report for the following day.

Having obtained permission from his boss at the shoe factory where he and Rose both worked, George made some hasty arrangements for a train trip to London to try to make sense of the chaos Violet had left in her wake. With no immediate threat of more snow, he managed to secure tickets for himself and Lydia on the 8.00 am train the following day to try and resolve the puzzle of where Violet had gone.

The train journey was strangely poetic. De-commissioned steam trains had been brought back into use as they were heavier than their newer, diesel replacements and there was no risk of the diesel freezing in the fuel tanks.

Trains stranded on the main railway route would restrict the movement of food and other provisions across the country and thousands of railway staff and volunteers had turned up to help. Even the army had been drafted in to keep the main railway lines clear and the trains rolling.

The steam train was packed. After all, snow had fallen nearly every day since Boxing Day, and now the weather seemed to be improving, folks visiting relatives for Christmas needed to get back to their homes and jobs, frustrated by the protracted disruption to everyday life. The weather had disconnected them from reality and imprisoned them in a strange, white other-worldliness, but it had also brought people together in true British spirit and folks shared snow stories about dustbin lids freezing to hands; burst gas mains; mountainous snowdrifts and power cuts, chatting like old friends as they chugged their way out of their personal snow globes and back into reality.

Once they were on the train, George and Lydia made their way to the breakfast carriage, where businessmen sat, warm and cosy in their smart suits, drinking tea and eating toast whilst watching lines of railway workers flashing past, clearing sidings and defrosting frozen points with over-sized shovels and sledge hammers, their hands almost blood-red from the cold as they worked to keep the country going.

The swaying of the carriage and the chugger-chugger of the engines was hypnotic, a panorama of fascinating snapshots rolling past. Dirty, sooty snow gave way to fields of pure whiteness; a train on a parallel distant track snaked its way across the white plains like a huge, billowing caterpillar while cows huddled under snow-laden leafless trees, dirty white and black, reluctant to move in the knee-deep snow.

'Look at the depth of these snowdrifts,' Lydia said to George as she tucked into a plate of toast. 'They are like frozen white cliffs. I didn't realise it was so deep.'

'It's the wind: it's blown it into the cuttings, where it's built up over a few days,' George replied. The railway line has been dug out of the snow. That's why it looks like a cliff.'

Another train passed by and Lydia flinched as the world outside turned pure white in a singularity of steam and billowing snow. When it cleared she sat spellbound as a lone snowman, with eyes of coal, a carrot nose and a red scarf flashed past, lonely and abandoned by the children who had built it. As they chugged through a built-up area, children were sledging on a slight incline, periodically tumbling off, rolling around like swaddled puppies and kittens.

The other-worldliness intensified periodically when they approached towns and villages, sometimes stopping to pick up more passengers. Traffic signs in the distance stood like short-sticked lollipops sprinkled with icing sugar. Garden gates to homes beside the railway line were frozen half-open like knives stuck in stale loaves of bread. At one point Lydia and George giggled out loud at a row of old ladies wearing grey balaclava helmets under floral headscarves, following each other carefully on a narrow frozen footpath, waddling like ducklings in their wellington boots as they followed the leader. Cars had been abandoned on a road beside the railway, the drifting snow piled up around them almost to the tops of the doors. A couple of men, having dug out a vehicle, slipped and skidded as they tried to push it free, exhaust fumes billowing high into the air as the engine revved and the wheels spun, flinging the powdery snow into their red faces.

Nine hours later, back safely in Cornwall Road, George blew on his hands, while Lydia slipped off the wellington boots she had borrowed from Rose onto sheets of old newspaper spread out by the back door. She tucked her frozen hands under her armpits, almost in tears. She had never been so cold in her life and she was certain she would never again be able to feel her feet.

Once they had settled by the fire in the living room with steaming cups of cocoa and some warmed up leftover stew and chunks of bread, George began to tell the story of their trip to London.

'We managed to get a key from Violet's landlord,' he began. 'You wouldn't believe the terrible conditions these poor children have had to endure.'

'I tried to keep it clean,' Lydia interrupted guiltily, but George put up a hand to stop her mid-sentence.

'I could see you did. But you can't make a silk purse out of a sow's ear, can you, lass, so the less said about it the better.'

Lydia bit her lip and looked away, embarrassed. 'We found some old photographs,' she said. 'But I said that if our parents don't want us, then I don't want them either, and so we left them behind.'

'Yes, we left them behind,' George echoed. He reached into the inside pocket of his jacket. 'Well, all but this one. I saved it for you – it's one of your grandmother and grandfather, Doris and Walter, and I thought you might like to keep it.'

Lydia took the photograph and rubbed her thumb over the image. George had explained the truth of her grandfather's circumstances to her on the train back from London, and she had mixed feelings about him. Nevertheless, she felt a thread of connectivity stir inside her.

'Do you think we might look for him? After all he might still be alive,' she asked George.

'All in good time, lass,' Tom muttered.

George picked up Lydia's brown cardboard suitcase by his feet. 'We collected up some essential documentation and some of the children's belongings. We managed to find Lydia and Tim's birth certificates, but Violet's has gone. We asked one of the neighbours if they had seen her. Apparently, she turned up at the flat just after Christmas and told the neighbour she had recently reconciled with her husband after finding out he was living in Northamptonshire and was moving away to start a new life '

'Is that the truth, do you think?' Tom asked.

'Did you bring some more clothes with you?' Rose interrupted.

George shook his head almost imperceptibly and shot a

look at his wife that told her not to pursue the matter. 'Nah,' he said. 'We couldn't find anything warm enough, so I reckoned we'd just go out shopping this weekend and buy them some more suitable clobber to be going on with.'

Lydia cringed. George had watched her sort through their clothes and muttered several swear words under his breath. Then, she had seen him wipe the corner of his eye before declaring that the next place they were going to visit was *Top Pop Fashion Shop*, where she could buy the popover top and slacks she had chattered about on the train earlier that day, and a warm, navy blue anorak to be going on with. He had then taken five pound notes out of his wallet and given them to her.

'The headmaster at Tim's school was a nice chap,' George continued, pulling a large brown envelope out of the bag. 'He's given us his school records and a letter so that he can transfer to the Grammar School, and another letter personally recommending Lydia for a place at the High School, if she wants to go. She's only missed a term, and if she is accepted, he reckons she will easily catch up if she works hard.'

A few days later, the family crowded into the living room – there were not enough chairs so the men stood whilst the women sat down. Children of various ages had been banished to the front room with the game of Housey-Housey and a handful of pennies and ha'pennies as prize money. Tom hauled himself to the table, his crutches creaking. He slapped his hand on the edge to gain everyone's attention.

'We are gathered here today,' he said solemnly, squinting through his cataracts as he swayed unsteadily, 'to decide how this family is going to provide for young Lydia and Timothy now their mother and father have deserted them. They're our flesh and blood and we should all take some of the responsibility.'

Tom drew in a sharp breath and puffed out his chest with importance as he lifted his glasses menacingly, peering at everyone in turn so that they could tell he meant business.

An hour later, the children's future had been mapped out. They were to continue to live at Cornwall Road but everyone would contribute or help out as much as they could. To give Rose and George a bit of a break, as they would be assuming the responsibility of being the children's main guardians, they would spend Saturdays with Daisy, Bill and the three boys.

Tom took off his cap and put it in the centre of the table. He extracted one arm from his crutch and reached into his jacket pocket, 'Here y'are,' he said to Bill, handing him his wallet, swaying on his remaining crutch, 'take a couple of quid out and put it in there.' He nodded in the direction of the upturned cap.

The men all looked at each other with raised eyebrows. Two pound notes was a lot of money when you only earned around eight pounds a week, and it was hell of a lot of money to find just after Christmas.

'Well, come on!' Tom said, picking up his cap and shaking it, 'kids don't come cheap, you know, and both of them need decent overcoats, some new clothes and school uniforms. George reckoned the clothes he found at the flat in London were only fit for the rag factory, didn't you George?'

George nodded his head slowly. 'I never thought I'd see the day when members of our family lived in such poverty,' he said. 'And I, for one, intend to make sure those poor kids want for nothing now.'

No-one daring to argue with Tom, the families all contributed as much as they could afford, and Margaret's husband, Brian, generously offered to buy both children second-hand bicycles so they could get to school.

Lydia's future had begun, but it was to be weeks before she could use her new bicycle to get to school, as the very next day after the family conference, having got up early to lay the fire so that her Auntie Rose could have a bit of a lie-in, she opened the back door to find herself staring open-mouthed at a wall of snow, a fifteen foot snowdrift having formed outside the back door during an overnight snowstorm.

Chapter Eight

The harsh winter of nineteen sixty-three not only enfolded families into its womb-like intimacy, it brought the country together in a determined community spirit that knew no boundaries in its quest to keep fires burning, food on the table and milk on the doorstep every day. There was not one street in Kettering where pavements were not cleared daily, as residents undertook to maintain their own little patch of Great Britain. Piles of dirty, sooty ice by the side of the road grew taller and taller while huge twinkling icicles hung dangerously from the eaves of rows of terraced houses, forcing people to glance up anxiously as they hurried about their daily lives. Someone, it was rumoured, had ended up comatose in hospital after being hit on the head by a giant icicle, although no one could say exactly who this person was or where they lived.

Schools battled endlessly to make sure pupils were kept warm during lessons. Bottles of frozen milk were placed by radiators to defrost by playtime, children overjoyed at finding an icy chunk of cream floating in watery milk, which was sucked up greedily through yellow, red and blue striped straws. Uniform policies were relaxed, so that pupils could wear warm clothes and concentrate on their lessons, no matter how terrible the weather was outside. Blizzards raged for days at a time, but still the country battled on: teachers taught; shopkeepers opened their shops; librarians stamped books and farmers dug out livestock from snowdrifts, battling endlessly against the elements, determined not to let the big freeze get the better of them.

Behind closed front doors, people huddled in front of

open coal fires, speculating on just when the terrible winter would end, gasping in shock at never-ending news reports of people being gassed in their homes by broken mains, dynamite being used to blast railway tracks free of snowdrifts in Scotland and the sea freezing over in Kent and Hunstanton. An urgent appeal went out for milk bottles, as stocks fell to critical levels with many being frozen into deep snowdrifts and therefore temporarily lost.

Lydia's past receded further beneath her feet with every flake of snow that fell in those first three months of the New Year. It was as if each and every day she made permanent, fresh footprints on the journey towards her future. The winter wonderland of sparkly new emotions and the rich togetherness of the Jeffson family gradually drew her out of herself and, for the first time in her life, she began to feel excited and optimistic. She hardly ever thought about her mother or wondered where she had gone. Secure in the knowledge that she and Tim were now part of the Jeffson family, and having obtained a Saturday job in the local branch of Woolworths to help pay their way, she was determined to make the most of their good fortune and her second chance to secure a good education.

Shortly after her sixteenth birthday in March, Lydia lost her appetite, couldn't sleep and had a constant gnawing feeling in the pit of her stomach. Despite all the love given so freely by the Jeffson family, it was as if she constantly craved for more. Like her mother before her, she found herself persistently drawn towards her Aunt Daisy and Uncle Bill and their three sons who lived in Windmill Avenue, and was never happier than when she spent time with them, joining in with their relentless male-orientated banter and crazy, hair-brained adventures. She made a pact with herself – if she was lucky enough to ever have a home and a family of her own, she would make sure she was just like her Auntie Rose and Aunt Daisy, who were the loveliest and most kind-hearted women she had ever met in her life.

In March, just as the Great British spirit was beginning to wear a little thin and wane somewhat, with townsfolk going about their business on a permanent, irritable short fuse, the snow quickly melted into a dirty slush and then evaporated away, revealing the green shoots of spring.

One Sunday afternoon, Lydia sat on her Aunt Daisy's back doorstep, enjoying the warmth of the sunshine, reading a book, while a few feet away Trevor tinkered around with an old moped. They were talking about her mother.

'If you ask me, she had a screw loose somewhere,' Trevor said as he reached in his toolbox for a spanner. 'I never met her but I know pretty much what happened to her when she was a child from my mate, Rob Potter.'

Lydia knew Rob Potter. He was Trevor's best friend and had a shiny new motorbike, on which she fully intended to ride pillion now the weather had improved. Rob Potter's new motorbike was the sole reason Trevor was determined to mend the old moped and have some wheels to ride of his own, but unlike Rob Potter's parents, his were not rich enough to buy him even a second-hand motorbike or scooter.

'How does *he* know about my mother,' she replied. 'He's nothing to do with our family, is he?'

'Nah. He's not family. But his dad, Billy Potter, lived in Cornwall Road as a child and his mum was at junior school with Violet. His mum had polio when she was a little girl and used to walk with callipers on her legs. You must have seen her before – she often sits drinking tea in the back room of the bakery with Aunt Sarah.'

'Oh yes, I know her. She's a really nice lady. She knitted Tim a balaclava helmet when we first arrived in Kettering. And Rob Potter's grandma comes round in the afternoons to have a cup of tea with Auntie Liz. Her name's Evelyn.'

Trevor sat back on his heels and squinted at Lydia in the sunshine. 'That's right. Evelyn Potter. Apparently, it was through your mum that Rob's parents ever met in the first place.'

'Really? How come?'

'Well – as I said, your mum has always had a screw loose, even when she was a little girl. Apparently, she cut off all her own hair when she was nine. Then her mother made up this cock-and-bull story that she had alopecia – you know, it's where all your hair falls out? Your grandparents made her have her head shaved every Sunday and even used to shave off her eyebrows, too.'

'That's dreadful,' Lydia said, shocked at the new revelations about her mother. No matter how heartless Violet had always been towards her and Tim, she knew she would never have done anything as cruel as that to them.

'Anyway, Rob Potter's mum, Mary, was asked by the Headmaster at their school to try and make friends with your mother, because she hadn't any hair and he thought she needed a friend, but Rob's mum said Violet was having none of it, was horrible to her and used to call her a cripple.'

'My mother always said she never had any friends as a child,' Lydia said with a shrug. 'I never heard her talk about anyone called Mary.'

'They weren't friends, but Rob's mum always felt sorry for her, even though she used to call her a cripple. One day, Violet was off school and someone said it was because she had cut her own arms and legs herself with a kitchen knife. Rob's mum decided to try one last time to make friends with her, and so went and knocked on her front door.'

'My mum *cut* herself?' Lydia said, flabbergasted.

Trevor nodded. 'I told you she always had a screw loose. Anyway, Rob's dad, Billy, had found her in Gramp's workshop, covered in blood. She'd taken the knife out of the drawer in the kitchen and cut herself with it. Then, when the police were called, she lied and said it was Rob's dad that had done it to her.'

'That's awful. What happened then? Did Rob's dad get arrested?'

'No. It wasn't long before the policeman got the truth out of Violet and she owned up to doing it herself. Rob's mum and dad had never met before, but when everything came out about what your mother's parents had done to her – making her have her head and eyebrows shaved off for almost a year – they both felt really sorry for what she had been through, and coincidentally turned up at exactly the same time to visit her and try to become her friend. Rob's mum was only ten years-old and his dad was in his twenties, though. Because his mum had walked a long way with callipers on her legs and given herself blisters on her hands using walking sticks to visit Violet, his dad pushed her home on his bike. And that is how Rob's parents met. It was all through your mum cutting herself.'

'You seem to know a lot about my mum,' Lydia said, uneasily. 'I suppose everyone's been gossiping since we arrived in Kettering at Christmas.'

'Yeah. They have,' Trevor admitted. 'Rob's dad told me the story only the other week when me and Rob went for a pint in the club with him.'

'But if Rob's mum was only a child, and his dad was grown up, how come they eventually got married?'

Trevor shrugged. 'I dunno.'

Daisy appeared in the doorway, a duster in her hand. Lydia stood up as she flicked it out of the door, embarrassed because it was obvious Daisy had been listening to the conversation about her mother.

Daisy leaned on the door jamb, folding her arms across her flowery apron as she took up Trevor's story.

'Rob's grandparents, Mr and Mrs Summers, used to be quite wealthy. They're retired now. They live in a big house in Rockingham Road – it's ever so posh. Anyway they were really taken with Rob's dad because he'd been so kind as to push little Mary home on his bike that day. Billy was a gifted carpenter and joiner and later did some work for them, making some furniture and kitchen cupboards. Anyway, a couple of years later he was beginning to make a bit of a name for himself in the town, and so they put up the money for him to set up in business as a carpenter. It was the making of him. Then, when Mary grew up, she married him.'

'That's a lovely story,' Lydia said. 'And to think it all came about because of my mother.'

Daisy folded her arms across her chest. 'Rob is a lucky lad to have the Potters for parents. They are such a lovely family, despite them both being handicapped.'

'Handicapped?' Trevor said, screwing up his eyes. 'No they're not. They're really nice.'

Daisy laughed. 'Well, Mary's now in a wheelchair, in case it escaped your notice.'

'Oh yeah,' Trevor said. 'It's just that I've never really thought of her like that. She's always done all the usual mum stuff, just like anyone else's mum. She cooks great dinners – her jam roly-polys are yummy and her Yorkshire puddings are enormous.'

'You said they both had disabilities.' Lydia said. 'What's up with Rob's dad, then?'

Daisy hastily changed the subject, wishing she hadn't mentioned it. Billy Potter had done so well over the years, she didn't want to have to tell Trevor and Lydia that he was regarded as one of the town's simpletons as a boy, with people calling him names and poking fun at him. He now ran a successful business and only a few people knew about his difficulties with reading and writing, because Mary did all the business accounts and correspondence.

'I loved your mother when she was a child,' Daisy said. 'She was treated very cruelly by my aunt, and yet she was so bright and intelligent. She was the prettiest little thing with her blonde hair and blue eyes. I often wonder how she'd have turned out if she'd had decent parents and a bit of luck in her life. Quite differently, I suspect.'

Lydia gave a sad, wistful shake of her head. 'I wish I had known about her awful childhood. Why on earth did she never tell me?'

Daisy tucked her duster into her apron pocket, untied the headscarf around her head and shook it off. 'After the incident with the kitchen knife, we took her in and looked after her for a few months, but we were only eighteen ourselves and needed the money her parents paid us for her keep. Your Auntie Eileen was just a baby and we were ever so hard-up. To be honest, though, it was the making of us. I've no idea how we would have afforded to furnish this house without the money we got from your grandparents for looking after your mother. She was no trouble, either. A lovely little girl and so bright and intelligent.'

'How long did she live here?'

'About seven months. Your grandmother was pregnant at the time and her doctor had recommended that Violet stay with us until the baby was born because of all the upset.'

'Do we have another auntie or uncle, then, if my grandmother had another child apart from the one who died?' Lydia said, raising her eyebrows speculatively.

'I'm afraid not, Lydia,' Daisy said, placing a hand on her arm. 'It was a little boy, but it hadn't formed properly in the womb and had a terrible defect. The poor soul didn't live very long. And it badly affected poor Violet because the doctor blamed her for the baby's defect and said it was the shock of your grandmother seeing Violet with her arms and legs covered in blood at a crucial time for the baby's development in the womb. It was a complete old wives' tale, but the doctor was elderly and old-fashioned and believed it, even though your grandmother's midwife spoke out and said Violet couldn't possibly be held to blame.'

Lydia's mouth fell open as she felt a painful tug of sympathy for her mother. Inexplicably she wished she could go back in time, put her arms around her mother as a child and make everything right in her life. She shook her head slowly, for the first time feeling as if she was actually getting to know the woman who had given birth to her.

'I knew nothing of this.' Lydia said eventually.

'Your mother's life has been one big series of tragedies,' Daisy explained. 'It's no wonder she's turned out as she has. I just wish people would stop speaking badly of her and remember what she's been through in her life.'

'Someone once said my mother was dead behind the eyes,' Lydia recalled out loud. 'And I sort of knew what they meant. It was as if you couldn't get through to her – I never knew what she was feeling or thinking. It was like she was just acting out her life, whatever we did or wherever we went.'

'If things had been different for her,' Daisy went on, 'she wouldn't have turned out to be such a wrong 'un, of that I'm certain. Life hasn't been kind to her, and she confided in me years ago that she feared she had inherited her own mother's lack of maternal instinct. She's to be pitied – not vilified. She needs help.'

'I don't know how many times she told me she wasn't cut out to be a mother,' Lydia said. 'If only she'd told me about her awful childhood, I feel sure I could have helped her come to terms with everything, but I can't think of a single time she ever let down her guard, even with us – her own children.'

Daisy hugged Lydia to her. 'Perhaps one day, love, you'll get the chance to do just that. She'll be back – you mark my words. You see, I'm probably the only person in the world who really knows her. I can see straight through that tough veneer to the real Violet underneath, but for now we need to concentrate on your education and make sure you and young Tim don't go down the same path as your poor mother.'

'If you are taking Physics and Chemistry, why don't you come to Mr Perry's Astronomy Society?' Daisy's eldest son, Stuart, suggested. 'You're spending too much time with my oaf of a brother and that mate of his.'

Lydia was quick to defend Trevor. 'Don't call him an oaf. He's really talented, getting that old moped going when your dad said he hadn't a hope in hell.'

Stuart glanced sideways at her as they walked to school together, his black hair flopping over his forehead. His stomach churned with jealousy. Lydia spent so much time with his younger brother and although she was perfectly polite and amicable during the few conversations they had shared, he couldn't help thinking she preferred Trevor to himself.

Lydia gave a nervous laugh, which Stuart then echoed uncomfortably. He couldn't believe he was actually walking to school with her. He'd hung around that morning, in a forced casual pose as if waiting for someone else. She had glanced over both shoulders as she hurried towards him. He'd stood up from the wall where he'd been sitting with his forearm casually bent across his knee, trying to look relaxed. It was the very first time he'd waited for her. Usually he strode on in front without even acknowledging her presence but acutely aware of her eyes boring into his back.

'I only wanted a ride on Rob's new motorbike,' she explained. 'If truth be told, the pair of them bore me senseless with their endless talk of motorbikes and football most of the time, but they can be great fun and a distraction from all my homework.'

Stuart gave a condescending sniff into the air. 'If you want to be a doctor, like me, you'll have to knuckle down. It's bloody hard work in the upper sixth – you won't have time to go swanning around on the back of greasy old motorbikes. I'm serious, Lydia – if you're interested in astronomy, join the Society. It will help you no end with Physics. There are a few girls go, so you won't be the only one. Please? I'd really like it if you'd join.'

Stuart held his breath. It had taken him great courage to ask her along to the Astronomy Society. Almost as soon as he'd uttered the words, he regretted it. Lydia might be clever, but she also liked to enjoy herself and she had brought a breath of fresh air into his male-dominated household. They walked along in silence. Lydia didn't answer, but shot him a wonky smile, which told him she wasn't quite sure about the Astronomy Society.

As they hurried towards the school, their similar appearance struck Stuart. They had the same thick, dark hair and brown eyes. They both wore glasses and were tall and slim. It was probably clear they were related, but she was only his second-cousin. His grandmother and her grandmother had been sisters. It wasn't like she was his actual cousin. And a chap was allowed to fancy his second-cousin. He knew, because he had checked in a law book in the school library and had discovered to his surprise it wasn't even illegal to marry your first-cousin, so it couldn't be that bad, him falling for Lydia in the way he had.

'Okay,' she said tentatively. 'I'll give it a try. But I'm not sure I want to be a doctor – I'd like to eventually go into social work, I think. Perhaps become a Child Care Officer.'

'Great,' said Stuart, pleased. He had been attracted to her from the moment he first set eyes on her last Christmas, when she'd been squeezed up against him for Christmas dinner. In the beginning, though, he had kept well away from the shenanigans at his grandparents' house, staying on the periphery of the crisis. He knew there were some dark secrets about his Aunt Violet, and that she had left Kettering about the time he was born, but it was something the family had never talked about.

Eventually, he had casually made a slight detour on his way home from school one evening and called in on his grandparents, on the pretence of telling Tom all about the Astronomy Society. He had chatted to Lydia about the High School and asked her what subjects she was taking for her 'A' levels, and after only a few minutes of conversation had felt as if he had known her for years, which was an odd feeling for him as he usually found it very difficult to make friends.

The visit had also reaped rewards in the form of a new, state of the art telescope from his grandparents for his eighteenth birthday, which, his Auntie Rose had told him with a disdainful sniff, had cost an absolute fortune.

They approached the school, side by side, in step with each other, neither of them knowing what to say next.

'I'll meet you out here after school and we can go and see Mr Perry if you like.'

'All right. I'll see you, then,' Lydia finally managed to mumble.

'Hope you have a good day,' Stuart replied over his shoulder, blushing as a couple of younger lads made fun of them.

A few weeks later, one Saturday morning, Daisy, Rose and Millie from the bakery were sitting in Daisy's kitchen, drinking coffee. They were talking about Stuart and Lydia and their blossoming relationship.

'I'm a bit worried about all the time they spend up there,' Daisy mused, motioning upwards with her eyes. 'I'm not so sure it was a good idea our dad buying Stuart that telescope. The last thing he wants right now is distracting from his exams. I love Lydia as if she was my own daughter, but Stuart's besotted with her.'

Rose took a bite of chocolate biscuit and grinned at her sister. 'Remember when you and Bill hid from our dad in Lily's wardrobe?'

The sisters burst out laughing.

Millie raised her eyebrows. 'What? You hid from your father in a wardrobe?'

Gales of laughter drifted from the kitchen as Daisy retold the story of how she and Bill had given Tom the slip by hiding in a wardrobe as teenagers.

After a few minutes Daisy said, 'No, seriously, I really like Lydia. Stuart's come out of his shell and blossomed since she's been here. You know what a loner he used to be.' She leaned forwards and whispered. 'But I must confess I'm worried about the ... well ... *relationship*.'

'Oh, I don't think they'd be doing anything like that yet,' Mille reasoned. 'She's only just turned sixteen for goodness sake, and Stuart's only eighteen.'

'So was I,' groaned Daisy. 'And look what happened to me – pregnant with our Eileen and chucked out of the house by my own father onto the streets. Anyway I didn't mean *relationship* in that way, I meant them being related.'

'They're not that closely related, are they, if their grandmothers were sisters? It's only second cousins,' Millie speculated. 'And it's not as if that's illegal or anything, even if they did end up together. Look at royalty and how they are all interbred?'

Rose and Daisy shot a look at each other.

Rose leaned forward onto her elbows.

'Millie ... we know our dad had a bit of a fling with Violet's mother, our Aunt Doris. We think that Violet might be our half-sister. But for goodness sake keep it to yourself. No one ese knows.'

'How do you know that?'

'I was a bit of a scallywag as a child,' said Daisy. 'I was eight at the time and I was somewhere I shouldn't have been – hiding under the bed in an empty house.'

'Hiding under the bed in an empty house?' Millie repeated incredulously. 'How come?'

Daisy told her the story of how she had been playing with Rob Potter's father, Billy Potter, when, in a childish prank, he had accidentally locked her in the empty house, and then later, her father had turned up for an illicit extra-marital liaison with her Auntie Doris.

'They were at it like a pair of cats, right above my head,' Daisy said. 'And I heard Doris say it was because she wanted a baby and her husband couldn't give her one.'

'And then,' Rose continued, Violet was born just about exactly nine months later.'

'When was this?' Millie asked.

'It was on Easter Saturday in nineteen twenty-two,' Daisy replied. 'I've had nightmares about it ever since. Our brother died of the consumption the same year, as well as Rose's young man, Bert. It was a horrible year.'

'My dad died in nineteen twenty-two,' said Millie, lowering her eyes and swirling the dregs in her coffee cup. 'I wish I could have known him, but I only have very shadowy memories because I was only five.'

Rose and Daisy glanced at each other. Daisy raised her eyebrows enquiringly. Rose shook her head and mouthed a long *"No."*

Millie looked up. 'Anyway, even if the old tomcat did run

up your Auntie Doris's alley and Violet's really his daughter, they would share the same grandfather, that's all. That makes them first-cousins as you and Violet are really half-sisters, too. Oh, now I see what you mean. It's a bit of an odd relationship, but I wouldn't have thought it was illegal or anything ...'

Millie took another chocolate biscuit and furrowed her brow, deep in thought. The three women fell silent, each musing over the strange family connection between Stuart and Lydia.

'... although I think it *is* supposed to increase the chances of having a handicapped baby,' Millie added looking from one sister to the other as she bit into the biscuit. 'Doris had a deformed baby, didn't she?'

'Oh, let's not speculate,' Rose said, standing up to clear away the coffee cups. 'They are just a couple of kids enjoying each other's company, looking through a telescope and learning about astronomy, and here we are marrying them off and having babies.'

Later, when Millie had gone home, Rose and Daisy discussed their friendship with Millie and whether they should ever reveal the deepest of secrets they shared – that Millie was the daughter of a man they suspected was really their half-brother, Frank Haywood.

Daisy was keen to get the secret out in the open. 'I just feel so bad, knowing that Millie is probably our niece, and she doesn't know a thing about it. It just seems a bit immoral, after all these years. I think the time is right to tell her.'

Rose shook her head. 'We can't, Daisy, we have to think of our mam ... and Millie's mam too. Sarah's not getting any younger and it would break our mam's heart to think that Dad had a secret son all those years ago and she didn't know. She's never really got over all the scandal with Violet. And remember, Dad doesn't know that *we* know either. It would be risking too much upset after all that's happened since Christmas, with Violet clearing off and leaving those kids. It would just be too much.'

Pretending to study the tea leaves in the bottom of her cup, Rose continued to reason with Daisy. 'Let's just let sleeping dogs lie, after all, what good would it serve?'

'I suppose you're right,' Daisy conceded, taking the empty cup from her sister's hands. 'But I'm still a bit worried about Stuart and Lydia. I just don't want them to make the same mistakes that Bill and I made. It was damned hard having a baby at seventeen, and Stuart needs to get good grades in his exams if he wants to get into Medical School. I just don't want him distracted right now.'

Chapter Nine

June 1965

It was with great excitement that eighteen year-old Lydia jumped on the pillion of Trevor's Lambretta Scooter after work one Friday evening in early summer. Stuart was coming home from university and she was so proud of him she was fit to burst.

'Thanks for picking me up, Trev,' she said. 'I've not been able to concentrate all day. I can't wait to see Stuart.'

'Do you want to go home first, or come straight to ours?'

'Your mum said I can stay for tea if I like, so I told Auntie Rose not to save me anything.'

Lydia loved being at Daisy and Bill's house. It wasn't that she was unhappy at home, living with Tom, Liz, Rose and George – it was just that they were all so *old*. Tom, now aged eighty-eight, was in good health, but all he did was listen to sport on the radio and then sit in the evenings watching television, his nose just inches from the screen as he battled with his failing eyesight. Liz was becoming increasingly frail and although she was a little younger than Tom, she looked much older. Rose and George were both now in their sixties, and Lydia could see that caring for herself and her brother took it out of them and mostly they just sank thankfully into their armchairs at the end of each day and went to sleep. Caring for the family was so tiring for her Auntie Rose, but Lydia loved her dearly and tried to do as much as she could around the house to help out.

In contrast Daisy and Bill's house was full of fun and laughter. The years in age that separated her two favourite aunts had never seemed greater – whilst Rose seemed to be always worn-out, Daisy, in her early fifties, was still full of energy and even though she worked part-time at home as an outworker for one of the area's boot and shoe factories, Lydia and Tim were always welcome and spent every moment they could in the happy Windmill Avenue household.

Bursting with excitement at the prospect of seeing Stuart, Lydia jumped off the back of Trevor's scooter, ran down the garden path and let herself in the back door. 'Hello,' she called out. 'Only me'.

Daisy met her in the kitchen, hesitant and apprehensive. 'Hello, love.'

'Where is he?' Lydia extracted a comb from her handbag and ran it quickly through her hair. She stood on tiptoe and looked around Daisy into the living room.'

'He's ... umm ... not here. I'm sorry, Lydia. I don't know why –'

'Oh, I expect his train has been delayed? When's the next one due in? Trevor, can you give me a lift to the station so I can meet him?'

Daisy rubbed at her forehead. 'I don't think there's any point, love. He rang earlier and said that he's not sure when he'll be back. From what I could make out he's staying in London for a while.'

Lydia was puzzled. 'Why? I spoke to him on the phone only last week. He's really looking forward to coming home.'

Trevor had been listening to the conversation from the back doorway, his crash helmet hanging from his hand. He turned to Lydia. 'I told you not to get too involved with him, but did you listen? I said you would be better off having a good time with me and Rob instead of moping around like some love-struck heroine from a slushy film waiting for him. He's probably gone and found himself another girlfriend in London.'

Lydia stood still, her heart beating wildly. There had been no clues, no difference in the tone of Stuart's voice on the telephone. Only last week he had told her how much he loved her and was looking forward to spending the summer with her.

Her voice sounded squeaky and not like her own. 'What makes you think that? You're just winding me up, Trevor. He'll be home soon. He's probably just got some stuff to do first.'

Trevor spoke through a mouthful of biscuit. 'He told me he's been seeing a Maureen. Or was it Doreen. Can't remember her name. A bit older than him, I think.'

Lydia felt a flush of heat envelop her face and neck. 'Maureen? She's not a student – she's one of his lecturers. Psychiatry, I think. It can't be her – you've made a mistake, Trev.'

Daisy frowned at Trevor. 'How do you know all this?'

'The last time he was home he told me he was seeing someone else, a few years older than him, and said her name was Maureen – or Doreen.'

Daisy was shocked. 'It's not funny, Trevor.'

Trevor shrugged. 'Do you see me laughing? It's true, but I didn't say anything to you because it's none of my business.'

Lydia's wobbly legs gave way beneath her and she sank down onto a kitchen chair, feeling suddenly sick. Daisy put her arm around her. 'Oh, Lydia. I'm so sorry. I know how fond you are of him. Trevor needs to learn to think before he opens his big mouth. I'm sure it's nothing –'

Lydia absent-mindedly ran her comb through her hair again. She opened her mouth to speak, but nothing came out as tears began to fill her eyes and nose.

Daisy shot an accusing look at Trevor, who shrugged his shoulders.

'It's none of my business,' Trevor repeated as he turned to walk back into the living room, looking at his watch. 'When's tea ready? I'm going round to Rob's later to fix his motorbike and don't want to be late.'

Rose knocked softly on the front room door, which now

served as Lydia's bedroom.

'Can I come in?'

Hearing a mumble that might have been a *"yes"*, she let herself in the door and shut it behind her. Lydia was curled up on her side, facing the wall. Screwed tightly shut, her eyes were red and her face blotchy.

'He's just rang me,' she said, her voice nasal and shaky through her blocked nose. 'Trevor was right, he's found someone else. It's all over, Auntie Rose.'

Rose sat down on the bed.

'When I was your age I thought my world had ended, too,' she began, uncertain as to how best to comfort Lydia. 'I had a boyfriend called Bert, and on Easter Sunday in nineteen twenty-two he asked me to marry him. He brought me an expensive bracelet – I'll show it to you sometime. The next week we went out and bought an engagement ring. Our wedding was to have been in May the following year. It was all planned, with bridesmaids and everything. His father had even bought us a house.'

Lydia turned onto her back, sniffing. She wiped her eyes with a handkerchief and looked up at Rose. 'What happened? Why didn't you marry him?'

Rose shook her head. 'It wasn't to be, Lydia. I married George, and we've been very happy. I couldn't wish for a better husband.'

Lydia sat up, interested to hear her aunt's story. She wiped her eyes again and blew her nose.

'He died,' Rose said simply after a few seconds. 'I was heartbroken. He became ill and died within a matter of weeks.'

'What was wrong with him?'

'The consumption.'

'Oh, Auntie Rose, that's really sad.'

'He passed away only a few months after my brother, Arthur, died of the same thing.'

Lydia put her hand on Rose's arm. 'That's terrible.'

'I suppose what I am trying to say, Lydia, is that your first love will always be special. I cried and cried until there were no tears left in me. Then, for a time, I was annoyed with Bert for dying and leaving me, just the same as you are angry with Stuart.'

'That's the worst thing. I'm so annoyed that I'm the last to know. He hadn't even had the guts to tell me himself. He might have phoned, but he didn't. And I am absolutely *furious* with Trevor for not telling me the truth, when he knew all about this other woman all along. She's loads older than him, Auntie Rose. She's one of his lecturers. I feel so humiliated.'

Rose shut her eyes momentarily. 'I know this sounds like a bit of an old cliché, but you will get over him. There are plenty more fish in the sea. I must say I'm surprised at him though. I would have thought he'd have done the decent thing and at least explained things to you face to face instead of letting you down like this over the phone.'

'It would be bad enough if it was another girl from university – but I'll be a laughing stock when my friends find out he's finished with me for an old woman.'

Rose sighed. 'More the fool him. He'll learn. He'll come running back, you see.'

Lydia blew her nose. 'I don't know if I'd want him to, now. And after hearing your sad story about Bert, I feel a bit pathetic.'

She swung her legs out of the bed. 'Come on, Auntie Rose – let's go and watch *The Likely Lads*. I'll be all right. After all I've been through in my life, I'm not going to let something like this get me down.'

'That's my girl!' Rose patted her on her hand. 'Hold your head up high and maintain your dignity. He'll soon realise what he's lost.'

There was a tentative knock on the door. Trevor's voice was croaky and uncertain. 'Can I come in?'

'I suppose so,' Lydia said with a sigh. 'But you should know that you are not my most favourite person right now.'

Rose stood up as Trevor peered around the doorway, his hair tousled and untidy. 'Hello, love. What brings you here – pleading for the life of your brother, are you?'

Trevor's usually grinning face was pale and serious. 'There's been a terrible accident. Rob Potter's been taken to hospital. I need to go round and tell his grandma. Will you come with me, Auntie Rose?'

Lydia stared at her fob watch, holding Rob Potter's limp wrist between her thumb and forefinger, checking his pulse. It felt strange, holding the wrist of a patient she knew so well. He'd not yet regained consciousness and there was much concern about the head injury he had received, as well as the serious injury to his right arm and broken leg. It had been a freak accident: a combination of circumstances that had overwhelmingly come together at the wrong time and at the wrong place for poor Rob as he had made his way home from work the previous evening on his motorcycle.

Lydia recorded his heart rate on a chart, hung the clipboard over the foot of his bed and quietly left, wishing she could say something comforting to his mother and father who sat, ashen-faced at his bedside.

A male voice whispered in her ear. 'You know him, don't you?'

She looked around nervously. The voice belonged to Dr Fraser, a recently qualified junior doctor. If the ward sister saw her, a second year nurse, talking to a doctor about anything other than patient care, she would be in for a rocketing. Satisfied that Sister was busy behind a closed curtain at the far end of the ward, she replied to the doctor's question.

'Yes, he's my boyfriend's ...'

Lydia gulped, unable to continue as her eyes filled with tears. She had momentarily forgotten that Stuart was no longer her boyfriend. 'Well, rather my ex-boyfriend – he's Stuart's younger brother's best friend. I've known him since I first came to Kettering when I was fifteen.'

The young doctor's face was grave and he shook his head slowly. 'I'm so sorry. It's hard to remain professional when you are nursing someone you know personally.'

Lydia blinked back her tears, unsure as to whether the doctor was being critical or sympathetic. She glanced over her shoulder. Billy Potter, Rob's father, was holding his head in his hands in despair, while his mother sat, still as a rock in her wheelchair, staring through thick-lensed glasses at her son's battered and bruised face.

Rob's mother's pain, her hopelessness at her inability to make everything better in the way she had done when he was a small boy with a grazed knee, snaked its way into Lydia's heart and closed around it until her eyes filled with tears. She couldn't help comparing Mary Potter with her own mother, who hadn't ever made contact with her since the day she abandoned her.

Lydia groped in her pocket for her handkerchief as tears spilled over her eyelids. She would give anything to have had a mother like Mary Potter. She gulped, determined to drive down her emotions. The doctor would think she was a nervous wreck, totally unfit to be looking after her patient. And Sister would be furious if she saw her crying.

'I'm so sorry – I'll be all right in a minute.'

The doctor glanced up at the clock. 'Are you due a break?'

'No, not until twelve.'

'Are you able to carry on?'

Lydia sniffed and blew her nose. 'Yes, I'll have to be. There are patients to look after. I'm not usually like this – it's just that he's such a decent guy and I'm so worried about him.'

Billy Potter patted her on the shoulder at the same time as the doctor smiled, winked at her and said: 'That's my girl. Watch out for Sister, though, she can be a bit of a battle-axe, so I'm told.'

Lydia hurried off into the ward kitchen. One of her jobs was to make tea for the relatives of seriously ill patients. At the discretion of the Matron, relatives were allowed extended visiting hours to sit by the bedside of their loved ones, and Rob's parents had been there ever since she started her shift early that morning.

When she returned carrying a tray, Rob's father was pulling the curtains around his bed.

'I've made you and Mrs Potter some tea and toast,' Lydia said, trying to appear cheerful.

'Oh that's grand. Thank you. We've not had any breakfast. We've been here since the early hours, but until he comes round there's not much we can do.' Billy gestured helplessly towards Mary in her wheelchair. 'The missus is very upset.'

'I know. I can tell she is. Rob is a lucky chap, though, to have his parents by his bedside, and he's in the right place. I'm sure he's going to be fine. It just might take some time.'

Mary Potter smiled weakly at Lydia over her handkerchief and nodded an acknowledgement.

'Trevor told me what happened,' Lydia said. 'I'm so very sorry. Rob's like a brother to me.'

Billy Potter's eyes watered as he shook his head slowly in despair. 'It was a miracle our Rob was ever born at all, given Mary's health problems, and now this has happened. I can hardly believe it. And it will kill his grandmother if he doesn't pull through this – she dotes on him.'

Lydia smoothed a wrinkle out of Rob's bed cover. 'Auntie Liz is sitting with Evelyn today, so she's not on her own. And I'll pop round to see her tonight to put her mind at rest if that will help.'

An hour later, Lydia sat alone in the hospital recreation hall, close to a table of final year student nurses, who were tucking into their lunch, chatting about boyfriends, pop stars and fashion. She pushed away her sandwiches, unable to even contemplate eating. The sight of Rob Potter's mother at her son's bedside had saddened her more than she could ever have imagined it would. It was such a simple thing, but somehow every emotion she had ever felt was wrapped up in that image, which refused to erase itself from her mind.

Odd thoughts had been stalking her all morning, too.

Could it be through all the tears and heartbreak, a small part of her was actually relieved Stuart had broken off their relationship? Surely not. They had been going out together for over two years and she loved him. They had talked endlessly about their future and Stuart had said it made sound sense for her to become a nurse as he was to become a doctor.

She rubbed at her forehead, trying to think clearly and make sense of the unexpected feelings of relief that were seeping into her deepest thoughts. Her inner voice whispered to her: *at least you won't have to worry any more about any children you might have inheriting his dark side.* There – she had actually allowed it to rise to the surface of her thoughts. Stuart's dark side: the shadowy, unfathomable part of him that was mostly shut away behind a curtain of cobwebs, but sometimes it would pull her up sharply and she'd get a momentary glimpse of a flawed and imperfect future with him.

She'd touch his arm – he'd flinch and pull it away. *"What's wrong?"* she'd say. *"Nothing,"* he'd reply, his eyes as unreadable as cracked mirrors of smoked glass. He'd sit, drawing grids on a piece of paper and then fill them with numbers. *"What are you doing?"* she'd ask, knowing she wouldn't get an answer. He'd then bend over almost double, scratching away with his pencil until the sheet of paper was complete with grids full of numbers. Although she tried to tell herself this strange behaviour was in connection with his studies, deep inside her she knew it wasn't normal.

Even Aunt Daisy was sometimes worried about his strange moods and odd behaviour. *"He's always been like it,"* she'd say, shaking her head. *"Just leave him alone and he'll snap out of it soon."*

In contrast, Stuart's younger brother, Trevor, was one of the most uncomplicated people she had ever met. Easy going and fun, she enjoyed his company and loved being with him. Why couldn't she have fallen in love with Trevor instead? Why had she been drawn towards Stuart when there was so much about him that had worried her?

A movement in front of her made her look up. Dr Fraser was standing with a cup and saucer in one hand and a greaseproof paper bag of sandwiches in another.

'Do you mind if I sit here?'

'No, of course not, but –'

Dr Fraser winked at her. 'I know. It's not the done thing for doctors to sit with other staff, but to be honest, Nurse Smith, most of the other doctors in here are bordering on the geriatric, and anyway, I wanted to make sure you were all right. You were pretty shaken up earlier.'

'I know, and I'm so sorry, Dr Fraser. I let my guard down. I wasn't very professional, was I?'

'Don't beat yourself up. You'd had a terrible shock, finding yourself nursing someone you know who is so seriously injured.'

Lydia tried to smile. The words were out of her mouth before she could stop them.

'I'm not sure I even want to be a nurse now.'

'Why? You're very good. You're well-regarded by Matron, and I happen to know that your exam results last year were outstanding. You are the brightest second-year student we have. Don't let this morning put you off. It happens to us all.'

'It's not that,' Lydia said. 'I let myself be persuaded to become a nurse when really I'd have liked to have worked with children – disturbed children who've been through a traumatic time. I wanted to train to become a Children's Officer, but my boyfriend – now my ex-boyfriend – is a medical student at University College in London and he talked me into becoming a nurse instead.'

'Oh dear. What happened to turn your boyfriend into an ex-boyfriend?'

Lydia shook her head, embarrassed. She didn't want to have to explain it all to Dr Fraser. She sub-consciously checked that stray strands of dark hair hadn't escaped from beneath her starched cap. She imagined he might be wondering what she would look like with her hair shaken free from the clips and grips and with a hint of make-up on her face. She bit her lip. It wasn't appropriate to be wanting to flirt with someone else when she had only just broken up with Stuart.

'How long were you with him?'

Disconcerted by Dr Fraser's persistence, Lydia blurted out the first thing that came into her mind.

'Too long, it seems. He was supposed to be coming home yesterday, but he didn't turn up. Then later he rang me to tell me everything was off and he's staying in London. Then poor Rob Potter having his accident just about finished me off. It was an awful day.'

'Oh dear,' Dr Fraser said.

She changed the subject. 'Do you think Rob will be all right?'

Dr Fraser fidgeted uncomfortably in his chair. Lydia knew he was wondering how he could he answer without scaring her.

He eventually spoke, his forefinger circling the rim of his teacup as he gave a carefully measured answer. 'Well – we are doing everything we can for him. Do you know what actually happened in the accident? Were there any witnesses?'

'Well, I understand the back wheel on his motorbike locked up, just as he was going round a sharp bend on his way home from work. The driver of the car that hit him said his motorbike just slid away from underneath him and there was nothing he could do to avoid hitting him. The sad thing is that Rob was driving on a country road that is usually deserted. Had the car not been coming towards him on that bend, the police said it was likely he would have just come off his motorbike and would probably got away with just cuts and bruises.'

In the months that followed, Lydia couldn't help herself assimilating her own life to the healing of Rob Potter's broken bones. At first, there had been the constriction of blood cells to prevent any further bleeding around the injury sites: that was at the same time she put all her energy into her work, leaving little time or opportunity to dwell on the past or think about Stuart. As the cells within the blood clots degenerated and died away, and new tissue regenerated, the deepening friendship with Dr Martin Fraser blossomed into a reparative phase of healing. When new cells formed the scaffolding on which new bone would form, it coincided with the time that Lydia began to believe in a future without Stuart and find herself hardly thinking of him at all.

During this phase she and Martin would sit in front of the screen of the Granada cinema in Kettering, enjoying epic films like *The Sound of Music* and *Those Magnificent Men in their Flying Machines*. They would spend idyllic Sunday afternoons in the hot summer sunshine, lazing around on the grass at Wicksteed Park making daisy chains and feeding ducks, eating raspberry jam sandwiches, followed by tubs of Wicksteed Park's own delicious ice cream before cooling off in the outdoor swimming pool.

As leaves fell and summer drifted aimlessly into a burnt orange and gold autumn, so the next phase of the healing began. While Rob Potter's fractures were slowly but surely remodelled into new shapes which closely duplicated the original shape of his bones, Lydia and Martin shared their first proper kiss, their relationship already cemented by friendship. However, as is common with the healing of fractures, there was one fracture which refused to conform to the usual process of healing, despite the ideal conditions of the patient's recuperation. The supracondylar humerus fracture he had sustained to his right elbow refused to heal, and in the same way Rob's recovery from his accident was blighted by the restricted functionality of his right arm, Lydia instinctively knew that despite her growing love for Martin, the situation with Stuart was not fully healed or resolved. She could feel it every time they met briefly over the next few months when he returned from London to visit his family, their bodies and polite conversation giving nothing away, but the blood pulsing through their veins carrying a toxin that, if not eradicated, threatened to destroy her future.

Chapter Ten

15th June 1968

Daisy had a pin in her mouth as she smoothed down the dress, trying to pin it to exactly the right length as Sandie Shaw belted out *Puppet on a String* on the radiogram in the corner of the room.

'Stand still and stop fidgeting!'

'Sorry, I was just trying to see over the hedge in the front garden.' She stood on tiptoe on the dining chair. Daisy sighed, exasperated. 'How can I pin the hem when you keep standing on tiptoe!'

'Sorry. I'm sure I just saw Stuart across the road.'

'No. You can't have done. He's not coming back until the day before the wedding.' Daisy gave up and took the pin out of her mouth, sighing in frustration at the fidgety Lydia.

'Yes, it is Stuart!' Lydia jumped off the chair in her wedding dress and ran to the front door. She opened it just as Stuart inserted his key.

'Hi – we weren't expecting you for a fortnight.' Lydia flung her arms around him and gave him a sisterly kiss on the cheek. Stuart drew away, his arms held stiffly to his sides, his glazed eyes fixed on a picture on the staircase wall.

Daisy appeared in the doorway. 'Lydia – mind that dress! What are you doing back home so early; we weren't expecting you for another two weeks.'

Stuart turned around, deliberately avoiding looking at either Lydia or his mother as he picked up his heavy bag from the doorstep and pushed past the two women before dumping it onto an armchair. Lydia shrugged and raised her eyebrows at Daisy, who shook her head in exasperation as she shut the door. Time was running out – and she needed to finish the dress.

Lydia gathered up the full skirt of her dress, holding it in front of her, and traipsed through the living room to the kitchen.

'What's up ... why are you back early?'

Stuart looked away, absent-mindedly opening a cupboard door hunting for food. 'Nothing. Just had the chance to get away before I'd planned, that's all.'

Lydia stood, statuesque in her wedding dress, blocking the doorway, holding the gathered satin and lace material in her arms like a trophy as Daisy peered over her shoulder.

'You'll ruin your tea, eating all those.' Daisy nodded at the handful of biscuits Stuart had grabbed. He looked down at his hand as if it didn't belong to him and put the biscuits back in the tin.

'You should take that off before you get it dirty.' Stuart said to Lydia looking away.

Lydia glanced down at her wedding dress. She had forgotten she was wearing it in the excitement of Stuart's return. She turned around without saying a word and ran upstairs to take off her dress. Why had he come back so early? And what on earth was wrong with him?

Downstairs in the kitchen, Daisy picked up the kettle and set it under the tap. 'What's the matter?' she asked. Shall I send Lydia home if her being here is bothering you?'

Stuart sighed and covered his face with his hands as he sank down at the kitchen table.

Daisy made the tea in silence as Stuart sat, motionless, staring at the tablecloth. After a while he said: 'I need to talk to both you and Dad together. I've got something important to tell you.'

'What is it, love?' Is it your finals? Is it Maureen?'

Stuart looked up and fixed his eyes on a tiny star-shaped blemish on the wall. He had a sudden urge to pick up a pen and trace round the mark, which then took on the form of a sharp-bladed dagger before his eyes, a macabre symbol of the shame, the stigma and destruction his terrible news would bring to his family.

Lydia reappeared at the door, now dressed in a checked cotton shirt and tight-fitting slacks, with the unfinished wedding dress over her arm.

'There's something wrong isn't there, Stuart? I can tell,' she said. She stood momentarily with one hand resting on the back of the chair, waiting for an answer. 'Why are you back so early?'

'No. Nothing's wrong. Just go away and leave me alone.' Stuart continued staring at the blemish on the wall, as Daisy took the wedding dress from Lydia.

She sat down next to him. 'Come on Stu. You can tell me. I'm not going anywhere.' Lydia raised her eyebrows and turned to look over her shoulder at Daisy.

Stuart's voice was flat and unemotional. 'There's nothing anyone can do. No-one can help me. And it's none of your business anyway.'

'Do you really want me to go?' Lydia cocked her head on one side so that she was in Stuart's line of vision.

He looked away. 'Don't mind. Do what you want. Don't really care whether you stay or go.'

'I'll go then. But just because we once went out together doesn't mean we can't be grown-up about things now, does it?'

Daisy nodded in agreement. 'We're a family – it doesn't matter – whatever it is – we'll sort it out.'

'I don't think so, Mum. Just leave me alone. I've got some bad news, but I'll tell you what it is in my own time.' Stuart turned his look directly at Lydia for the first time since arriving home, but his eyes were cold and blank, giving nothing away.

'You go back to Martin,' he added, putting the emphasis on *Martin.*

A sudden and irrational feeling of anger washed over him, dragging behind it a thunder cloud of dark loneliness brought about by seeing Lydia in her wedding dress. The feeling was unexpected and overwhelming. It wasn't as if he didn't know she was getting married. It wasn't as if he didn't know that the man she was going to marry was a doctor. Why was he almost crying? Crying was something he never indulged in, no matter how devastating the news.

Lydia sighed. 'Please don't be like this with me, Stuart. Especially now I'm getting married in a fortnight. I thought we had both moved on. It's like your mum says, we are family ...'

Lydia's angry words tailed off and she shook her head sadly before adding: '... and you are all precious to me.'

Daisy sat down at the table and placed her hand over Stuart's. 'Have you broken up with Maureen? Is that what it is?'

Stuart couldn't look at his mother. She wanted answers and he didn't know how he was going to give them, especially as there was no Maureen and never had been. He rose suddenly, the sound of the chair scraping on the kitchen floor shattering the brittle atmosphere. He pushed the chair back under the table, grabbed his bag from the armchair and left the kitchen without speaking or even a cursory glance in Lydia's direction.

Daisy called out anxiously. 'Where are you going?'

There was no reply. The front door slammed.

Ten minutes later, Stuart let himself in the back door of his grandparents' house, Liz and Tom were sitting alone in the living room. Tom was squinting at a small television screen at his side, trying to watch a cricket match, his face only a foot or so from the screen. Liz put down a pair of scissors she was holding, about to cut out a recipe from a magazine.

Tom looked around, raising his glasses onto his forehead. 'Hello, lad. What a lovely surprise. What brings you home so soon? We weren't expecting you yet.'

'I know – for another fortnight.' Stuart interjected, sighing loudly. He really didn't want to have to explain to anyone why he had been forced to return from London.

'Grandma. Please can I talk to Gramp on my own?'

Liz frowned, furrowing her brow, sensing the tension in the air. 'I suppose I can find something to do in the kitchen. I'll put the kettle on.'

Stuart exploded. 'Why does everyone always put the bloody kettle on?' 'Why do they think that *tea* will make everything all right? It's so stupid.'

'Well, have a cup of coffee then,' Tom said, bemused at the outburst. 'Don't speak to your grandma like that.'

'Sorry, Gramp. It's just that I ... I've had some terrible news.'

Stuart sank into Liz's armchair opposite Tom, who switched the television off. 'What's up?'

Stuart closed his eyes. It was said there was a dark, mysterious planet somewhere on the very edge of the solar system. In the black, private world behind his eyelids he was that planet speeding through a lonely star-studded space and his grandfather was the sun, twinkling brightly in the distance, but far, far away. His mind became fixated on the imagery and he began to sway slightly in his chair. If he was the lonely, dark, lost planet, then Lydia was surely Venus, the brightest planet the black space behind his closed eyes.

'Well?' Tom said impatiently.

Stuart kept his eyes shut. If was as if an unseen enormous force was mandatorily closing down his five senses and he was powerless to resist. His bad news was all-consuming; a huge black ball of nothingness, obliterating his once bright future.

'I've had to give it all up. I can't be a doctor. I'm done for, Gramp. Done for.' Overwhelmed by inadequacy, he resisted the urge to kneel on the floor and wail into his knees, his arms over his head. He wished he could become his grandfather; swap places with him, become instantly old and almost blind and speed forwards in time to the twilight years of his life. If he was his grandfather, he wouldn't have to face an endless future of a life outside medicine and without the love of his life by his side.

How could he have let it all slip through his fingers so easily?

Tom's voice drifted in and out of Stuart's consciousness – he couldn't concentrate. Surely Tom was speaking in some foreign language.

Tom's old eyes were filled with moisture as he leaned forwards in his armchair, his elbows resting on his knees, his hands clasped together in anguish. 'Why? You're doing so well ... top marks ... glowing future ... think about it ... you'll break your poor mother's heart ... don't give up now ....the brains of the family ... all so proud ...'

'Well, what about it?' Tom continued, raising his eyebrows, waiting for an answer.

'What?'

Stuart's confused mind had neither heard, nor understood his grandfather's suggestion, but when he finally opened his eyes, his consciousness flooded back like a tidal bore rushing down a river.

'Having a year off, getting yourself back on track? For goodness sake, Stuart, you can't just chuck five years of medical training down the drain. Just a few more months and you'll be a fully qualified doctor.'

'No I can't. I have to give up completely.'

Tom unclasped his hands and held them out to Stuart, palms upturned. 'Why? Come on. You can talk to me. I might be an old codger, but I care about you, lad, you know I do.'

Stuart put his hands over his face, shaking his head slightly.

'I have schizophrenia. Gramp. Do you understand what that means?'

'What?' Tom cupped a hand behind his ear. He hadn't heard him clearly, as Stuart had his face buried deep in his hands, his fingertips digging into his eye sockets in a desperate attempt to bring back the dark, private world of unseeing eyes.

Eventually, he took his hands away, opened his eyes and

looked up reluctantly. 'I suffer from schizophrenia. I'm mad. Off my head. A shilling short, as they say. With mental health problems, I can't be a doctor. There's no way out of this.'

'No! No! What bloody idiot has put that idea into your head? You're such a clever lad – a bit quiet – but whoever has said that, they've got it all wrong!' Tom's eyes blazed with indignation that someone could have dared to suggest such a terrible thing to his clever, favourite grandchild.

In a low, strained voice, Stuart told his grandfather how, at first, he had become obsessed with calculating mathematical ratios in physical objects and had withdrawn into a stark, cold world consisting entirely of physics and astronomy. At the same time he had been plagued by creeping and crawling sensations on his skin, and had been unable to sleep, imagining that cockroaches were crawling all over his body. He had visited his doctor in London, thinking the stress of his work had affected him. He had taken ever-increasing doses of Librium anti-depressants which hadn't made any difference to his symptoms, and then attended appointments with a psychiatrist and other specialists. Then, in one crushing afternoon, the verdict had been delivered and the prognosis offered as coldly as if they were talking about someone else. He scratched his shoulder sub-consciously as he told Tom about the crawling sensations on his skin.

'The medication makes me a bit better – but I still can't be a doctor. Believe me, I've tried. I've appealed and pleaded, but it's no good. I have to give it all up straight away.'

Tom put his head in his hands, shaking it slowly from side to side. 'I should never have bought you that telescope. I'm sorry, lad. It's my fault, It's that blasted contraption – twisting your head thinking about outer space and all that rubbish. It doesn't do you any good to keep thinking about that sort of thing all the time.'

'No, Gramp. It's got nothing to do with astronomy.' He thumped his forehead hard with the flat of his hand. 'It's a mental defect – a malfunction of the brain. A chemical

115

imbalance.'

'Can't they give you something for it – you know - cure it?' Tom furrowed his brow. 'I would have thought this day and age they would have a cure for this schizowhatsit.'

Stuart felt the bitterness rise into his throat at the decision not to allow him to continue with his studies and take his final exams. 'There's no cure. It's no good, Gramp - my career is finished before it's even started.'

His grandfather spoke quietly. 'Do you get voices in your head, then?'

Stuart gave Tom a disparaging look. 'Huh ... that's what *everyone* thinks.'

'Well, do you?'

'I don't want to talk about it anymore.'

The conversation between Tom and Stuart ended abruptly a few minutes later when Lydia arrived home. Liz appeared in the living room doorway behind her, leaning on her walking stick with one hand and holding a cup and saucer in the other. Her hand shook and the tea spilled over: she had been listening at the kitchen door and had heard every word of Stuart's bad news.

Stuart gazed at Lydia. She was, indeed, Venus, her light and warmth beckoning to him. An aura seemed to glow all around her as she stood before him, breathing heavily and with faintly flushed cheeks from running home.

'Do you want to talk?' she said softly. 'We can go into my room if you like, can't we Auntie Liz?'

Liz shrugged, shook her head sadly and gave a deep sigh. Stuart stood up.

'Does our Daisy know?' Liz directed the question at Stuart, but glanced at Tom, who stared at her blankly, bewildered and tearful.

Stuart shook his head. 'I'll tell her later,' he said, 'when Dad gets home from work.'

In the front room, Lydia shut the door behind her and leaned on it, subconsciously blocking Stuart's route of escape. She folded her arms, trying to be brave and yet feeling full of fear. Something was wrong. Badly wrong. She had never before seen him in such an agitated state. He stood still in the centre of the room, his back to her, staring at her reflection in the mirror over the fireplace. Although it was difficult not to look away, Lydia deliberately maintained her gaze in the reflection and they stood, silently for a few highly charged seconds. She couldn't help feeling in some way responsible for his distress, even though she knew whatever was wrong with him couldn't possibly be her fault.

'What's the matter?' Why did you run out like that?'

'I have schizophrenia. I can't be a doctor. I'm finished, Lydia. Finished.'

Without warning, Stuart spun around and threw himself into Lydia's open arms. They stayed still for a while, breathing heavily and holding each other tightly.

'I'm sorry I rushed out on you like that.'

Stuart pulled away slightly and the sight of her burned into an image in the blackness behind his eyes. The pocket of emptiness and loneliness began to dissipate and a warm, pleasant feeling began to spread from somewhere deep within his pelvis. He opened his eyes and looked at her.

'I've missed you,' he whispered.

'I've missed you, too.' Lydia breathed in sharply, and then held her breath and closed her eyes, her lips slightly parted.

Stuart shuddered, conscious that the familiarity of her in his arms once again was more intoxicating to his body than the strongest drug. If a career in medicine was now lost to him, could Lydia be his consolation prize? The fact that she was marrying someone else was of almost no consequence to him as he clutched her to him, breathing in a future filled with bright light. The strange euphoria slowed time until it stopped and then gradually began to reverse over the last two years.

Lydia rested her head on Stuart's shoulder. Something like

a sob rose up from her chest, and her breath caught in the back of her throat.

'I still love you,' she said, softly. 'I don't care about the schizophrenia.'

'I'm so very sorry for what I did to you, Lydia.'

'I know,' she whispered.

They held each other, tenderly and silently. All the carefully planned words that had floated redundantly inside Lydia's head throughout the last two years disappeared into a world devoid of time and space. Over the last two years, she had rehearsed words of anger, words of desperation, endless questions, all of which she felt shuddering their way through Stuart's body as they left her, unspoken but understood. He turned his head slightly and his lips almost imperceptibly brushed her cheek with a light and gentle kiss. Tears of sadness brimmed over her eyelashes and slid down her cheeks.

She felt his hand caressing the back of her neck and his fingers twisting through her hair and she closed her eyes, disappearing beneath the waves of the familiar sound of his breathing.

'We didn't even say goodbye to each other,' he said. 'We didn't ever get proper closure, did we?'

'No. I've wanted to say so many things to you, but because you never said anything, I felt I couldn't too.'

'For me,' he said, looking straight into Lydia's eyes,' it was so beautiful, so perfect, I almost felt it was a dream. I just couldn't find the words and as time went on it was safer to not say anything to you. I knew I had made a dreadful mistake letting you go, but my feelings were so chaotic and out of control. I wanted to tell you about my problems, but then you met Martin, and I could see you were happy, so I just didn't say anything.'

'Yes,' Lydia agreed, nodding her head slightly. 'For me, too, it was just the same. I couldn't ever say anything to you because I thought you were happy with Maureen.'

Stuart grimaced. 'There's not a day goes past that I don't think of you and the time we spent together.'

Lydia couldn't reply. The rehearsed words just wouldn't form.

'I've craved and ached for just one more moment of time together, such as this,' she finally managed to whisper.

As they reluctantly disengaged the embrace, his thumbs caressed the backs of her hands as he turned away and sank down into an armchair.

Lydia hesitated, watching him as he traced the outline of the floral pattern on the arm of the chair with his forefinger. Her eyes fleetingly darted to her divan bed that doubled up as a daytime sofa, but Stuart looked up at her, patting the arm of the chair, indicating she should sit down on it. Self-consciously she slid beside him, her arm around his shoulders. He put both his arms around her waist and buried his face between her breasts.

She slid her hand up to his dark hair as she rested her head on his shoulder.

'This is really hard for me to say,' Stuart mumbled pulling away slightly. 'I love you, but I can't ruin your life as well as my own. You've got to walk away from me, Lydia – for your own sake. You *have* to go ahead and marry Martin because there can never be any future for us. It's enough for me knowing that you love me. I can live my life alone as long as I know that.'

Lydia raised her head to look him in the eye.

'I don't understand, Stuart. What are you saying? Why say we have no future? I haven't married Martin yet.'

Stuart lowered his eyes, and stroked the back of Lydia's hand with his thumb.

'I can never marry you – or anyone. I can never have children. I can't risk passing this on to the next generation.'

Lydia's shoulders dropped in relief and she broke the whispered conversation with a normal tone. 'You of all people should know that there's lots that can be done for schizophrenics. Haven't you learned anything at medical school? People manage to lead relatively normal lives with help – it's part of you, Stuart, and I love you – schizophrenia and all.'

She kissed him gently on the cheek. 'It really doesn't matter to me. I'll be right here by your side. It doesn't matter, Stu.'

She waited for a reaction that didn't come. 'Can't you see what I'm saying? I'll do whatever it takes to be with you. I'll break off my marriage. I like Martin – but I don't love him. I love you, and I always will.'

Lydia shifted uncomfortably. 'Say something, Stuart. Please? Say something.'

Stuart shook his head and looked into his lap. 'I can't do it to you, Lydia. I sometimes can't control myself. I have such weird thoughts and do weird things.'

'It *can* be controlled. We'll beat it together.'

Stuart shook his head.

'Please? Please, Stuart, let's try?'

He shook his head again.

They sat for a few moments in silence. Lydia twizzled her hair around her index finger. She jumped up, all rational thought disappearing in a moment of recklessness. While she unbuttoned her shirt, Stuart sat motionless in the chair, mesmerised into paralysis as it slid over her pale shoulders. She took off her slacks, letting them fall to the floor before removing her bra. She sat on the edge of the bed, naked, before him, looking at her feet. Still he didn't move.

'What about Gran and Gramp?' he said.

'Auntie Liz won't come in. She thinks we are just talking. And Uncle Tom can't walk very far. We're safe in here. And I don't care anyway.'

'Are you sure? This is not like you, Lydia. I think you should just get dressed. You'll regret it afterwards.'

Lydia slid into bed. 'I told you – I don't care. If, afterwards, you still don't want to be with me, then I'll accept it. But I want you to change your mind. I'll give everything up for you.'

She shivered with a sudden self-consciousness and pulled the sheet up around her. She knew she was doing wrong. She knew she would have to live with her conscience. She understood exactly what she was about to do, but, as Stuart levered himself up from the armchair and lay down on top of the bed beside her, it was as if she was giving herself a gift of justification or redemption. It was something owed; something accepted as consideration for her loss and settling for second best.

'You're perfect,' he said. 'Just perfect.'

Half an hour later, they allowed themselves just a few minutes to hold each other and talk quietly before they dressed. Lydia just had time to make the bed before there was a tap on the door.

'Do you two want a cup of tea now you've had time to talk?' Liz enquired hesitantly.

Later, she would say to Tom: *"And her about to get married too – that's a bit of her mother coming out if ever I saw it."*

Chapter Eleven

Martin Fraser inspected himself in the mirror, straightening his tie. He smiled at his reflection humming softly to *The Happening* that was playing on the radio in the kitchen. His mother walked into the room, clipping on her earrings.

'Should I wear my gloves, or carry them?' she mused.

Martin looked at her mirror image and laughed. 'How the hell do you expect me to know? I'm a man.'

His mother put down her bag and gloves and walked over to join him. They stood side-by-side staring at their reflections in the mirror.

'You look lovely, Mum.' Martin grinned. 'Yellow really suits you. Makes you look younger.' His mother smoothed a stray wisp of hair with her index finger, obviously pleased at his remark.

'Do I look silly in a hat?'

'No. Well ... everyone looks silly in hats, don't they?'

Elsie grimaced. She gave him an affectionate slap on the arm, just as the best man walked into the room, looking wooden and uncomfortable in his suit and tie. 'I wish your father was here. It's so hard being a widow, even after all these years. I still feel self-conscious being on my own.'

As his mother hurried off to find some aspirin to put in her handbag before the car arrived to take them to church, Martin felt a fleeting sense of sadness and loss. He'd never known his father, other than through stories of heroes and lamentations about the terrible waste of life and the ultimate sacrifice. As a boy, he'd tried to feel love for the shadowy images in fading photographs clutched to his mother's heart as she grieved. His childhood and teenage years had seemed to run their course ahead of time, somehow, as he'd placed his small feet in his father's big shoes and tried to run in them before he could even walk properly.

He drew himself up, proud of the man he had become, despite the lack of paternal guidance. He and his mother had made a good team since the war had stolen his father away when he was three, and they'd been left to cope alone. He'd have to make sure that she wasn't too lonely from now on – it was going to be a big change for her too, especially as she was moving to Kettering to be near to him and Lydia and was leaving all her friends behind in Scotland.

'Don't worry, Mum. You'll be just fine. You're sitting next to Rose and George at the reception and I'm sure you'll have plenty to talk about.'

Martin carried on humming, thinking of his Lydia. He couldn't believe he was actually marrying her. He felt a sudden lurch in his abdomen and he couldn't quite decide if it was excitement or apprehension. Lydia had been quiet in the past two weeks and he'd been worried about her. He'd constantly fought a fizz of irrational annoyance since Stuart Roberts had returned home early. The life-changing news that he was suffering from schizophrenia had been like a giant sponge, absorbing all Lydia's family's enthusiasm for their big day and had, he felt, taken something precious away from him. His bride had been bubbly and excited about their wedding before Stuart's return. Now she was quiet and thoughtful, worried because he would now never realise his lifelong dream of becoming a doctor. He knew the news had come as a shock to her – after all they had used to be quite close as youngsters. He was certain Lydia loved him, but there was a tiny, niggly maggot of fear, buried deep inside his heart, that she still harboured feelings for Stuart Roberts.

He stared in the mirror again and re-knotted his tie, smoothed back his quiff and adjusted his buttonhole yellow carnation. It must be pretty normal to feel a sense of fear and trepidation when you are about to get married. After all, he was in unchartered territory now. If only he had a father to confide in, he was sure he would feel more confident about the day ahead.

Elsie walked carefully down the garden path to the wedding car to join Rose and George, rubbing her temples with her fingertips. It must be all the excitement that was giving her a mild headache, she thought to herself as she slid into the back seat next to Rose, who greeted her with a huge, welcoming smile and comforting comments about how lovely she looked.

During the short drive to the church she began to feel faintly nauseous. She checked her handbag, making sure she had popped a packet of aspirin tablets inside, and blinked as her vision became slightly distorted. With a thump of panic in her chest, she hoped she wasn't about to suffer from one of her migraines, on today of all days.

When they arrived at the church, Elsie shivered as she slid out of the car, holding onto George's arm to steady herself.

'You all right, Elsie?' he asked.

'I think I'm just nervous,' she said, rubbing at goose bumps on her arm. 'I always feel tense on big occasions. I really miss my Alfie at times like this.'

George patted her arm. 'You stay with Rose and me; we'll keep you company.' He leaned forward and whispered conspiratorially in her ear. 'Rose fancies herself as mother of the bride but Daisy's made the dress and I think she does too – we'll just watch and see who wins!'

Elsie chuckled. George was a kind, thoughtful man and she knew that Lydia's family would be right there, supporting her during her imminent move to Kettering from Scotland. Another, more intense, wave of nausea washed over her and she swayed slightly, grateful to hold onto George's arm as the three of them walked into church and took their places in the front pews. The sun made a brief appearance through darkening clouds, and the ray of sunlight that fell on Elsie's face through a high window in the church bothered her. She put her hand up and adjusted her hat, blocking out the rude brightness that was making her feel as if she was going to be sick.

There wasn't a prouder man in the whole of Kettering than Tom, who had been thrilled to be asked to give Lydia away. Standing in front of the mirror over the fireplace, he adjusted his tie and brushed a fleck of dust from his jacket, balancing precariously on one crutch. He gazed at the reflection of the elegant young bride behind him, seeing nothing of Violet in her. Lydia had taken off her glasses, and without them she looked stunning.

Tom, whose own eyesight was very poor, patted his breast pocket. 'I've got your glasses in here, but I think you'd better put them on for the reception. One of us at least needs to be able to see properly.' He checked his trouser pocket for his speech, written out on several sheets of writing paper by Liz in big bold letters so that he could read it easily. He slid the crutch off his arm and picked up the two walking sticks he had been practising with for the last month.

'Are you sure you are going to be all right with those?' Lydia asked Tom's reflection, concerned that he would struggle to walk her down the aisle without his crutches. 'Perhaps we could ask the driver to put the crutches in the boot of the car?'

Tom was relieved. It was painful for him to walk, even using crutches, and he knew it would take a big effort to walk Lydia down the aisle using just walking sticks. 'Good idea, young lady. Why didn't I think of that?'

'I know you're nearly ninety, Uncle Tom – but you don't look it. You don't look a day over seventy in that smart suit.'

Tom turned to face her and she gave him a quick affectionate kiss on the cheek. His eyes filled with tears of pride. 'You and young Timothy have brought so much sunshine to our autumn years. I'm so glad Violet brought you back to Kettering.'

Lydia's smile faded and her expression hardened. 'I know you worry about my mother, and I know that, despite what she has done, you still care about her. But I'm glad she's not here, Uncle Tom. I don't even think about her now. I don't need a mother, not when I have three aunties like Liz, Rose and Daisy.'

Uncomfortable, Tom felt he needed to defend Violet in some small way. After all, she was his daughter, even if no-one else knew that.

'Your mother wasn't always bad, you know. She was a lovely little girl. Looking back, I think it all went wrong when your grandfather walked out. I could never abide him, but, give him his dues ...'

Tom wagged his finger in the air, aware that for the first time in his life he was about to pay Walter Grey a compliment. 'Walter was a very good father to your mother, but I think the difficulties they faced as Violet was growing up affected her more than anyone in the family realised.'

'I wish I could have traced my grandfather.' Lydia sighed and carefully sat down on the edge of a chair so as not to crease her wedding dress. 'I don't hold anything against him, you know – for being gay and all that.'

Tom gave her an odd look. 'Gay? As I recall, Walter always had a serious look on his face – not a jolly type of fellow at all!'

Lydia laughed. 'Uncle Tom – gay is another term for homosexual!'

'Hummph. Poofters – that's what I call 'em. Gay! Whatever next.'

Tom knew that Lydia was laughing at him, but he didn't care. He chuckled with her. 'All this new-fangled language – I can't make head nor tail of it.'

Waiting in the church for the bride to arrive, Elsie was feeling increasingly ill. She sat down gratefully next to the best man, intensifying waves of nausea sweeping over her as she blinked to try and clear her blurred vision. Beads of sweat began to form on her upper lip and she leaned forwards to acknowledge Daisy, across the aisle, hoping that the migraine would soon subside. She glanced at Martin's wristwatch and then searched in her handbag for her powder compact so that she could apply a little more powder to her perspiring face before the bride arrived. Lydia's bridesmaids were giggling at the back of the church and the tinkling laughter of teenage girls echoed and ground on her nerves almost as much as the bright sunlight had done.

Exactly on time, there was a low murmur from the congregation and the church organist struck up the first bars of the wedding march. Elsie felt dizzy when she stood up, and her heart beat faster as she watched her son trying to resist looking round at Lydia. A slight movement caught her attention and Martin glanced momentarily to one side. Elsie followed his gaze. With some consternation she was surprised to see Stuart Roberts, still seated on the opposite side of the aisle when everyone else was standing, tapping his fingers on the back of the pew in front of him. He was staring straight ahead seemingly oblivious to his youngest brother, Neil, who sat beside him trying to haul him to his feet as Lydia walked slowly and carefully down the aisle on Tom's arm.

Elsie felt hot – much too hot. Tom and Lydia drew level with her and, with a shaking hand, she fished in her handbag for a handkerchief before the service started. Filled with panic, she mopped her sweaty, pallid face, hoping she wasn't going to be sick in the church.

The minister began to address the congregation and Elsie sank down thankfully onto the pew.

Lydia could feel Stuart's gaze burning on the back of her neck and struggled hard with the urge to look around at him. Instead she turned to Martin and gave him a bright smile as he squeezed her hand reassuringly.

Stuart's voice was a mere whisper, but loud enough for everyone to hear. 'Please don't marry him, Lydia.'

Lydia froze as the minister looked up in annoyance and fixed his eyes on a point just behind her and to her left. She knew he was glaring at Stuart. With a pounding heart she looked at her feet, willing Stuart to be silent.

'Don't do it. Please?'

Martin, tight-lipped, stared straight ahead his eyes glazed with repressed anger.

Stuart sat on his hands rocking backwards and forwards in the pew. His dark hair had flopped forwards and was now obscuring his field of vision, spread like a spidery veil over his black-rimmed glasses and his face was set in an animal-like grimace. Neil gave him an embarrassed nudge. The tense, fragile atmosphere in the church began to snap and crackle as Lydia squeezed Martin's arm in an effort to reassure him, but when she looked at his face she knew he was furious, his jaw stiff as he strained to maintain control. She turned around. Stuart's father, Bill, nodded at her and then stood up and placed his order of service on his seat behind him. He edged behind her, patting Tom on the shoulder as he passed him. Neil edged along the pew behind to let his father slide into his seat beside Stuart, who was now leaning forwards, his elbows on his knees, clutching his head with both hands. Lydia tried to tear her eyes away from him but couldn't.

He looked up, and the gaze they shared for a fraction of a second seemed to charge the atmosphere with static electricity. Behind his glasses, Stuart's eyes were bright. She knew he was breaking up, dissolving in regret and disappointment. She shuddered as she became aware that the moment was all-defining, a peculiar kind of reality encapsulated in a tiny fragment but with enormous consequences for her future.

Stuart's pain was her pain. It cut her cleanly in two – one part with Stuart, one part with the man who was about to become her husband.

Lydia's heart urged her to gather up the full skirt of her

wedding dress, go to Stuart and tell him that everything was going to be all right. She must face up to what she had to do and explain to everyone in the church that she was making a mistake and that she couldn't marry Martin after all, because Stuart was her soul mate, the love of her life and always had been from that very first Christmas she had spent with the Jeffson family. But she hesitated, rational, her head pulling her back to the sobering reality that life with Martin would be so much more serene and easy.

But her heart danced and sang so loudly her head couldn't resist the pull. She tugged on Martin's arm. 'I'm so sorry, Martin ...'

Simultaneously, she heard Bill's voice behind her. 'Come on, son. Let's go outside.'

Stuart stood up.

Lydia met Martin's reproachful glance with teary eyes, before staring straight ahead. *Just shut up. Shut up.* Her inner voice repeated itself over and over in her head. She pressed her lips together to stop herself speaking, and closed her eyes so she couldn't see either Stuart or Martin. It was too late. Stuart had missed his chance. She would have called off her wedding two weeks ago, but he'd walked away. She had stood, naked, before him and given him a second chance on the day he came back to Kettering. He hadn't taken it.

But she loved him, didn't she? And it wasn't too late, was it? She hadn't married Martin yet. She hadn't vowed to love, honour and obey him until death parted them.

'I'm so sorry,' Bill announced loudly to no-one in particular. 'My son is ill. He needs medication and he probably hasn't taken his tablets. I'll take him out.'

Bill led Stuart like a disobedient child to the back of the church and out into the churchyard. Lydia glanced over her shoulder again, and watched as Stuart hung back before leaving the church.

There was another moment, then, when Stuart stopped, turned around and stared at her from the entrance to the church. With the brief suspension in time, the muscles in her legs tensed, ready to turn and run down the aisle to be with him. But then Martin reached for her hand and it was soft and warm on hers. He turned his head and smiled at her, and the anger melted away from his face.

She repeated the first of her earlier words in a whisper. 'I'm so sorry, Martin ...'

She closed her eyes. 'I love you. Let's just get on with it.'

Outside, with the clouds overhead darkening, Stuart wrenched his arm from his father's grip. 'Leave me alone. What do you know about anything? Why did you drag me out of the church like that?'

'What on earth made you do it?' his father said.

'Do what?'

'Whisper like that in the church. You had your chance with Lydia two years ago and you blew it.' Bill paced up and down, with his hands in his pockets. 'You've got to accept that she's marrying someone else.'

Stuart mumbled and turned away from Bill, determined to go back into the church. 'I didn't whisper anything. Now *you're* imagining things, Dad!'

Bill grabbed Stuart's arm to stop him. 'You did! You whispered *don't do it* over and over again and asked Lydia not to marry him. Everyone heard you. I've never been so embarrassed in my life.'

'Did I?' Stuart put his hands over his face. 'I didn't know. Oh God, this is awful. I'm not usually this bad. It must be the stress ...'

'Did you take your tablets this morning?'

Stuart shrugged his shoulders. 'I can't remember.'

Bill tutted and shook his head as Stuart shoved his hands in his pockets and jingled loose change nervously. 'You fool! You absolute bloody fool! How are you going to live with this condition if you can't even remember to take your tablets?'

'I'm sorry, Dad.'

'You're going to have a lot of apologising to do. Poor

Lydia. Let's just hope you haven't ruined her wedding day. Martin was furious. It was a wonder he didn't come over and punch you in the face.'

Inside the church, as the service continued with no more hitches, Elsie felt claustrophobic and nauseous in the confined, stifling atmosphere of the church; everything seemed as if it was going on far too long. The organ and high-pitched singing of hymns pierced her eardrums and jarred her senses until she could hardly bear it. Dark clouds overhead parted and bright sunlight streamed through the high window, multi-coloured sunbeams falling on her face, boring into her eyes like burning, sharpened fingernails.

Eventually, after what seemed like hours, the minister announced that Lydia and Martin were now man and wife. The congregation chorused its *oohs and ahhs* as they kissed. Elsie felt saliva flood into her mouth and knew she could fight the nausea no longer. She mumbled to Rose that she needed some air and rushed down the aisle with her handkerchief over her mouth, the congregation staring at her in surprise. She only just made it to the churchyard before she vomited onto the grass.

Bill, who had lit a cigarette, rushed over to her, shocked and concerned.

'Oh dear. Elsie love ... here hold onto me.'

Elsie heard his voice and blindly groped for his arm. Feeling shaky and faint, and coughing as cigarette smoke curled around her, she grabbed hold of his suit jacket. Bill took his handkerchief out of his trouser pocket and passed it to her.

'I feel so embarrassed,' Elsie began to say between coughs and gulps. 'I felt ill before we went into church. It's a migraine – on today of all days. Oh, I feel absolutely dreadful and now I've completely ruined the wedding.'

'You and me both, then.' Stuart said, shoving his hands into his pockets, looking at his feet. 'I apparently need to apologise. I sort of – well – can't tell the difference if I'm speaking or just thinking. I honestly didn't mean to ruin everything and I'm sorry if my behaviour made you ill.'

Elsie began to feel a little better as a cooling breeze blew over her hot face in the shade of the church. She smiled at Stuart. She felt sorry for the serious young man and his parents. They must be so worried about him.

'Oh, don't worry, love. It wasn't you. I felt ill before we even got to the church. People will understand. It's just that if you had a broken arm, everyone can see that, but something like the illness you have is hidden away.'

Elsie put her hand out and steadied herself on the roughly hewn stone wall of the church, unable to continue talking, her handkerchief over her mouth. She closed her eyes, feeling guilty as she realised that she was actually quite relieved that Stuart had shown himself up. After all, they could hardly blame her for being ill when Lydia's side of the family had caused an upset in the church too.

'Should we go back in? Do you feel well enough?' Bill said, smoothing down his jacket.

Elsie shook her head. 'Let's all wait here – they'll be out soon once they have signed the register. We'll only draw attention to ourselves.' She smiled sympathetically at Stuart. 'And we don't want that do we?'

After the photographs had been taken, the wedding party made its way to the reception. Lydia and Martin stepped out of the car into the hustle and bustle of Saturday shoppers, some of whom stood still and stared at the bride and groom as they entered the reception venue. Inside, white, starched tablecloths covered long tables and shiny silver cutlery and cut crystal wine glasses sparkled in the beams of sunlight, which streamed through the glass roof lights, illuminating the top table and flower arrangements of sweet peas, freesias and yellow roses.

Tom, having retrieved his crutches from the wedding car, stood in the entrance to the reception hall, creaking every time he shifted his weight to shake someone's hand. He stood, proud and upright, his family's patriarch; a sentry guarding his domain.

Stuart arrived, flanked by Daisy and Bill. His brother, Trevor held out a tray of sparkling wine and he took a glass, without looking up.

'Ought you to be drinking that?'

Stuart glared at Trevor. 'Probably not – but I'm a big boy now. Anyway, it's none of your business.'

'Has he had his tablets?' Trevor asked his mother.

Stuart looked at his feet, his dark hair flopping over his eyebrows. He took off his glasses and scrubbed his eyes with his fingertips. 'You don't have to treat me like a child.'

'Well, what a show-up.'

'Just shut up, Trevor.'

Stuart smiled in sympathy at Elsie as she arrived, holding onto Rose's arm, but his eyes were glassy and expressionless. His newly-diagnosed disorder had him in its grip, the chemistry within his brain tensing his muscles and drilling a steel-like rod down the length of his backbone right into the floor.

He watched, unable to move, as Elsie and Rose made straight for the Ladies' toilets.

Wedding guests stood around in the foyer, a mosaic of coloured outfits and hats bobbing about as people sipped their drinks, mingled with each other and made small talk. Stuart was left in the care of his brothers while his parents stood with his older sister, Eileen, and her family. Then, after a few minutes Lydia's brother, Tim, joined them.

No-one appeared to notice that Stuart had disappeared as they stood around laughing and chatting. Watching from the shadows as his mother whispered in his Uncle George's ear, Stuart rubbed at his temples trying to eradicate the sensation of withdrawal from the world around him. The insignificance of his absence amongst his family caused a pang of disconnection inside him so intense it felt as if it was about to burst its way out of his chest and into his throat. He gulped, his Adam's apple bobbing as he watched his Auntie Rose and Uncle George hanging around in the doorway with his grandparents, greeting the last few guests as they arrived. Then they, too, joined the family group.

George stood on tiptoe, looking all around the hall. Stuart knew he was looking for him, wondering where he had gone.

He slipped further into the shadows, pressing himself into the wall as he glanced towards the ladies' toilet door. Martin's mother was in there. She'd steady and soothe away these horrible feelings and tell him what to do to make sure he didn't cause any more trouble. He finished his wine and set the empty glass on a ledge before edging towards the door, fighting an overwhelming urge to hide himself away where no one could find him. How could everyone in the world be so happy and joined-up when he was so sad and disconnected? He had never felt so alone in his entire life, and the loss of his precious Lydia was causing him more physical pain than he could ever have imagined. He shouldn't have come to the wedding. He should have stayed away.

He opened the door hesitantly, peering into the cloakroom before slipping inside.

The door shut with a soft click. For the first time that day, Stuart felt safe.

'Has anyone tried the gents?' George said helpfully.

'Yeah. He's not in there either.'

'The kitchens?'

'Doubt it – but we'll go and have a look.' Trevor and Neil walked towards the kitchens, acknowledging guests as they walked across the hall looking for their brother.

'It's my fault. I should have kept my eye on him, but he's a big boy now and I need to be a mother to Lydia today,' Daisy said to her daughter, shaking her head, her voice full of remorse. 'I can't believe he didn't *know* he was whispering in the church.'

'You can't watch him all the time, Mum.' Eileen said. 'It's going to take time for us to work out how best we can support him.'

George clapped his hands and then rubbed them together as he took charge of the situation. 'Righty ho. He's got to be in this building somewhere. He can't have gone far in fifteen minutes, for goodness sake. And we've all been standing by the door, greeting people, so we would have noticed if he'd gone out. Let's look lively and split up. We'll soon find him and then we can all sit down and enjoy the reception.'

In the ladies' toilets, Elsie heard the door open and someone enter the cubicle next to her. Once the door lock had been slid into place, there was no sound. She couldn't even hear anyone breathing. It was as if a ghost had entered the cubicle. A little frightened, Elsie opened the cubicle door and hurried into the adjoining small cloakroom where Rose was waiting for her.

Rose adjusted her hat and leaned forwards, peering at her reflection in the mirror. 'How are you feeling now, m'duck?'

'A little bit better, thank you, Rose. I'm so annoyed at this blinkin' migraine – and at my son's wedding too. I feel terrible for ruining their special day.'

'Don't be silly. You haven't ruined it. These things can't be helped. Shall we just wait here for a minute or two? They are not quite ready to sit down for the meal yet.'

Rose moistened a clean handkerchief with cold water and passed it to her. Elsie patted her face with it, the mild lavender fragrance infused in the white cotton making her feel slightly better. The two women sank down onto the chairs in the tiny cloakroom.

'There's someone else in here.' Elsie mouthed, her voice barely a whisper. She nodded her head towards the door that led to the toilets. She put her mouth close to Rose's ear. 'I heard them come in but they haven't made a single sound.'

Rose stood up, opened the door quietly and then bent down to look under the cubicle doors – there were no tell-tale shoes to give a clue as to who was inside. She frowned, puzzled, shaking her head.

'I can't see any feet,' she mouthed.

Elsie stood up, tiptoed over to the end cubicle and pushed the door gently with her index finger – it was most definitely locked from the inside. She knew she had not imagined it.

'Hello,' said Rose, her voice echoing in the silence. 'Are you all right in there?'

There was no reply. Rose shrugged, her palms upturned.

Elsie and Rose fell silent, listening. Inside the cubicle Stuart sat on the closed toilet seat, hugging his knees.

'Wait here,' Rose mouthed to Elsie, who shook her head, alarmed at the thought of being left alone with the ghostly being in the end cubicle. Elsie motioned towards the exit door with her hand.

'How strange?' said Elsie as she folded the wet handkerchief into a square and patted her brow with it as she and Rose walked out into the hall for the reception. 'I hope it's not a pervert.'

Martin strode over to his mother, relieved she seemed to be recovering from the untimely migraine. He was worried about her – it was not like her to make a fuss. 'Are you feeling better, now, Mum?'

'A bit. I'm so sorry, Martin, for being ill at your wedding.'

George spotted Rose talking to Martin and Elsie and edged his way through the guests to join them. He took her to one side with a worried frown on his face.

'Stuart's missing. Have you seen him?'

'There's someone in there,' Rose said, motioning towards the ladies' toilets. 'We think they've locked themselves in, but they didn't answer when we asked them if they were all right. It must be Stuart.'

'The Ladies! My giddy aunt – what on earth is he thinking of!' George hurried off to fetch Bill.

'Let's just keep it to ourselves for a while,' Rose said to Elsie, looking towards Lydia. 'No point in letting Stuart upset her even more on her wedding day. He's done enough damage as it is.'

Martin swore under his breath, his composure stretched to breaking point. He fought down his anger, hurrying across the room to join his new wife. He held up a spread hand to Rose, gesturing above the din of laughter and jumbled voices. 'Five minutes?' he mouthed.

Rose nodded and made off towards the toilets, followed by Elsie, George, Bill, Trevor and Neil. To Stuart, who just wanted some time alone, it was a small army. And an invasion was the very thing he didn't need.

Bill climbed up on the toilet seat in the next cubicle to Stuart, his arms resting on the partition between the two cubicles. His voice was low, calm and compassionate.

'Look, Stuart. I know this is hard for you, but please don't ruin this wedding any more than you already have.'

Stuart didn't move, or even look up.

Bill's patience fell apart. 'Get out of there right now! You're behaving like a spoilt child. What on earth will people think of us?'

Stuart hugged his knees tighter, staring straight ahead at nothing in particular. 'Leave me alone,' he mumbled. 'Just leave me here.'

Bill sighed, fed up and exasperated. Short of tearing the cubicle door off its hinges, there was nothing else he could do. He looked at his watch and jumped down, just as the cloakroom door opened abruptly and hit Rose's back as a wedding guest tried to use the toilets.

'Full up, I'm afraid,' Rose said cheerfully and shut the door in the woman's face.

Bill stood with his hands upturned. 'What on earth do we do now?' Everyone shrugged their shoulders.

'Leave him,' Trevor said. 'We'll just keep a look out and if he comes out, one of us can deal with it.'

Bill and Neil nodded at each other in agreement. 'All right, we'll leave him,' Bill said as he stepped back up onto the toilet pan and peered over the cubicle partition. Stuart still hadn't moved.

'We're going into the reception now, Stuart. You can come with us, or you can stay here, but whatever you do you are NOT to make any sort of scene. Do you understand?'

'OK. I'll just go home, then.'

'Not on your own you won't.'

'All right then, I'll stay here.' Stuart's voice was flat and unemotional. The interesting pattern he had found in the flecks on the Formica toilet door would keep him occupied for hours.

Chapter Twelve

Having been shown to their seats, guests were seated ready for the wedding breakfast to be served. Heads turned in amusement as Bill, Trevor, Neil and George opened the door of the ladies' toilets and one by one strode across the floor, followed by a worried-looking Rose with Elsie on her arm.

Bewildered, Lydia stared straight ahead. As the smart waitresses filled up crystal wine glasses from heavy decanters, people were talking and whispering amongst themselves and Lydia knew there was some sort of crisis. She wasn't stupid. She'd seen what was going on and it was obvious they were all trying to shield her from the truth – whatever that was.

Martin leaned over to whisper in her ear.

'I love you,' he said.

Her wedding day was turning into a complete fiasco. 'What's going on?' she asked him, blinking back tears.

'Daisy feels dreadful because of what Stuart said in the church and my mother thinks she's ruined our wedding because she's not very well.'

'Where is he?'

Martin shrugged. 'I don't know. I think he might have gone home. Does it matter?'

Lydia forced a smile and shook her head. She stretched across the table to pat Daisy comfortingly on her hand. 'Don't worry about the church. I understand. I know he's ill and I'm worried for him, but everything will be all right in the end once he gets his medication sorted out. Let's just get on with the rest of the day and try to enjoy ourselves.'

She then turned to Elsie, sitting by her side. 'Feeling

better now ... Mother?'

Elsie beamed. It was the first time Lydia had called her *mother*. It was clear she was being forgiven for being ill and spoiling the service.

'I'm so sorry I've ruined things for you, love.'

'Don't be silly, you haven't.'

George motioned for everyone to be quiet and stood up, patting his bald head and smoothing down his non-existent hair. He gave a nervous cough as he glanced around the room, trying to catch everyone's attention. He tapped his knife on the table and cleared his throat.

'Before we begin to celebrate the marriage of my lovely niece, Lydia, and we welcome Martin into our family, I'd like to let everyone know that unfortunately there is a problem with the ladies' toilets.' He motioned towards the door and cleared his throat again as all eyes turned towards the waitress who was affixing a handwritten *Out of Order* sign to the toilet door.

George gave directions to alternative facilities with a false smile and exaggerated hand movements. 'We're sorry for any inconvenience, if you'll excuse my choice of words!'

"It is a great honour for me to be asked to be Lydia's father-of-the bride."

Tom's voice drifted through to the ladies' toilets and Stuart unfurled himself inside the cubicle, his legs stiff and heavy from sitting on the hard floor. He took off his glasses and rubbed at his eyes, surveying his handiwork of the last two hours. It was a bit of luck he'd found a pencil in the top pocket of his jacket, which meant he had been able to join up the patterns in the Formica door in a most satisfactory manner. He nodded his approval. It had been a good way to pass the time until it was time to go. He smoothed back his hair and slid his glasses back over his nose, straining to hear Tom's speech.

A harsh, inner voice vibrated inside him, and his hand trembled as he reached out and rested his thumb on the door lock. He felt the smooth metal beneath his thumb and forefinger and caressed it for a while before gradually applying pressure and almost silently slipping the bolt back. He took a couple of steps towards the cloakroom door and put the flat of his hands against the thick layers of paint. He leaned in slowly, turning his head slightly until his ear was pressed up against the cool paintwork.

He could hear laughter. He felt a sudden rush of pride for his ageing grandfather, standing up and delivering a speech in front of nearly a hundred people. At the same time he felt a wild and uncontrolled envy. In the last fortnight, Lydia had clearly taken his place in Tom's affections. Remembering all the special times he had shared with Tom when he was a child, it didn't seem fair that she had now pushed him clean out of his family.

A roar of laughter hammered against the door in Stuart's ear, bringing with it a series of tiny, glinting knives cutting through raw nerves. His eyes turned to glass as he watched, someone's hand grasp the door knob and turn it with a slow twist of the wrist. Was it his hand, or someone else's? He pulled the door slightly towards him and it yielded with a squeak of rusty hinges. In the hall outside, the laughter died down in increments as if it was gradually being switched off.

Everyone turned their heads to look at the creaking door.

His father stood up, his chair scraping against the wooden floor. Bill dashed across the room as Stuart flung the door wide open and stood motionless gazing into space. He stared at his hand, bemused as it remained suspended in mid-air. The hand belonged to that other person, the one who had just opened the door; the one who screamed at him from the mirror in his mind and wouldn't let him rest, not even for a minute.

'Come on, lad. I'll take you home now.' Bill's voice was almost a whisper. Stuart didn't move. He couldn't hear his father above the din of screaming voices in his head.

Trying his hardest to be discreet, Bill hissed. 'Now!' But everyone was silent and could hear, eyes averted in embarrassment.

143

Stuart cast dull eyes towards his father and, in slow motion, the person that might have once been him clenched his right hand into a fist to make sure it really did belong to him and wasn't just a ghostly apparition of part of his own body.

From the top table, Tom saw Stuart clench his hand into a fist.

'No!' he bellowed, breaking the silence in the room like a clap of unexpected thunder. He hauled himself up, quickly pulling his crutches onto his arms. He limped noisily and painfully across the hall floor towards the ladies' toilet door, followed by Daisy.

On the top table, Lydia put her hands over her face and shut her eyes, shaking her head from side to side in disbelief as her new husband snaked his arm around her shoulders and drew her into him.

Stuart stared at Tom. Why was a bull bearing down on him, its head distorted and angry, snorts of anger spraying forth from its mouth in loud, rhythmic squeaks? He counted the squeaks. *Eighteen, nineteen, twenty ...*

The bull stopped in front of him; there were beads of sweat on its brow and its chest was convulsing, ready to devour him. It released its gnarled and twisted hoof and touched him on the shoulder as if to steady itself. He stepped back, away from the salivating, angry bull which now appeared to be choking on gallons of putrid, foul-smelling saliva.

Stuart blinked and when he opened his eyes, he was horrified to see his grandfather in the place the bull had been, crumpling to the floor, crutches awry. Tom coughed. Blood trickled from his mouth and then splattered explosively across the floor as his whole body heaved with terrible gurgling sounds that reminded Stuart of a dog about to throw up.

Surely he hadn't just hit his grandfather, had he? Panting with shocked revulsion at what he might just have done, Stuart turned and fled.

Guests gasped and looked on in horror as Tom collapsed.

Several people jumped up and ran over, mobilised by the sight of the blood that had just splattered from Tom's mouth as forcefully as if it had just been detonated by an unseen firing pin.

Stuart stopped running when he reached the main door. He stared at his hand in front of him, turning it over and over, twisting his fingers before his eyes before finally clenching it into a fist. He tried to speak but nothing came out. He was drifting, floating, swirling around in the air above himself like gathering mist.

He heard his grandmother's hysterical voice shout: 'Tom! Tom!'

Stuart's vision cleared and his feathery, disconnected body melted back into himself. As his mind cleared, the horror of what he might just have done forced adrenaline into his limbs and flooded his consciousness.

Shaking himself free from those who were trying to comfort him, Stuart ran out of the door and down the steps into the busy main street, dodging between bemused shoppers and almost falling over a small boy on a toy scooter who happened to be in his way.

'Call an ambulance!' he heard someone shout behind him. Then there was a familiar voice behind him, calling his name. Then, he could hear nothing but his heart in his ears and his breath forcing its way in and out of his lungs.

Beating.

Thudding.

Pounding.

A weightless but urgent inner voice in his head screamed at him. The voice became louder. It was now beside him – shouting at him to *run, run, run, faster, faster, faster.*

A large green shape appeared out of nowhere. It had a face with two eyes, a wide stubby nose and a lop-sided grin. It was strangely welcoming. Once he reached it, he knew he would once again become Stuart Roberts, gifted medical student, eldest son of Daisy and Bill Roberts, brother of Eileen, Trevor and Neil. But most of all he would be the ecstatically happy newly-wed husband of Lydia. He was certain everything in his life would snap back to normal when he reached the green face.

Faster, faster, faster.

Feet pounding.

Chest gasping.

Head buzzing.

A man shouting.

Hooter sounding.

Women screaming.

Brakes squealing.

Finally, his mother shouting his name.

Silence.

'Stuart!' Daisy yelled at the top of her voice as astonished shoppers looked on. 'Stuart. Stop. For God's sake, stop!'

An eerie *"ooohhhhhh"* drifted on the wind at the sickening squeal of rubber on metal followed by a loud hiss of air. The green double-decker bus juddered to a stop, rocking slowly from side to side, skewed slightly across the road.

In Daisy's head, everything sparkled red and silver and then went black.

Neil caught up with Daisy and grabbed her just as her legs crumpled like broken twigs beneath her, but people were rushing past them, jostling them as they ran towards the scene of the accident. A large group formed around the front of the bus and two or three men tried to reach Stuart, who was trapped underneath.

The two of them were dragged along by the crowd, seemingly in slow motion, towards the gory scene. A man appeared from nowhere in front of Daisy, obscuring her line of vision.

'I wouldn't look, love – it's pretty gruesome!'

Someone shouted hysterically. 'Can somebody call an ambulance?'

Then someone else said: 'Tell them not to rush. There's no point.'

After just a few agonising minutes, the piercing sound of

an ambulance siren in the distance intensified and then people looked up in surprise as it sped across the junction behind the accident and up the road in the wrong direction.

Someone had fetched a chair for Daisy. She stared blankly at her two sons as they crouched down in front of her, holding and stroking her hands. Behind her, Eileen's arms held her steady against the chair back, and she could feel her daughter's face burying itself into her neck.

Daisy was cold, shivering ... or was she? She tried to speak, but only a series of disjointed whispers came out. Behind her, Eileen murmured into her felt wedding hat and she felt her daughter's voice vibrate through the material.

A policeman arrived and gave an exaggerated cough. 'Is this the young man's mother?'

Daisy tried to swallow the foul-tasting lump that had suddenly manifested itself in her throat, preventing her from speaking properly.

'Can you bring her in here?' The policemen spoke in the general direction of Eileen, and pointed to a nearby shop. 'We need to get her inside and off the road.'

The shopkeeper shut the door behind them, locked it and pulled down the blinds. The shop was a sweet shop and the sickly smell of boiled sweets and sherbet mingled with exhaust fumes from the queue of vehicles outside that had begun to form after the accident.

The policeman took off his helmet.

'I'm afraid,' he said, 'that it appears that your son may have ... um .... he might be ...' He took out his notebook and pencil. 'Could you give me some basic details?' He looked at Eileen. 'Just name and address will do for now?'

'Take me to him.' Daisy heard herself say. 'Please?'

'Of course I will, madam. But I'm pretty sure that your son is, er ...he's likely to be ...' He turned to Eileen for help and shrugged nervously.

'I understand,' Eileen said.

'Dead.'

Daisy heard the policeman whisper the word and she saw him shake his head. The word bounced around like a hard rubber ball in her head. *Dead. Dead. Dead. Dead.*

'Dead?' she repeated, her voice surprised. But the words wouldn't stop coming and forming themselves in her head in a merciless chant.

Something snapped inside Daisy's abdomen, in the region of her navel, and the pain caused by the snap was, so intense, she thought she was going to die, right there in the sweet shop. It caused her to double over and, at the same time, a primal, animal wail escaped from her chest. Subconsciously, she grasped the air before her as if trying to find something tangible to hold onto. She was Stuart's mother just minutes ago. Now there was nothing but air where the invisible cord had been. He had gone. She knew it. Gone and was never coming back. Just like little Oliver all those years ago.

After a while she opened her eyes and looked straight at the policeman, her eyes dry and her mind strangely clear.

Her voice, though, was wild and disjointed. 'Oliver was mine. She might have given birth to him but I was his mother.' She set her face in a determined pout and her voice became louder. 'And now, Officer, I've lost Stuart, too. My strong, clever boy, born on the same day as my Oliver was taken.'

She began to shout as she viciously pulled the hat from her head and threw it on the floor. 'IT'S JUST NOT FAIR! THERE IS NO GOD! HOW CAN THERE BE WHEN HE TAKES ANOTHER CHILD FROM ME?'

Daisy's angry shouts reverberated right out into the street as she tore her silver crucifix from her neck, trembling with shock. Someone thrust a lit cigarette into her hand. She put it to her lips and drew the smoke into her mouth. Spluttering and coughing, she threw it to the floor. She had never smoked before in her life, so what was she doing accepting a cigarette?

She stared at the crucifix and silver chain twisted through her fingers and drew her arm slowly back.

There was a mirror on the wall behind the tiny counter of the sweet shop. A beam of sunlight intruded through the blinds in the shop window and reflected itself in the mirror, as if taunting her. Daisy took aim at the light. With the full weight of two lost sons behind her, she flung her crucifix at the mirror. It struck the reflected sun full in the centre before falling to the floor behind the counter.

Shaking uncontrollably, her head slumped forwards until it was bowed deep into her knees. She heard Eileen explain to the policeman about baby Oliver, who had died all those years ago and whose loss was still raw inside her. She looked up briefly and saw him shake his head in sympathy, but he was obviously too young to remember the terrible tragedy that had been in all the newspapers at the time.

The shopkeeper brought out cups of tea on a tray as, in a shaky voice Eileen gave the policeman a summary of events at the wedding and explained about Stuart's recent diagnosis of schizophrenia.

There was a tentative tap on the shop door. The policeman unlocked it and opened it a couple of inches.

'Can I come in?' a voice said.

'Are you the lad's father?'

'Yes.'

Safely inside the shop, Bill's face crumpled and he, too, began to cry, loud racking sobs forcing their way through his fingers as his hands, shaking violently, covered his face. Eileen locked the door behind him. Daisy lifted her head. This was not really happening. Any minute now she'd wake up from this horrific nightmare.

'I'll take you all to the hospital in my car,' the policeman said, squeezing behind the counter to retrieve the discarded crucifix. He straightened up and pressed it into the shopkeeper's hand, whispering to him that he should try and find a family member to give it to.

Trying hard to maintain her self-control for everyone's sake, Eileen spoke, concluding her story.

'Then my grandfather collapsed. Someone said he was vomiting up blood, but I didn't see that as we were all running after Stuart.'

It is not uncommon in family tragedies for one person to be so profoundly traumatised they have to run away, as far as possible, in a primal fight-or-flight instinctive reaction. They can usually be seen standing on the periphery, seemingly cold-hearted and unconcerned. But, deep inside, unable to grieve, powerless and unable to come to terms with a catastrophic event, they have to run and keep on running – as far away as they can – to the other side of the world, if necessary.

Neil Roberts was that person. The youngest of the three Roberts boys, he had just left school after obtaining a clutch of perfect exam results and had secured a place at university to study to be a civil engineer.

Someone said to the shopkeeper that the dead man's brother was standing in the middle of the road, staring after the ambulance as it drove away from the scene with a police car carrying the man's parents and sister following close behind. The shopkeeper had gone over to him and pressed the crucifix into his hand, explaining that his mother had torn it from her neck and thrown it at the wall.

That night, Neil clutched his mother's crucifix in his fist and held it close to his heart. He had offered it to her at the hospital but she'd just turned her tear-stained face away, telling him to throw it away. She didn't ever want to wear it again because there was no God. If there was, He wouldn't have taunted her by giving her another son on the same day He had taken one away, only to wrench that son away from her twenty-one years later.

A month later, with Daisy's crucifix around his neck under his shirt and nothing to his name but a cardboard suitcase of clothes and a wallet containing the remainder of the money from his post office savings account after he had bought a one-way ticket, Neil boarded a plane for Canada.

And Daisy had lost another son.

Chapter Thirteen

'I'm afraid it's cancer.'

'Stomach cancer?'

Martin nodded. 'And at his age – or any age for that matter – there isn't really anything can be done for him.'

Lydia bit her lip. 'Does he know?'

'Yes.'

'How's he taken it?'

Martin looked down at his shoes. 'As you'd expect. He's a bit shocked, but he told the consultant he had been vomiting blood on and off for a few months. He must have been in terrible pain, and I think mostly now he's just relieved to get some medication.'

'I feel awful,' Lydia said with a sigh. 'He must have only kept himself going so that he could walk me down the aisle. He never said a word to anyone about how ill he was feeling. And we should have done something about him losing weight, but he always insisted it was because he was getting old. Does Auntie Liz know?'

'No, not yet. They'll call her in and explain the diagnosis. You should get Rose to come in, too. And perhaps George. I don't know what it will do to poor Daisy in the state she's in already – probably best to break the news to her separately.'

'Can I go in and see him?'

Martin nodded. 'Okay.'

'Do you think we should cancel our honeymoon?'

Martin shook his head. 'We've missed the first couple of days, but I think we should still go. There's nothing more we can do. And Tom's life isn't in imminent danger now we know what caused him to collapse. He'll be discharged in a couple of days, and he'll be much more comfortable being at home.'

Lydia shook her head sadly. 'I don't know how Auntie Liz is going to survive without him. They are devoted to each other.'

Two days later, Tom came home from hospital.

From a calm acceptance of the diagnosis that, in a few weeks' time – a couple of months at the most – he was going to die, he was becoming more and more frightened and agitated. Grieving over the death of Stuart was affecting every member of the family, their anguish exacerbated by having to wait for an inquest into the circumstances of his death. Although shocked by Tom's terminal diagnosis, the family's energies were being drained and channelled in another direction and no one was listening to Tom's lamentations about Stuart's schizophrenia.

'It must be hereditary,' he said to Rose one day. 'Can you find out if it is? Can you ask someone? Please – I have to know if it was my fault before I die.'

'Why? What's the point? It will only upset Daisy if she finds out I've been asking questions,' Rose replied. 'It's not as if Stuart had any children he might pass it onto.'

Tom's eyes began to leak moisture and he grabbed at Rose's hand. 'Please, Rose?'

'How can it be your fault? It's another awful tragedy, and God knows this family has had enough tragedies to fill a bookshelf in Kettering library.'

'I might have passed it onto him. After all, I'm the only one in this family to have knocked on the door of the funny farm.'

'Well, there's nothing anyone can do now, is there? We have to try and keep you as comfortable as possible, and worrying is doing you no good at all. And Mam is not well, either. Everything is taking its toll on her, too.'

'I've been a bad man, Rose. I've done so many terrible things to people in my life. I'm really scared of dying ...'

'I know,' Rose said, patting his hand in comfort. 'But everyone's frightened of dying, whoever they are, and whatever they've done in their lives.'

'Can you ask our Lydia to come and see me?'

'She's gone on her honeymoon. They missed the first couple of days, but there was no point in them hanging around because there's nothing more that can be done about Stuart's funeral until after the inquest.'

Tom's voice was croaky. 'Can you ask her to come and see me as soon as she gets back, then? It's important, Rose. There are things I have to tell her about our Violet. She has to know; she has a right.'

Overwhelmed by exhaustion, Tom fell back onto his pillows. Rose waited until he closed his eyes and then left the front room, where he was, in his own words *"waiting for the Grim Reaper"*.

Just two weeks later, Tom's physical condition had markedly deteriorated, although his mind was still much too active, everyone said. If Tom had ever wished for an easy exit from this life into the next, he knew now he wasn't going to be granted his wish and be allowed to die in peace.

A constant stream of visitors filed into the front room, everyone knowing that Tom didn't have long to live. His days consisted of clutching at hands, apologising for various wrongdoings. There was an endless stream of confessions for things he had done, or failed to do. He grasped at imaginary straws, shouting up at the ceiling for forgiveness, convinced that he was destined to go to hell.

In desperation, Rose called in the local vicar, hoping that he could offer some words of comfort to her father. He emerged, an hour later, saying he'd done his best but he feared that Mr Jeffson was not enough of a believer to accept that, whatever he had done in his life, his sins would be forgiven and he could die in peace.

'But he believes he was once touched by an angel,' Rose implored. 'It was thirty-six years ago when he tried to commit suicide with ant paste poison and nearly died. It was the turning point – it was when he decided to get treatment for his psychopathic tendencies and become a better man. Surely that shows that he's a believer, despite what he says.'

'God will be his judge,' the sour-faced vicar said. 'There's no doubt he tried hard to make amends, but I'm afraid there is nothing more I can do to help Mr Jeffson, especially given the foul language he has just spoken to me.'

'He didn't mean it, I'm sure.' Rose said apologetically. 'I'm sorry he swore at you, Vicar, but he's so frightened of dying and there's nothing anyone can say or do to make him feel better about it.'

Almost at the end of her tether and exhausted from single-handedly caring for Tom, clearing up after him and making sure he was always clean and comfortable, Rose sank down into an armchair, her head in her hands. George slid around the door and joined her in the room.

'When's it going to end, George? I can't take any more.'

George sat down on the arm of Rose's chair and put an arm around her shoulders. 'I don't think it will be long now, love.'

'It's so horrible. There's blood everywhere. He only has to hiccup and it bubbles and splatters out of his mouth. I can't keep up with all the washing. If only our Daisy was able to help, it wouldn't be so bad.'

'She can't, Rose. She's totally in bits. Inconsolable. Neil rang from Canada today. He says he's never coming back. Bill's nearly going out of his mind. They're in a mess, Rose. Just as much of a mess as we are.'

'Lydia will be back from her honeymoon today. I've got a feeling Dad's just hanging on until he can see her.'

Tom's weak voice drifted from the front room, interrupting their conversation. 'When's she coming, Rose? Tell her to be quick.'

'How the hell did he hear that?' George said, grimacing. 'He hasn't got his hearing aid in.'

'He hears everything just lately,' Rose said with a sigh.

'Tell her to hurry up.' Tom groaned.

'I'll ring her at tea time,' Rose said to George. 'Perhaps he will be less agitated once he's spoken to Lydia.'

A few hours later, Lydia and Martin arrived to visit Tom, but he'd been vomiting blood all afternoon and, near to tears and almost collapsing with exhaustion, Rose had to admit defeat.

'Can he be taken somewhere?' she pleaded. 'Just to give me a bit of a break for a couple of days?'

'I'll ring the hospital,' Martin said. 'He'll have to be admitted. You can't cope on your own with all this.'

'It's no good, he can't talk to me,' Lydia said as she emerged from the front room shaking her head. 'I think he must be suffering from delirium. He keeps saying something about my mother and harping back to Easter Saturday in nineteen twenty-two, but I can't understand what he means. He's confused and thinks I'm his grand-daughter. I think we need to get him on stronger medication to calm him down and make him more comfortable before he can be moved.'

Martin picked up the telephone to dial the hospital. As he started speaking, Liz appeared barefoot at the top of the stairs, dressed in a long nightdress. Frail and clutching the handrail, she carefully negotiated the stairs, step by step, helped down by Lydia.

When they reached the bottom step, there was an almighty rumbling growl from the front room. Rose screamed out. 'Oh God help him! Lydia, Martin, you'd better come quickly.'

Liz was unnaturally calm when she entered the room and shuffled over to Tom's bedside, where, appearing not to notice that the bed was covered in blood and clumps of cancerous tumour expelled from Tom's stomach, she reached across him with thin, sinewy arms and rested her head on his chest.

'Oh Tom. I forgive you,' she whispered. 'Shush. There, there. You have nothing to fear.'

Tom's body relaxed and he closed his eyes for the last

time.

He had died in exactly the same manner as he had lived.

When tragedy strikes, it overwhelms senses, smothers lingering suspicions with explanations and wipes clean the hurt from brain cells to enable human beings to move on and recover. After a perfunctory calculation on her fingers, Lydia rationalised that the honeymoon baby she was carrying was most definitely Martin's and she was ecstatic with the unexpected turn of events. When the news was made public a few weeks later, Rose had commented, in an attempt to inject a hint of optimism in the face of adversity: *"you know what they say, one out and one in."*

She couldn't bear to think about Stuart. And she had only happy memories of Tom, who had welcomed both her and her brother into his family as abandoned, homeless children. His death had deeply saddened her, but he *had* been very old, after all.

She gave birth to a daughter, Naomi Rose, in early March nineteen sixty-nine and the happy event dragged the family out of the sultry, oppressive doldrums into a pleasant warm spring, the fragrant blossom and new buds lifting their spirits with lungs full of new clean air. Everyone agreed that a new baby was the best antidote to the mind-numbing malaise that had followed the tragedy of Stuart's accident and Tom's death from stomach cancer, which hadn't been helped by Liz passing peacefully away in her sleep just weeks after her husband had died.

Something had been bothering Millie of Haywood's Bakery for almost a year, and now that Lydia's baby was here and thriving, she knew she was going to have to say something – if only for her own piece of mind. She decided to wait until Lydia next came into the shop, which she did with regularity due to her fondness for pink iced buns. She didn't have to wait long, because, just after she had made her decision,

Lydia turned up the very next day.

'Hello,' Lydia called out cheerfully as she put the brake on Naomi's pram outside the cake shop.

'Hello, love.' Millie wiped her hands on her apron and walked around the shop counter to the open door. 'Let's come and have a look at the little princess.'

Three-month-old Naomi was awake, lying on her back in her pram. Her huge brown eyes gazed at Millie as she peered into the pram and she gave a gummy smile and waved her arms, kicking off the pram blanket with enthusiasm.

'Oh, just look at her. Pretty as a picture. Bring her in. I'll put the kettle on if you have time. I'll shut the shop door and then I'll hear the bell out the back if a customer comes in.'

'That would be nice. I could do with a cuppa,' Lydia said as she picked up her daughter from the pram and buried her face in Naomi's fine black baby hair, breathing in the smell of Johnson's baby shampoo.

The two women made their way through the shop to the back room. Millie looked at the clock on the wall. It was just after four thirty and the shop shut at five.

'I won't be a minute,' Millie muttered as she decided to shut the shop early and hurried back through to put up the *closed* sign.

When she returned, Lydia was spooning tea into the teapot with one hand while holding Naomi.

'I'll fetch us a cake each, shall I? Millie was nervous, putting off the inevitable difficult conversation she knew she had to have with Lydia. She disappeared back into the shop. Her hands shook slightly as she collected the tray of pink iced buns from the display counter. She returned to the back room, put down the buns on the table and then reached for her handbag, which was hanging on a hook on the door.

'Lydia, love. I've been meaning to give you this – but the time has never been right. I swear to you now, I have absolutely no idea what is in it.'

Lydia stared at the writing on the blue Basildon Bond

envelope. She immediately recognised it as Stuart's.

Millie continued. 'Stuart came to see me just before your wedding. He broke down, here in this room. From what he said to me, I think he was worried he would end up in an institution because of his illness.'

'Why didn't you give it to the Inquest?' Lydia said. 'You really should have done.'

'Because it was yours – wasn't it? And Tom was in hospital. And then you went off on your honeymoon and when you came back, poor Tom died. Then it was Tom's funeral, followed by Stuart's, and soon after poor Mrs Jeffson passed away in her sleep, bless her soul. After all that dreadful tragedy, it was unthinkable to give you the letter while you were expecting. It's never been the right time, until now.'

'Why did he give it to you? Why not to Rose or Daisy – or someone in the family?'

Millie shrugged. 'I really don't know. I think it might be because I was just far enough away from the family, and yet close enough to be able to carry out his wishes if his fears were realised.'

'You've never read it?'

Millie was indignant. How could Lydia think that she would do such a thing? 'Of course not! What do you take me for?'

'Sorry. I'm not thinking straight.' Lydia turned the envelope over, but hesitated before she ran her finger along the flap.

'Are you going to open it?'

Lydia bit her lip. She shrugged her shoulders.

'Do you want me to take Naomi and go into the shop so you can read it in private?'

Lydia nodded.

Millie lifted the baby from Lydia's arms and went back into the shop with her. She shut the door between the shop and the back room, perched on a stool behind the counter and switched on a small transistor radio, singing along to the tune, jiggling baby Naomi up and down on her knee.

Just a minute later, Lydia opened the inner door again. 'You all right, love?'

Lydia nodded and held up the letter for Millie to see.

'It's back to front, I think. Have you got a mirror?'

Millie stared at the letter in disbelief. 'Only a powder compact. What on earth ...?' Her words tailed off as she screwed up her face in disbelief. 'It's in my bag, behind the door.'

Lydia turned around and shut the door behind her without speaking.

It was almost ten minutes later when Lydia re-emerged, her eyes moist. She handed the powder compact back to Millie.

'Well, the inquest was right. It was an accident. He wasn't intending to take his own life.'

Millie knew she shouldn't ask, but burning curiosity had finally got the better of her and she blurted out one question after the other as she sub-consciously rocked a sleeping Naomi back and forth.

'Did you manage to decipher it? What did it say? Why did he write it back-to-front?'

'Nothing much. Just private things – you know ...'

She felt she needed to give Millie more of an explanation. 'In a way it's answered lots of questions, but I was beginning to put the whole thing behind me and now it's brought it all back again.'

'It's bound to.' Millie put her free arm around Lydia. 'What matters now are the living – you, Martin and little Naomi. We can't do anything about the dead.'

'I know. This reversed handwriting is just weird. If anything, it demonstrates how severe his illness must have been. I couldn't have read it without a mirror.'

Lydia shook her head and leaned on the table, scanning the letter once more. Her action was slow and deliberate when she tore it up, the sound ripping through the silence. She crumpled the pieces and held them tightly in her hand for a few seconds before throwing them into a waste bin.

'Thank you for carrying out Stuart's wishes, Millie, but

I've got Naomi to think of now. I have to put him firmly into my past, because what's done is done. I can't change anything, so what's the point in even thinking about it.'

Twenty minutes later, staring at the waste paper bin, Millie faced a fresh quandary. Yes, she was curious, she admitted that. She sighed, not knowing what to do. Eventually she rifled through the contents of the bin until she found every screwed up piece of the torn up letter. She fetched a paper bag from the shop and carefully put the pieces into it, folding it over at the top. She had never intended to piece together the letter and read it; after all it *was* private, but she did know that at some point in the future, Lydia might regret ripping up what were, after all, some of the last words written by Stuart.

Chapter Fourteen

Two years later

Winter 1971

Millie's granddaughter, Suzy, laughed at Janet, who was Rose's granddaughter, and pulled a face. 'Nah ... you absolutely *hate* Cherry B. He knows that, doesn't he?'

'I know, but nothing else rhymes except *"me"* and that's so corny. All right clever clogs, you come up with something.' Janet rolled over on her bed and passed the pen to Suzy.

'Right, what about this.'

Suzy scribbled out the next line.

Both girls burst out laughing. Janet leaned over to grab the scrap of paper but Suzy snatched it away.

'Or this ...'

The girls rolled around on the bed in mock agony. 'I don't think we should send any Valentine's cards,' said Janet, pretending to choke. 'It's only going to end badly, and it's a soppy thing to do anyway.'

Janet and Suzy were friends, as were their mothers, Joan and Margaret and their grandmothers, Rose and Millie. Although they were at different schools, the two fifteen-year olds spent much of their spare time together. Wherever they went, people who didn't know them assumed they were sisters. Once, when they were younger they had pretended to be twins.

'Hey,' Janet said, grabbing Suzy's arm and examining it. 'I didn't realise you had that little crease on your forearm, just below your elbow?'

Suzy studied her arm. 'I've got it on both arms – look.' She held out her arms and Janet inspected them. She pulled up the sleeves on her own jumper.

'I've got them too. I hadn't ever noticed you had them.'

Suzy frowned. 'This is just so weird. We are too much alike in other ways for it to be a bizarre fluke.'

After a few minutes, the girls sat, cross-legged on the bed staring at a list they had made of their similarities.

'There's loads more too, if we think about it. 'We like the same things and even our voices sound the same on the phone.' Suzy chewed the end of the pen, deep in thought.

'Yeah,' agreed Janet. 'When I rang to let Mum know I was going to be late the other day, she thought I was you, and said: *"Janet's not here at the moment, Suzy, you'll have to ring back later."* '

'Talking about your mum, you'd better start tidying up or else she won't let you go to Four Seasons on Monday,' Suzy said, pointing the pen in her hand at a book, which lay open on the floor, along with scattered various editions of *Jackie*, odd socks, empty crisp packets and a pair of knee high black boots with mud on the heels.

Janet uncrossed her legs and sat hugging her knees, picking at the candlewick bedspread. 'I think it's time we investigated this.'

Suzy must have been thinking the same thoughts because she said in a quiet, serious voice, 'Or perhaps not.'

Outside, the late afternoon sun was surrendering its deep red hue to a purple-grey dusk, and Janet stood up and flicked on the light switch. Both girls stared at each other blinking as Janet said, 'We'll have to do it secretly.'

'That's just what I was thinking,' Suzy agreed. 'We mustn't upset anyone – especially our parents.'

Before the evening drew to a close, and Suzy pulled on her coat to walk home, the girls had hatched a plan to get to the bottom of their lifelong similarities once and for all.

The following evening, the girls were back in Janet's bedroom. This time though, there was a third person in the room. David, Daisy's grandson, sat uncomfortably on Janet's dressing table, swinging his legs and biting his lip. They had tricked him into the impromptu meeting by telling him they had a Party Four – which was just a trick to get him there. He was almost a year older than them, and was trying to grow a moustache, which for some reason had caused them both to roll around on the bed in tears of laughter. Although the three of them had played in this room many times over the years he suddenly felt self-conscious and very much aware of the femininity that the room exuded, and it wasn't just the smell of Avon Honeysuckle and Aqua Manda perfume, either.

The evening was turning into an uncomfortable interrogation.

Janet studied him closely, and he knew she was trying to spot any sort of non-verbal reaction. 'Has your mum or your gran ever said *anything* about me and Suzie and how alike we are?'

David shifted position and sat on his hands. 'No.'

Suzy pulled up her sleeves and, taking the cue, Janet did the same.

'Can you see – we've got the same arms?'

David leaned forward. After a few seconds he said: 'What? It's just arms.'

Janet, unable to hide the tone of suspicion in her voice, pointed to the crease on one of her arms and then to the crease on Suzy's. 'There,' she said, 'it's just there.'

David sighed and looked at each girl in turn. He shrugged his shoulders. 'What's so special about that? I've got them too.'

David pulled his jumper over his head, his tie-dyed t-shirt coming off with it. The girls took an arm each and ran their fingers over the creases. He felt increasingly uncomfortable and jumped down off the dressing table, alarmed, as if something had suddenly bit him. He shrugged them off.

'Leave me alone! I think you're both mad – and paranoid. Talking of Paranoid – have you got my LP you borrowed last week?'

Suzy ignored him. 'We made a list last night – look!'

David took the list and shrugged again. 'Look. I did hear Gran and Auntie Rose talking about something years and years ago. Something about Gramp and tomcats up alleyways. I think she meant the old boy must have put it about a bit.'

He punched Janet on the shoulder playfully. 'You could ask your grandma, couldn't you? Remember when Gramp and Grandma Liz died and we found out that they had lied about the year they got married, meaning that Grandma Jeffson was pregnant?'

Janet thought back to Tom and Liz, and the shocked faces of her grandma and great-aunt Daisy when they had come across their parents' marriage certificate and realised that the lavish diamond wedding anniversary they had celebrated had been held a year before it should have been.

'Aunt Daisy was really upset, wasn't she?' Janet sympathised, 'especially because Gramp threw her out when she found out she was expecting your mum at seventeen.'

'Yeah,' David agreed. 'Gran and Grandad had to go and live in a horrible room in King Street, where the ceiling leaked on the bed when it rained and the toilet stank of wee.'

Suzy raised her eyebrows at David. 'That was a bit hypocritical, wasn't it? Throwing your poor grandma out of the house just because she was up the duff, when he had done the same thing to your great-grandma years before?'

David turned to Suzy. 'There's lots of secrets in our family, isn't there Jan? Gran always calls them *skeletons in the cupboard* and refuses to talk about them. Look, why don't we try and get Auntie Rose and my gran together in the same place one afternoon and then pay them a visit. 'You can come too, Suze. We'll all three of us go.'

Janet picked up the list. 'We'll take this list. As evidence.' She jumped up and ran downstairs. 'There's no time like the present,' she yelled.

Having dialled Rose's telephone number, she inspected her nails while she waited for her to answer.

'Hello, Grandma. How are you?'

'Janet. I'm glad you've rang. You know that jumper I'm knitting for you? I need to measure your arms. I want to get it done. It's absolutely freezing outside and they've forecast snow. You're going to need it if you won't wear a vest.'

Janet grimaced down the phone. 'What colour is it.'

'It's the same colour as that hideous wallpaper you've got in your bedroom. I thought if you liked it on the walls, then you'd like a jumper in it.'

Janet grinned. 'Thanks, Grandma. I love purple.'

'What did you want, anyway?'

'Oh, I nearly forgot in the excitement of having a new purple jumper. I want to talk to Aunt Daisy about some sewing I'm doing at school. When will she be there?'

'Oh. How nice. Daisy will be thrilled to help you with your homework. She'll be here on Wednesday afternoon, as usual. I'll pop round the bakery and get some iced buns. I'll ask her to wait for you after school. Don't let me forget to measure you, though, will you? Got a memory like a sieve these days.'

'Can Suzy come too? And David?'

'David's not doing sewing homework as well, is he?'

'I don't know. He might be, but I don't know what they do at the boys' school. All boys at my school do girls' stuff at school nowadays, Grandma. Next term, I'm going to do technical drawing. We had a choice between woodwork, metalwork and technical drawing. The boys are either doing needlework or cookery.'

'Oh. That's good. I think it's a lovely idea. In my day, boys didn't know how to sew or cook, and didn't want to learn, either.'

Janet knew her Grandma Rose would be looking forward to the visit. She always said teenagers' gossip cheered her up no end.

'I'll look forward it, love. I think it's smashing that the

three of you are such good friends. Now mind you don't let me forget to measure your arms and I'll see you on Wednesday.'

The three teenagers arrived separately as they were all at different schools. David was the first to arrive and he parked his racing bike in the back yard, untwisting the school scarf from his neck and shaking his shoulder length, wavy black hair free of his parka jacket.

'Hello, Auntie Rose,' he called out as he opened the back door. 'It's only me.'

George appeared at the living room door, smoking his pipe.

'Hello, lad. Auntie Rose and your grandma have just popped down the cake shop for some buns – I expect they're gossiping with Millie and Joan as usual. They'll be back soon.'

George shuffled through to the kitchen in his tartan slippers, his large trousers pulled up to his chest, suspended on braces. Even so, his trousers were too long. George had always been short, but now he was approaching seventy he seemed to be getting smaller than ever. David spotted a half-eaten rice pudding on the kitchen table.

'Can I have this, Uncle George? I'm absolutely *starving*.'

'Go on then. I'd hate to deprive a growing lad.' George smiled and took his pipe out of his mouth to cough, as David plunged a spoon into the solidifying rice pudding, making a satisfying gloopy noise in the process.

Janet opened the back door. 'Hey, you gutsy pig! I always finish off the rice pudding. Grandma saves it especially for me.' She grabbed the dish and spoon from a protesting David and tucked in, just as Suzy joined them, dressed in the green uniform of Rockingham Road Girls' School.

'Hi ... want some?' Janet handed over the spoon and dish to Suzy.

George shook his head. 'I hope none of you lot have anything catching, sharing a spoon like that. Our Rose will go mad. You know what she's like about hygiene.'

Suzy pinged George's braces and kissed him on top of his bald head. 'Don't worry, George. If we have caught lurgies off each other, then at least we get some time off school.'

George filled the kettle, water slopping over the top of the stove as he set it down and lit the gas.

'I suppose you all want a cup of tea to go with the non-existent iced buns.' He looked at his watch. 'Where the devil have they got to? They went out at three o'clock.'

The teenagers were laughing and making jokes about *The Magic Roundabout* on the television, when Rose and Daisy walked in.

'Well, this is nice,' Rose said as she took a handkerchief from her coat pocket and blew her nose. 'Oohh, it's cold out there. I wouldn't be surprised to see some snow tonight.'

Once they had eaten their buns. Janet stood up and went to fetch her leather satchel from the kitchen. David and Suzy looked at each other. Now the time had come to ask some questions they were nervous.

Janet took the list out of her satchel and unfolded it.

'Now. Grandma? Aunt Daisy?' she began dramatically. 'We want to ask you something and we don't want to upset mum or Auntie Eileen or anyone else for that matter – that's why we want to speak to you both first in private.'

'Is it about your sewing?' Daisy asked.

Janet gulped. She didn't feel so brave now she had started. There was no going back now. 'There *is* no sewing Aunt Daisy. We all just wanted to talk to you. You know how alike Suzy and me are. We made a list of all the similarities – look.'

David interrupted as Janet passed the list to Daisy. 'And I've got the creases in my arms.' He rolled up his school shirt to show his Auntie Rose, who was sitting next to him.

Janet took over again. 'We just wondered if there was, well, an explanation for it. We think it's too much of a coincidence.'

George, who was normally a man of few words, bent

down to put his pipe on the hearth. He cleared his throat and, before Rose and Daisy could open their mouths to respond, he looked directly at his wife and sister-in-law.

'Don't you think it's about time, you two, that the truth came out?'

Daisy crossed her arms across her chest and shivered, perceptibly shrinking into the cushions of the sofa in embarrassed silence.

'Well? Do you want to tell them, or should I?' George waited for Rose or Daisy to reply.

Suzy, Janet and David fell silent too, their identical brown eyes wide as they flashed from Rose to Daisy and then to George.

George turned to Suzy.

'Suzy, love. This family has some skeletons in its cupboard. But your mum doesn't know, your gran doesn't know and most important of all – your great grandma, Sarah, doesn't know. But yes, you *are* distantly related to Janet and David.'

Suzy's face drained in shock.

'How? Oh my God, it's not my mum, is it?'

'I don't know where to start!' Flustered, Daisy looked at Rose for an answer. 'Where do we start, Rose?'

'How about at the beginning – it's as good a place as any,' George said.

'Oh hells bells. This has come completely out of the blue. It was your Gramp, Janet. He had a secret son,' Rose began.

The teenagers stared at each other, remembering Tom, who played lotto with them for money, despite the protests from their mothers, and treated Suzy and her younger brother just the same as his own great-grandchildren.

George cleared his throat before continuing, letting the revelation sink in.

Janet's voice was thin and trembly. 'Who was Gramp's secret son?'

George glanced at Suzy, who despite herself, was starting to smile, her eyes bright with moisture.

'His name was Frank Haywood and he was your great-grandad, Suzy. He died when your grandma Millie was just a little girl, so she probably doesn't remember much about him.'

'Is this for real, man?' David's eyes were wide with disbelief.

Suzy's broad grin split across her face. 'I knew it. I just knew it. We're sort of second cousins, then. How great is that?'

David breathed a sigh of relief. 'We were worried it might have been a bit closer to home. That's why we didn't mention it to our parents.'

George leaned forward to speak quietly to David over the babbling of the girls, who were hugging each other and crying into each other's hair.

'They don't know either, so don't go mentioning anything just yet.'

Janet and Suzy stopped bouncing up and down, arms still around each other.

'What! How come?'

Rose spoke quietly and looked at her hands.

'George found out first, years ago, at the time Janet's mum was born, but he didn't say anything to me until the end of the war.'

David was curious now. 'Does it have anything to do with Lydia and Tim?'

George picked up his pipe from the hearth. 'Indirectly, lad. Indirectly. By the way, they don't know either. Nobody does. So you mustn't say anything to anyone.'

Rose was becoming more and more worried.

'What shall we do, George? Now the kids know, it's really let the cat out of the bag. We can't just let *them* tell Sarah, Millie and Joan – and Margaret and Eileen, too. The shock could kill Sarah – she's not in the best of health she's so frail a puff of wind would blow her over, let alone anything like this.'

George sighed. 'If Tom was here, he'd call a family conference.'

Rose ignored him, her mind in turmoil. 'If we're going to

tell them the whole story – let's tell them now, George. After all the kids are the only ones who don't know about Oliver and Doris. It's just that we all swore not to talk about it after it happened. They'll just have to know – that's all.'

George drew breath. He didn't know where to start.

Daisy covered her face with her hands. 'I can't bear it,' she said.

Rose touched her sister's arm. 'We can't ignore it now. It's got to come out, Daisy, no matter how bad it makes us feel for keeping it a secret all these years.'

George leaned forwards, his elbows on his knees.

'In September nineteen forty-six, Lydia's mother had a baby, which was kept a secret. She was sent away to have the baby. Her mother, Doris - Lydia and Tim's grandmother - pretended to be expecting a baby, and secretly adopted the little boy, who was to be brought up as her own son. He was called Oliver.'

George paused. Daisy had begun to cry silently, her hands shaking as she grappled in her skirt pocket to find her handkerchief.

'Oh, dear God, this is awful.' George was becoming upset himself. He was usually so calm and rational, but the memories were pulling all the old emotions from him. He scratched his head, and turned to David.

'Look. It's upsetting your grandma. She loved little Oliver as much as if he was one of her own children. I'm going to have to ask you to keep quiet about all this for a few days. I think we do need to call a family conference. If the skeletons are about to fall out of the cupboard and go waltzing down the street, then we ought to make sure everyone hears about it at the same time.'

'When?' David said. 'I'll help you organise it, Uncle George. I don't think we can do it here – this house is too small for all of us.'

'We'll have to make a list of all those who are affected.' George said, thinking out loud.

'It should be quite soon,' Janet suggested, 'and not somewhere in public.'

'My house is the biggest,' David added.

'Yes it is,' Daisy agreed, holding her handkerchief to her nose. 'We could open the doors into the conservatory. I'll have to talk to our Eileen first and then see if she will host a bit of a get together. It's Sarah I'm most worried about ...'

Daisy grimaced and turned to face the teenagers to explain.

'At first, it was Grandma Jeffson mostly that we couldn't risk finding out about Frank Haywood. She didn't know that, as a sixteen year-old, Gramp had a secret son with a woman over twice his age. It would have destroyed her. Not only that, Gramp didn't know that we all knew. Now poor Sarah is in such bad health, well, I just don't know how *she'll* take it, finding out that Tom was her father-in-law all along and she never knew.'

David questioned his grandmother. 'Surely Gramp must have guessed you all knew about Frank Haywood. After all, Suzy's family have been friends of our family for years.'

George shook his head. 'No, lad. He didn't. He confessed it to me when he was blind drunk. He'd hinted at it before when he was delirious after falling down a drain and breaking his hip, but I never knew the identity of his son until then. That awful day in nineteen forty-six when little Oliver died in Wicksteed Park lake, was the first time we ever met Sarah and Millie in the cake shop, I guessed Sarah was Tom's secret daughter-in-law and then I told Rose just who they were.'

'The baby died in Wicksteed Park Lake?'

'Yes. He drowned. With Lydia and Tim's grandma.'

'I told Daisy what I knew,' Rose went on.

'And I told your grandad and no-one else in the world.' Daisy said to David.

David frowned. 'So you, Grandad, Auntie Rose and Uncle George are the only people alive who know?'

'Yes,' said Rose and Daisy together.

David puffed out his cheeks and exhaled, raising his eyebrows. 'It's a good job we decided to ask you and not our parents. That really would have caused ructions if they don't know about Suzy's family, either.'

Suzy had become quiet and thoughtful. 'I think it's a good thing it's all going to come out. I know my grandma and my mum feel very lonely, not having any other family apart from a distant aunt and cousins on my dad's side – and there's not many of them either.'

Rose and Daisy looked at each other. Rose leant forward and patted Suzy on the hand. 'We've always been really fond of *all* of you. Sometimes it was very hard not to say anything.'

Suzy shook her head in disbelief. 'It's all so sad! I used to dream that Janet, David and all the others could be my cousins – Lydia and Tim, too. I used to lie and tell girls at school who didn't know me that I had loads of cousins.'

The family gathering was hurriedly arranged for Friday evening at Eileen's home. What started out as a simple get-together quickly escalated into something more, with Eileen and Margaret preparing food, hasty negotiations with Eileen's neighbours about parking and wildly speculative telephone calls to a tight-lipped Rose and unyielding Daisy from various members of the family who were trying to find out what the urgent family gathering was really all about.

Finally, with everyone assembled apart from Daisy and Bill's son, Neil, who was still living and working in Canada, George stood up, a piece of paper quivering in his trembling hands. He decided to begin with an apology for his bad judgement in keeping a long-lived secret, which had affected each and every person assembled. He then read out Janet and Suzy's list of similarities eliciting a nervous laugh from those gathered.

Once the laughter died down, he said simply,

'The reason for these similarities is that Janet and Suzy *are* related. Tom had a son before his marriage to Liz.' He looked at Sarah Hayward. 'That son was Sarah's late husband – Frank Haywood.'

George paused as a low murmur grew into chatter and

everyone's eyes fell on Sarah. Frank Haywood's elderly, frail widow seemed to be in a trance, nodding her head in silent agreement as if mentally piecing together a jigsaw.

There was not a dry eye in the room as four generations of mothers and daughters hugged each other, united in realisation that they did have a family, after all.

George had planned to give an explanation. He had carefully drafted notes to help him tell everyone how he had been the first person to discover that Frank had been Tom's son. He wanted to explain that Liz had not known, and that Tom had never realised that his daughters and his sons-in-law had discovered the truth. He had planned to go to great pains to set out logically the reasons why the secret had remained buried for so long.

He watched as Millie, happy tears streaming down her cheeks, broke away from her mother, daughter and grand-daughter and grasped Rose and Daisy's hands, realising for the first time they were her aunts. Joan embraced Margaret and Eileen, their close friendship since birth fertilised, at long last, with the knowledge they shared the same genes.

The scene that would stay forever in George's memory, though, was the reaction of the children. David, Janet and Suzy were joined by their siblings and cousins. They all hugged each other and rolled up their sleeves, looking for forearm creases and inspecting each other's chins for dimples. They compared freckles, hair colour, eye colour, music tastes, likes and dislikes, their excited chatter mingling with grown-up emotions in a happy commotion.

George folded his pieces of paper and tucked them into his pocket. Bill took his hand and shook it, smiling.

'It doesn't matter, George,' Bill shouted above the din, 'explanations and post mortems can come later. It's out in the open, mate. Out in the open, where it should have been years ago!'

A few minutes later, David's voice boomed above the chatter and laughter.

'Could everyone be quiet, please? My Great Aunt Sarah would like to say a few words.'

All heads turned towards silver-haired Sarah, who had struggled to her feet. She stood up, still remarkably elegant in her navy blue skirt and cardigan, and cast her watery eyes around everyone in the room before she spoke.

'I'd just like to say a few words on behalf of my Frank, who sadly is not here in person to share this wonderful evening. Frank died when he was only twenty-five, and I'm sure that if there is an afterlife, he is right here with his family, of whom I know he would be rightly proud.'

Everyone clapped, and waited as Sarah thought about what she was going to say next.

'Frank was a lovely husband and father. He was a good man, and worked hard. I'd rather have had seven years of happy marriage with my Frank than seventy years with anyone else. He didn't have a happy childhood and rumours of his mother's behaviour always haunted him. He often used to say to me that he wasn't really sure who his father was, and with hindsight, I wonder if he once suspected it was Tom Jeffson. He admired Tom and I know that he would have been proud to have called him his father.'

Sarah began to look uncomfortable standing up, so Bill pushed her chair up behind her and motioned for her to sit down.

'I haven't finished, yet, Bill,' she said indignantly. Everyone laughed as she settled in the chair.

'Now I'd like to say something about Tom Jeffson. When my husband became ill with tuberculosis, Millie was only four years old. Mr Jeffson was very kind to us and often used to pop round to check we were all right and had enough money. I always wondered at the time why he did it – I always thought it was because he was friendly with Frank at the factory and he felt sorry for us. It was so hard for me to make ends meet when Frank died. That's one of the reasons I started to make cakes for people – it was something I could do at home. There was no-one prouder than me when, helped out by Tom Jeffson, we managed to scrape together enough money to rent the cake shop, which was the best thing we ever did, because it has now reunited us with our family.

'I know that over the years Tom Jeffson got into some trouble and he made bad judgements in his life, but I want all of you to know that, to me and our Millie, he was the kindest gentleman I have ever known.'

When Sarah had finished speaking, Eileen's husband asked everyone to collect themselves a drink from the kitchen, as he wanted to propose a toast.

Once everyone had reassembled, with full glasses, he continued:

'For this toast, I'd like to pick up on Sarah's speculation of an afterlife, if members of our family who have passed away are here – somewhere ...' he gave an exaggerated look around the room and up towards the ceiling, '... then we'd all like to drink to your peace and contentment now this secret is finally out.'

The room was silent; even the children were quiet and solemn as he spoke.

George put an arm around Rose and whispered in her ear, '... and Bert. We mustn't forget your Bert.'

Grateful for the acknowledgement, Rose leaned into him. One of the most generous of her kind husband's traits was that he always acknowledged Bert as her first love. He had never minded her talking about Bert, remembering him, and he even accompanied her to the cemetery on the anniversary of his death each year.

George was determined to have the last word. He raised his glass. 'I'd like everyone to remember a chap called Bert too. He was Rose's first love and never got the chance to have a family of his own, because he died of tuberculosis, too. He was a friend of Rose's brother, Arthur, and he was Frank Haywood's friend, too. The three young men all died at about the same time of the same disease. We mustn't forget how terrible it must have been for Tom to lose two sons and a son-in-law to be within just a few weeks of each other.'

Much later, Eileen opened the front door to say goodbye as one by one the family began to leave. The ground was covered in a sparkling, pure white twinkling layer of fresh crisp snow, the whirling, swirling flakes mirroring the mingling of genes inside the house.

Outside, in the back garden, Lydia and Tim stood alone, arm in arm.

'Did you notice that no-one mentioned our mother?'

Lydia pulled her open jacket around her and snuggled up to Tim, shivering as snowflakes fell silently around her. 'Yeah. It made me feel somehow further apart from her than ever.'

Tim sighed. 'We're so lucky in lots of ways that we have been accepted by our family but people do seem to forget that we don't have a proper mother.'

Lydia nodded in agreement. 'I know just what you mean. It's as if we are one link in the chain away from everyone else now.'

'Do you think we should try to find her?' Tim looked to his sister for an answer.

'I don't know, Tim. She abandoned us. It should really be up to her to find us.'

Brother and sister stood in silence, listening to everyone saying goodbye to each other at the front door.

'I've never told you this before,' said Lydia, 'but just before mum took us away from London, she said to me without thinking: *"your grandfather's pockets are deep enough."* Then, just before he died, Uncle Tom was trying to tell me something about our mother. He was very confused and kept saying I was his grand-daughter.'

Tim screwed up his face against the snowflakes. 'What? I thought our grandfather was a Walter Grey and no-one knows what happened to him.'

Lydia shrugged her shoulders. 'It's just made me wonder, that's all. Wonder if Uncle Tom was really our grandad?'

Chapter Fifteen

Six years later

May 1978

The long-awaited day of celebration dawned bright and clear, tiny multi-coloured flowers beginning to bud on the summer bedding plants that George had planted early in the borders of his neat lawn in Cornwall Road.

He walked up and down the garden path a few times in the early morning sun, smoking his pipe and surveying his immaculate garden. George felt happy and contented as he paused, gazing at the exact spot on the lawn where, fifty-five years earlier he had sat with Rose on the very first day they met, drinking wine out of tea-cups and making a long daisy chain. He couldn't believe how quickly the years had flown by.

The smell of frying sausages and bacon wafted into the garden from the kitchen, where Rose was cooking breakfast. George's mouth watered. Rose always made a cracking good fry-up on special days and at weekends. He bent down, wincing as his arthritic knees creaked, and knocked the residue of tobacco out of his pipe on the edge of the cobbled path. He tucked his pipe into his pocket and then strolled back to the house.

'Don't you go far, George. Your breakfast is nearly ready.'

On impulse, George turned and hurried back into the garden. There were a few crimson blooms on his rose bushes. He carefully selected six perfect flowers and buds and cut them neatly with his penknife. He took his handkerchief out of his pocket and wrapped it around the stems, so that they didn't scratch his hands, and shuffled back into the kitchen.

'Here you are. Roses for my Rose.' He held them out to Rose who beamed as she wiped her hands on a tea towel.

'Aw, how lovely,' Rose said. 'Fifty years and you still give me flowers from the garden.' She took them carefully from his hand and put them in a vase of water.

George sat down at the kitchen table, as Rose placed the vase in the centre. 'I was just standing out there, remembering the first day we met.'

'We made a daisy chain, didn't we – a very long one?' Rose said, remembering.

'We haven't had a bad life, have we, love?' George leaned back in his chair watching Rose put the breakfast on two warm plates as golden fried bread sizzled in the frying pan.

'Any regrets?' Rose asked him.

'It would have been nice to have had more children,' George speculated. 'We did have young Tim and Lydia though. And I feel as if they are our children, too, as well as our Margaret.'

'Oh, I don't know. It's probably a good job Dad stopped us from having more children. It would have been difficult having more than one, living here with Mam and Dad. No – my only regret is that we never had our own house when we were young.'

Rose placed George's breakfast in front of him and poured him a cup of tea from a flowery porcelain tea pot.

'Me too. And my only regret is tied up with your only regret. Because if we'd had our own home, we would have had more children, wouldn't we, love?'

Rose put the sugar in George's tea and stirred it for him. 'Yes, we would have, I suppose, but I don't have any regrets on that front now – after all, as well as Lydia and Tim, we've got two lovely grandchildren and I don't suppose it will be long before we are great-grandparents now our Janet has married Rob. We've got a lot to be thankful for.'

Rob Potter had married Janet, three years earlier.

Despite major difficulties with his right arm, he had recovered well from his accident. Since the marriage, Rob's parents, Billy and Mary, were frequent visitors to Rose and George's house, as was Rob's grandmother, Evelyn, who had lived just a few doors away from them for most of their married life.

After finishing his breakfast, George stood up and stretched. He shuffled through to the front room, and opened the sideboard drawer as the chiming clock on the wall struck eight o'clock. He pulled out a blue leather jewellery case and opened it up. Inside was a twenty-four carat gold gate bracelet, an engagement ring and a wedding ring, together with a small, sepia head and shoulders photograph of Rose's tragic fiancé, Bert. George took out the photograph and stared at it for a few seconds. He tried to imagine the type of man Bert had been when he was alive. He studied the angle of his jaw, his friendly but firm expression, his hairline and his eyes. Most of all his eyes. For fifty-five years he had wanted to know what Bert had been like. Sometimes he had experienced a very strange feeling, as if all he needed to do was to extend his hand into nothingness and Bert would somehow take it, give it a cordial shake, and say: *"thanks, mate, for looking after her – for giving her the life that I couldn't."* He felt like that now. He caught a subliminal movement out of the corner of his eye and jumped, startled, before giving a low chuckle as he realised it was only his own reflection in the mirror over the mantelpiece. Staring at the image he took a step forward. The elderly gentleman staring back at him blurred a little and he blinked, trying to clear his vision. He looked at his own milky grey eyes, etched with a lifetime of emotions. His eyes somehow seemed to detach from him, taking on a personality of their own. Kind, caring, benevolent eyes, without malice or criticism. They were the eyes of a reliable friend – a confidant and mentor. Strange words and phrases drifted into his mind and he felt light-headed and distant.

George sub-consciously put out his hand to steady himself on the mantelpiece, still mesmerised by the reflection of his eyes.

"You're a big man, George. A diamond. Priceless." The voice in his head was so strong, it was almost as if someone had said the words out loud.

George blinked two or three times as his eyes came back into focus. He was relieved. He must have had a funny turn, and it just wouldn't do to have a funny turn today of all days.

He shut the case with a purposeful click as he snapped out of his daydream.

In the kitchen, Rose was finishing her cup of tea as she mused over the crossword in the daily newspaper. She still had on her pink dressing gown and her hair was in curlers, encased within a hairnet, a slight frown on her face as she tried to work out a clue. George slid back into his chair, catching his breath as his knees creaked. He placed the blue leather case centrally on the table, his hands trembling with emotion.

'Here you are, love. Fifty marvellous years you've given me. I'd like you to wear this today.'

Rose stared at the box. She slowly picked it up and opened it, lifting out the heavy gold bracelet, twisting her fingers around the links in the chain.

'Bert,' she said simply with a smile.

George leaned forward and gave her hand an affectionate and sympathetic squeeze. 'I've always felt that I owed Bert. In the early days I used to feel guilty that I was only with you because he lost his life so tragically. He has always felt like a friend. I certainly never resented you being with him or wanted to take away the time you spent together, even if I could have done. It just feels right, Rose, that you wear that bracelet today as a thank you to Bert for the last fifty, glorious years of wedded bliss.'

Rose's eyes filled with tears as they sat, holding hands across the table and the years fell away. 'It's always been the biggest wonder to me, George Foster, how such a big heart can fit into such a slightly-built man.'

George reached into his trouser pocket for his pipe and

tobacco while looking at his watch. 'We'd better get cracking soon, love.' Time's getting on, and folks'll start arriving at eleven.'

Rose folded her newspaper and jumped up, clearing the table. 'Better wash up, get dressed and get these curlers out then.'

Rose and George had a busy day ahead. They had announced to everyone that the day of their golden wedding anniversary would be an open house, and people could drop by at any time for a cup of tea and a home-made slice of cake. Margaret and her husband, Brian, had also organised an evening celebration at the USF club for over fifty people and Rose had enjoyed a fun and laughter-filled afternoon at the shops with her daughter and grand-daughter to choose their outfits.

The back door was flung open and banged on the wall as Janet suddenly burst in with her little dog, which wagged its stumpy tail furiously and scampered round the kitchen in excitement.

She kissed George on the cheek and hugged him.

'Happy anniversary, Grandma and Grandad.'

Rose bent down to stroke the little dog and give him some tasty left-overs from breakfast. 'What time is Margaret coming?'

'Soon. But she's always late – you know Mum. Tell her a time that's half-an-hour before the time you really want her to be ready and then she'll be about right.'

Janet picked up the antique blue leather box from the kitchen table. 'What's this?'

'Look and see', Rose smiled.

'Grandma! This is absolutely gorgeous.' Janet carefully picked out the gold bracelet. 'I haven't seen this before. Did Grandad buy you it? You are such a little sweetie, Grandad!'

George shook his head and put his arm around Rose. 'No, I didn't buy it for her. A chap called Bert did. He gave it to your grandma on Easter Sunday in nineteen twenty-two on the day he asked her to marry him.'

'What?' Janet said, puzzled. 'What happened? Did you fall out?'

Rose pulled out a chair. 'No. We never fell out. George, put the kettle on again – let's have another cup of tea and I'll tell Janet the story of my bracelet.' Rose took out the rings and the photograph and pushed them across the table to Janet, whose eyes widened.

'Oh, Grandma. Tell me what happened. Was he killed in the war or something?'

Rose laughed. 'What, in nineteen twenty-two? Didn't you learn *anything* at school? The war ended four years before that.'

Janet shrugged her shoulders. 'I know.'

'And now, your grandad wants me to wear it today, as a gesture to Bert's memory, because if he hadn't died, you and your mum wouldn't exist.'

'Scary!' Janet looked at Bert's photograph. 'He looks nice, Grandma. He's got sexy eyes. Really handsome.' She jumped up and hugged George again. 'I'm glad you're my grandad though.'

George stood on tiptoe and kissed her on the cheek. 'And I'm glad you're my grand-daughter!'

'One day, that bracelet and the rings will be yours,' Rose said to Janet. 'I want you to have them when I'm gone. And then you can pass them onto *your* daughter.'

'I might not have a daughter, Grandma,' Janet laughed. 'We might end up with a house full of boys.'

Lydia was annoyed.

'What the hell were you playing at young lady?'

Naomi's dark brown eyes were defiant. 'I want to be a mechanic when I grow up and I'm only helping Uncle Bill mend his motorbike.'

'Look at your clothes … your knees … and your hair. Oh, Naomi. That oil will never come off your face before tonight! It's the golden wedding party and goodness knows what people will think.'

Daisy appeared from upstairs with Naomi's dress over her arm. It was deep red with a delicate paisley pattern in blues and greens and Lydia had paid a fortune for the material, which Daisy had made into a smart new dress, especially for the occasion. The rich colours complemented Naomi's dark, straight shiny hair and her pale complexion with a smattering of freckles. Although only nine years-old, Naomi was tall and looked at least two years older.

Daisy couldn't believe that a child – a girl at that – could get so filthy in only a few minutes 'Oh my word! What on earth have you been doing?'

'I was helping Uncle Bill!' Naomi's face broke out in a childish giggle as she stood on tiptoe and looked at her face in the mirror. 'Oo-er,' she said. 'Still if I'm going to be a mechanic when I grow up, then I'll have to get used to being dirty.'

Daisy put the dress carefully over the back of the sofa. Lydia grabbed a wriggling Naomi's hand and dragged her into the kitchen, roughly pulling off her oil-stained cardigan and dress. As Naomi stood in her vest and pants, Bill opened the back door, wiping his oily hands on a rag. He chuckled.

'I don't know what you're laughing at, Bill Roberts! What on earth were you thinking, letting her get filthy like that?'

Bill winked at Naomi, who stuck her tongue out cheekily before her mother yanked her vest over her head. 'Looks like it's the Vim for you, young lady,' he chuckled.

Daisy filled the sink with warm water and Lydia lifted up an unwieldy Naomi onto the draining board.

It took almost fifteen minutes to eliminate the oily stains from Naomi's fair skin, and she ran around the living room with bright red knees from having them scrubbed.

'Good Lord,' Bill said, opening his mouth in a mock expression of shock. 'Those knees match your new frock!' Naomi stuck her tongue out at Bill again behind her hand. He stuck his out back.

'Bill!' Daisy remonstrated. 'Don't do that – she'll pick up

bad habits!'

The chaos was exacerbated by the telephone's shrill ring. Daisy answered it.

'Neil,' she screeched, her face lighting up. 'How lovely to hear from you. What time is it over there?'

'Are you sitting down, Mum?'

'No. Yes. Why?' Daisy sank onto the bottom step of the stairs, the receiver glued to her ear.

'I've got a surprise for you.'

'Oh. Come on then, what is it. Are you coming home? Or is it something else?'

Standing in a telephone box in Kettering town centre, Neil was imagining the scene in his childhood home. After his brother's tragic death, this was the first time he had returned.

'Put the phone down, Mum. I'll ring you back in a minute. I've got to go now.'

'Neil?' Daisy was puzzled as the phone went dead. 'Are you still there?'

She shouted to Bill.

'Bill – that was our Neil – but he's just rung off.'

'Leave it a while. He'll probably ring back. If not we'll try and call him in Canada.'

Ten minutes later, Daisy was becoming agitated, waiting for Neil to ring again. Bill strode through to the hallway and picked up the phone. He dialled the operator and had just begun speaking to her when the doorbell rang. Daisy opened it.

'Neil!'

She flung her arms around her youngest son, tears of joy streaming down her face. It was the first time she had held him in her arms for ten years.

Neil explained that he had taken two weeks' holiday as a surprise for his parents to coincide with his Aunt Rose and Uncle George's golden wedding anniversary. He had hoped to arrive the previous day, but his flight from Canada had been slightly delayed.

Naomi stood still in the kitchen doorway; a child

suddenly conscious of her semi-naked state for the very first time in her life. She stared at the man who she had heard lots about, but had never met. She noticed his striking, steely-blue eyes, moist with emotion. She felt a sudden funny feeling in her tummy which made her uncomfortable and confused. She wanted to run back into the kitchen and get dressed quickly, but she somehow couldn't tear herself away.

Rose and George stood on a raised platform, waiting to cut their golden wedding cake. Margaret's husband stood behind them, with a microphone in his hand. In a few days' time, Lydia and Martin would celebrate their wedding anniversary, too. Their tenth.

Although Stuart was not a constant occupant of Lydia's thoughts, very few days passed by without something reminding her of him, such as gazing up into the sky on a crisp, clear night and recognising the pinpricks of light that represented the star formations they had studied together. At such times she imagined the touch of his hand on hers, as he grasped it, pointing out various constellations. The same brands of soap and shampoo that Daisy still used to this day reminded her of the smell of his skin and hair. Sometimes, when she was alone in the house, she would put her special collection of old records onto her record player, close her eyes and be transported back to the magical days of their teenage years, tears spilling out of her eyes, her nose, her mouth, until she felt she would drown in bittersweet reminiscence. She could remember the taste of his lips whenever she drank coffee, which reminded her of trying to stay awake in the long evenings of studying whilst eating Mars bars, Crunchies and Polo mints. Even to this day she was never without a packet of Polo mints in her handbag or pocket.

It seemed to Lydia that he lived on – forever encapsulated in all her senses. So where was he now, she thought, when she needed him, her thoughts in knots and trepidation surging through her arteries with every beat of her heart?

In contrast to Lydia, Daisy was happier than she had been for a very long time. She had all her family around her at long last and apart from the constant dragging feeling in her heart that was the loss of Stuart and Oliver, she felt contented as she sat next to Neil, now back by her side after the tsunami-like events that had taken place on Lydia's wedding day ten years earlier.

Daisy couldn't resist reaching out her hand and touching the curls at the nape of Neil's neck, studying this face. His eyes were like her father's; but whereas Tom could stop an army in its tracks with a cold disapproving stare, Neil's seemed to captivate and mesmerise, exuding vitality and a unique type of perception.

Daisy leaned her head against his shoulder, breathing in the heady smell of his expensive aftershave. For the first time, as the DJ played a memory-stirring tune that had been in the charts ten years before, she didn't feel like putting her hands over her ears and shutting out the memory of the terrible day when she lost her first-born son under the wheels of a double-decker bus. Daisy found herself humming along with the tune and drumming her fingers on the table with the beat.

Bill covered her hand with his. 'Happy, love?'

'Oh, yes. You?'

Bill nodded. 'I can't believe you're here, son,' he said to Neil, shaking his head in wonder. 'I know we write, and speak on the phone regularly, but to actually have you here ... well ... I just can't describe how happy we are.'

Bill bowed his head and discreetly wiped his eyes with a forefinger as Neil surveyed his parents with a guilty, half-smile.

'I'm so sorry. I just couldn't bear to come back,' he said. 'It's taken me all this time to get over what happened. I was traumatised and kept having flashbacks to that awful day and eventually had to see a doctor and get some help.'

'Let's not dwell on it.' Daisy forced a smile. 'It's Rose and George's special day.'

Daisy's eyes were inexplicably drawn upwards towards the ornately decorated ceiling. She imagined Tom, looking down on his family, with Liz by his side, and felt a sudden, unfamiliar rush of affection for the intensely complicated man who had been her father. In her hand she clasped a silver cross. Missing from her neck for ten years, she now felt able to wear it again. She stroked it with her thumb. The cross had travelled half-way across the world and back again, waiting for her to regain her faith.

Daisy refocused her attention as Rose and George prepared to cut their golden wedding cake. She stood up, clapping enthusiastically as George gave Rose a peck on the cheek. She hoped they would enjoy their holiday next week in Clacton, which was where they had spent their honeymoon fifty years ago.

A gold bracelet on Rose's wrist glinted and the links in the chain shifted slightly as, together, she and George forced the knife through the hard, white and yellow icing on the cake. Daisy recognised the bracelet in an instant. Hadn't Rose once told her that she would never, ever wear it again?

So why was she wearing it today, of all days?

Chapter Sixteen

The grey Humber Hawk did not look out of place in the street. Although the car was twenty years old, it had been well looked after and the polished chrome, unblemished paintwork and vibrant red leather interior exuded a bygone luxury and opulence. Its two passengers watched the funeral cortege from their vantage point as mourners began to leave the front door of a house a few yards away.

The woman in the car was heavily made-up, her trademark bleached hair, blue eyelids and bright red lips belying her true age. She leaned across the male passenger and opened the glove compartment with a manicured hand; as she did so, her hair fell forwards, a hint of greying roots just visible along the parting. Red fingernails clicked on the lacquered walnut dashboard when she closed the glove compartment and the male passenger inclined his head slightly to get a better look at her cleavage.

She leaned back, ripping cellophane from a new packet of cigarettes. After extracting one with the tips of her long nails, she waved the packet in the direction of her companion. He lit her cigarette with a silver lighter, then his, taking a deep drag before exhaling slowly, his eyes playing up and down her bare legs.

'Who do you reckon it could be, then?'

Violet shrugged her shoulders. 'My Uncle Tom and Auntie Liz would definitely be dead by now. I suspect it's either my cousin or her husband.'

She glanced down and scratched her bare leg, deliberately allowing her hand to drag up the hem of her short skirt which exposed more of her thigh. She glanced sideways at her companion, checking for a reaction.

Her voice was without emotion as she speculated on the identity of the body in a hearse parked a few yards away. 'My kids will both have flown the nest by now. After all, it's been sixteen years since they came to live here.'

Violet took another drag on her cigarette and nodded towards the house. 'Look, there's Daisy and Bill just coming out of the front door.'

'Who's Daisy and Bill?'

'Daisy's my cousin. Well – she's supposedly my cousin, but she's probably really my half-sister. Uncle Tom was a proper tomcat and once had an affair with my mother, most likely resulting in *moi*.'

'How old is she?'

'Daisy? Oh, nine years older than me. Why?'

'She must be well into her sixties, then. She looks good for her age. Who's that other woman with them?'

'Oh, that must be Eileen, their daughter. Blimey, she's aged a bit since I last saw her. And I suppose those two spotty-faced lads are her kids.'

'Just your average family, then. But I like that. It wouldn't do if your family were anything out of the ordinary, and likely to blow our cover at the drop of a hat.'

Violet smiled seductively under her eyelashes and put her hand on the top of the man's leg. She desperately needed this business partnership, and would go to any lengths to get it.

A bumble bee buzzed passed the open car window and Violet flinched, thinking it was about to fly into the car. She waved her hand in a reflexive action, and the cigarette fell from her hand.

'Bloody hell,' she grumbled, as she slid along the leather seat searching for the cigarette. Finding it, she slung it out of the window, just as more people emerged from the house.

'Well, it can't be George who is dead, because he has just come out with his daughter, Margaret.'

Violet and her companion watched as a black-suited funeral attendant opened the passenger door of a shiny black limousine, and a slightly built, elderly man slid into the front seat.

Violet looked genuinely surprised. 'It must be Rose who has died. Blimey. Who'd have thought she'd have popped her clogs before weedy little George?'

'Who's that?' The man nodded towards a tall, striking dark-haired young woman. 'Classy. Very classy.'

Violet didn't answer.

As Lydia emerged from the house, an uncanny sixth sense drew her eyes to the old, grey car parked a few yards away across the road.

Charlie gave a low whistle as the young woman stared straight at them. 'That young lady with the black hair. She's a stunner. Very, very nice.'

Violet glared at her companion.

The man pursed his lips, enjoying Violet's discomfort, testing her level of self-control. 'Oh, is that your daughter, do you think?'

Violet didn't answer. Whatever self-disgust she, herself, was feeling, she couldn't help but feel proud of the woman Lydia had become.

'We didn't get on,' Violet said in a robotic voice. 'She was a feisty piece. I had no option but to let her and my son live with Uncle Tom and Auntie Liz. They were nothing but trouble.'

'And how old were they when you *dumped* them?'

'I didn't dump them. It's not as if they were little kids' Violet lied. 'They'd almost grown-up.'

The man raised his eyebrows again. He was enjoying seeing Violet squirm, his artificial tough streak complementing her contrived indifference to her offspring.

'So, exactly how old was your daughter, then?'

Violet took another cigarette, and lit it before answering. She looked him in the eye as she exhaled deliberately into his face.

'Fifteen. She was fifteen. So they weren't exactly babes in arms, were they?'

'So how many kids do you have, all told?'

Violet leaned forwards and rested her arms on the steering wheel, staring at Lydia, her husband and Tim, who had just emerged from the house with a slightly-built woman on his arm.

'Do we have to talk about my bloody kids?'

'Well, if you're going to front-up my business I need to know these things.'

Violet tutted and inspected her fingernails. 'Well, if I must, but just you remember who's putting up the capital for this venture. It might be your house, but it's my money.'

Charlie Kingston wound down the passenger window and threw his cigarette butt out onto the pavement without stubbing it out. He sniffed and rubbed his chin with his hand.

He made his mind up about Violet. 'All right. If you want this partnership, then it's strictly on my terms. And I want the money in cash.'

Violet flashed a triumphant smile at her new business partner.

'Thanks Charlie. I won't let you down. You won't regret it. As far as folk will be concerned, I've come back to Kettering to be with my family.'

Daisy and Bill sat in the limousine immediately behind George. No-one could quite believe that the body in the coffin in the hearse in front was Rose.

'I should be in there with her,' George said, his voice thick and emotional. 'I shouldn't be in another car while she's all alone in front.'

Daisy opened her bag and extracted a folded white handkerchief. She used it to wipe her red-rimmed eyes.

'Oh George. What are we all going to do without her?'

George turned around.

'I don't know, Daisy. I just don't know. I still can't believe it.'

Daisy, Bill and George sat in silence while Margaret and her husband, Brian, slid into the seats behind them and the remainder of the family filled the two limousines and various other cars parked in the street.

George spoke again. 'I don't think she's alone, you know. She'll have her Bert by her side to keep her company. I know they will be reunited in death, but it's no consolation for me, is it?'

Daisy opened her handbag, replaced the handkerchief, and shut it with a soft click of the clasp remembering the day Rose had met George. She had not expected to find someone else to love after her fiancé, Bert, had tragically died, but George had slipped effortlessly into her life and they had, after all, shared fifty years of a happy marriage.

'I've never said this before, George, but I know Rose wouldn't have been as happy with Bert as she has been with you.'

'Aw. That's a lovely thing to say, but you were only a little girl ...'

'I might have been only eight years old,' Daisy interrupted, 'but I was a nosy little madam and I don't think she would have been completely happy. They were too different. Not like you and Rose at all.'

Daisy blew her nose again. It didn't take much to set her off crying since Rose had passed away, having suffered a sudden heart attack in the middle of the night on the day before they were due to go off on holiday.

'Is the hotel in Clacton giving you a refund?'

'Aye,' George replied. 'They were very kind when Margaret rang to cancel the booking. I'm going to give the money to Janet and Rob. They are planning to start a family soon. It would be what Rose would have wanted.'

'That's a nice thing to do. Rose would approve of that.'

George gave a sad sigh, gazing at the house, where fifty-five years earlier he had met his wife.

'I was a lucky man to be married to Rose. But I think I always knew I'd only borrowed her, and would have to give her back to Bert one day.' He looked down at his knees and shook his head. 'I really don't know what I shall do without her.'

Bill, who was sitting beside Daisy, interrupted the conversation: he'd not been listening, but instead watching the couple in the old Humber Hawk parked on the opposite side of the road.

'You see that old car, over the road. Who do you think it is?'

Daisy sat upright. 'I don't know.' She fumbled in her handbag for her glasses, and put them on. 'I don't recognise them. Probably nothing to do with us at all.'

'I reckon it's your Violet with some bloke.'

'No!' Daisy and George said in unison, studying the distant figure more closely.

Bill took a deep breath. 'I'm sure it's her. I've been watching them for a minute or two now.'

George's face crumpled into a grimace 'If it is, she's got a bloody cheek. Coming back today of all days.'

Daisy shook her head. 'It can't be her, Bill! How did she know Rose has just died? Who would have told her? No-one knew where she was.'

'She might have read the announcement in the paper.'

The driver of the funeral car slid into his seat. He adjusted the rear view mirror, glancing at George. 'Are we ready then?'

'Aye,' George said, sighing, his watery eyes fixed on the coffin in the hearse in front. 'Let's get this over with.'

The funeral cortege pulled out and drove slowly past the Humber Hawk. In the car behind Daisy, Bill and George, Lydia's dark eyes locked momentarily with those of the blonde woman.

'It's her,' Lydia whispered to Martin in shock, craning her neck around to get a second look.

'Who?'

'My mother!'

Two hours later, the wake was well underway. George was bearing up well after the shock of finding his wife cold and still beside him, only two days after their golden wedding anniversary celebrations. He couldn't believe that in the space of just over a week he had celebrated fifty years of marriage to Rose and then buried her.

His grand-daughter, Janet, found him in the garden. She slipped her arm through his. 'Grandad, why don't you come and stay with us for a while.'

George laughed for the first time since his wife had died. In his mind's eye he had sudden vision of staying in Janet and Rob Potter's chaotic, noisy house which always seemed to be full of young people and blaring pop music. Their garden was a mess and George had been itching to get his hands on it.

'Aw, love. That's a very nice thing to offer, but I really don't think a young couple in their early twenties want their old grandad under their feet. I tell you what, though. I'll come and do your garden for you. That'll keep me out of mischief for a while and give me something to take my mind off things.'

'Aw, Grandad. Thanks. That'll be great. We were planning on getting it done before we try for a baby, anyway.'

George's daughter, Margaret, joined them in the garden and stroked his shoulder. 'Are you all right, Dad?'

George nodded and reached into his pocket for his pipe and tobacco. He filled it carefully before lighting it with a match. 'I am now I've got you two with me.'

'Dad, I know now is probably not the time to talk about this, but now Janet's married and moved out, Brian and I thought you could come and live with us if you wanted to. What do you think?'

George smiled, but shook his head. 'I'll be fine, Margaret. I want to stay here. It's my home. If I can just get through the next couple of weeks, I'll be all right.'

'Well, there's no rush. You know the offer's there.'

After a few minutes, Margaret turned away and hurried back into the house, leaving Janet with George.

Bill passed Margaret at the back door. 'I'll just go and have a word with George before we go,' he said to her.

George winked at him when Bill arrived by his side and extracted a silver hip flask from his jacket pocket. Bill poured a measure into the little cup that doubled up as a cap. 'Here you are mate,' he said. 'We wondered if you'd like to come and stay with us for a while. It's been such a shock, Rose dying so suddenly. You're more than welcome.'

George smacked his lips. 'Thanks, Bill. That's right kind of you both, but I really think I'd like to stay put, if you don't mind. Like I said to our Margaret just now, this is my home ...'

'Are you coming back in, Grandad?' Janet interrupted.

'In a minute. You go back in, love. I'll just finish my pipe out here and have a chat with Bill. I'm all right.'

George was pleased Janet had made the offer for him to stay with her for a while. It meant that he'd feel comfortable visiting her and Rob in the future.

'I'm going to make myself busy and do our Janet's garden for her,' he said to Bill. 'This time next year it'll look a picture, and who knows, it might just contain a baby in a pram.'

After Bill had gone back inside the house, George stepped over the neat border from the lawn to the cobbled path that ran the length of the long, narrow garden. Since he had inherited it from Tom, he had turned the bottom end into a vegetable garden, and given up Tom's allotment. He walked slowly up the path to the very end of the vegetable patch and then reaching the top of his long garden, turned to face the house and reflect back on his life, puffing on his pipe.

He looked up into the sky. 'Well, Bert, me ol' mate. You've got her back now. I don't know where that leaves me, but I suppose it all works out somehow. I couldn't have loved any other woman as much as I have loved her.'

He felt a painful pang of loneliness, but a slight breeze blew away the morose feeling and he knew he was not alone. He could sense Rose all around him, comforting him, telling him that she was all right. He spoke out loud again.

'I know you're here, Rose. I can feel you. I'm glad you

didn't suffer, but I wish I could have held you as you passed away. You should have woken me up, love. Rest in peace sweetheart.'

George took a last puff on his pipe, and then bent down to knock the spent tobacco out on the edge of the path, a stray tear falling from his cheek. He straightened up and brushed his eyes with the back of his hand. He didn't feel too bad at all, all things considering. He knew the tears would come eventually, but, touched by the offers for him to stay with Janet, Margaret and Daisy, he could also feel the love of his family, which he knew would see him through the difficult weeks and months ahead.

Lydia sat alone in the front room, the sounds of chinking china cups and occasional stilted chuckles and conversation drifting through from the living room, where the last of the mourners were finishing the sandwiches. The front room had not changed since she first came to live in this house as a fifteen year-old. It had doubled up as her bedroom, and it was the place where she had spent an unforgettable illicit afternoon of passion with Stuart. Since the golden wedding party, she'd thought about him constantly, the unscheduled arrival of Neil from Canada unsettling her. Sitting in one of the two brightly patterned armchairs in the room, she ran her hand over the smooth fabric, closing her eyes, trying to remember every single second of that afternoon. Now, today, the memories were more intense than they ever had been. One of the biggest regrets of her life was when, in a moment of anger in Millie's cake shop, she had ripped up and thrown away the letter written in reverse handwriting; his only legacy to her, other than the memories.

Now, she needed Stuart's words of comfort more than anything because just two weeks ago, as she'd dressed for Rose and George's golden wedding party, she had found a lump in her breast. It was quite a large lump and Lydia had wondered how it was she had not felt it before. She ran her hand across the top of her left breast, just beside her breastbone. It was still there. She had told no-one about the lump, preferring to shut it into a box in her head labelled *lump* and squirrel it away, out of sight and out of mind. Today, the box had rattled and shaken itself open as she dressed in black clothes for the funeral and she knew she could ignore its dark, ominous presence no longer.

She stood up and stepped over to the mantelpiece. Staring at her reflection in the mirror, once again she ran her fingers over the lump. The door opened behind her. It was Martin.

'You okay?'

Lydia nodded and turned around to face him. Kind, solid Martin.

He stepped towards her and encircled her with his arms. She rested her head on his shoulder and felt safe. The words were out before she could stop them.

'Martin, I've found a lump.'

'A lump? Where?'

Lydia pulled away from him and unbuttoned her blouse. 'Here.' She ran her fingers over the top of her breast.

'When did you notice it – just now?'

'No. It was when I was getting dressed for the party last week. Then Auntie Rose died and I put it out of my mind because Rose was really the only mother I've ever known and I was so upset. But it's still there.'

Martin's kind eyes were filled with concern. 'Why on earth didn't you tell me? You'll have to see a doctor. We'll get you an appointment tomorrow. Try not to worry. It's probably just a cyst.'

Lydia nodded, and rested her head on his shoulder again, relieved that Martin would take charge. She was lucky he was a doctor and would make everything all right, wouldn't he?

'You're only thirty-one, Lydia. Age is on your side. The chances of it being anything serious is remote.'

Lydia shook her head as her own medical training put the words in her mouth. 'Any woman of any age can get breast cancer, and even men can get it too.'

She changed the subject. 'I came in here to look out of the window. That big grey car's gone now. It probably wasn't my mother. She'd have relished in making a grand entrance and stealing all the limelight, even at a funeral.'

At the same time her long-abandoned daughter was confronting her fears in the arms of her husband, Violet Grey was inspecting her new home a mile away. She let out a low whistle. Set back from the main road, the house was huge. The gardens had been landscaped and the house had a double aspect, with two gravelled driveways meeting outside the front door. The smell of fresh paint and modern new shag-pile carpets throughout told a story of an expensive renovation.

'I can do something with this place, Charlie. Oh yes! This house will be the classiest whore-house in Northamptonshire. Only the best girls will do, with discretion absolutely guaranteed.'

'There's a small car park about a hundred yards away –'

Violet interrupted, impatiently. 'Yeah, I know! I did used to live in the town, remember?'

'So punters can be dropped off here, at the front door, and then their drivers can park up there for the rest of the day or night.' Charlie finished his sentence, annoyed at Violet's habit of interrupting him mid-sentence. 'There'll be a maximum of four punters per twenty-four hours, by strict appointment. You'll deal with the appointments yourself. I don't want any nosey undercover coppers trying their luck.'

Charlie swatted at Violet's hair with his fingers.

'You need to dye this brown,' he added, 'and get rid of those painted fingernails. You'll have to cut them short. And you'll need clothes. Smart, tweed suits; summer dresses and some trouser suits. You'll wear your hair up in a bun, and get some glasses to make you look intelligent. You'll put on only a minimum of make-up. Chuck that red lipstick away. You won't be able to wear it again. And make an appointment with a dentist to get those awful teeth fixed. Remember, from now on you are a widow with a perfectly legitimate book-keeping business which you run from home. If anyone turns up at the door and wants a bit of book-keeping doing, then I'll get it sorted.'

Violet put her handbag down and wound her sinewy arms around Charlie's neck. 'Do I *really* have to dye my hair, Charlie? Can't I just get a wig?'

'No you can't. You need to take a leaf from my Marigold's book. She always dresses down. Remember? This place is for the upper crust. The most elite of the elite. It's vital that punters feel safe and secure, so you need to look like their wives, not their slags. And just you make damned sure you re-acquaint yourself with your family.'

'It will take time but, yes, I shall. I'll work hard on being the perfect mother and aunt. Hell – I'm probably even a grandmother by now.' Violet gave a snort of laughter. 'That would go down well with the new image, wouldn't it?'

Charlie put his hands on Violet's shoulders without responding. He pushed her back against the wall and leaned on her, as he unzipped his trousers and then yanked up her skirt.

'And you'll tell them you've made good ... made money in Spain when your husband died ... have bought a house?'

'Yes Charlie. I will.'

'And you'll make sure your girls always dress on the premises, and look respectable when they leave the house?'

'Yes.'

'You won't let me down?'

'No, Charlie, Never!'

Less than a minute later, Charlie grunted and exhaled. Violet grimaced, and rested her chin on his shoulder, inspecting the red painted nails that were going to have to be sacrificed.

Charlie stepped back, zipping up his trousers. 'Good,' he said as he walked off, straightening his tie, unable to look her in the eye.

He stopped at the front door and looked back at her over

his shoulder, throwing her a frown that made his eyebrows appear joined in the middle.

'I've put everything I have into this venture. I have a wife and daughter to keep in the manner in which they have become accustomed. So if you do let me down, I'll break your fuckin' neck.'

Chapter Seventeen

The sun shone all the way through the school summer holidays as Naomi Fraser made friends with Lottie, a girl of the same age who lived in the tree-lined road on the outskirts of the town where her parents had recently bought a new house. They had Captain Birdseye fish fingers for tea, permanently skinned knees and not a care in the world as their mothers took them to the cinema to see *Close Encounters of the Third Kind*, to Woburn Safari Park to see the lions, swimming in the sea at Hunstanton and, on the odd day it was raining, played Monopoly and Cluedo with them, while all the time the two nine year-olds whinged they were bored.

Lottie's mum was older than Naomi's, but both girls had no brothers or sisters and their lives and routines were similar: their families were comparatively well off and their mothers stayed at home while their fathers worked long hours to give their families a decent standard of living.

On Saturday afternoons, Naomi always visited Grandad George in Cornwall Road and stayed with him while her mum, and sometimes her dad, went into town to do some shopping. She knew he wasn't really her grandad, though. Technically speaking, he was really her uncle, but she had grown up calling him *"grandad"* and there was no way she was going to admit to Lottie that he really wasn't.

Lottie's dad seemed to be a very important businessman in Kettering. She had learned he was on the Council, had built lots of houses and was very rich. Her mother had said that in a couple of years he would be Kettering's Mayor, which was, she deduced, the most important person in the town. Naomi knew her father wasn't as rich as Lottie's. Naomi liked Lottie's mum and dad – her mum especially because she was big and round, kind and smiley and had a lovely sunny name – Marigold, or Goldie for short – and although she was quite a bit older than her own mum, she had made friends with her.

Jimi Singh, Naomi's other best friend, was an only child, too. His aunt and uncle lived next door to Naomi's Grandad George, and they looked after him on Saturdays, because both his parents were at work in a shop. When they played together in the street outside her grandad's house in Cornwall Road, Naomi would often hear mysterious comments such as *"poor little lad"* and people would refer to him as a *"half-caste"*, but any inquisitive questioning on her part was always met with narrowing of eyes and a reverberating silence of disapproval. Naomi sensed something sad about shy Jimi Singh who wore a handkerchief on his head and wondered if peoples' comments about his brown skin upset him as he lingered outside in the street on Saturday mornings, waiting for her to arrive at her grandad's house so they could go out to play.

Until he had made friends with Naomi at school last year, Jimi had told her he didn't have many friends, but now he had loads. Before she died, Grandma Rose had said it was because of her being so kind to him, but she didn't think so. It was because of his interesting stories and vast knowledge of dinosaurs and time travel.

Now her grandad lived on his own after Grandma Rose had died, he would often send the two of them to the corner shop for something he called their Saturday contraband – a twenty-pence mix of rubbishy sweets and an Incredible Hulk comic for Jimi and a Misty comic for her. She thought she would never, ever tire of Jimi's interesting stories about his dad, who was something called a Punjabi and came from Pakistan, and his mum, whose name was Linda and came from Halifax. She loved going to his house to play and did so often, after school.

Sometimes, she wished her dad was not just a boring old

doctor and her mum a housewife. There was nothing interesting to talk about with *her* family, apart from her mum having breast cancer.

In contrast to Jimi, Lottie Kingston was rich. Sometimes, when the three of them were playing together at her house, she would laugh at her and Jimi for looking forward each week to their Saturday contraband. Lottie had a new bike, a pony and only had to open her mouth and her dad would buy her as many sweets and comics as she wanted. He called her his *little sugar plum*, which she loved. Naomi always wanted to laugh when she heard Lottie's dad call her that, because, like her, Lottie was a big girl for her age, and comparing her to a fairy was funny. Lottie always told Naomi that she'd give up everything, even her pony, to have a normal, proper dad like Naomi's, but she never could understand what Lottie meant, because Mr Kingston treated her like a princess and bought her loads of presents all the time, whereas her dad, who was just a boring doctor at the hospital, made her earn her pocket money by doing jobs.

Just before Naomi had made friends with Lottie and Jimi, her Aunt Daisy had given her a telescope that had once belonged to her son, who had died. Naomi couldn't understand why her mum acted in a very strange way when she was around the telescope. She had set it up in Naomi's bedroom for her, and on more than one occasion she had caught her mother stroking it, or taking it off its stand and clutching it to her chest. She had once caught her talking to it and even kissing it. Naomi supposed her mum was doing such things because of the cancer. Jimi said it might be because telescopes somehow captured cosmic rays which would kill cancer cells.

Lottie, Jimi and Naomi loved the telescope. In the daytime, its main use was to spy on people going about their lives far away in the distance. But at night, when Naomi's parents were asleep and everything was still, dark and quiet, she would sneak out of bed to look at the moon and stars and wonder just how far infinity was, because everything had to have a beginning and an ending. When she had asked Jimi about infinity he had told her it was like a Mobius strip, and had made one for her to colour in, just so that she could understand that infinity had no ending – it just went on and on and on. Jimi was so wise and clever. She knew that when he grew up he would fulfil his dream of being something called an astrophysicist.

One Saturday morning in September, just after the new school year had started Naomi and Jimi were playing outside in the street in Cornwall Road. A large, very shiny, old-fashioned grey car glided gracefully around the corner and then stopped right outside Naomi's grandad's house.

Naomi watched from the other side of the street as the lady inside the car adjusted her make up in a small mirror before she slid effortlessly out of the driver's seat and then reached back inside to pick up a dazzling white summer jacket, which she threw around her shoulders over a snake-print summer dress which was so long it reached her ankles. She patted her hair and tucked a loose strand behind her ear. Her hair was brown, immaculately swept up on top of her head, secured with a clasp that was made of carved wood with a pin through it.

The snake-lady stepped into the front porch of her grandad's house and rapped the door knocker sharply. Naomi skated up to the porch on her roller skates from her vantage point. 'That's my grandad's house,' she said. 'He's up the garden on the veggie patch so you'd better go round the back, 'cause he won't hear the door.'

The lady looked round at Naomi. She smiled with her mouth but not with her eyes.

'Okay,' she said. 'Can you show me the way?'

Although the lady looked like a snake, she reeked of perfume, and Naomi noticed when she smiled her front teeth were bad, which was not a good thing for a posh-looking lady. Naomi decided she didn't like her dress. Or her thin lips. But her bad teeth were the worst thing about her.

'What's your name, then?' the lady said, her discoloured, mottled teeth making Naomi's stomach churn.

Naomi didn't answer. She had been told not to talk to strangers.

'Will you just show me round the back, then? I need to speak to George Foster, your grandad.'

Jimi and Naomi skated noisily into the entry between the two houses followed by the snake lady.

'Grandad!' Naomi shouted. George appeared from behind his runner bean canes at the top of the garden when he heard Naomi's voice. 'There's a lady come to see you.'

Naomi skated with difficulty up the uneven garden path and did an expert turn as she slid her hand into George's. She felt his grip tighten protectively.

'Who is it?' she whispered.

George put his arm around her shoulders and pulled her into him.

'Bloody hell,' he said to the snake lady. 'What do you want after all these years? It's like flipping déjà vu. What are you going to abandon here this time?'

From her Grandad's words and tone of voice, Naomi realised in an instant just who the snake lady really was. Her grandmother. The woman who abandoned her mum and Uncle Tim when they were just children.

She began to feel sick and squeezed George's hand tightly, before sliding backwards so that she was hiding behind him.

'Hello George,' Violet said as she extended a limp, pathetic hand towards him. She gave another false smile, showing her disgusting teeth.

George didn't take her hand to shake it. Instead, Naomi felt George's arm pushing her behind him even further, protecting her from her wicked grandmother.

Her grandad gave a big sigh and then said: 'What do you want this time?'

Her grandmother crooked her neck around George to look Naomi up and down and smiled again. Naomi felt she was sure to be sick, right there by the runner beans.

'So what's your name? Whose daughter are you?' Violet grinned at her, lips parting over rotten teeth making a shiver of fear run down her arms and spine as Violet spoke directly to her.

'And who is this?' she continued, looking at Jimi.

Jimi's voice was clear and brave.

'My Auntie lives next door. I'm Naomi's friend from school.'

'Naomi?' Violet said, and held out her hand. 'I'm pleased to meet you.'

Naomi couldn't think of anything to say to Violet in reply, because all she could think of was that she could no more have touched her grandmother's hand than plunge her fingers into a can of wriggly worms. A nasty taste suddenly filled her mouth at the sight of the horrible bad teeth.

Then she was sick; the sick spraying all over her grandmother's bare feet and white sandals. It was brown sick, because she had eaten chocolate-covered cereal that morning. She even managed to get some on her grandmother's white jacket, a feat she was instantly very proud of.

'Ugghh.' her grandmother said and grimaced as she jumped back, more like a nimble footed cat than the sly snake Naomi had likened her to when she had slid out of her car.

Her grandad let go of her and pulled his white folded handkerchief out of his trouser pocket, mumbling under his breath. 'Oh my word, Naomi. What the hell have you been eating?'

Naomi wiped her mouth on George's handkerchief and then held it there to conceal the small, satisfied smile as she stared at the horrible snake-lady grandmother with her sick-covered feet.

Naomi didn't understand why having breast cancer meant that her mother had to go into hospital to have it cut out. Everyone said that she would be all right once she had the operation so Naomi wasn't too worried, despite often seeing her mum crying on her dad's shoulder when they thought she wasn't looking.

Her dad said she needn't go to school while her mum was in hospital. He still had to go to work each day, and her school was too far away from either Grandad George's house or Grandma Elsie's house to walk to and from on her own. Instead, her dad had gone into her school and spoken with the headmaster, and it had been agreed that she could have a few days off school, so her dad didn't have to worry about getting her to school on top of everything else.

It seemed that, because things were "complicated", her mother would have to stay in hospital for about two weeks. She was to stay with Grandad George for one week, and Grandma Elsie for the other week. Everyone had laughed at her suggestion that Grandad George go to stay with Grandma Elsie for two weeks so they could all be together, but Naomi thought it was a very sensible option. Grandma Elsie lived in the next street to her grandad's other, grown-up, grand-daughter, Janet, and Grandad George had promised to make her garden nice. To Naomi, it was very simple. She and grandad could work on the garden at Janet's house all day while Grandma Elsie stayed at home and cooked the dinner and did the washing.

Soon, the morning arrived when it was a school day and she didn't have to go to school because her mum was going into hospital. Her dad was very quiet in the car on the way to Grandad George's house, and it had upset her to say goodbye to her mum, even though she had promised that in two days' time she would be able to visit her in hospital.

It hadn't taken her long to put away her clothes for the week and soon, she was drinking orange juice and eating toast at George's kitchen table.

'Guess what?' George said as he poured himself a cup of tea. 'I rang your other Grandma yesterday and we thought you might like a bit of a day out today. So Grandma Elsie is making us all a picnic and we are meeting her at Wicksteed Park.'

Naomi jumped up and did a little dance around the kitchen, her toast in her hand. 'Brilliant. Can we go on the water chute?'

'I don't know about that, although we might be able to go round the lake on the train. We can take a cricket bat and ball and have a game of cricket if you like.'

'Can we go now? It's so exciting – going to Wicksteed Park when all my friends are at school.'

George laughed. 'Just as soon as I've washed up and tidied the kitchen. Your Grandma Rose will come back as a ghost and smack my bum if I don't keep up her high standards in the house.'

George pretended to be a ghost and chased Naomi around the kitchen, waving his arms at her. 'I'll help,' Naomi said, squealing as she tried to ward him off.

'We can take a plastic bag and see if there are any blackberries if you like. And then tomorrow we can make a blackberry and apple pie,' George said.

Naomi couldn't believe her luck. The suggestion about Grandad George and Grandma Elsie living together so they could both look after her while her mum was in hospital had obviously had some results. Everyone must have thought she would be so upset about her mum going into hospital, they were bending over backwards to keep her happy.

It wasn't until they had set off, carrying the cricket stumps, a bat and ball in a plastic carrier bag, George realised that for the first time since Rose had passed away, he felt happy again. He felt slightly guilty that he might be betraying Lydia, but he had dialled the telephone number Violet had left him and made his peace with her since her first visit. Last week, he had even been to her grand new home for afternoon tea. After all, if Rose was here she would never have turned her back on her, even though she might have had a few grumbles and angry words to say.

He was the only one, though. No one else had yet accepted Violet's offers of reconciliation with her family. She had been to see everyone in turn, extending her olive branch. Daisy had quickly taken up the baton of protecting Lydia, saying to Violet that it was the last thing her daughter needed to worry about, with an operation date looming large on the horizon. Daisy had also told her that her son, Tim, had now emigrated to Canada to work at the same company as Daisy's youngest son, Neil, and so all Violet could do was to write him a letter. She had pleaded with Daisy to let her have her Tim's telephone number, but Daisy had been resolute. If she wanted to reconcile with her son, it shouldn't be through a telephone call. She would have to put pen to paper and try and make her case. It would then be up to Tim whether or not he contacted his prodigal mother by telephone.

Despite everyone else's misgivings, George's generous act of kindness towards Violet had made him feel good. He felt good about today, too. He was sure Rose would be happy for him to be looking forward to a pleasant day out with Elsie and Naomi. Elsie was good company and they always found something to chuckle about, even the most silly things, and Naomi loved nothing better than to hold both their hands and walk between them, the three of them straddling the pavement.

George didn't want to tell Naomi that he had been to tea with Violet, though. On the day she had turned up at his house for the second time in her life after a long absence, Naomi had been very upset when she had gone, and it wasn't just having been sick either. She had yelled at him at the top of her voice, and asked him to make sure her snaky rotten-toothed grandmother cleared off and didn't ever come back.

But, the next time Violet called on him, he hadn't told her anything of the sort. He was much too polite to do that, and in any case, he must uphold Rose's standards at all costs. Instead, George had been pleasant to her and showed her lots of photographs of Lydia and Tim when they were teenagers. The box containing the photographs had not been put away again until last Saturday, when Naomi had visited.

George had then lied when Naomi asked him why he had been looking at the photographs. He had said he had been looking for pictures of Rose, but had felt sickened to the core when he realised just how Naomi would feel if he told her that he had shown her grandmother old pictures of her mum and uncle, when really she'd given up all such rights to see them, having abandoned them in cold blood when they were just children.

It was an impossible situation. He couldn't see how Violet's family would ever forgive her for what she had done, and it was the last thing Lydia needed right now. Martin had definitely done the right thing in keeping the news of Violet's return from her until she had recovered sufficiently from her operation, and swearing his nine-year old daughter to secrecy about the unexpected turn of events.

Violet replaced the telephone receiver and sank down into an adjacent armchair in shock. She hadn't expected this turn of events. Charlie hadn't said anything either, which suggested he knew nothing about it.

She gave a cynical chuckle and shook her head in amazement. Then, when she had recovered sufficiently to make the call, she dialled Charlie's office number and asked his secretary if she could speak to him.

'What's up?' Charlie said when she was finally put through to him.

'I've just had a call from your wife. She's invited me over to your house for afternoon tea on Sunday.'

Charlie swore. 'How the hell did she get your number?'

'From your address book, apparently.'

'Oh, yes. I remember I did put it in the book on my desk at home. There's family numbers in there too, as well as some of my business partners' details.'

Violet twisted the telephone cable around her fingers. 'She seemed to know all about me.'

'Yes, I told her that you were a widow and that you were

my partner in the new book-keeping business. She won't suspect anything. I can guarantee it. It's just so typical of my Marigold. She's got nothing better to do than fuss around people, doing her good deeds.'

'What shall I do, Charlie? I told her I would check my diary and ring her back'

'I think you should come along. If you don't, she'll wonder why. You'll get on all right with her. She's not the sharpest knife in the drawer, but she'll make you welcome. She will probably just bore you to death with recipes and knitting patterns.' He laughed. 'But once you've tasted her Victoria sandwich cake you'll be spoilt. She makes a grand cake, does my Marigold.'

The following Sunday afternoon, Violet decided she would walk rather than take the car. When she arrived at Charlie's house, she patted her hair in place before ringing the doorbell. Marigold answered straight away, as if she had been waiting for her. When Marigold hung up her jacket on a peg in an adjacent cloakroom, Violet took the opportunity to have a quick look around while her back was turned. Charlie's house wasn't as she expected it to be. It was homely and lived in – the type of place you would look forward to coming back to after a hard day at the office.

'Thank you for inviting me,' she said to Marigold. 'I've been looking forward to it. Your husband tells me that once I've tasted your delicious cakes, I shall be spoilt for life.'

'Oh, that's typical of my Charlie.' Marigold patted her stomach as she closed the cloakroom door. 'He loves his food – it's why I'm this size. All this cooking and baking makes us both put on pounds.'

Marigold showed Violet into the front room, where Charlie sat reading a Sunday newspaper. 'Hello, Mrs Smith,' he said with a warm smile, scrambling to his feet to kiss her on the cheek. 'We are really pleased you could join us.'

'We've got another visitor, too,' Marigold said. 'Our daughter, Lottie, has invited her friend over this afternoon, so I'm afraid things might get a bit noisy, although they will probably eat their tea in the playroom, so it shouldn't be too chaotic.'

'Oh, that's all right. I don't mind. I like children.'

'Do you have any of your own? Mind you, I suppose yours will be all grown up by now. I didn't have my Lottie until I was forty-five, so I'm a really old mother to her.'

Violet smiled. 'Yes, I do – two – but you're right. They are all grown up now and off doing their own thing. I don't see much of them, I'm afraid. My son lives in Canada.'

'Oh. What does he do?'

'He's a civil engineer, working for a big company. He's done very well for himself.'

Charlie frowned, clearly puzzled. Violet knew he couldn't tell whether she was lying or telling the truth about her son. 'That's a brave move,' he said, with a hint of sarcasm in his voice. 'It must have been a big decision to desert his family and move abroad.'

'He works with my nephew, Neil, so he's not all alone out there,' Violet retorted quickly, pleased to have scored a rare point over Charlie Kingston.

Violet's polite laughter drifted through to the kitchen, where Lottie and Naomi sat at the table playing Monopoly, urged by Marigold to not make too much noise because they had a visitor.

'My grand-daughter's a bonny girl,' Naomi heard the woman say in the other room. 'Tall, like my daughter, but much more heavily built. In fact, she's a bit chubby. I think my daughter should put her on a diet before it's too late.'

'That woman is talking about her grand-daughter,' Naomi whispered to Lottie. 'I wonder who it is she's talking about. We might know her.'

'Let's listen some more and try and find out,' Lottie replied. 'Hey, wouldn't it be great if there was such a thing as a listening telescope and we could hear people talking miles away?'

The girls giggled, and then fell silent listening to the grown-up conversation in the front room.

'And where does your cousin live?' Marigold asked.

'Not far from Wicksteed Park in Windmill Avenue. We lost touch for a while because I was living in Spain. When my husband, Richard, passed away last year, my cousin's friend urged me to come back to England and use the money from the sale of our business to set up a business of my own. I still need to work, you see. I can't afford to just do nothing.'

'It was fortunate Mrs Smith was put in touch with me,' Charlie interrupted. 'I've been looking for a good book-keeper for years, and once we had discussed things, it seemed to be an ideal opportunity to go into partnership and it would help her out, too.'

Marigold patted her husband's arm. 'He's such a good man,' she said. 'So sensitive and kind. You won't regret going into business with him. And I hope we can be friends, too. What about your daughter, where does she live?'

'She lives here in Kettering. Her husband is a doctor at the hospital.'

'Oh, that's nice. You'll get to see lots of your grand-daughter, then, now you've moved back to England.'

'Yes. I hope so. My family means everything to me. Richard and I were very happy in Spain, but now he's gone they are all I have left.'

'What's your daughter's name?'

'Lydia.'

In the kitchen, where she had been listening to the conversation, Naomi's head jerked upwards in shock.

In the lounge, Marigold fanned her face with her hand. 'It's really hot in here,' she said. 'I think I'll open the French doors and let some air in.'

The lady spoke again, her words cutting and sharp like slivers of glass. Naomi was almost sure it was her grandmother, but her next words confirmed it.

'My other cousin, Rose, died suddenly a few weeks ago. I was so upset. Rose and I were very close once. She was quite a bit older than me, but she was a kind soul. Her husband, George, invited me for tea the other day and we had a very pleasant afternoon, looking through old photographs of my son and daughter when they were children.'

Naomi couldn't help herself shouting out: 'I want to go home now,' she cried.

Her chair scraped noisily on the vinyl kitchen floor before she flew out of the kitchen into the hallway, blazing with indignation, unable to contain herself. She found her pathway blocked by Lottie's mother, who grabbed her by the waist, hoisted her up and plonked her back down in the kitchen, kicking the door shut behind her.

'Oh dear,' Violet said in the front room. 'She's a little firecracker, isn't she? Is that your daughter?'

'No,' Charlie said. 'That was her friend. I expect they've had an argument. Marigold will sort them out.'

Naomi found herself pressed between Lottie's mother's breasts, wondering if a little girl could go to prison for killing a snake-grandmother. The hatred rising from her stomach made her mouth water and before she could stop herself, she had been sick again, all over the kitchen floor.

Later, Lottie's mother took her home. She had given her a good talking to, saying that sometimes big twists of fate happened and that, usually, it wasn't anyone's fault. It was just a coincidence that Lottie's dad just happened to be her long-lost grandmother's business partner. When Naomi had calmed down, Marigold tried to explain that she, too, hadn't known that Violet had any connection with her at all when she had invited her to tea.

'I knew as soon as she said her daughter's name was Lydia and her husband was a doctor that she was your grandmother. You see, your mum has told me everything since we've been friends with each other. I knew your grandmother abandoned your mum when she was a child.'

'But I can't believe Grandad George has met up with her again since that day when I was sick on her shoes,' Naomi wailed, her face streaked with tears. 'And he has shown her photos of mum and Uncle Tim. She's got no right, has she?'

Marigold sighed and hugged Naomi once more. 'Look. I know how you must be feeling and how confused you are. Let me try to sort it all out for you. I'll speak to your dad and grandad. Don't worry about a thing. The most important person is your mum. We mustn't worry her with any of this. We all need to protect her so she can recover from her operation.'

'All right,' Naomi conceded. 'But I don't want to see my snake-grandmother ever again. I hate her.'

The next day, Naomi had been invited to Jimi's house to play after school. She had to have someone to talk to, or else she would have snake nightmares again, like last night.

With her eyes filling with tears and a quivering bottom lip, she told him about the disastrous Sunday afternoon at Lottie's house.

'And she said I was fat. I heard her say to Lottie's mum and dad that her grand-daughter was chubby and needed to go on a diet.'

'No you're not,' Jimi whispered, alarmed by her watery eyes because he had never before seen Naomi cry. 'Don't listen to her, Naomi. You're not fat. I don't think I like her very much.'

'Neither do I,' Naomi said.

'I thought Rose was your grandma? And Granny Elsie?'

Naomi shrugged her shoulders, unable to find the right words to explain the complicated family relationships to Jimi. She couldn't find the right pieces to fit into the jigsaw puzzle they were doing, either, and carried on forcing the small cardboard shapes into places they just didn't belong, eventually banging them into place with a tightly clenched fist.

'My family is hard to understand,' she said without looking up at him.

Later, when her dad came to fetch her from Grandad

George's house after his shift at the hospital she listened to their conversation.

'Lydia just can't take any more,' her dad said to Grandad George, pushing up the glasses on his nose like he always did when he was nervous, and then smoothing back his hair with his hand.

'Let's leave it until after she's recovered from this latest setback and see how she is before we say anything,' George said.

Her father had nodded, deep in thought. 'She's having the next operation tomorrow, and should be coming home next week. It's been a long old job, though. Lots of complications. I just hope they've got it all out, now.'

Naomi knew they were talking about the cancer. It was the biggest word in her life at the moment and it wasn't right she was having to think about her snake grandmother when all she should have to worry about was her mum being in hospital with cancer.

'Violet looks quite respectable now,' George said. 'She's got rid of that bleached blonde hair and toned down the war paint. I think she's turned over a new leaf.'

He turned to Naomi. 'She was interested in looking at the old photograph albums and was so sorry about your Grandma Rose.'

Naomi wanted to shake her grandad's arm. Did he really not realise just how wicked her grandmother was? She was amazed to see her dad nod and agree with him. Her mouth must have fell open because her dad had then said: 'If the wind changes, your face will stay like that and people will think you've turned into a fish.'

Her grandad had then patted her dad's shoulder and said: 'we should do the Christian thing, Martin, and not turn our backs on Violet. I really don't know what Lydia and Tim will think about their mother returning to Kettering, but we need to let them make up their own minds.'

Granny Elsie had then come out of the toilet. Naomi hadn't realised she had come with her dad to pick her up. Her heart soared, surely she would be on her side, but she could hardly believe her ears when she agreed with them, shaking her head and commenting that *"two wrongs don't make a right"* and *"blood is thicker than water"*.

'It must have been very hard for her to swallow her pride and come back,' Granny Elsie said. 'We shouldn't stand in her way, George. It should be up to Lydia, and then the family should abide by her wishes.'

Naomi stared at the three grown-ups in turn. Why couldn't they see what she could? Why didn't they understand that her grandmother, Violet, was evil through and through, and would never, ever change?

The next week, just before her mother was due to come out of hospital, George and Elsie had arranged to take her on an organised bus trip to a country park for an afternoon cream tea. Pippin, Elsie's Yorkshire terrier ran around chasing his ball as the grown-ups all sat around on deck chairs in the autumn sunshine. Naomi sat on a tartan blanket on the grass, throwing Pippin's ball for him and making a daisy chain.

George and Elsie almost forgot she was there, she was so quiet, but she was listening to every single word they said about her nasty grandmother and, although some things she found hard to understand, she filed everything away in her brain for future reference. At the end of the afternoon, Naomi was certain of one thing: she hated her grandmother and nothing and no-one would ever make her change her mind.

Chapter Eighteen

The world buzzed and fizzed as Lydia clawed her way back
to consciousness. She felt something being removed from
her throat and swallowed, the sharp stinging soreness
reminding her that she had survived the latest operation.
She wanted to raise her right hand to her chest, but the
anaesthetic had not quite worn off and she couldn't manage
to co-ordinate the action.

'Lydia. Lydia.' She heard a female voice calling her name
in the distance. 'You've had your operation, and it all went
well.'

Lydia tried to nod her head in acknowledgement and her
eyes flickered open momentarily before she drifted away
again, relieved that it was all over.

Later, she woke in the ward, with Martin by her side,
holding her hand. She felt nauseous and uncomfortable.
She wanted to move her position but knew that it would
hurt her.

'Has it all gone?' she mumbled.

Martin nodded. 'Yes, it's all gone. Let's just try and get
you better now.'

Lydia closed her eyes tightly, but not tight enough to
squeeze back the tears that escaped through her eyelids
and rolled down the sides of her face as she lay on her back.

Both her breasts, complete with the cancer, had now
been removed.

For some inexplicable reason Lydia wanted her mother.
She had not heard from Violet for sixteen years and yet now,
frightened and in pain, she just wanted to feel a mother's
arms around her telling her that, no, she wasn't any less of

a woman without her breasts, and yes, she would get over it in time. But there was a big empty hole, just under the place that used to be occupied by her left breast, and she knew Violet would never occupy that special place.

Elsie was one of her first visitors and she rubbed Lydia's back as she was sick into a bowl after the anaesthetic, and held her hair out of the way. Elsie was the one who stayed all afternoon and washed her face for her, combed her hair and spoke a mother's words of reassurance. Elsie was the one who kissed her cheek gently when she left, taking away her dirty washing and leaving clean, fragrant nightdresses and underwear in its place. Lydia finally realised, lying in her hospital bed, that her kind-hearted, gentle mother-in-law had become her mother. But it still didn't fill the big empty hole left by Violet, who had abandoned her, and Rose, who'd died.

In contrast, her Aunt Daisy was her friend, confidante and the person who cheered her up with expensive fragrant soap and a hand-made delicate bed-jacket, love crafted into every stitch. Daisy was the one who made her laugh with daft jokes and tales of funny family stories of days gone by; and she was the *only* person with whom she could talk about Stuart, without feeling guilty or uncomfortable. Daisy cut out amusing snippets from magazines and newspapers, and brought her books to read – light hearted romances and easy to read sagas – never depressing literary tomes that would encourage Lydia's concentration to wander, allowing fear and pain to creep into her welcome moments of escape amongst the comforting pages of a good book.

Forever Amber, a book Daisy had read secretly in the dark, depressing days of 1947, trying to take her mind off the tragedy of her Aunt Doris's suicide and baby Oliver's death, was the first book she brought for Lydia to read.

The absorbing tale of Amber St. Clair was delectably inappropriate for an unhappy woman recovering from a mastectomy, but Daisy knew that the novel's passion and the main character's strength, courage and determination in the face of terrible adversity would seep from the pages of the novel into Lydia's subconscious mind, take her mind off her own situation and help her to recover from her operation, whilst relieving the boredom of a hospital stay and making her chuckle at the bawdy scenes.

When Naomi visited, her childish innocence gave Lydia permission to rise above her own worries in an effort to protect her daughter from the enormous grown-up word that was cancer. Naomi's pictures, cards and chattering about her friends, Lottie and Jimi, raised Lydia's mood and infused in her a dogged determination to survive the illness for the sake of her daughter.

In contrast her heart sank when Martin visited. He did nothing wrong; he said all the right things, did all the right things and listened to her talk in all the right places. But he wasn't Stuart. She didn't feel the type of love for her husband that she still felt for the love of her life, forever unobtainable and yet strangely close. She liked to sleep; because in sleep she dreamed of Stuart, untarnished by the schizophrenia that steered him into an untimely death, strong and vibrant and more than anything ... alive.

Then there was her Aunt Millie, a family friend until seven years ago, when her true relationship and a family secret had wriggled its way to the surface. Now she was a proper, real-life auntie.

Millie didn't mind if she just went to sleep, clutching her hand. Millie represented comfort and reliability and, if she wanted to cry, rant and rave and shout at the cancer that had stolen her breasts and made her feel incomplete, then that was just fine. Mille would sit by her bedside for hours at a time, often in silence as Lydia slept. She would open her eyes and Mille would just smile, brush a wayward strand of hair from her eyes with a gentle hand and help her to get out of bed and sit in a chair.

It was on one of Millie's visits that Lydia raised the question of Stuart's letter.

'Millie?'

'Yes, love?' Millie looked up from her knitting. She had thought that Lydia was sleeping.

'I wish I hadn't thrown Stuart's letter away.' She opened her eyes and turned her head to look at Millie. 'I ripped it up and threw it away.'

'I know,' Millie said. She took her glasses off and placed them on the bedside table and then tucked her knitting into her bag. She'd known that this day would come eventually. She'd always sensed that retrieving the torn up pieces of letter from the waste paper bin was the right thing to do.

'After you left on the day I gave you the letter,' Millie began, 'I took all the pieces from the bin and put them in a paper bag. It's now well hidden in my wardrobe.'

Millie leaned forwards and stroked Lydia's forehead. 'I swear I've never read it; I've never even opened the bag since that day.'

'When I get home, can I have it back?'

Millie nodded. 'That was why I kept it for you – I knew you'd ask for it one day.'

'Thank you so much for keeping the pieces. I loved him, Millie. You are the only person who knows just how much. I wouldn't have married Martin. I told him that his schizophrenia didn't matter – that we'd somehow live with it and make the best of things. But he was having none of it and wouldn't listen.'

Millie patted Lydia's hand. 'I know, he told me. He loved you too – that's why he wrote the letter and gave it to me for safe-keeping. I was to give it to you only if he was taken away, sectioned and institutionalised. It was his biggest fear, you see. He had known his condition was getting worse and was so worried about it. He didn't ruin your wedding on purpose in some spectacular destructive display of madness. Whatever happened to him that day, he couldn't control it. He wouldn't have hurt you like that for the world, I'm certain of it.'

Lydia stared at Millie. She inhaled and opened her mouth, but then exhaled without speaking. She had come close – too close – to telling Millie her dreadful suspicions about Naomi. But something held her back – something niggled in the back of her mind that she must never, ever tell anyone about Naomi.

Charlie Kingston was impatient; and when Charlie was impatient, he became tense; and when he became tense he just had to release the tension in the only way he knew how. With a woman.

'I tell you Charlie, I already *have* made contact. I've been to see George and met my grand-daughter – I can't remember her name for the life of me, but she's a feisty little madam, just like her mother. George has even been round here for tea.'

Violet flicked a speck from her smart, brown, flared trousers and ran her hands over her hips before nervously fingering the belt that was buckled tightly over her cream polo necked jumper. She squinted; her eyes were not yet accustomed to her new large-lensed fashionable glasses. Her image perfectly fitted the stereotype Charlie had created in his head. Last week, she had even had her top front teeth crowned.

He rubbed his chin and nodded slowly in admiration. 'Not bad, Vi, not bad at all.'

He pursed his lips, glancing around the reception area Violet had created and liked what he saw. The bright room at the front of the house was tasteful and yet business-like. No one would ever guess that it was not a waiting room for clients waiting to collect their ledgers and files after Violet had produced the balance sheets necessary for them to run their businesses successfully.

'You've done a good job, I'll give you that.'

Violet plucked a stray hair from Charlie's expensive suit jacket.

'I said I would, didn't I? And I said I'd meet your deadline. And I have, haven't I? Everything is ready.'

Charlie clenched his teeth. Before he had stepped through Violet's front door he had been irritated by a difficult Council meeting and the tension was showing no signs of easing, coiling around in his head like an angry rattlesnake.

He suddenly stepped back as if he had been punched in the stomach. This was all wrong. He could no more throw Violet on the floor or up against the wall, unzip his trousers and release his tension than induce a pig to fly. He tried to visualise Violet in fish-net stockings, suspenders and gaudy, cheap underwear, but the image did not cause even a tiny rush of blood as he expected. The fact was, the woman who stood before him looked almost *too* respectable.

Disconcerted, he tried to make conversation.

'What did George say when you turned up?'

Violet grimaced. 'He was fine, but my grand-daughter was with him and the little bugger chucked up all over my white sandals.'

Charlie forced a laugh. 'That's kids for you.'

Violet smirked with a self-satisfied half-smile.

'George was a push-over – he always was. Very easy-going. I've met my daughter's husband and his mother too. It's too early to tell if they'll accept me, but at least they were polite and that's a good start. But I haven't met my daughter yet. She's in hospital, apparently, and they won't tell her I'm back in Kettering until she comes out. They don't want to upset her while she's recovering from her operation.'

Charlie turned to look out of the bay window, his back to Violet as he tried to escape from his worrying lack of ardour. 'What's wrong with her?'

'I don't know. They wouldn't tell me. Told me to keep away until she was well enough to cope.'

As Charlie pulled back the net curtain slightly, he gave a low chuckle as it suddenly dawned on him that this was exactly what he had been trying to achieve. A front-line woman who would make his punters feel as if they were with their wives. Suddenly he didn't feel quite so bad at his apparent impotence.

The road was only just visible from the house, as foliage from trees and shrubs at the twin ends of the long driveway concealed the view. He grunted to himself in satisfaction as he realised that most of the trees were of the evergreen variety, and would not shed their leaves in winter.

He briefly fantasised about throwing Violet to the floor and ripping off her clothes to see what underwear she had on underneath the sensible, boring trousers and sweater. He turned back to look out of the window, locking his eyes on the road, mentally noting how many cars passed by.

'Look. I'm having a bit of a get-together at my house to let two or three people know about this place before we open for business. It's just a few friends and the mother-in-law, but there'll be one or two punters there who can quietly start to spread the word. You can –.'

'When?'

Charlie threw his eyes skywards. He hated being interrupted.

'I thought perhaps Saturday. I'll tell my Goldie you are coming. Wear what you're wearing now if you like. We can light the smokescreen and then get this show on the road.

'All right. I'll be there. But you need to stop fussing so much, Charlie. I've got everything in hand. Anyway, come and see what I've done with my little flat at the top of the house. I'll get these stuffy clothes off and put something more exciting on ...'

Lydia was alone for the first time since leaving hospital two days earlier. She took out a brown paper bag from her handbag.

Sitting at her dining table, she carefully withdrew the torn, ragged pieces, placing them together like a jigsaw before setting a small make-up mirror at a slight angle at the side of the mutilated letter. After a while she reversed the pieces and read the other side of the page.

"22nd June 1978
Dear Lydia
    I have given this letter to Millie for safe-keeping.
    Firstly, can I say that I love you with all my heart and

soul, but that is the last time I shall say it because a few days from now you'll be marrying another man.

If you are reading this letter, it means that the other side of me, the side that is a mirror image of the real me, but shut away and imprisoned, has finally won this war inside my head and I have probably been admitted to the mental hospital in Northampton.

I'm not stupid. I know that it is not possible to completely control schizophrenia. I might religiously take my medication, but there will always be relapses and I am so frightened of the man I become when I have a psychotic episode. That's why I walked away last week after we had made love. It was for your own good. But there is something else. Even if you had broken off your marriage, and we had married each other, there would have been the question of children. You see, Lydia, my grandfather told me I can never marry you, because of a secret – he is really your mother's father, which means that we are much more closely related to each other than you realise because our grandmothers were sisters, too. Schizophrenia can be inherited. I can't risk passing this living hell on to anyone else and I know how much you want to have children.

It just simply wasn't to be. It wasn't another woman that came between us, it was our genetics. There was no other woman – I just made it all up so that you would get on with your life. I want you to know that there only ever was you.

So, I find myself, sitting here, writing this letter in a script that looks all right to me but all wrong to everyone else. But I know you will absolutely understand why I wrote this letter in mirror image.

So, Lydia, I have given this letter to Millie to give to you and entrusted her to know just exactly when that time should be, if ever.

Don't give up. Persevere with your marriage. Martin is a good man – the man I should have been without this constant curse hanging over me. If you are blessed with children, love them and nurture them. It is enough for me to know that you are safe, secure and have the means to lead a happy life

without me.
   Love always,
   Stuart."

Lydia's tears began to bubble out of her nose and mouth. The hairs on the back of her neck prickled and before she knew it she was laughing and sobbing all at the same time. So it was true that Tom Jeffson had been her grandfather all along, as she had always suspected.

'I love you Stuart,' she said out loud, as she rose from the table to find some tissues.

A few minutes later, she sat down again, and re-read the letter. At that moment she knew she would survive the cancer. She owed it to him to smile and be cheerful now. Lydia gazed at the torn fragments for a few more minutes, the earlier tears replaced with a resolute determination to make the most of the rest of her life. The first time she had read this letter in Millie's cake shop, she had torn it up and tossed it away, recoiling in horror from it because it meant her precious baby girl might inherit schizophrenia. Now, at the age of nine, there was no question that Naomi was fine. She knew that because there was no greater authority than her, having read everything there was to read about how to spot the signs of schizophrenia in a child.

Her eyes played across the torn scraps of paper, assembled on the table like a ragged jigsaw puzzle. She'd stick them together with Sellotape, she thought. But not yet. She wasn't quite ready to start sticking together a perfect future from an imperfect past. She needed to recover from the operation first.

On impulse, she grabbed an ancient cookery book she had inherited from Rose. She placed all the ragged scraps of paper back in the brown paper bag, folded it over at the top and then placed it between the pages of the book before writing the name "Daisy Roberts" on the front cover. She tucked the book in between several other cookery books on a shelf in her kitchen, flinching with a sharp pain in the place that used to be occupied by her breasts.

A while later, as the clock struck four, the sound of running feet was accompanied by the back door being flung open as Naomi and her friend Lottie burst into the kitchen.

'Mum!' Naomi shouted, excitedly.

Lydia threw her a tired smile.

'Hello girls. Have you had a good day at school?'

Naomi looked concerned for a moment at the sight of her mother's blotchy face and red-rimmed watery eyes. She knew her mum had been crying again. 'Mum. Is it all right if I go to a grown-up party round Lottie's house on Saturday? It's called a barbecue and they are going to cook sausages outside in the garden.'

'A what?'

'A bar-bee-cue.'

'Won't it be a bit cold to sit outside eating sausages?'

'We don't have to eat the food outside if we don't want to,' Lottie explained. 'Dad will just cook it in the garden, and there will be fireworks and things, and we will just eat our food with our fingers. It was my mum's birthday last week and Dad wants to surprise her with a brand new barbecue.'

Marigold Kingston's heart felt as heavy as lead. The last thing she wanted was an impromptu birthday party in the form of one of those new-fangled barbecue bashes where people pretended they had reverted back to the dark ages and ate food with their fingers. She would have much preferred to have gone out for a quiet meal, or even just spent the autumn evening in the garden, sipping wine and watching the sun go down.

'Thank you, Charlie.' she had said when he plonked the huge box containing the new contraption in front of her. 'You're so thoughtful. I've always wanted one. I don't know why other people don't have them. They are so much fun for the children.'

What sort of a man bought his wife a barbecue for her birthday? Of course, he had already given her flowers that made her sneeze and gaudy jewellery that made her feel like a prostitute, but the barbeque, she thought, was the last straw. He'd wanted one ever since the Chairman of the Planning Committee had invited them to a barbecue a few weeks ago.

'Nothing's too good for you, my little flower,' Charlie had said to her as he kissed her on the cheek. 'I've arranged for caterers to cook the food, so you won't have to lift a finger.'

Marigold sighed and closed her eyes. She was tired. Tired of the constant talk of business deals. Tired of all the evenings spent alone while Charlie was at business meetings, Council meetings and goodness-knows-what-else meetings. Tired of his dogged determination to be selected as Mayor of Kettering (thus filling her with dread at the thought of having to be Mayoress). Tired of all dinner parties, garden parties, Tupperware parties and political parties, and having to put on flashy make-up all the time and have her hair done every week. She hated the way Charlie called her *"his little flower"* and Lottie *"his little sugar plum"*, and she absolutely despised the name Goldie. She wanted a more genuine life, and to let her clipped feathers grow again. She didn't want to feel like a wife on paper; merely someone to own all his assets so that the taxman or the courts couldn't touch him if things went wrong. She wanted to save up for a holiday, or for a new pair of shoes, using her own money, earned from a little a part-time job; and to savour a small piece of independence and be able to buy things without having to ask Charlie for money all the time.

Charlie's distinctive, gravelly voice interrupted her thoughts.

'Anyway, Goldie, are you listening to me? I've arranged everything for tomorrow night. You'll have a lovely party, I can guarantee it, even though it is all a bit last minute.'

The barbecue was in full swing when Violet swung open the wrought iron gate at the side of Charlie's home, the huge garden lit up with hundreds of fairy lights. Classical music was playing softly in the background, just audible above the sound of polite conversation, voices punctuated occasionally by brittle laughter. White smoke rose from a corner of the garden and she caught the faint smell of fried onions on the breeze.

Violet stood still, taking in the scene. She took a deep breath to steady her nerves before she stepped forwards and then gave the gate a hard shove, so that it clattered heavily behind her as it latched.

The voices and laughter stopped and heads turned as she glided down the garden path, swaying confidently, her breasts bouncing slightly as she thrust her chest forwards.

A printed silk red, orange and yellow flowery dress that came down almost to her ankles floated and billowed around her slim legs; high, wedge-heeled white leather sandals clicked and clacked on the concrete surface; a delicate, white crocheted shawl tied casually around her shoulders was complemented by the white straw hat she wore on her head, her hand holding it in place as she swayed along. She carried nothing in her hands: no handbag, purse, birthday present or contributory bottle of wine. She knew she looked classy, elegant and rich, and by the look on Charlie Kingston's face, he was more than pleased with her choice of clothes.

Marigold, sitting on a rustic bench beside her elderly mother, who was cradling a half empty glass of wine as if it was a new-born baby, stared at Violet as she walked across the lawn towards Charlie, her hand outstretched. She caught her husband's admiring expression and her heart sank. She and Violet were the same age, yet no one would ever have guessed it. She glanced down at herself. Her navy blue trousers, although smart, were plain and dowdy and her white blouse had come from Marks and Spencer. She wished she'd not just scraped back her shoulder-length hair and secured it behind her ears with hair grips and had made the effort to get a last-minute appointment at the hairdressers to have it put up. Embarrassed by her dowdy appearance, she felt the heat rise from between her breasts and spread up to her face.

She watched Charlie shake Violet's bony hand. She noticed that the skin on her face was heavily caked and powdered but she wore very little eye make-up and almost-colourless lipstick, which didn't somehow fit with the image Violet was trying to project. Could it be that Violet was actually, underneath her confident façade, as nervous as she was?

'Hello, Marigold. Happy birthday.'

Marigold took Violet's outstretched hand to shake it politely, but Violet stepped forwards and caught her by the arm, bending forwards to kiss the air at the side of her cheek instead. She was just about to reply that her birthday had been the previous Sunday when her daughter came running across the lawn, followed by their yapping, small white dog.

'Mum ... mum! Come quick. Naomi's been sick.'

Marigold shut her eyes briefly as she remembered Violet was Naomi's estranged grandmother. How on earth was she going to keep Naomi away from her this time with so many people to entertain? She sighed. Should she even try? It was none of her business, after all.

Chapter Nineteen

Daisy leaned forwards with purpose, her fingers interlocked so tightly in her lap, her knuckles blanched almost pure white.

'I know it's a shock, love. We wanted to let you recover for a few weeks before we told you, but events have overtaken us.'

Lydia sat with her hands clasped either side of her head in shock as Daisy and Millie, sitting side by side on her sofa, crinkled their eyes in concern and flinched uneasily at her reaction. 'I only came home last week. I really can't cope with having to think about *her* on top of everything else.'

'Well, there was apparently some trouble with Naomi. She had a bit of a run-in with her last Saturday night at the Kingston's barbecue. It seems Violet is one of his new business partners and is running a book-keeping business.'

'Why doesn't that surprise me? She was always on the fiddle when we were children. And what's Naomi been up to now?'

Daisy unclasped her hands. 'You would hardly recognise your mother now, Lydia. She's a much different woman to the one who abandoned you. She's even started going to church with Millie. Naomi was only protecting you, love. I shouldn't worry about it, but she gave her a right mouthful, apparently.'

Lydia raised her eyebrows and gave a sardonic chuckle. 'I'll have to have words with that young lady. She seems to have lost all her manners while I've been in hospital. And church? My mother's going to church? You have got to be joking.'

Millie nodded. 'She's donated a large sum of money, too. Apparently, it's the same church she used to go to when she was a little girl. Everyone thinks she's a lovely woman.'

'She was sitting outside in an old grey Humber as we left for Rose's funeral. I just knew it was her, but Martin said I must have been mistaken.'

Daisy edged forwards in her seat. 'Bill saw her, too, but I said it must just have been someone who reminded him of her.'

'What does Bill think about all this?'

'Oh, you know Bill, cynical to the last. He reckons he knows her as well as anyone and that she's more than capable of putting on an elaborate show or a brave front. Don't forget she lived with us for a while when she was a little girl.'

Lydia gave a laugh that was laced with irony. 'The next thing you'll be telling me, Aunt Daisy, is that *you've* started to go to church with her. Now that would be a turn up for the books, wouldn't it?'

Daisy fingered her silver cross, back around her neck after its long-term trip to Canada with Neil. She shook her head. 'Small steps, Lydia, small steps. I might be re-acquainting myself with God after he took Oliver and Stuart and then sent Neil to the other side of the world, but we're on nodding terms only at the moment. I'm not going to church with Millie and Violet. Not yet, anyway.'

'So has *everyone* in the family met her then? Everyone apart from me?'

'Yes'.

'Even Tim?'

'Yes. Briefly. When he flew back to visit you in hospital three weeks ago.'

'What does my brother think, then?'

'Well, he says he won't make up his mind either way until he has spoken to you. You'll have to ask him yourself.'

Lydia chewed her lip. 'I'm glad you didn't spring this on me before my operation. I'd never have coped.'

'I know,' Daisy and Millie said simultaneously.

'Well. You'd better tell her to come round, then, but don't expect me to welcome her with open arms.'

Two days later, Lydia watched through the window as the grey Humber stopped outside her house. The driver's door opened and a slim, brown-haired, well-dressed lady stepped out of the driver's seat and hesitated for a moment when she locked the car door. Her navy trouser suit was immaculately pressed and the pale blue silk blouse was clearly expensive. Lydia shook her head in surprise. Surely this elegant woman couldn't be her mother?

Lydia waited until she heard a soft tapping on the door knocker. Through the reeded glass of the front door, her mother's outline was sliced and distorted and Lydia's heart thumped painfully with apprehension as she opened the door. At the first sight of her mother standing before her, the string holding together sixteen lost years snapped like a broken string of pearls, and pent-up anger fragmented and scattered inside her so that it stung everywhere in her body and not just in her heart.

The two women stood in silence, absorbing each other's appearance for a few seconds. It was Violet who spoke first.

'Lydia, my dear girl ...' she said simply, her eyes beginning to fill with tears. She fumbled with the clasp on her handbag, pulling out a white, lace-edged handkerchief and dabbed at her eyes. 'You don't know how much this means to me. Thank you for agreeing to see me.'

'Come on in, then,' Lydia heard herself say coolly as she stepped aside to allow her mother into her home.

She watched in frigid silence as her mother dabbed at her eyes and snivelled, overcome with something Lydia wasn't sure was real emotion. She could have just been play-acting.

'I've missed you so much. I don't know if I can find the words to say how sorry I am for leaving you like I did, but I was ill at the time. I had a nervous breakdown, you see ...'

Lydia was unconvinced. 'What? Lasting for practically all

my life?'

'Even longer than that. I was mentally ill for a long time – even going right back to my childhood. But it was losing Oliver so tragically that was the start of my breakdown. I suppose they've told you all about Oliver.'

'Yes.'

Lydia felt a pang of sympathy for the slightly built woman before her. She tried to imagine how she'd feel if Naomi had died so tragically. She quickly slammed down the sympathy before it could take hold and distort her view of a mother who could abandon her children in cold blood.

'But you left us.'

'I tried so hard with you and Tim when you were small, but your father was an alcoholic and got himself into trouble with some bad people. I did my best, but I fell into bad ways, too. It was just a vicious circle. I knew you both deserved more, and so I tried to earn my way out of poverty, but I wasn't well and made some really bad judgements. I couldn't see the wood for the trees ...'

'But you abandoned us, didn't you?' Lydia interrupted as bubbles of hatred collected in a lump in her throat and she swallowed hard. Subconsciously, she clenched her fists. The fury that had been coiled inside her was slowly unwinding; it dragged stilted, wooden words out of her mouth that barely stretched across the chasm of bitterness.

'Did you know how awful that made us feel?' Lydia's voice was low and her eyes full of loathing as she turned her head so that she didn't have to look at her mother's face. 'We felt as worthless and rejected as one of your fag ends, ground under your shoe.'

Violet dabbed at her red-rimmed eyes again. There was no doubt now the tears were real. Lydia closed her eyes. Her mother might be upset and she might be genuinely sorry, but she just had to say the harsh words she had been rehearsing in her head since she had been fifteen years-old.

'We knew what you were ...'

Violet interrupted. 'I only did it for you and Timothy. To put food on the table and clothes on your back. Don't you *ever* think I actually enjoyed what I did. I loathed myself. That's why, as soon as I could, I made sure I could earn my living from other girls and wouldn't have to suffer such degradation myself.'

Her protestation fell on deaf ears. Lydia was determined to say her piece. She pursed her bottom lip and shook her head in disgust. 'That's even worse in my eyes. Some of those poor girls must have been as desperate as you were. You left us alone in that awful place, and you stole my childhood away from me.'

'I knew you would be better off with the Jeffsons. I wasn't worthy of being called your mother –'

'I don't mean when you abandoned us here,' Lydia shouted in exasperation. 'Cornwall Road was a palace compared with that disgusting hovel in London. I was forced to grow up before my time because you were never there to look after us. I had to practically bring up my own brother …'

Violet folded her arms over her head protectively, her voice thick with tears of regret. 'I was never cut out to be a mother. I'm so sorry. Please believe me, Lydia.'

'Where did you go after you left us?'

'Spain.'

'With our father? Was at least *that* part of your story the truth?'

Violet gulped and blew her nose. 'I can't tell you any more lies, Lydia. I left you and Timothy because I truly believed I could never be a good mother and I was terrified bad things were going to happen to you if we stayed in London. You were far better off without someone like me. I'll admit it now, I never did intend to come back for you because I'd reached the end of my tether. I might have hated what I did, but it made me steel-plated. Hard. I couldn't actually *feel* anything for anyone – not even my own children. But I'm not like that now. I genuinely want to say sorry, but I'm not expecting that you will forgive me.'

'Did we *really* have a father who lived in Kettering?'

Violet shook her head, her eyes closed against the brutal

truth. 'No. Your father was murdered when we lived in Croydon. He had taken part in a high profile bank robbery and the perpetrators thought he was the weak link because of his alcoholism, so they killed him and told me they had dumped his body in the North Sea, weighted down so that he would never be found. Until that happened we all rubbed along all right. You must remember, Lydia. I don't think I was always a bad mother, was I?'

'Is that when you had your breakdown?'

'Yes. Well – probably one of many. I'd always been prone to depression, especially during the time of year that Oliver was born and died. But when I was told in no uncertain terms to keep quiet, or else they would come back and kill us all, I was petrified. I couldn't sleep for fear we would all be murdered while we slept in our beds. I couldn't eat, either. I smoked and drank myself nearly to death.'

Lydia nodded, recalling her childhood. 'I remember,' she said. 'I know that we did once have a nice home, and when we lived with our father things weren't too bad.'

'When I left you in Kettering that Christmas, I went to Spain with a man who had faked his own death. He took on your father's identity because, to all intents and purposes, your father *was* still alive and so it was easy for Sergio to pretend to *be* him.'

'Sergio?'

'Yes. Sergio de Luca. Do you remember him? He was a famous pop star.'

'Oh my word. *Him!* Everyone thought he drowned in Thrapston gravel pits. It was on the telly for years because he'd gone missing. He was involved in the Profumo scandal, wasn't he?'

'Yes, he was. But it doesn't matter now. Look Lydia. I'm telling you all this because I want you to know the truth. It took a lot for me to find a way to come back to Kettering after Richard died last year. I've had to sell-up and make lots of sacrifices to come back, face you and make my apologies for the wicked things I have done in my life.'

'Richard? Who's he?'

'Sergio. He was Richard in Spain because that was your father's name. I never did call him Sergio again. You see, Lydia, once we got to Spain we both finally came to realise what dreadful things we had both done in our lives and wanted to start afresh. We did eventually fall in love and had a wonderful life together. The last sixteen years have healed me. I'm a completely different person now. I know everyone thinks it's all a big front, but it's the God's honest truth.'

'But how could you even think of dumping your children, Mother? You are a disgrace to your gender, no matter how you try to justify your actions. Leaving children is just disgusting, no matter what the circumstances.' Lydia's voice was forced and her eyes blazing with bitterness. She knew she had to keep calm, otherwise she would lose her temper and scream and shout at her mother to get out and never come back. She had imagined this moment in her head a million times, but the well-rehearsed words had taken flight, and she couldn't for the life of her think of a single further thing to say to the woman before her.

'I hate you,' she said eventually, before bursting into angry tears.

'I don't blame you,' Violet whispered. 'I've been so worried about you because the rest of the family wouldn't tell me what was wrong. Why did you need an operation and why you were in hospital for so long?'

'I've had breast cancer,' Lydia said, unbuttoning her blouse slowly. 'And now I look like this.' She pulled her blouse open, revealing a flat, white bandage in the place that should have been occupied by a lacy, white bra.

Violet's hand flew up to her mouth in genuine shock. 'I had no idea, Lydia. I'm so sorry.'

Lydia sank back into the sofa and put her hands over her face. She was all cried out. The anger had gone, to be replaced by relief; she had finally confronted the woman who had left her to care for her younger brother without even a backward glance. 'It's been so hard, not having a mum,' she said through her fingers.

Violet sat down, perching tentatively on the edge of the sofa beside her daughter. 'I didn't have a mother, either,' she said. 'When I was a little girl, she might have been there in person, but she was no mother, believe me.'

'I know. I've heard the story a thousand times and I can understand why the things my grandmother did would have pushed you over the edge, even without you losing your little boy in such tragic circumstances. I've researched the old newspaper reports from the nineteen forties, Mother, so I know exactly what happened.'

Lydia took her head out of her hands and glanced at the women who sat uncomfortably beside her. Violet looked much smaller and more vulnerable than she'd remembered.

'Tim and I would have helped you, had we known what awful things you had suffered. We were a family, Mum. Even though we had no money. You didn't have to become a prostitute, for goodness sake. If only you had confided in me when I was a teenager, I'm sure the three of us could have worked something out rather than you have to degrade yourself. And it was wrong of you to keep us away from our family when we were growing up, when they could have helped.'

'But Tom Jeffson would have stolen you away from me,' Violet interrupted quickly. 'Just like he stole Oliver –'

'Aunt Daisy loved Oliver, too, Mum. She told me that she and Uncle Bill had made up their minds to adopt him when it became obvious my grandmother couldn't cope. She was devastated when he died, even though she wasn't his biological mother. If you'd stayed around, you and Daisy could have been a great comfort to each other. You shouldn't have just taken off and turned your back on the people who loved you.'

'Daisy and Bill were so good to me when I was a child. Did they tell you that I lived with them for a while? They were only eighteen when they took me in, but those few months I spent with them were the happiest days of my childhood.'

'I know all about your childhood. And about the awful

242

things your mother did to you –'

'I'm not looking for excuses, Lydia. I know I have inherited my mother's lack of maternal instinct.'

Lydia briefly closed her eyes. This conversation was painful, but she wasn't about to stop now. 'Why did you leave us here? Everyone was much too old to look after us.'

'Oh Lydia. Surely you can understand why I took you to them. Just look at you now! A beautiful home, loving husband and a daughter you have every right to be proud of. Naomi properly put me in my place at the Kingston's on Saturday. She might only be nine years-old, but she knows her own mind all right. She'll go far. And that's not to mention Timothy going to university and landing himself such a good job in Canada with Neil. I couldn't have given you all this, Lydia.'

Lydia gave a deep sigh in reluctant understanding.

Violet swivelled around, tentatively placing both her hands over Lydia's. 'Your Uncle Tom did *everything* in his power to make sure my baby stayed in the family and wasn't put up for adoption, as I'd originally wanted. I had no choice in the matter. I was sent away to a home for unmarried mothers to give birth, and there was a doctor and his wife all set to adopt my little boy, but Uncle Tom scuppered my plans with his grand scheme. Then I saw how he was with Oliver when he was born and understood why he wanted to keep him in the family at all costs. He always loved children. When I was little, he spent a fortune on a brand new piano for me because it was said I had a talent for music. Where Tom's family was concerned, money was no object. I knew he was the best person to leave you with, even though he was elderly.'

Lydia withdrew her hand from Violet's. 'But it was so hard for everyone. Auntie Rose and Uncle George bore the brunt of having two children thrust upon them. Rose worked her fingers to the bone, permanently exhausted even though I did help around the house as much as I could. Do you know, she couldn't even afford to retire from the factory when she reached sixty? She had to carry on working to keep me and Tim in school.'

'*You* went back to school?' Violet's eyes widened in astounded surprise. 'I thought you managed to transfer to Kettering Woolworths.'

'Auntie Rose persuaded me to go back to school and take my exams. She was so good to us. I only worked in Woolworths on Saturdays to help contribute to our keep.'

Violet swallowed hard, and Lydia knew she was feeling guilty about forcing her to get a job as soon as she could when they lived in London, believing further education was a waste of time for a girl.

Lydia shook her head. 'Look, Mother. I appreciate you coming here, and for finally explaining everything to me, but don't know if I can forgive you just because you've said sorry for what you did.'

Violet leaned forwards and grasped Lydia's hand again.

'Look. I promise I'll be truthful from now on, whatever you want to ask, I'll give you straight answers. I'm not expecting forgiveness, but I want to look after you now in the way I should have looked after you for all the lost years. You need me, Lydia. You need me to help you get strong again after your operation. Please, at least let me be a mother to you while you recover. And then, I promise I'll just bow out gracefully from your life if that's what you want.'

'I understand you've reconciled with everyone else in the family while I've been in hospital?' Lydia said, a hint of bitterness still evident in her voice.

Violet nodded. 'I have. Apart from Naomi, that is, but I'm planning to work on that. Like I've just said, I would have visited you earlier, but they told me you were too ill …'

'I need to speak to them all before we go any further with this,' Lydia interrupted.

'Of course you do. I understand. I'll leave you in peace now, but I just need to ask you one thing. Please don't do anything about Richard – Sergio. He's dead now and there's no point in digging up the past. Like I said before, we faced a long journey together to come to terms with the terrible things we both had done in our lives. We grew to love each other and lived quietly and peacefully together until he passed away. It's the only part of my entire life I don't regret, and it's the part that has made me strong enough to come back and try to make my peace with you and Timothy. Do you know, Richard wanted to send for you so many times? He desperately wanted to be a father to you both and for us to be a proper family. But I couldn't let you live another lie, not when I knew you were happy and doing so well in your new lives in Kettering. In your place, I wouldn't forgive the mother who abandoned me, either.'

'How did you know we were doing well? Who told you?'

Violet sighed and closed her eyes. 'Nobody. Whenever I came back on a visit to England, I always came to Kettering for a weekend to make sure you were both all right. I'd go into Woolworths on a Saturday and watch you serving people. Then I'd hang around in Cornwall Road and try to catch a glimpse of Timothy. On one of my yearly visits I found out that you were getting married, purely by chance from eavesdropping a conversation in the corner shop. I managed to find out the date, and then Richard and I made sure we came back so that at least I could see you married. We tramped around all the likely churches in the town, trying to find out where the ceremony was. We were there, Lydia, watching from across the road to catch a glimpse of you when you came out of the church. I sobbed like a baby in Richard's arms afterwards, and when I read in the newspaper about poor Stuart Roberts dying on your wedding day in that terrible accident, I was so upset for you.'

Although Lydia sensed the barriers had now started to erode with the revelation that her mother had been present at her wedding, it felt as if she had been climbing up an incline of sand and reached half-way up to the top before sliding nearly all the way back down again. It probably hadn't been a good idea for her mother to reveal her secret visits over the years. Now she knew about these visits, each and every time her mother had walked away felt like another abandonment.

Chapter Twenty

Four years later

November 1982

Thirteen year-old Naomi stared at the cheque in her hand.

'I'm sorry, Violet, but it wouldn't be morally right for me to accept this.'

'Please? It's for your future. I'm not trying to buy your affection, Naomi. I know you don't like me, but I want you to be able to afford to do special things with your life,'

Naomi wanted to tear the cheque into tiny pieces and throw it back in Violet's face, but she was far better than that. She had principles and standards, unlike the woman before her who she steadfastly refused to refer to as her grandmother.

'Look, Naomi. Let me try to explain what I mean ...'

Naomi rolled her eyes and sighed. 'All right then. But please don't expect me to change my mind. I know you have the best of intentions, but you know the score. Everyone else in this family may have put the past behind them, but I'm sorry – I can't be a hypocrite. You abandoned Mum and Uncle Tim, and I just don't know how any woman could possibly do that.'

With tears in her eyes, Violet nodded as she tucked the cheque back into her handbag. 'In a couple of years, you will be the same age as your mother was when I left her in Kettering twenty years ago. You see, Naomi, when we lived in London I'd forced her to sell herself short, to forget about her hobbies and interests, not bother about exams and get a job as soon as she left school, even though I knew she was clever enough to do anything she wanted with her life. I can't turn back time, but I can admit I was very wrong in those days and at least make sure my only grand-daughter has the means to make the most of her life now she is growing up.'

'Look,' Naomi said, looking Violet straight in the eye. 'Don't take this the wrong way; I do respect you for coming back to put things right with Mum. I've always been polite to you, haven't I? I've not made trouble in the family in the name of my own stubbornness. I could have refused to speak to you, but what would that have achieved? Please just leave it there and accept that I don't want a grandmotherly relationship with you. I know I'm only thirteen, but I won't pretend. I'm just not made like that, Violet.'

Violet tapped her handbag. 'I admire you, Naomi. But I want you to promise me that if you ever change your mind about this money, you will ask me for it. I want you to be able to go on that school trip to France your dad told me about. I want you to be able buy a cello and play in the band. Did you know I used to play in that very same band when I was a girl? I had a boyfriend called Theo and we used to play together.'

'If I want money to go to France, then Dad will give it to me. If I want a cello, then he will buy me one. He's not short of money.'

Violet sighed again. 'I just want to be able to be a proper grandmother, Naomi.'

'You can't just buy back the past, Violet. I think you are trying to do that by giving me the opportunities you should have given to Mum.'

'Well, you're entitled to your opinions. I shall set up a separate bank account. This money can go in there in case you change your mind.'

Naomi shot a half-smile at Violet, keen to keep the peace with her for her mother's sake, despite the conversation they had just had. Lydia hadn't been well just lately and she didn't want her mother to have anything else to worry about.

'Well, thank you, anyway. When are you going on your holiday to Spain?' Naomi asked, changing the subject.

'On the Wednesday before Christmas. I get the keys to my new house just a few days before I go, so it will all be a bit hectic for the next few weeks.'

'Jimi and I will help you move, if you like. I don't want Grandad George and Grandma Elsie to fuss around and feel they have to help out, not at their age, and Mum's recovering from pneumonia. I'd rather help you myself than have my family feel obliged to help you move.'

'Thank you,' Violet said. 'That's very kind. Tell that nice young man of yours I'll make it right with you both.'

Naomi gave a big sigh, exasperated. 'Jimi and I don't want your money, Violet.'

Later that day, Charlie Kingston sat down heavily on a dining chair and opened his cheque book on the table before him with a flourish.

'So, is that it then, Vi? Is this where we part company?'

'We pulled it off, didn't we?' Violet smiled.

'We did. We've had four extremely good, lucrative years. Are you sure you won't change your mind?'

'No. I've earned my retirement. When I came back to Kettering, I promised myself that I would stop working at sixty. I might have thought about staying on for another couple of years, but after what happened in September, I just want to be out of it now. I've earned enough money to fund my retirement without anyone finding out what I've really been doing to earn it, and I've reconciled with my family – well, everyone apart from Naomi ...'

Charlie interrupted her with a loud chuckle. 'She's a hart nut to crack, I'll give her that. She's going to be a handful for her parents when she starts to spread her wings.'

Violet shook her head. 'I love her to bits, but I don't doubt you're right, Charlie. Naomi is the only one who won't forgive me for abandoning my children.'

'I just hope we've heard the last of that Italian nutcase,' Charlie said.

Violet shook her head. 'He's not just a nutcase, I reckon he's a psychopath. Tamika's still off work after what he did to her in September. She was in hospital for a fortnight. Did you know, he kicked her in the back so hard she had to have one of her kidneys removed?'

Charlie puffed the air out of his cheeks and shook his head. 'I didn't know that. Some might say the risk of being roughed-up is an occupational hazard, but we've never tolerated violence on that level from our punters. What did you say after you'd called the ambulance?'

'I went with her to the hospital and said she had turned up at the house after being beaten up by her new boyfriend. Then when the Old Bill came round here to take a statement from me and asked how I knew her, I said I was her employer – which, of course, was true – and that she did some typing for me now and again.'

'Are the Police still investigating?'

'They did for a while, but because Tamika gave them a made-up name, the trail went cold very quickly. I think we are in the clear.'

'Well. Make sure she's well looked after, won't you?' Charlie said. 'If she needs money, let me know. Tamika's one of our best girls. She's intelligent and able to play whatever part she is asked to play. In fact, she's a lot like you.'

'Oh, I don't think she'll be coming back to work,' Violet said. 'She's a tough one all right, but she told me last week she wants a different life now. She's had enough of the punters after that Italian creep, no matter how respectable they are. I've told her she can stay with me for a while when I move out into my new house if she needs somewhere to go.'

Charlie leaned back in his chair, palms together under his chin, deep in thought. 'She could take over from you here, couldn't she? I'd like to see her all right after losing a kidney. And she knows the score; how we like things to be run. She'll keep up our high standards.'

Violet shrugged her shoulders. 'It's a good idea, Charlie, but I thought you wanted to go to London to find my replacement.'

'Not necessarily. It all depends on whether we've seen the last of our Italian friend. I wouldn't want him to come back and find her in charge.'

Violet laughed. 'I should think he's long gone, after what I did to him. He'll not show his face around here again – or anything else for that matter.'

'What did you do?' Charlie asked, intrigued.

'You don't want to know,' Violet chuckled. 'He wasn't happy, I can tell you. The only thing hurt was his pride, but I know he'll never come back.'

Charlie handed over the cheque he had just written out.

'Well. That's it then. The next time we see each other, you'll be plain old Violet Smith, sipping coffee and eating cake with Marigold at my kitchen table. I'm so glad you've made a friend of her. You've done her the world of good since we have all known each other. In fact, you've done me good, too. I know I'm a much nicer person than I was before you came into our lives.'

'That's a lovely thing to say, Charlie. Thank you. But I have a confession to make. In the beginning, I was just using you as a means to settle myself back in Kettering doing the thing I knew I did best. I always hated what I did back in London, but I knew I was good at it. I led a good, honest life in Spain, but I was prepared to come back to this sort of life because my prime focus was always on reconciling with my family.'

Charlie laughed. 'Don't you think I didn't know that? It's been a privilege to do business with you, Vi. I know our business is illegal, but over the last four years you have made it respectable. You've treated the girls well, been discreet and professional with our clients and built up something we can both be proud of. I hope you have a long and happy retirement and we stay friends. God knows, you deserve it.'

'I don't want to go back into hospital,' Lydia whispered to Martin. 'Please let me stay here.'

Martin lay down on the bed beside her and propped his head on his arm. 'It's your call, Lydia. Whatever you want, I'll make arrangements for you to have the best care there is.'

Lydia stroked his arm. 'How long do you think I have?'

Martin's head dropped onto his chest and he shook his head slowly, his voice thick with grief. 'Let's not talk about it. I can't bear it.' His chin began to wobble and his face cracked as tears threatened. 'It's just not fair,' he whispered. 'Why you?'

'Why not me,' Lydia breathed.

After a while, Martin sat up. 'We need to make plans; get things in order so we can carry out your last wishes; and work out how on earth we are going to tell Naomi her mum is going to die.'

'I don't want her to know.'

'We should tell her ...'

Lydia shook her head. 'No. I don't want her, or anyone else, to know.'

Martin shook his head. 'So you want to keep the fact you have only a few weeks to live a secret? You can't do that. You can't keep it from people who love you.'

'It's my life. I can do what I want with what little of it I have left, can't I? Please let me do this my way.'

'What are we going to tell everyone, then?'

'Well, I've just had pneumonia, haven't I? People can take weeks to recover from pneumonia.'

When Martin shut the bedroom door behind him, Lydia was asleep, exhausted from making a list of her belongings and who she wanted to have them. As he studied the list in his hand, his legs buckled beneath him, and he slid down the closed door until he was sitting on the floor, sobbing into his bare forearms crossed over his face.

Two weeks later, Daisy was visiting George and Elsie, who were making plans for the traditional party for the children in the family to take place on the Sunday before Christmas. Three years ago, to everyone's delight, George and Elsie had married in a quiet registry office ceremony, and were now enjoying good health, good fortune and sharing their twilight years living in George's house in Cornwall Road.

'She's not getting any better,' Daisy said to Elsie. 'I'm really worried about her. I think she should go back into hospital.'

'So do I,' Elsie replied. 'I said as much to Martin the other day, but he says she is insisting on staying put. They set up a drip yesterday, and the district nurse comes in to check on her four times a day. Martin's taken some leave from work and does everything for her. He won't even let me or Violet help her change her nightie.'

'Well, I suppose he's best placed to look after her, being a doctor,' Daisy mused. 'Perhaps we shouldn't worry. She's in good hands.'

'I'm so glad Lydia's finally reconciled with her mother,' Elsie said. 'Perhaps now Violet is going to retire, she will be able to spend a bit more time with her when she gets better, making up for all those missing years.'

'Making up for lost time has been the story of Violet's life,' Daisy said, as she walked over to the sideboard in the living room and picked up a framed photograph of Violet as a child. The sideboard was crammed full of family photographs, which Elsie carefully dusted every other day.

'That's a lovely photo of Violet,' Elsie said, standing beside her. 'George found it in Rose's album, and I went to the Co-op and bought a nice frame for it. I wanted her to see it on our sideboard and know that she's part of our little family now. People shouldn't be vilified all their lives for making mistakes. Life's too short.'

'I remember this photograph being taken,' Daisy said. 'It was while she was living with us when she was a little girl.

She's wearing that headscarf because she cut off all her hair, and her parents shaved her head and told folks she had alopecia. We were all fooled for months, until she broke down and screamed out the truth in front of the doctor.'

Elsie shook her head in sympathy. 'I know, George told me all about it. It's no wonder the poor woman turned out like she did.'

'Rose always said she would come back one day,' Daisy said.

'Do you think Rose would have forgiven her?' Elsie asked.

'Oh yes. Rose was like that. She hardly ever spoke badly of anyone.'

Elsie smiled and picked up a photograph of Rose and George on their wedding day, stroking it with her fingertips. 'Rose was such a lovely woman and a real friend to me when I first moved here in the aftermath of Martin and Lydia's awful wedding day. I talk to this photograph all the time, because every single day I thank her for George. We are so happy, Daisy. I never thought I'd love another man after my Alfie, but I do. And I love their Margaret like she was my own daughter.'

'You both deserve to be happy,' Daisy said, picking up the photograph of Elsie and Alfie. 'I never knew your first husband, but he feels so familiar with seeing his photograph every time we come round.'

'You deserve to be happy, too.' Elsie said. 'After all the tragedy you've had in your life.'

'I am happy,' Daisy replied. 'Even though Stuart's gone and Neil's living in Canada, I'm so lucky to have Eileen and Trevor and their families living nearby. I count my blessings every single day.'

Daisy put down the photograph and glanced around the homely living room, the decorated tree sparkling in the corner and the Christmas cards festooned around the walls.

'Who would have ever thought that it is exactly twenty years ago next Sunday that Violet first came back to Kettering and left Lydia and Tim here, in this house?' she said.

Chapter Twenty-one

Falco Conti, better known as The Falcon, was proud to be known as a gangland thug. In his world of fantasy and make-believe, and with his contrived tough and taciturn ways, his idea of a girlfriend was a pair of handcuffs and plenty of rope. It gave him a kick to dress in snappy clothes and flash wads of cash around, and to give the impression that he was so much more than just a small-time crook who still lived with his mother and took her shopping on Saturdays. It gave him even more of a thrill to pay a prostitute for sex rather than bother to find himself a girlfriend, something of a long-term habit he would find hard to break now he was well into his forties with nothing to show for his life so far, apart from an impressive paunch and the dubious attribute of being the man who boasted of being so hard, he even killed his own name.

The Falcon was not an intelligent man. Someone had once told him that vengeance was a dish best served cold and his misinterpretation had been literal. Since his encounter with Violet on a passing visit through Kettering in September, he had been biding his time, waiting for winter. No one got away with humiliating him in front of The Mamba, and now everyone in his microcosmic gangland world had renamed him Fanny Falcon, reeling with laughter every time they saw him, it was something he was definitely not going to put up with for much longer.

He pressed himself into the branches of neatly-trimmed conifers in the wide shrubbery beside the front door, waiting for someone to come out. He had been humiliated and defamed by the snooty Madam in charge of this high-class brothel. He'd make sure she got her just desserts all right. Nobody would dare laugh at him and call him Fanny Falcon then. He lit a cigarette and blew the smoke high into the air while he waited for an opportune moment to snake his way through the shadows to work out how exactly how he was going to gain access to the house and execute his revenge.

Eventually, the front door opened and a frail, elderly gentleman dressed in a smart suit carefully picked his way down the steps, helped by a young girl. A few seconds later, a shiny black Jaguar swept slowly down the driveway to the front of the house, its tyres crunching on the gravel.

The Falcon, just a few feet away in the bushes, pressed himself further into the branches of the conifer so that he couldn't be seen.

'There you go, Mr Atkinson,' the girl said. 'Take care of yourself, now.'

The elderly gentleman raised his trilby hat and slid over the smooth leather seat into the passenger side of the car. 'I'd like to give a small gift to show my appreciation to Madam Violet on her retirement,' he said. 'I would be most appreciative if you could tell me her new address so I can pop a cheque in the post.'

'That's so good of you, Mr Atkinson. I'm sure she will be very grateful for your kindness.' The girl then dictated Violet's new address to the chauffeur in the driving seat, which he wrote down in a notebook.

'We are going to be a bit thin on the ground this year,' George said as he and Elsie made their way slowly back home from the bus stop, carrying laden shopping bags. 'There'll only be our Margaret, Janet and the little 'uns unless Naomi and Jimi come too.'

'We should still keep up your family's tradition for a children's party on the Sunday before Christmas, though,' Elsie said. 'I'll make a few sandwiches, some sausage rolls, and a nice trifle, and I'm sure we will all have a good time. I was talking to your Daisy about it only the other day. Did you realise it's exactly twenty years since Lydia and Tim first arrived in Kettering?'

'Aye,' George said, 'how could I ever forget?' He then made Elsie chuckle out loud as he relayed to her how Rose had sent him out on Christmas Eve to buy last minute presents for Lydia and Tim.

'It's forecast bad weather for Sunday.' Elsie said. 'We might even get some snow, so they say.'

'Good job you've bought enough food to feed an army, then,' George said. 'Because I for one won't be venturing outside if it's going to be treacherous underfoot. We don't want any broken limbs in this household, especially not at our age.'

Elsie giggled. 'I'm looking forward to Christmas this year with your Margaret and Brian. I just wish Lydia could feel better soon. It won't be much of a Christmas for them, will it, with her still hooked up to that contraption with a drip in her arm? Apparently, she's spoken to Jimi's parents and made arrangements for Naomi to spend Christmas Day with them, so this blasted pneumonia doesn't ruin Christmas for her. She just wants a quiet day at home, alone with Martin.'

George fell quiet as they reached the back door. Once they were inside he said: 'I don't know about you, love, but I get the feeling Martin's hiding something from us. I think there's more to Lydia's pneumonia than they're telling us.'

The removal van pulled up outside the newly built house, which stood resplendent at the end of the cul-de-sac as if it had just been painted on a blank canvass, waiting for the bland garden to be filled with an assortment of colourful plants, shrubs and saplings.

Soon afterwards, Violet pulled up in her new car behind the removal van, jumped out and began overseeing the move into her new house. Later, after school, Naomi, Jimi and Lottie paid a visit, running from room to room, their school shoes echoing on the wooden floorboards and uncarpeted staircase, excited about the new house with its trademark magnolia walls, new kitchen and bathroom and gleaming white doors and door frames.

'I'm not going to unpack too much of this stuff before I go away,' Violet said to Naomi. 'I've got to go to London tomorrow to sign some papers, so I won't have an awful lot of time to get things straight before I fly out to Spain next Wednesday.'

'We can help,' Jimi said. 'If you leave a key with us, we can have things ready for when you get home from Spain in the New Year.'

Violet laughed and waggled her forefinger. 'I don't think so, young man. I appreciate your offer, but I wasn't born yesterday!'

'You should leave a key with someone in case of emergency,' Jimi said with wisdom beyond his years. 'Why don't you leave one with my parents, after all we only live round the corner?'

'What emergency? I can't see that there'll be any sort of emergency in a brand new house.'

'Well, it's going to be cold, according to the weather forecast. So you might get burst pipes, that sort of thing. We had burst pipes last year and we live in a new house, too.'

'Were you planning on coming to Grandad's on Sunday, Violet?' Naomi asked. 'Only it's the twentieth anniversary of when you abandoned Mum and Uncle Tim, and I don't think you should be there.'

'If you don't want me there, then I won't come,' Violet said. 'I understand how you feel. I'm not heartless.'

On the way home, Jimi tugged on Naomi's arm. 'Hey,' he said. 'I thought you were going to try and be nice to your grandmother.'

Naomi shrugged his hand off her arm. 'I don't want her there on Sunday,' she said firmly. 'Mum's told me enough times what it felt like, being abandoned by her mother on the Sunday before Christmas. I'm sorry, Jimi, I can't be a hypocrite. Mum was only a little bit older than us. Can you imagine it?'

'Well, I think you are being blinded by self-centred pride,' Jimi said. 'My dad is a Sikh. He says that no matter how wicked and evil someone's been in the past, everyone is capable of changing and showing remorse.'

'Yes, but it makes me so angry whenever I think about it,' Naomi retaliated. 'I won't rock the boat for Mum's sake, but I can't ever forgive Violet for what she did. I have my principles.'

'My dad says anger and pride are two vices to be avoided, too,' Jimi said.

Naomi stopped walking and looked at him. 'Do you really believe that?'

'Yes, I do,' Jimi said. 'I hardly ever get angry. I just take a deep breath and count to ten. Then the anger magically goes away.'

Naomi sighed and slipped her arm through Jimi's. 'What do you honestly think of Violet?'

'I think she was very hurt and damaged inside when she first came back,' Jimi said. 'But that was four years ago; and the love of your family and their forgiveness is making her strong again. I like her. She's always really nice to me.'

'Well, I promise I'll try harder, then. But I can't promise to call her Grandma, Nan, Granny or anything else other than Violet.'

'Excuse me,' said The Falcon to the driver of a blue Ford Transit van that had just pulled into the driveway of Violet's new house the next day. 'I'm looking for the new owner.'

The driver pulled open the back doors of the van and hauled out a roll of carpet. 'She's gone out and will be back sometime after five. If you want to see her you'll have to be quick, though. She's going on holiday on Wednesday and won't be back until the New Year. She wants the entire house fitting out with carpets while she's away.'

'Cheers, mate,' The Falcon replied. 'I'll catch her later,

then.'

The Falcon walked down the drive and up the road, deep in thought. It was all right for her – she'd obviously made a packet out of blokes like him over the years, judging by the smart new house she'd just bought for her retirement.

He lit a cigarette, heading off towards the off-licence to buy some beer. Now he'd discovered the location of Violet's new house, the long-awaited vengeance for the humiliation he'd suffered was close. It might snow at Christmas, according to the weather forecast. Vengeance was a dish best served cold, so they said. Well, soon he'd finally make sure Violet paid for what she had done to him. No one would dare call him Fanny Falcon then.

Chapter Twenty-two

'Lydia and Martin are coming, too,' George said to Elsie as he put down the phone. 'I hope we are going to have enough food.'

'Oh, that's grand,' Elsie replied, clapping her hands together. 'I'm so pleased. Hopefully she's turned the corner now.'

'Yes. Martin just said she was feeling much better. He's going to get the car warmed up before she gets in it, and then we can sit her by the fire when she gets here. It will be lovely for our two families to all be together.'

Later, with the living room table laden with food ready for the family to arrive for the traditional pre-Christmas party for the children, George and Elsie waited for Martin and Lydia to arrive, a fireside chair for Lydia being made ready, complete with a tartan blanket,

Naomi's footsteps pounded in the entry and she burst in through the back door, her cheeks and eyes glowing with excitement. 'Mum's here. Dad says can you open the front door and he'll carry her in.'

Elsie frowned at George. 'Carry her?'

George shrugged and shuffled off to open the front door. In the street, Martin was helping Lydia out of the front passenger seat of their car. As George stood by the open front door he felt a sudden tingle of fear in his chest. Although it had only been less than a week since he and Elsie had visited Lydia, her face was pallid, her hair lacked its usual lustre and she was struggling to get herself out of the car. Martin slid his arm under her knees and picked her up gently, carrying her through the front door.

'Let me take that,' George said, taking a plastic shopping bag from Lydia's hand.

'Thanks, Uncle George,' Lydia said. 'I've been in bed with this pneumonia for so long, my legs refuse to work properly. Did you realise that it's twenty years today – ' Lydia began.

'I know, lass,' George said quickly. 'I don't know where the time's gone, and you're still as pretty as a picture –'

'Oh, Uncle George. I look a wreck, but never mind. I'm here, and that's all that matters.'

George chuckled and winked at her. 'No more of a wreck than when you first turned up and I had to go out shopping on Christmas eve, face that battle axe of a shop assistant in Learner and Woodward's and try to explain why I was buying underwear suitable for a fifteen year-old girl.'

Lydia laughed. 'You were great, Uncle George. And Auntie Rose, too. It was my best Christmas ever.'

'Well, thanks to Elsie, we shall have another one now you're feeling better. And it starts right here.'

Three hours later, George stood at the kitchen sink, his sleeves rolled up ready to start the washing-up. Elsie shut the door behind her.

'She's dying, George,' she whispered, shaking her head in anguish as her eyes filled with tears.

George bowed his head. 'I know, love.'

'She couldn't even hold her own cup to her lips. Martin had to help her.'

'Aye.'

'Naomi doesn't know, does she?'

'No. I don't think she does. Nor does anyone else, and we should respect that,' George said, his voice almost a whisper. 'We shouldn't say anything.'

'I don't know what to say anyway ... or do,' Elsie said, clutching onto George's arm for support. 'I'm Martin's mother, and I can't comfort him because I'm not supposed to know his wife is dying.'

'Do you think our Margaret knows?'

'No,' Elsie replied. 'I don't think so. She's been in the front room all afternoon playing with Janet and the kids so that Lydia can have some peace and quiet.'

'I reckon if and when Martin needs help, he'll ask for it,' George said. 'We might not be spring chickens any more, but we are perfectly capable of looking after Naomi at short notice if we have to.'

'Lydia wants to speak to you,' Elsie said. 'In private.'

George raised his eyebrows, rolling his sleeves back down. 'Oh. Right. I'll just go through, then. Where's Martin?'

'In the front room, with everyone else. Naomi's apparently organising a game of bingo.'

George opened the door to the living room, forcing himself to throw Lydia a cheerful smile. 'What's all this about then? An early Christmas present?'

'Something like that,' Lydia said weakly, as she reached down for the plastic bag at her feet. 'I just wanted to show you this while we are on our own.'

George's heart missed a beat as Lydia held out an old, battered desk-sized diary, closed with a gold clasp.

'Do you remember it?' she said.

George took it from her, running his hand over the silky material cover. 'Aye. It was one of your Christmas presents twenty years ago.'

'When I'd written the entry for Christmas Day in nineteen sixty-two, you asked me if you could read it.'

'Oh, I was only joking,' George said with a laugh. 'I was pulling your leg. I didn't really want to pry –'

'I know you were,' Lydia said. 'But I want you to read it now. While it's just the two of us. Please?'

George sat down beside her. 'Have you got the key?'

'It's not locked.'

George opened the tiny clasp with his thumbnail.

'You need to turn to the end,' Lydia said. 'Remember – I started this diary on Christmas Day. It's not specific to any particular year, so it didn't really matter what time of the year it was started.'

George leafed through the pages, all crammed full to

bursting with Lydia's small, neat handwriting in various coloured pens. Some pages were decorated with little pictures, doodles and hearts with arrows through them. When he got to 25th December, he stopped and looked at her.

'Are you absolutely sure you want me to read it?'

Lydia nodded.

George began reading. After a minute or two he stopped, reached into his trouser pocket and drew out his handkerchief, before lifting his glasses and dabbing at his eyes.

He put his finger on the page and leaned over to show Lydia which part of the entry he was reading. 'Your Auntie Rose didn't mind me giving you that five pound note in your new purse. It was just that when I told you to keep quiet about it, I didn't want you to open it up in front of everyone else. When I told her afterwards, she put her arms round me, gave me a big kiss on the cheek and said: "I wondered if you'd remembered to put some money in that purse. It's bad luck to give a purse as a present with no money in it." She was more worried about you having bad luck than she was about the five pound note, which was a lot of money in those days.'

'It was a fortune,' Lydia said. 'Over half a week's wages for a factory worker, like you. I couldn't believe you'd given me so much money when you'd only just met us.'

'I just felt so sorry for you both,' George explained. 'You had nothing. When you unpacked that suitcase and took out your spare underwear, and we saw it was full of holes, I thought our Rose's heart was going to break, she was so upset about it. I just wanted to buy you some dignity, no matter whether your mother came back for you or not. It wasn't about the money, really. It was all about your self-respect.'

Lydia's lips began to quiver and she shook her head, remembering. 'I don't think I have ever been as overwhelmed in all my life as I was that Christmas morning. I remember Auntie Rose gave me an old cardigan to keep me warm, and it smelled of so many good things – lavender, vanilla – everything that was homely. I'd wrap it round me, hug it when I went to sleep at night and even when I got married, I took it with me when I moved out. It was like my comfort blanket growing up.'

George continued reading. 'Oh, Rose,' he whispered without looking up. 'I miss you so much, especially at Christmas. You always did have a weakness for chocolate liqueurs and Harvey's Bristol Cream.'

Lydia touched his arm. 'Do you know, she even thought to write out a card for us? I kept it for years. I still have it at home somewhere.'

George shook his head, reminiscing. 'She always made sure everything was perfect for everyone else,' he said. 'She'd work her fingers to the bone to give all the family a good Christmas and end up so exhausted, it would take her until New Year's Day to recover.'

'I love you, Uncle George.'

George took a deep breath as he closed Lydia's diary, his eyes brimming with tears. 'I love you, too, Lydia.'

Lydia held out her arms for George to help her stand up.

'Thank you for giving me and Tim such a good life,' she said, her arms around his neck, burying her head into his shoulder. 'When I stepped over the threshold of this house twenty years ago, and I asked if you were my father, I want you to know that I couldn't have had a better one, even if you had been able to say "yes" to me that day.'

In her new house, Violet glanced at her watch and then switched on the television. Culture Club singing "Time" flooded the room, echoing off the walls as if it was prodding her rudely with a sharp stick. She bit her lip to stop it quivering as tears threatened. She seemed to be doing a lot of crying these days, despite her self-affirmation as a hard woman who never cried.

Why had her life been so hard and rocky when other peoples' lives seemed so smooth and easy? On Christmas

Eve she would be sixty years old and almost an old lady. More than anything, today, she had wanted to take her place in her family and join Lydia, Martin and Naomi in the family home in Cornwall Road for the traditional celebration on the Sunday before Christmas. It had been important to her that she should, it being twenty years since she had made the biggest decision in her life, right or wrong as that may have been.

Lydia had spoken to her on the telephone, anxious for her to join the family that afternoon. But Violet had been business-like and off-hand, brushing away the invitation, using the excuse that she had so much to do before she went away to visit her friends in Spain for Christmas. Then Elsie had rung, trying to persuade her to change her mind, saying that everyone wanted her to be there. She had said to Elsie that perhaps it was better that she stayed away, it being exactly twenty years since she had abandoned Lydia and Timothy in Kettering, but Elsie had said that everyone felt that because it was twenty years, she should be part of the celebrations.

Violet's head dropped on her chest and she rubbed at her aching head. Although she had almost changed her mind, she couldn't upset Naomi – not when her grand-daughter had expressly asked her not to go. She loved Naomi with all her heart and was full of admiration for her strong spirit, honesty and dogged determination to achieve the absolute best she could in her life. She didn't even mind that Naomi always called her Violet and refused to acknowledge her as her grandmother. All she wished for was Naomi's forgiveness for the decision she had taken twenty years ago, but she knew that as long as she lived, it would never be forthcoming.

"... Time is like a clock in my heart ..."

The poignant lyrics echoed around the characterless room and Violet shivered. Soon, Lydia and Martin would be back at home, having been at the party in Cornwall Road all afternoon. She would give Lydia some time to rest and would pop round later and sit with her for a while. In the

New Year, when she was fully recovered, she would treat her to a day out at one of those new-fangled spa places, where she'd be pampered and made to feel good about herself again after being so ill. She'd already sent for the brochure, and when she got back from her holiday, she'd talk to Lydia about it.

She brushed tears from her cheeks and stood up. No matter how much she fussed around and cared for Lydia, she was still a bad mother; nothing would ever change that fact. She had, that afternoon, put her grand-daughter's feelings before her daughter's invitation to the party. What sort of woman did that make her? And what sort of masochistic lunatic, having turned her life around to achieve something decent and worthwhile, then returned to the seedy life she had despised and fled from sixteen years ago, just so that she could try to mend something that could never, ever be fully repaired?

At least she was well out of it now, she thought. Never, ever again would she have to prostitute herself, or others under her control, in the name of making a living.

The Falcon zipped up his black leather jacket against the cold wind, staring at the light in Violet's window. He thrust his hand in his pocket, fingering the smooth key he had found under a ceramic planter by the front door. Was she stupid? Everyone knew that if you were going to leave a key for carpet fitters, it was the place everyone used. He'd wait until she had gone out before slipping inside. He knew she was going out because he'd let himself in earlier and was hiding upstairs when she'd been on the phone and had heard her say: "I'll pop round when she's had a chance to have a rest. Is seven o'clock all right?"

It gave him an unbelievable thrill to be in Violet's house, either while she was out or when she was there, with the risk of being caught. In fact, he had almost willed Violet to discover him, enjoying the kicks it gave him by only just making it upstairs to one of the spare bedrooms before she'd opened the front door, which had happened a few times over the past couple of days.

He stood up and strolled off towards the off-licence a few streets away. He'd buy himself a few beers and make himself at home while she was out.

As he walked, he tried to work out just how he would settle the score with Violet; what misadventure would befall her to make her pay for ruining his life. He thought back to the day in September when she had lured him back into the whore-house with a promise of favourable terms to compensate for not being given the full three hours he'd paid for on his previous visit.

She'd shown him into an amazing room, full of every single object imaginable for his own pleasure, telling him to undress and then another girl would make up for the time he had paid for and hadn't received. It was on one condition, though: that he didn't repeat his previous rough behaviour with the girl.

Afterwards, he hadn't been able to find his clothes, which he was sure he had folded and placed on a chair in the room. Violet had given him a luxurious velvet bathrobe and told him to wait downstairs while she looked for them. When he'd been shown into the waiting room, it had been empty, but a few minutes later he'd been shocked when two other members of his gang had appeared, winking at him and nudging each other. He'd felt good for a while, boasting about the good time he'd just had for free when they were going to have to pay – even though they had apparently been given a huge discount.

Then, while he was bragging to his comrades about how the girl the previous week had not been able to keep up with him, and had been carted off in an ambulance under a blue light, Violet had reappeared with a pile of clothes in her hand.

"Miss Falcon?" she had said to him. "I've located your clothes. Please feel free to use one of our changing rooms just down the corridor. I hope you've enjoyed your stay with us this afternoon."

She had then placed the pile of clothes, complete with a wig of long, blonde hair and a pair of huge stiletto-heeled shoes, on a coffee table in the centre of the room. His two companions had fallen on them in an instant, laughing as they held up the black mini skirt and sequinned top against themselves and teetered round the room in the size nine shoes, wearing the wig. He'd been mortified, and tried to protest, saying that he'd been set up, but they were having none of it. Just a few days later, the story of how he'd been caught wearing women's clothes in a whorehouse had been spread far and wide, and everyone was calling him Fanny Falcon, wolf-whistling him as he passed by, blowing kisses at him.

He was nothing but a laughing stock, and Violet was going to pay dearly for it.

Lydia sank down into the pillows and closed her eyes. She had just one more thing to do before getting on with the business of dying. It had been hard to leave her diary from nineteen sixty-two with Uncle George, and even though she hadn't looked at it for years, she had felt a strange attachment to it. At first, he hadn't wanted to read it all, saying that it was enough for him to read the entry for Christmas Day, but she'd insisted. He must read it all. Everything. Because she wanted him to know just how grateful she was for all he and Auntie Rose had done for her.

'I wonder why my mother didn't want to come to the party this afternoon,' she said to Martin, her voice croaky and weak.

'She said she's been really busy with the move and getting ready for her holiday, and couldn't possibly make it. But she'll be here to see you about seven,' Martin replied, looking at his watch.

'I'll need more morphine soon.'

'Is the pain bad?'

'Yes, but not unbearable yet. If I have some now, I'll be

asleep when Mum gets here, and I want to tell her something.

'What do you want to tell her?'

'Something about my Uncle Tom.'

Martin nodded, deep in thought. 'I still think we should talk to Naomi, love,' he whispered.

'No,' Lydia said, grimacing as she shifted slightly in the bed. 'I don't want her to have bad memories about this Christmas. She'll be better off with the Singhs, enjoying Christmas day with Jimi. I've spoken to Linda Singh and she's quite happy to have her. It'll be good for them both, being together.'

Martin sighed. 'It's your call.'

There was a knock on the front door. Martin squeezed Lydia's hand before going to answer it. 'I'll leave you alone with your mum, then, shall I?'

Lydia nodded, closing her eyes in pain. 'Then I'll have some morphine.'

Violet opened the door to Lydia's bedroom.

'Hello', she said. 'Did you have a nice time at the party?'

Lydia nodded. 'Yes. I'm tired now, though.'

'I'm so sorry I didn't come. I'm up to my eyes in it.'

'I understand. Never mind, you're here now.'

The unexpected churning feeling started somewhere in the region of Violet's navel. It rose up through her chest and when it reached her throat, she gasped audibly and put her hand to her mouth, her eyes widening with the intensity of it. Her hand groped for Lydia's under the bedclothes and when she found it, she grasped it tightly. Was she having a heart attack? The pain was the worst she had ever felt, and it had come on so quickly.

'What's the matter, Mum?'

'I ... I ... Oh, Lydia.'

Violet screwed up her eyes, but the tears leached quickly through her eyelashes. Neither of them spoke. Both were now weeping, silently, gripping each other's hand.

'Why?' Violet mumbled. 'Why didn't you –'

'Because of Naomi. She's my daughter and I love her. Every second I can spare her from the hell of knowing what is to come is worth it.'

Violet shook her head and without saying a word, lifted the bedclothes and climbed in beside Lydia. She didn't protest. Even when Violet slid her arm under her thin shoulders and pulled her into her breasts, she didn't complain.

'But you're my daughter, Lydia,' she breathed. 'And I've always loved you. How long have you known?'

'About a month.'

'Where is it?'

'In my lungs, my spine, my liver ... everywhere.'

'I'm not going to Spain. I'll move in here and look after you. I'll look after you all.'

'No, Mother. If you love me, you'll carry on as normal. Go on holiday. Please? For Naomi's sake. I need everyone to do this for Naomi.'

Violet buried her head into Lydia's shoulder, breathing in the fragrance of her, unable to stop herself shaking with fear. 'Does anyone else know?'

'Just Martin. Please don't say anything to anyone.'

'But why ...?'

'I have to do this my way. I'm okay. At least I get to prepare –'

Violet began to sob, interrupting her quickly. 'I know just what you mean, Lydia, about sparing Naomi. I understand, really I do.'

'You're not a bad mother, you know.'

'Oh, I am. I've never forgiven myself for what I did to you.'

'Only now can I fully appreciate and understand why you did it,' Lydia said. 'And I want you to know I forgive you completely. You're only sixty. Put everything behind you now, and try to enjoy the rest of your life. You've put things right by coming back, and that took enormous courage.'

'Thank you,' whispered Violet. 'That means so much to me.'

'Now, get out of my bed, smooth the covers over, sit on that chair and let's both put on a brave face for Martin and Naomi and try to act normally,' Lydia said.

Violet wiped her eyes. 'All right. I'll call down in a minute and ask him to make me a cuppa – is that normal enough?'

'Yes. And now I need to tell you something about Uncle Tom before I have my medication.'

'Is it that Tom was really my biological father?' Violet said. 'Because if it is, I already know that.'

'Did you always know?'

'No. And I can't remember actually being told when I was a girl, either. I think it was something I gradually came to realise.'

'I suspected as much after Naomi was born,' Lydia said. 'But what I want to tell you is that when Uncle Tom died, Auntie Rose and Aunt Daisy decided not to put a memorial in the Book of Remembrance for him.'

'So you want me to arrange for a memorial?' Violet asked. 'Of course I will, if that's what you want.'

Lydia shook her head. 'I just couldn't bear to listen to everyone saying what a tyrant he'd been and hearing the tales of the bad things he had done in the past. So, just after he died I went to the Crematorium, filled in a form, and put it in myself, pretending to be a next-of-kin. I've been to the Chapel of Rest every year on the anniversary of his death to pay my respects to him, but nobody else in the family even knows it's there.'

'So what do you want me to do, love?'

'Will you go in my place?'

'Yes, of course I will.'

'Every year?'

'I promise.'

Lydia sighed, exhausted. 'But don't tell anyone else, will you. I really had no right to do it.'

Chapter Twenty-three

Two days later, with her heart weighing heavily in her chest, Violet heaved her suitcase over the threshold and locked her front door behind her. The taxi driver opened the passenger door for her before putting her suitcase in the boot. She sat in the car, staring dispassionately at the house she had bought. She wasn't sure she was going to like living there. It felt spooky and eerie, even though it was brand new. She couldn't quite put her finger on it, though. Several times, she had felt as if someone was watching her, but that was impossible because she was completely alone.

'Are you all ready, then?' the taxi driver asked. 'Not forgotten anything?'

'No. But I'm not entirely sure I should be going anywhere.'

'Why? Jetting off somewhere nice for Christmas would be a dream come true for me,' the driver said, making conversation.

'Well. I've got some serious family problems. I'm having second thoughts.'

'How long are you going for?'

'Oh, just a week. It's my birthday on Christmas Eve, and my friends in Spain invited me over to celebrate and spend Christmas with them. I used to live there, you see.'

'Well then. A week's not going to harm anything, is it? You'll be back soon. I'd just enjoy it if I were you. Drink plenty and eat plenty. You only live once.'

Violet smiled at the driver. He seemed like a friendly sort of bloke.

'What are your plans for Christmas, then?' she asked.

'Oh not much. Me and the missus are going to our daughter's for dinner, and then I expect I'll just put my feet up in front of the telly.'

Violet rubbed at her eyes.

'Are you all right?' the driver said.

'Just a headache. I suppose it's all the rushing around. I only moved into my house a week ago, and I'm not sleeping too well. I've got a lot on my mind.'

'It's a lovely house, if you don't mind me saying.'

'I don't know whether I'm going to like it,' Violet said. 'It doesn't somehow feel right. I think it might take some getting used to. I don't even have any carpets yet, but the carpet fitters are going in tomorrow and Friday, so when I get back it might feel more homely.'

'Oh yes, I'm sure it will,' the driver replied. 'There's nothing like a nice bit of carpet to turn a house into a home. And once you get on the plane, with a glass of wine in your hand, you'll feel a lot better, mark my words.'

'More like a nice cup of tea or a glass of fruit juice,' Violet said. 'I don't drink – I used to, but I gave it up on Christmas Eve in nineteen sixty-two and haven't touched a drop since, apart from the odd small glass of wine, just to be sociable.'

From his vantage point, The Falcon watched Violet leave in the taxi. After a few minutes he emerged from the shadows at the end of the road and, looking over his shoulder to make sure no one was watching him, hurried down her garden path, retrieved the key from under the ceramic planter and let himself in.

He shut the front door behind him, his pock-marked, unshaven face split into a cheesy, wide grin. She was going away for Christmas which meant he'd got plenty of time. Now, what could he do to this lovely new house to make her pay for what she had done and rescue his reputation?

Making himself comfortable in the lounge, he put the television on, opened a can of lager and lit himself a cigarette. He shivered. Why not have the gas fire on? After all, it wasn't him paying the bills. He picked up a Christmas card from the mantelpiece, and finding he still had his lighter in his hand, flicked it until there was a small flame.

He'd always been fascinated by fire. As a child he'd kept a box of matches in his pocket, chatting to himself as he played his fiery games.

'I'm the master of the flame,' he said out loud as he held the Christmas card close to the lighter to see just how close he could put the flame to the card before it began to scorch.

After a few minutes of playing with the card and the flame, he became bored and began poking around in Violet's living room, opening sideboard drawers, looking for alcohol and finding not even a drop. He searched some more – surely there was some money in the house? Everyone kept cash, didn't they? Especially a whore. He supposed she'd have plenty of cash squirrelled away somewhere, but all he could find was a cheque for five hundred pounds, tucked behind a clock on the mantelpiece.

'Can I go to Jimi's?' Naomi asked her father as she put the phone down. 'His dad's just bought a new VHS video recorder for Christmas and he's invited me round to watch a film with him.'

Martin raised his eyebrows. 'A new video recorder? VHS? Crikey, they cost a fortune. You'd better ask your mum if she minds you going.'

'She's asleep. She's been asleep all morning. I think it's that medicine you keep giving her.'

'She needs it, Naomi. Pneumonia is painful and leaves you exhausted.'

'I just want her to get better now,' Naomi whined. 'She's been ill for ages. Violet told me that once she's better, she's going to treat her to a spa day of pampering. Do you think I'll be able to go as well? If we tell them I'm sixteen, they might let me in.'

'What's a spa day?'

'Oh, it's just a place where you sit in saunas with face

packs on, then someone massages you and rubs you all over with smelly oils. Then afterwards you have nice stuff to eat and sit around in white robes, drinking wine and reading all day. I saw the brochure round Violet's.'

Martin laughed. 'It's the first I've heard of it. Whatever next?'

'Can I go round Jimi's to watch a film then?'

'All right. But make sure you're back before tea time. I don't want you walking the streets in the dark.'

Back at Violet's house, The Falcon was making himself at home, surrounded by empty lager cans. When he reached a certain state of inebriation, he became morose and sentimental and, fuelled by a photograph of two children on Violet's sideboard, began reminiscing about his childhood.

He'd not been a happy child. Struggling academically, he'd been an easy target for bullies and his fiery, overbearing mother only made things worse by bursting into his classroom, brandishing her clenched fist at his teachers on more occasions than he could remember.

He'd stand in the playground on the periphery of a group of children playing marbles or conkers, connected to them by age but disconnected in every other way, listening to their chatter, trying to understand what they were talking about, but then getting it all wrong. Everyone would turn and laugh at him when he made a stupid comment, calling him names like Freaky Falco or Creepy Conti.

Fire became his only companion; the means of disposing of friendship gone wrong. His only control over the raw feelings of rejection and suppressed passion was to burn the belongings of his enemies, or those of the girls who'd laughed in his face, their breath smelling of chewing gum, when he'd asked them to go out with him.

The lighter fuel, an accelerant which gave him unexpected sexual pleasure, the searing pain of failure attenuated by the smell of burning flesh, wood reduced to charcoal – all of these things warmed his cold heart and gave him the power he craved.

Then, one day when he was sixteen, he'd set fire to a building and watched from a distance with such heightened pleasure, it had been better than the most addictive drug. He'd stood still and silent, spellbound as choking clouds of noxious fumes billowed around him, plumes of black smoke rose high into the air and the flames licked seductively against window panes with their orange tongues, dancing and flirting with him, beckoning him with sly, mesmerising fingers to go inside, feel the searing heat and revel in the comedy of tragedies being played out inside.

He'd spoken to fire fighters when they had arrived, blue lights flashing, getting in the way as they had aimed their hoses at the mocking flames, pulled on breathing equipment and protective clothing and dashed inside to save the screaming human beings who were trapped. He'd bent over a body, charred and reeking, before being pulled away by a policeman, and had danced around in ashes, falling like snow around him, as the fire rolled and tumbled around inside the building, people screamed and a family pet was given oxygen, along with two small children who had been pulled from the house, still and lifeless.

He'd not been caught for his crime.

The Falcon gulped down another can of lager, remembering the thrill of that first fire. He'd got away with murder that day, but only because his mother had told the police he was an imbecile and had special needs, cloaking him with flabby arms, stinking sweaty breasts and stained aprons as she kept him safe from the long, spidery arms of the law.

The girl who had spurned him had lived, but the scars ran deep. So deep, in fact, that she had tried to kill herself months later, unable to come to terms with the deaths of her father and her younger brother and sister in the terrible tragedy.

It had been all her own fault. She'd led him on, talking to him; lending him a book on how to deal with bullies. Then, when he'd put his arm around her and tried to kiss her on the lips, she'd pushed him away, saying that she didn't fancy him, although she would always be his friend when he wanted to talk to her.

Bitch. She'd been no better than the others.

'Mr Singh?' Naomi said. 'I'm going home now. Can I use your phone to ring my dad to let him know I'm on my way?'

'Of course you can, but it's getting dark. Why don't you walk back with her, Jimi?'

'All right,' Jimi replied.

'Good,' said Jimi's dad. 'Young ladies should always be escorted safely home.'

The route from Jimi's house to Naomi's took them past the cul-de-sac where Violet's new house was situated. As they passed by, they noticed a dim light emanating from a crack in the curtains in the living room.

'Violet's left a light on,' Naomi said. 'Do you think she meant to?'

'I don't know,' Jimi replied. 'Perhaps we should go in and switch it off. She's left a key under the plant pot – I heard her telling my dad the other day. The carpet fitters are going in tomorrow and Friday. She asked him to pick up the key for safe keeping when they had finished.

'All right. We'll go in, switch it off, and then you should tell your dad when you get back home.'

Jimi bent down to retrieve the key.

'It's not here,' he said, straightening up.

'Perhaps it's round the back?' Naomi said. 'I'll just go and have a look by the back door.'

While Naomi was gone, Jimi peered into the window, trying to see through the crack in the curtains. Suddenly, at the back of the house, Naomi screamed.

Jimi shot off and sprinted down the driveway at the side of the house, just in time to see a man yank her over the threshold of the back door, his arm around her neck. The man gave a menacing laugh as he locked the door.

'Jimi ...' Naomi screeched. 'Help me.'

The man dragged Naomi into the hallway through the kitchen and kicked the door shut behind him.

'Help!' Jimi yelled at the top of his voice. 'Someone help me!'

Silence.

Panicking, Jimi realised the other houses in the cul-de-sac were all unoccupied, waiting for their new owners to take up residence in the New Year. He looked around for something to break the window with, but there was nothing; the flat, characterless, brand new back garden devoid of anything he might use.

He shouted out again, and then ran around to the front of the house.

'Someone please help me,' he screamed again, unable to decide whether to leave Naomi at the mercy of the man and run back to his own house to fetch his father.

The front door opened and the man stood before him, holding a struggling Naomi. 'Get inside, you loud-mouthed brat,' he said, grabbing Jimi by the front of his coat and pulling him inside the house.

Panting in fear, Jimi screamed in the broken voice of a thirteen year-old boy. 'Let her go. Just leave her alone.'

The Falcon pulled his arm from around Naomi's neck and instead grabbed her by the collar of her coat, laughing like a wild animal. The rough action caused her to flop against the wall like a ragdoll.

'I've got you now,' he yelled. 'And you can scream all you like, no one can hear.'

Violet waited by the big, glass window for the plane to disappear into the cloud cover. When it had gone, she turned around, picked up her suitcase and looked around for a payphone. The officer at the departure gate had not been happy when she had broken down in tears, and explained that she couldn't go to Spain for a holiday when her daughter was so gravely ill, and the plane had been held up while her suitcase was found in the hold and retrieved.

She rubbed at her abdomen. The pain she had felt when she had realised Lydia had cancer was back, and even worse this time. For some reason she felt compelled to get back home as soon as possible, a strange gravity pulling her back.

She pulled a business card out of her coat pocket. The kind taxi driver had written his home telephone number on the back of it, and told her that if she wanted him to fetch her back from the airport next week, she should ring it and he would make sure he was there to collect her.

She dialled the number carefully.

'Hello? It's Violet Smith. You've just dropped me off at Luton airport.'

'Oh yes,' the taxi driver replied. 'Are you all right? Has something happened?'

'Yes. No. Not exactly. But I was wondering if you could come and collect me again. You see, I've changed my mind about going on holiday. I just want to come home to be with my family.'

An hour later, Violet climbed into the taxi, and, once again, promptly broke down in tears.

Martin opened the bedroom door softly. Lydia was still asleep, the television on in the corner of the bedroom. He shook her shoulder gently, and her eyes flickered open briefly.

'I'm going to have to pop out, love. Naomi should be home by now. Jimi's father rang and said they left his house ages ago. I'm a bit worried so I'm going to take the car and see if I can find them. I won't be long.'

Lydia grunted an acknowledgement.

'I'll be as quick as I can.' Martin said apologetically.

'So if you reckon you're a Sikh, and are against violence,' The Falcon said to Jimi, 'why do you carry this funny little knife?'

Jimi didn't answer. Probably the most stupid thing he had ever done in his life was to brandish his Kirpan knife at the monster who had then forcefully removed his leather cross-belt and sheath from under his jumper, and twisted it around Naomi's wrists before securing it to a dining chair behind her back so that she couldn't move. He edged towards an old plumbers' blowlamp that sat menacingly at her feet, together with a plastic bottle of petrol the man had syphoned from Violet's car in the garage. If he could move quickly and grab the metal blowlamp, he could perhaps throw it at the window and try to attract some attention.

The Falcon put the tip of Jimi's curved Kirpan knife under his chin, forcing him to look up at him.

'I asked you a question, raghead. So answer it.'

'I don't speak English,' Jimi replied sarcastically.

'Oh.'

'You tell me then, if the raghead can't speak English,' the Falcon said to Naomi, flicking his lighter and staring at the flame.

'I don't know,' Naomi said with a gulp. 'It's something to do with his religion.'

'What's your name?'

'Naomi Fraser. My father is a doctor. He will come looking for me soon. I should have been home by now.'

The Falcon pursed his lips. 'Good,' he said. 'He'll be able to treat your burns when he gets here then.'

'No!' Jimi screamed as he grabbed the plastic bottle of petrol and threw it across the room, away from Naomi.

Petrol puddled on the bare floor as the cap flew off when it hit the hard floor. The Falcon jumped back, laughing, enjoying the power he had over the children.

'Now, now. Take it easy,' he said, wagging his forefinger at Jimi and Naomi before he picked up the bottle and threw the remainder of the petrol at Jimi, soaking his trousers and coat at the front. 'We don't want to start a fire, now, do we?'

The Falcon sat down on the floor, laughing hysterically, cutting up strips of Christmas card with Jimi's Kirpan.

'Not very sharp, is it?' he said.

At the very moment Violet jumped out of the taxi, screaming, Naomi became aware that she was still alive and Jimi's leather Kirpan belt had been removed from her wrists. Retching and choking, she tried to pull the oxygen mask from her face, while at the same time trying to sit up under the red blanket that covered her. Blue lights flashed all around her, firemen shouted instructions and then the whooshing of fire hoses being yanked from the fire engine brought her to full consciousness.

She became aware of strong arms encircling her, and her father's voice crying, 'thank God, thank God.'

'There's someone else in there,' Martin shouted to a nearby fireman. 'A young boy – Jimi Singh.'

'Someone stop that woman,' another fireman's voice yelled nearby.

Naomi, finally freeing herself from the oxygen mask, screamed. 'Get him out. Please, just get him out.'

She watched as Jimi's father, sprinting down the cul-de-sac, dodged a fireman who was trying to stop him. His anguished howl would haunt her forever as he was restrained by two strong fireman from following Violet into the burning house.

'Violet!' Naomi screeched as Violet's back view appeared from the billowing cloud of black smoke, dragging a burning bundle across the threshold.

She scrambled to her feet and wriggled out of Martin's restraining grip to stagger over to where firemen were frantically putting out the flames with a fire blanket. 'Jimi,' she yelled as simultaneously, Jimi's father fell onto his knees at his son's side.

The loud, approaching wail of an ambulance siren drowned out all other sounds as the vehicle pulled up at the scene. Soon, Naomi found herself being forced onto a stretcher, the oxygen mask back over her face, and her father's soothing voice beside her as she was loaded into the back of the ambulance.

'Jimi,' she shouted again, her breath misting the inside of the oxygen mask.

She heard her father taking over, shouting at the ambulance driver. 'I'm a doctor. This is my daughter, Naomi Fraser. She's not badly hurt, just smoke inhalation. We need to get Jimi to hospital first. He's badly burned. Also, my mother-in-law has burned hands and arms – her life is not in danger, but she needs urgent treatment for shock.'

Then her father disappeared into the smoke to attend to Jimi, and the next time she saw him, she was tucked up in a hospital bed with Grandad George and Grandma Elsie by her side and she hardly recognised him, he looked so old and haggard.

Violet had achieved everything she had always wanted: the forgiveness of her children for abandoning them; a new home, and the love of her family. Now, with the single flick of a madman's lighter, it was all gone, along with most of the skin on her hands and forearms.

She'd had no choice but to tell the police everything, especially as Naomi was able to give such a good description of the man they called The Falcon, who had been linked with several arson attacks in London in the past but had never been charged.

Violet wasn't worried about herself. As far as she was concerned, her life was over. She might have been hailed a hero, having saved the life of Jimi Singh, who had been air-lifted to a specialist burns unit in a critical condition, his distraught parents by his side, but in the process she had opened a repulsive, shocking can of worms, and she knew for certain her family wouldn't forgive her this time.

Once again, she was to be the cause of her family being featured in the national news, together with newsreel on the television of Councillor Charles Kingston, the Mayor of Kettering in Northamptonshire, being handcuffed and led away by police, charged with running a brothel.

Tomorrow, the news reports would be all about Sergio de Luca, missing presumed dead twenty years ago.

In the space of just two days, she was back to square

one, every bit as exposed and lonely as she had been at the age of nine, when her parents had forced her to shave her head every week. Only this time she was left as helpless as a baby, unable to do even the most basic of things for herself, because her burns were so severe, there was no guarantee doctors would be able to save her hands.

Until recently, Violet had hardly ever cried. It was a luxury she very rarely allowed herself. But now, with George and Elsie looking after Naomi, Martin looking after Lydia, and Jimi's parents looking after him, who was there to look after and care for her?

She doubted anyone would ever speak to her again now the disgusting truth about her had been revealed. Even the only friend she had ever made in her life, Marigold Kingston, had been caught up in the tragedy, too.

Still, at least this time, no one had died.

The next day, the door to Violet's sterile room at the hospital squeaked open. She opened her eyes, hardly able to believe that someone cared enough to pay her a visit, even though it was now Christmas Eve and her sixtieth birthday.

Once again, it was Daisy Roberts who plucked her from the jaws of despair, just as she had done fifty-one years ago. At first, she thought her heart was about to break for good when Daisy imparted the sad news that Lydia had passed away peacefully in her sleep the previous day, completely unaware of the drama of the past two days. Then she could hardly believe that Daisy had stayed with her, stroked her cheek, combed her hair for her and comforted her as she cried, sobbed and wailed for nearly two hours, as a lifetime of tears that had been welling behind her eyelids for weeks was shed in a single afternoon.

Then, exhausted by all the crying, she watched in surprise as the door to her room opened again to reveal two more visitors. Naomi appeared first, looking more vulnerable than she had ever appeared before, even at the age of nine when she and Violet had first crossed swords.

Then Martin had followed, encircling his arms around his daughter's shoulders.

'Oh Violet,' Martin said. 'What on earth are we all going to do without her?'

'Are you all right, Grandma?' Naomi had said, her voice hoarse and croaky from all the smoke she had inhaled in the fire.

And with that one, single word she had been desperate to hear, Violet's life flooded back into her in glorious technicolour.

Chapter Twenty-four

2007

The village church at Barton Seagrave stood slightly elevated, overlooking the village green. The cottage where Naomi's Aunt Daisy had lived decades before stood at the edge of the green, the bright spring sunshine picking out the pale yellow stone, adorned with an abundance of sugar pink, pure white, sky blue and deep mauve clematis clambering up the walls of the cottage like hundreds of bright sapphires, rubies and diamonds. Proud rhododendrons flowered either side of the front gate, the buttercup yellow and waxy red flowers filling the air with a delicious rose-like fragrance that mingled with wafts of early, fragrant honeysuckle that grew in abundance in and around the churchyard. It was as if the cottage had embellished itself in the brightest of colours having waited eighty-four years to be a guest at a Jeffson family wedding.

The leaves on the tall trees that rose majestically from the village green rustled and whispered as if serenading the bride and groom As the sun flirted with clouds overhead, wedding guests started to arrive, the women standing around in groups dressed in bright outfits and the men looking uncomfortable in suits they were unaccustomed to wearing. Laughter pierced the air as old acquaintances were renewed. A group of children played in the churchyard and were called back by their parents, worried they would get dirty and ruin their new outfits. Shiny, newly washed cars pulled into the crescent that encircled the village green and parked on the edge of the road.

Naomi Singh, still strikingly beautiful at the age of thirty-nine, stood on the periphery of churchyard watching the arrival of wedding guests. The atmosphere that surrounded her was somehow ethereal, as if she was an actress playing the final scenes in an epic story.

The bride's elder brother was chief usher and taking his duties very seriously. He looked at his watch, just as the bridesmaids and the bride's mother arrived

'Smile, mum – you're on camera,' he said to his mother as she alighted from the car, looking flustered as the official photographer took a snapshot of her.

People started to wander into the church in a thin disjointed stream, laughter and good spirits tinkling like a million wind chimes in the warm, spring breeze. The bridegroom looked pale and nervous when his best man patted his chest in mock horror as the pair made their way into church.

Soon, Naomi left her vantage point and slid into a vacant pew near to the back of the church. Her Uncle Tim looked around to see where she was. She smiled at him and gave a little wave just to let him know she was all right.

Naomi knew the bride wouldn't be late. She'd arrive exactly on time, radiant and happy and Naomi would, from her seat at the back of the church hear her declare to her proud dad that she was not nervous at all.

On cue, the scene was played out exactly as Naomi had imagined. The bride arrived, glowing with happiness on her father's arm as she waited in the doorway, Naomi turned and smiled at her.

'Hello, Emily,' she whispered. 'You look beautiful.'

The organ music changed, heralding the start of Emily's walk up the aisle on her father's arm. She carefully adjusted the position of an antique gold bracelet on her wrist so that it wouldn't be concealed by the wedding bouquet and glanced at her father: 'I'm not nervous, Dad,' she whispered. 'I'm really happy'.

After the service, the wedding party assembled in the

sunshine for photographs. As she was alone, Naomi hung back in the church until last, and watched the sunlight stream through the stained glass windows, splitting into a myriad of glorious multi-coloured beams.

While the wedding party were having their photographs taken, Naomi slipped out of the church, and made her way around the periphery of the church grounds, smiling at people she didn't know and acknowledging those she did. She soon spotted her Aunt Daisy, standing in a crowd of relatives by the church, looking straight at her. She raised her hand and waved, trying to catch her attention, but sensed Daisy hadn't noticed her.

She glanced over her shoulder, but all she could see were rhododendrons behind a gate a few feet away. She blinked, temporarily blinded by the sun.

When her vision cleared, there was a young girl standing only inches away from her on the other side of the gate, one hand delicately resting on the smooth time-worn timber of the top rail. She dressed in a striking, nineteen-twenties style, dropped-waist powder blue dress, her dark blonde bobbed hair shining and blowing slightly in the warm honeysuckle-laden breeze.

'Hello,' she said to Naomi. 'What's happening? Who's getting married?'

'It's a distant cousin of mine' Naomi said. 'Her name's Emily'

'Emily? Who's Emily? Why is she wearing my bracelet?'

The young woman had begun to cry, the tears rolling down her cheeks. Naomi fumbled in her bag, looking for a tissue.

'Here,' Naomi muttered into her bag 'Don't cry ...'

She looked up and held out the tissue.

The girl was gone.

As the photographer asked the wedding party to prepare for the group photograph, Naomi turned her attention back to the wedding, waving again at her Aunt Daisy, who at the age of ninety-two, looked magnificently regal in her navy blue suit and hat. Naomi felt proud of her – she didn't even need to use a walking stick, she was so fit. Then, her Aunt Daisy took her Uncle Tim's arm and walked purposefully back up the pathway into the church. She hadn't seen her, after all.

Naomi looked around for more familiar faces, not exactly self-conscious because she was on her own, but very much aware that two of the people she was supposed to be with had gone back into the church.

'Would you like a lift to the reception?'

Daisy's youngest son, Neil, stepped out in front of the tall woman who he'd noticed was on her own. He'd spotted her walking down the lane towards the church earlier as he'd driven past, looking for a parking place.

'Oh, thanks. That's really kind of you. I was hoping someone would offer me a lift. I'm supposed to be with my father, but he's a doctor and has been called away on an emergency.'

She decided to introduce herself, just in case he hadn't recognised her, and smiled self-consciously. 'I'm Naomi Singh, and you're Neil Roberts, aren't you? '

Neil was mesmerised. The second she'd mentioned her name was Naomi, he knew who she was, but he couldn't quite equate his last memory of her with the exceptionally striking woman who stood before him. She was perfectly proportioned, although she was the type of woman who would never be classed as slender. She was almost six feet tall, with flawless, slightly tanned skin, a hint of freckles across her nose and cheeks and straight, shiny brown hair. Her eyes were dark brown – so dark they were almost black. She wore a cream coloured tailored trouser suit that contrasted perfectly with her dark hair and eyes. She was not wearing a hat and the simplicity of her outfit and the fact she wore only the barest amount of make-up appealed to Neil.

'Naomi! Good grief, where *have* the years gone? The last time we met, you had just been stripped almost naked in my mother's kitchen sink howling because your mother had put Vim on your legs and had scrubbed them with a nailbrush. Your knees were bright red.'

'Don't remind me – I remember it well. I think I was about nine and had just got covered in motorbike oil. You'd come back from Canada, visiting your parents. You're back for good now, aren't you? Aunt Daisy told me you were coming back soon, but I didn't realise you would be here in time for the wedding.'

Neil stepped beside her and took her arm. 'My car's over there.' He pointed to a gleaming, brand new gunmetal grey Range Rover Sport.

Naomi's eyes widened. 'The Range Rover?'

'Yeah. Kinda nice isn't it? I treated myself when I got back.' Neil flicked the button on the key fob from a few yards away and the doors opened with a reassuring clunk.

Naomi slid into the sleek, cool passenger seat and inhaled the expensive smell of new leather. Neil took off his jacket and hung it in the back of the car. As he settled into the driver's seat she caught a whiff of distinctive aftershave. She stared at Neil's profile. Although by now he must be in his mid-fifties he'd weathered well, with just a hint of greying hair around his temples and a few laughter lines radiating from the corners of his eyes betraying his age. His designer glasses gave him an air of a distinguished successful businessman, which, she supposed, was exactly what he was. His hair was still thick and lustrous, well cut with just a hint of a curl around his collar adding a dash of vulnerability. When he spoke, his English accent was shot through with the merest hint of a Canadian drawl.

He flicked his thumb over the steering wheel controls of the CD player and, surprisingly, an up-to-date dance beat drifted out of the car's speakers. Naomi smiled – she had been expecting classical music, or perhaps some classic rock.

Neil, catching the smile from the corner of his eye, glanced at Naomi.

'What's so funny?'

'This music!'

'Why?'

'It's not what I expected.'

Neil leaned over and deftly opened the passenger side glove compartment. He rootled around and pulled out a CD case entitled *Ibiza Anthems*. He handed it to her without taking his eyes off the road and grinned.

'I'm not a decrepit old man, you know. There's still plenty of life in the old dog yet!' He rolled his eyes for dramatic effect.

'Ever been to Ibiza?' Neil asked her.

'No. My husband, Jimi, and I would have loved to have gone when we were teenagers, but he was badly hurt in a fire and so couldn't travel easily.'

'I remember hearing about that!' Neil said. 'Your grandmother was hurt, too, wasn't she?'

'Yes. She still can't use her hands properly. She saved Jimi's life, though. So I am always grateful to her for that.'

'I was so sorry to hear that your husband had died,' Neil said, wanting to spare Naomi having to explain everything. 'My mother told me.'

'That's all right. It was two years ago now. His lungs were always very weak because they were damaged so much in the fire. He caught pneumonia and that was that. I was a bit of a mess to start with after he died. Jimi meant everything to me. But I'm not even forty yet and I know I have to keep on living, somehow. No point in being miserable, is there, because you only make everyone around you miserable too. Anyway, enough about me. Have you ever been to Ibiza?'

Neil shook his head. 'No, I've never been – living mostly in Canada it's a bit too far – but the club scene aside, it is supposed to be the most beautiful island in the Mediterranean.'

Naomi laughed. 'From what I hear it's noisy, full of lager louts and swearing, litter-dropping Brits and bolshie Germans, and the drinks are a rip-off!'

Soon, they arrived at the reception. 'We'll continue our

Ibiza conversation over our meal,' Neil said.

'We might not be sitting together for the reception.' Naomi laughed. 'I am supposed to be sitting with my dad, Uncle Tim and his wife. I don't know when he'll get here, though. When he's out on an emergency there's no way of knowing.'

They walked a few yards to the hotel where the reception was being held. 'Well, I'll just sit in your dad's place, then,' Neil said. 'And he can sit in mine when he gets here. He won't mind sitting next to Mum will he? And Tim and I will promise not to talk about Canada all afternoon.'

After they had been greeted by the bride and groom at the door, Naomi walked over to a table laden with welcome drinks and picked up two glasses of white wine. She looked around for Neil whilst sipping from one of them. He was laughing and joking with the bride's mother.

She took a sip of wine and held out the other glass as he walked back over to her. 'I got this for you, but I don't know if you're drinking – or even if you like wine.'

Neil smiled. 'I love wine – but by the bottle, not the glass usually.'

They stood comfortably together, their arms almost touching. Although Naomi didn't feel obliged to strike up a conversation, she did so after a few seconds.

'Are you back for good, then?'

Neil put down his glass and motioned to Naomi to sit down at an empty table in the foyer. 'Yeah. I think so. You've probably heard, I've just broken up with my partner of over twenty years. The only thing was, I was also a partner in her father's business, so it made everything kinda awkward. That's why I've come back – to make a clean break.'

'Do you have any children?'

'Good God, no! We never got round to getting married let alone having any kids. Do you?'

Naomi shook her head and put her glass down before crossing her legs at the knee. 'No. Jimi and I would have loved children, but we couldn't ever have any because of his injuries.'

Neil gave a nervous cough and grimaced. 'I'm sorry ...'

Naomi shook her head. 'Don't be. It didn't make any difference to me, because I loved him. The most important thing was that he was alive.'

They sat looking at each other, neither of them speaking. Neil leaned forwards to place his wine glass on the table.

'Your mum died of breast cancer, didn't she? I remember because your Uncle Tim was devastated.'

'When I was thirteen. It was two days after the fire that nearly took Jimi's life.'

'That must have been awful for you, and so young to lose your mum. I can't imagine life without mine, even though I've lived in Canada since I was eighteen. We've always kept in touch regularly, though.'

'I absolutely love Aunt Daisy to bits – everyone does.' Naomi picked up her glass and took a sip of wine. 'I'm lucky I still have my grandma and my dad, though. Do you remember Dad? His name's Martin.'

'Of course I do. I was at your mum and dad's wedding.' Neil hesitated, unsure as to what to say. He decided to be frank and open about it.

'It was an awful day. Terrible. Absolutely horrific.' He shook his head, remembering.

'I know. I've heard the story. Dad still finds it difficult to talk about, even now.'

They sat quietly for a while, listening to snippets of conversation that drifted around them.

'I haven't given up hope of having a baby one day.' Naomi said as she took another sip of wine. Suddenly she realised what she had said, and how it could be taken by Neil, and giggled behind her hand, her eyes dancing and crinkling with laughter.

'What are you laughing at?' Neil held out his wine glass and glanced down at his shirt. 'Have I dribbled, or something?'

'No! I just realised what I said – about wanting a baby. I got a sudden vision of you taking off and shooting out of here like a crazy frightened puppy in case you thought I meant with you!'

Neil laughed. 'I'm afraid I'm no puppy. I'm fifty-six.' He got up and walked over to the wine table and took two more glasses. He continued the conversation where he left off as he sat down. 'I'd have liked to have had children too. Celia and I kept putting everything off, you know, going on holidays to the States, living something of a nomadic lifestyle, saying perhaps next year, but never really meaning it, and before we knew it we had both hit fifty. We just left it too late. Now she's gone off with a geeky twenty-three year old IT technician. Her father is livid.'

'Oh dear! Dumped for a younger man.' Naomi smiled cheekily. 'More fool her. I'd go for maturity and experience any day. So what are you planning to do now?'

Neil grinned at the compliment.

'I've already told you. I've made my mind up. I've always wanted to go, so a trip to Ibiza is the first thing on the agenda.' He put his glass down and clasped his hands behind his head, stretching out his legs. He shut his eyes and thought out loud. 'Tiny, deserted coves bordered by turquoise sea and pine trees; supposedly the best sunset in the world; snorkelling in warm sea; licking the salt off my lips ...'

He suddenly sat up straight, his eyes twinkling mischievously. He leaned forwards, cradling his wine glass, his forearms resting on his knees.

'Let's go together, shall we. Can you get some time off work?'

Naomi laughed. 'I could, but I can't really afford it.'

'Oh, shut up about money! There's far more important things in life. I'll rent a villa or something. Go on – it's the chance of a lifetime.'

He raised his eyebrows, waiting for an answer. The air seemed somehow brittle and fragile, and he thought that if he moved or spoke another word the moment would be broken and come tinkling down around him.

'You're really serious, aren't you? You're not joking?' Naomi said.

'Well, as far as I know we only live once – there might be reincarnation, but who knows?' He shrugged his shoulders. 'So, will you come? Please?'

'I've only known you for a couple of hours,' she giggled. 'Oh, all right then. I suppose meeting once when I was a child somehow qualifies us as having known each other for most of our lives.'

Neil threw back his head and laughed so loudly, people nearby turned their heads to see what he was laughing at.

What on earth was she thinking of, agreeing to go on holiday with a man she had only just met? She gulped, sensing that she had just made a big decision, flippantly and with no regard for a respectable passage of time to think about it. What if Neil expected more than just friendship? How would she cope with that?

She studied Neil's eyes and all she could see were laughter lines, crinkling his skin around the edge. The depth in them was clouded with betrayal, hurt and the merest hint of grief. It was evident he had suffered, too, probably just as much as she had. She supposed that if Neil looked into *her* eyes he would be unable to see what was underneath her grief for Jimi, because no matter how hard people tried, no one understood how much she had loved him. But Jimi was dead and never coming back, and she instinctively felt it was now time for her to move on and begin to live the rest of her life.

She took a deep breath.

'When?'

'If I can get us a villa, how about next Friday?'

Daisy appeared beside them, wanting to know what they were laughing at.

'Hello Mum,' Neil said, taking off his glasses to wipe a tear of laughter from his eye. 'I'm sorry to have abandoned you, but you were okay with Eileen, weren't you?'

'I see you've re-acquainted yourself with Naomi,' Daisy said. 'The last time you met her she was half naked in my kitchen, with bright pink knees.'

Naomi grinned. 'That was Uncle Bill's fault. He made me get dirty mending his motorbike.'

Neil motioned towards a spare chair. 'Why don't you sit down with us for a while, Mum?'

'Just how are Neil and I related, Aunt Daisy?' said Naomi. 'I can't remember. It's so complicated.'

Daisy puffed out her lips. 'Well,' she said. 'Neil – do you remember us talking about Doris?'

'Yeah,' he said. 'I think so.'

'Is that the same Doris who was my great-grandmother?' Naomi asked.

'That's right, Naomi. Doris was my mother's sister'

'We must be second or third cousins, then.' Neil said, turning to Naomi. 'See – it's perfectly respectable.' He swivelled around in his chair to face his mother. 'I've asked Naomi to come to Ibiza with me for a holiday. She's said yes.'

Daisy's heart missed a beat. Could it be that there was a spark between Neil and Naomi? She hoped not – it would be a disaster and couldn't happen. 'That's nice. It'll do you good to have a little holiday,' she said, despite herself.

Daisy knew immediately that Naomi had misread the unexpected look of consternation in her eyes from the wilting smile she shot her before turning to Neil.

'But there's one condition,' Naomi said quickly. 'I shall pay my own way. I don't expect you to pick up the bill for everything.'

Neil shook his head. 'I insist. I've plenty of money sloshing around from selling my share of the business, and I was planning to go on holiday anyway. It means I won't have to go alone.'

Chapter Twenty-five

It was slightly overcast when Naomi woke on the first day in Ibiza, the rising sun colouring the bubbly grey clouds in hues of mustard and butterscotch. The window was open and a breeze, laced with the aroma of pine trees, rattled the wooden blinds. Momentarily disorientated, she remembered where she was.

She could hear the rattle of cups in the kitchen, and the sound of soft whistling as Neil made coffee, the aroma of it gradually wafting throughout the secluded villa. She shut her eyes again, hardly able to believe she had agreed to come on holiday with a man she had met only seven days ago.

She yawned, almost awake now. Nice things like this didn't usually happen to her – Naomi Singh – too big to be a proper woman; too tall to walk beside most men without feeling self-conscious. Jimi hadn't minded, though. With Jimi her height had never been an issue because he had told her she was beautiful every day. She squeezed her eyes shut, determined that she was not going to cry over Jimi. Not today, anyway.

The door of her bedroom opened.

'Morning.'

Naomi levered herself up and her heart flipped. Neil's hair was uncombed and tousled, like a child's. He was grinning at her, his blue eyes sparkling and radiant, the sadness of a broken relationship chased away by the excitement of the first day of a holiday. His eyes crinkled, radiating years of experience, laughter and tears in a beacon of maturity. When he smiled, his energy was infectious.

His chest bare, he wore a pair of long shorts that stopped just short of his muscular calves. On his feet he wore unfastened brown leather sandals, slipped on with the childish exuberance of a little boy.

'Morning,' she replied, surprised at her lack of self-consciousness.

Neil placed the mug of coffee on her bedside cabinet, and sank onto her bed.

'Sleep well?'

Naomi nodded. 'Oh yes.'

'No regrets about coming here with me?'

She shook her head, pushing back sleep-tousled hair from her eyes. She could feel the warmth of his body on her leg and allowed herself the luxury of wallowing in the feeling. She hoped he would stay while she drank her coffee.

Seven days, she thought to herself. She'd only known him for seven days, but her body felt as if it had known him forever. She would have slept with Neil last night, had he asked her to. They'd given each other a platonic kiss before taking separate bedrooms, but Naomi had been willing. Part of her was relieved, because he'd shown her the type of respect that she knew was rare, but he'd only have had to say the word.

'Good,' said Neil.

He took her hand and gently pulled on her arm, before she could pick up her coffee. 'Come outside, there's something you need to see.'

Naomi slid out of bed, still holding Neil's hand. Padding barefoot through the open French windows, dressed only in her pyjamas, her eyes widened as she took in the perfect view. They were standing on a smooth patio and barbeque area; which was separated from the pool by white concrete ornamental balustrading. Steps led down to brilliant white marble slabs surrounding the clear, turquoise blue pool. A lush green lawn containing several sun loungers interspersed with planters and tubs of bright flowers surrounded the pool. Beyond the lawn an orchard of lemon and carob trees stretched as far as Naomi could see against the backdrop of pine clad hills in the distance. A breath of warm breeze shimmied across the still water of the pool.

'This must have cost you a fortune!' Naomi gasped. It had been dark when they'd arrived and she'd not appreciated either the size or the beauty of the location.

She realised Neil was still holding her hand when he gave it a slight squeeze. 'I need to say something to you,' he said. 'I want you to know that I don't expect ...'

He sighed and grinned at her, unable to find the right words. 'What I mean to say is that I've no ulterior motives.'

'I know,' Naomi said quietly, lowering her head at Neil's obvious embarrassment, but she was glad he'd said it. There was no pressure now. She needed to escape from the embarrassing moment, so she walked over to the balustrade and rested her hand on the smooth handrail. Out in the distance, nestled between hazy, pine-clad hills she spotted a dark blue-grey triangle, and with a tingle of excitement reminiscent of long-forgotten seaside holidays, realised she could see the sea.

'Oh, look,' she said, pointing towards the hills. 'There's the sea!'

Neil appeared beside her, his unfastened sandals flapping. He sat down onto the marble steps and patted the space next to him, inviting Naomi to join him. She sat down, hugging her knees. Her untidy hair fell across her eyes and she raised her hand to tuck it behind her ear.

Naomi stared at Neil's toes and then glanced at her own bare feet beside his, suddenly self-conscious as she realised that in the mayhem of the last few days, as they made last-minute arrangements, she had forgotten to paint her toenails. It suddenly seemed funny and she burst out laughing.

'Guess what,' she said, squinting sideways at Neil in a wry, lop-sided grin.

'What?'

'I must be the only female on the planet who would travel to Ibiza without painting her toenails.'

'That's exactly what I like about you.'

'What? That I don't paint my toenails?'

'No, silly. That you'd forget. It's something that is trivial and of no consequence, and yet most women I've ever known would think it was a priority and would spend long, boring hours plucking eyebrows, painting nails, exfoliating this, that and the other, putting themselves through agony getting waxed, stripped and goodness knows what. Celia would have done anyway. In fact, Celia would never have entertained going on holiday with less than at least two weeks' notice. I'm pretty sure that she used to enjoy the anticipation, packing and preparation more than the holiday itself.'

'I'm not like most women. That's the trouble. Even my marriage was unconventional.'

'What do you mean – trouble? You're good at the important things, Naomi. I know you visit my mother every week and through her, I feel we are more than just acquaintances, even though our paths crossed only once before.'

'I love Aunt Daisy. Everyone does.'

'What about your grandmother, though? After what she did to your mum and Uncle Tim, she doesn't deserve you, and yet still you don't have a bad word to say about her.'

Naomi felt defensive and embarrassed at the mention of Violet, who was now eighty-four years old and living in a nursing home.

'It wasn't always like that. I was horrible to her until I was thirteen, I hated her for what she did to Mum and Uncle Tim. But then Jimi gave me a good talking to. His parents were Sikhs and I admired so much of their religion. He said I was being self-centred and I should forgive her because everyone was capable of changing their lives. Then, after she saved Jimi's life in the fire, I realised my grandmother couldn't help her upbringing, or the terrible ordeals she had suffered. She led a hard life in London, too and spent a great big chunk of it under a dark cloud of depression. She's only got me, Aunt Daisy and Aunt Millie. Uncle Tim visits when he can, but he lives so far away.'

Neil's glance was full of admiration.

'You're one in a million Naomi.'

'No I'm not. Don't say that. You don't know me.'

'But you make me feel alive again. When I discovered Celia's affair I realised how hollow and superficial my life had been, even though we had been together for a long time. Do you know, she never once came back to England with me? She never even met my parents. It's as if the time between your parents' wedding day and the day Celia walked out on me is now just a blank void. It feels as if I've been living in some sort of vacuum, only to be thrust out into a world where I'm as naked and clueless as the day I was born. I'm fifty-six, Naomi, but emotionally, I feel as naïve as the awkward teenager who fled to Canada after witnessing his brother being crushed to death under the wheels of a double-decker bus. The only substantial part of my life has been my career, but even that was predicated on my relationship with Celia, because her father owned the company I worked for. Now, I feel like a lizard must feel when it sheds its skin.'

Naomi's heart thumped in her chest. She couldn't believe that her most private thoughts had been almost identical to Neil's. She'd also felt like she'd shed her old skin when she stepped onto the plane. She tentatively took his hand. He didn't pull it away, although she sensed a slight tightening of reticence, as if in self-defence.

'I felt exactly like that when we got on the plane last night, and again when I woke up just now and you stood in the doorway holding my coffee. My marriage was different, though. I loved Jimi and wouldn't change anything, even if I could. Our marriage was strong, despite his physical limitations. But I'm definitely not going to be a weeping, wailing widow all my life. I'm too young for that.'

The dark patches of clouds on the hills in the distance began to drift away as the sun turned the pine trees a shade lighter and the grey triangle of sea turned deep blue.

'Do you believe in fate, Neil?'

Neil didn't answer for a while, but eventually shook his head. 'No, I don't. Because if there was such a thing as destiny, fate, or call it what you like, it's stolen nearly forty years of my life. What do I have to show for it? No marriage; no children; and, now, no career. I wanted to get married and have children but the years drifted by, one by one, insignificant on their own, but collectively they turned into a huge chunk of shallow life, built around parties, holidays and socialising with people who were easy on the eye but hard to get to know or form friendships with. It was a lie, Naomi. My entire life in Canada, was an orchestrated, stage-managed lie, perpetuated by my strong drive to have a successful career and make lots of money. Now, I don't care about money because it can't buy the things in life I want, so my wealth has become worthless.'

'OK, then. Do you believe in love at first sight?'

Neil tightened his grip on Naomi's hand, frightened she would run away from him if he told the truth. He watched the sunlight creeping slowly towards the tangle of lemon and carob trees in the villa's untamed garden. Soon it would bathe them both in warm early-morning warmth. A breeze caught the water of the pool and the ripple captured sparkles of the approaching sun that were so bright they made him squint. He let go of Naomi's hand, carefully put his arm around her shoulders and drew her to him. She didn't resist. He could feel destiny begin to shake off his old, unsubstantial life as easily as a dog shaking water from its coat. If he hadn't spent most of his adult life in Canada he wouldn't be here now, with the woman who he was certain would become the love of his life. The chilliness of the marble steps beneath him and the sun's warming rays above him sandwiched him firmly in the moment and he allowed the unfamiliar feeling of security to overwhelm him.

A strange thought drifted into his mind. At the moment of Naomi's conception, had destiny whisked him away to a faraway place across the ocean out of harm's way? Had the wise hands of time then moulded and shaped her until the two of them fitted together perfectly. Was it fate that had brought him right here, right now into this moment. It must be. There was no other explanation.

His voice was almost a whisper as he gave his answer. 'Yes, to the second question on love at first sight, and I think I've just changed my mind on the first one about fate.'

A week after she had returned from her holiday, Naomi pulled up in her car outside her Aunt Daisy's house to a bright flash of lightning and almost simultaneous crack of thunder. Instinctively she cowered and folded her arms over her head, realising that the storm was right overhead. She decided to wait a while before making a dash for the front door. Grimacing at the sheets of rainwater coursing down the windscreen, she reached for her bag on the passenger seat and extracted her mobile phone to ask her aunt to open the front door.

There was no reply.

After a few minutes she decided to make a run for it. Realising she would be soaked through waiting for her aunt to open the front door, she dialled her Aunt Daisy's number again. Naomi frowned when, again, there was no reply, and tried once more. Perhaps she was upstairs? She pulled up the hood on her jacket, jumped out of the car and ran towards the house as quickly as she could, zapping the car on the run.

She rang the doorbell. When there was no response she tapped on the front window, peering through the slats in the blinds. The television was on in the corner of the room and there was a discarded newspaper and knitting on the sofa. Naomi frowned with increasing concern and wiped her wet face with the back of her hand as she opened the letterbox.

'Aunt Daisy. It's me, I'm getting soaked!' Naomi put her ear to the door. There was no reply. Worried, she went back to the front window. This time she could clearly see through the lounge to the kitchen and noticed that the back door was slightly open. She sighed and rang the doorbell again. Surely Aunt Daisy couldn't have forgotten the time. From the sound of her voice on the phone earlier, whatever she wanted to see her about was pretty urgent.

She ran around to the back gate and stood on a ceramic planter to look over the fence. She could see the back door was slightly ajar and detected a faint smell of roast chicken. She called over the gate.

'Aunt Daisy! Can you hear me? Can you let me in, I'm absolutely drowned.'

Feeling slightly annoyed, Naomi went back to her car. She looked at her watch – Aunt Daisy had said five o'clock when she had invited her to dinner in her urgent phone call earlier that day. It was now ten past five, so, she surmised, Daisy should have been waiting for her. She rang the number one more time on her mobile phone. Again there was no reply.

Sighing with frustration, she turned the ignition key and drove off. As she drove back home a niggling worry gripped her by the shoulders, arrested her thoughts and directed them back to Aunt Daisy. Could she have had an accident in the house, and was lying on the floor somewhere, unable to answer either the phone or the doorbell? She looked at her watch again and pulled over to the side of the road.

Waiting for a gap in the traffic so that she could turn around and go back, Naomi pulled out her mobile phone again and flicked through the contact list.

'Oh, blast!' she said out loud as she realised she didn't have her Auntie Eileen's phone number, or Daisy's other son, Trevor's, on her mobile phone. She sat and thought for a while. The only way she could get Eileen's phone number was to ring Neil. If she rang Neil, he would wonder why he was not invited to dinner, too. Daisy had been explicit – she wanted to talk to her alone and definitely didn't want her youngest son to know about it. She sighed. If Daisy didn't want Neil to find out, then she wouldn't have told Eileen or Trevor either.

In fact, Daisy had behaved very oddly when she had visited her with Neil last week, just after they arrived back from Ibiza. Although she had gone through the motions, expressing pleasure at the exciting news that they were now engaged, with plans to get married and have a family very soon, both she and Neil had detected a definite reticence, feeling they needed to state the obvious to her: that they were both single; neither of them was young or stupid, and if they wanted to get engaged after just three weeks, then there was nothing to stop them.

She should go back and climb over the gate. After all, the back door had been open and she could go in and check that everything was all right. She turned around quickly in the road and drove back to Daisy's house. By the time she arrived, the storm had abated and the sun had reappeared through a gap in the dark clouds, making it difficult to see in the glare of the steaming wet road. Naomi rang the front door bell, just in case Daisy had been unable to hear it above the noise of the torrential rain and thunder. When, once again, there was no reply, she clambered up onto the ceramic planter and then onto the lid of the wheelie bin. From there it was relatively easy to straddle the gate and lower herself down on the other side.

She pushed open the back door and a waft of heat from the oven hit her.

She gasped in shock. 'Oh, no! Aunt Daisy!'

Daisy was lying on the kitchen floor, her face grey, her eyes shut and her mouth open. She knelt down on the floor and with a trembling hand, felt Daisy's neck for a pulse. Her skin felt clammy and cold, even though the air outside was humid and muggy and the kitchen was warm. She put her cheek to Daisy's mouth to feel for her breath. She was breathing, but it was barely enough to make her chest rise and fall.

She dialled 999.

Twenty minutes later, after a rush of frantic telephone calls, the ambulance drove off, blue lights flashing, with Daisy inside.

Trembling with shock, Naomi went back into Daisy's house. With Eileen accompanying her mother in the ambulance, and Neil and Trevor both on their way to the hospital to meet the ambulance when it arrived, there was nothing more she could do. She decided to clear up in the kitchen and make herself a coffee to collect her thoughts before going home.

As she turned the oven off, and took out the roast chicken, she noticed a very old cookery book on the worktop. Naomi realised it was one that used to sit on a bookshelf in her mother's kitchen when she was a child. There was an envelope sticking out from amongst the pages, as if marking the place of a special recipe. Intrigued, Naomi picked up the book and slid out the envelope. It wasn't sealed, so she lifted the flap to see what was inside. Her fingers connected with a torn up, wrinkled sheet of paper, which had been stuck together again with Sellotape. Someone had obviously ripped it up, crumpled it in their hand and then thrown it away, only for it to be retrieved and painstakingly stuck together again.

Naomi smoothed out the letter, curiosity getting the better of her. Why was it written in mirror image? It was the strangest thing she had ever seen.

She wandered through into the lounge, absorbed in trying to decipher the back-to-front writing. Moving Daisy's knitting to one side, she sank down onto the sofa. Who on earth would write a letter in reverse? What was the point? And why had it been torn up and stuck together again. She looked up at the mirror above the mantelpiece.

'A mirror,' she mumbled.

She held up the letter and studied the reflection, noticing first the date. She frowned as she realised that the letter had been written only a week before her parents' wedding day. When she saw the letter was addressed to her mother, Lydia, her eyes refocused on the double-sided letter in her hand to see who had written it.

Stuart, Neil's brother who had died in an accident on her parents' wedding day, had written a letter to her mother.

Why? Naomi's hand shook as she held it up to the mirror, reading its message. Her heart began beating wildly.

The memories of a childhood spent as an only child began to make an unwelcome sense. She remembered Martin and Lydia's mysterious appointments, and then once overhearing her parents talking about giving her a brother or sister: something that had never materialised.

She continued to stare at her own reflection in the mirror and watched the tears form in the corners of her eyes and spill over her lower eyelashes. She looked around for a photograph of Stuart on the wall. The shadowy, unknown, shy youth she had never known seemed to animate before her eyes, and although she had seen the photograph many times, it was with a new perspective that she studied his haunting eyes and the shape of his nose and his chin. Staring at Stuart's face she recalled her mother's features - her dark hair, the shape of her face, her nose and eyes. She became aware of her own reflection in the glass, superimposed over the framed photograph as if the terrible secret had finally reached its destination after a lifetime of lurking in the shadows. Time slowed as her own eyes merged with Stuart's in the glass to be imprinted forever on her heart as if it had just been branded with a hot iron.

Then, as the thunderstorm, now way in the distance, gave a last weak, flash of lighting, her heart seared with a pain so forceful, it almost struck her down to her knees. If Stuart was really her biological father, then she could never, ever marry his brother.

Bile rose into her throat and made her gulp. Her hand flew to her mouth in horror. She might have committed incest – not just once or twice but many times in the past month. She clamped both hands over her mouth and bit into her palm hard as the tears spilled out of her tightly shut eyes.

Aunt Daisy knew. And this letter was the reason she had been summoned to her house for tea.

She looked at the first line of the letter:

"I have given this letter to Millie for safe-keeping ..."

Aunt Millie.' She said the name out loud.

Millie, now elderly, confused and suffering from dementia, was in the same nursing home as her grandmother, and she visited them both every week. Should she try and find out some more information? She shook her head. No, it was out of the question. With trembling hands, Naomi folded the letter and put it into her handbag. The probability was that the only people still alive who knew of the letter's contents, and therefore the possibility that Stuart might be her biological father, were Daisy and Millie.

The image of her kind and devoted father, Martin, materialised like a sobering spectre before her, and she realised with absolute certainty that there was no way in the world she was going to destroy him with the shocking knowledge that he might not be her father after all.

Naomi spent the next two days blanketed in a horrible nauseous feeling that constantly threatened to suffocate her. She couldn't eat; she had trouble stringing two sentences together and slept fitfully, her unconscious mind churning together her concern about Daisy following her stroke and the life-changing implications of the letter. She read and re-read it endlessly, until she could have quoted the contents, word for word, from memory. She realised on the second day that although the paper was yellow and obviously quite old, the Sellotape was newer – it was clear and had not aged at all, as she would have expected. That could only mean one thing – that it had been torn up a very long time ago and taped together again only recently. Closer examination revealed that the edges of the torn pieces had yellowed more than the rest of the paper, confirming her assumptions.

Daisy must have stuck it together. Millie could not have done, because she was too shaky and frail.

Finally, she made up her mind what she was going to do. She didn't know whether morally it was right or wrong, but she did know that she could never hurt the two most important people in her life – her father and Neil. Since Grandma Elsie had passed away peacefully in her sleep ten years ago, followed by George only twenty-four hours later, she was her father's only blood relative and his whole life. She knew it would surely destroy him to find out that he might not be her father after all.

DNA tests would probably be inconclusive as she and Neil *were* distantly related, his grandmother, Liz and her great-grandmother, Doris, being sisters. As she saw it, if Neil was her uncle – and it was only *if* – then they had already, unwittingly, broken the law. What really mattered was the question of children. In an effort to try to make sense of what had happened between her mother and Stuart, she researched schizophrenia on the internet. If seemed there was a real chance that any baby she and Neil conceived could inherit the condition anyway, even without the paternal uncertainty.

An even more complicated twist rose into her consciousness. She remembered past speculation about her grandmother's biological father. Her Aunt Daisy had suspected all her life that Neil's grandfather had also fathered her grandmother, Violet. If that were true, then that would mean they shared a lethal mix of genes. But she might be Martin's daughter, anyway. It was surely 50-50. There was no absolute proof Stuart was her father.

Exactly forty-eight hours after Stuart's letter to Lydia had come into Naomi's possession, she took it into her garden, lit a match and set light to it – watching wafts of smoke curl silently into the early evening air, the past disappearing into nothingness. She lifted her eyes skyward and whispered out loud.

'Well, Mum? If you are up there, watching, then this secret dies now. I can't give up Neil and I can't turn Dad's world upside down. I don't care about the genetics. The past belongs in the past.'

Early the next morning, Neil and Naomi were sitting quietly, eating breakfast, watching television. Having stayed over at her house the night before, Neil was exhausted and emotionally drained. Until he arrived late last night, he and his brother and sister had sat at his mother's bedside constantly since she had been taken to hospital.

On the television that week there had been a series of interviews on adoption and fostering on the early morning show. The timing couldn't have been better.

'Neil' Naomi said purposefully.

'Umm ...?' he replied through a mouthful of toast.

'I've been watching this programme all week. I know we said we would like to try to have a child together once we are married, but ...' She shook her head.

He nodded, swallowing his toast. 'I know. I understand.'

She knelt down on the floor in front of him and put her arms around him resting her head in his lap. 'I'm probably going to be over forty before we have a baby. I don't think I want a baby at forty – and you will be nearly sixty. It's too old, Neil. Too old for both of us. It might be what some women would want, but it's not for me.'

Neil stroked her hair. 'To tell you the truth, I was worried about that too. I feel the same. If you desperately wanted a child, then there would be no question – I'd be perfectly happy to try.'

Naomi lifted her head and looked him in the eye. 'It's funny that fostering and adoption has been on breakfast television all week. Why have one of our own, when there are so many older children out there who need parents? What do you think?'

'With Mum in hospital and the prognosis after her stroke so poor, we need to tread water with our wedding plans for a while anyway,' he said. 'Even if she does make some sort of a recovery she is going to be very disabled. Time is against us if we want our own baby, but I agree we do have a lot to offer an older child'

Naomi gave him a hug in reassurance. 'We'll cope. We'll all cope. Don't worry about the wedding. After all, it's not as if we were planning a big luxurious do, is it?'

Neil shook his head. 'I'm so glad I faced my demons and came back to England. If I hadn't come home I wouldn't have met you, and I wouldn't have had some precious time with Mum before she had her stroke.'

He bent his head and kissed her hair. 'It's a funny thing, is destiny. I feel at peace with myself and my life, even though my mother is so ill in hospital and I'm worried sick about her.'

'It was all meant to be,' Naomi sighed. 'My mother and Uncle Tim being abandoned, your brother's accident and even the fire; my mother dying of cancer and then Jimi leaving me a widow at the age of thirty-seven. Every single thing that has happened in this family has been destined. Who cares about what people did or didn't do in the past? Now, everything is about *us*, in the here and now. That's what matters. We shouldn't have a baby just because it's something we both once wanted, with different people, in a different life.'

'I couldn't have put it better myself,' Neil said smiling as he stroked her hair again.

'After all, it's only a seed – a tiny little seed. And a seed doesn't make someone a father.'

Chapter Twenty-six

An orange hue, peculiar to the early hour of the day, lit up the sky and flooded through the floor to ceiling glazing. As the rising sun danced and flirted with night's receding shadows it created a surreal, almost magical, view of the approaching visitors. Multiple footsteps invaded the eerie, golden silence.

Outside, the warmth of the watery light coaxed a fresh new day from manicured lawns. The garden was crammed with fragrant, colourful summer flowers that shimmered with a mysterious dewy iridescence as they basked in the sun's weak rays.

In the deserted corridor, a tall, well-dressed man was followed a couple of steps behind by an awkward, lanky youth. Uncomfortable in his best suit and tie, the young man's chestnut eyes were hidden behind black-rimmed glasses giving him an air of intellect. His dark hair flopped down over his forehead and with a nervous hand he pushed it back with a slight toss of his head. He was carrying a red-haired baby boy just on the verge of toddlerhood.

The older man hesitated for a moment as he reached the end of the corridor. Surrounded by an aura of dignity he turned to face his son, shrugging his shoulders with hands upturned.

'We didn't bring any flowers or anything,' he whispered. 'I should have arranged to bring her favourite flowers – she always loved daffodils, tulips and crocuses.'

'She won't be thinking about flowers, Dad, she's waited long enough to see us all again.'

The dispassionate, sterile corridor remained deserted as

the visitors observed two nurses tending an elderly lady through glazed door panels. Peaceful and breathing evenly she appeared to be sleeping as a nurse gently touched her wrist, measured her pulse and then smoothed down the sheets. The peace and quiet of the hospital ward was punctuated with an intermittent, but regular, beep of electronic monitoring equipment and the faint smell of alcohol gel hung in the air.

One of the nurses stroked the elderly lady's cheek.

'She must be a very special person,' she whispered to her male colleague. 'She has so many visitors. They come in their droves, young people, elderly people, children – it seems as if the entire town has visited Daisy since she was in here.'

Daisy's eyes flickered open and she raised her eyebrows at the young, male nurse. 'I'm certainly feeling nothing special stuck in this bed,' she said with a weary chuckle, 'but I really do feel much better today.'

She lifted her head slightly and smiled at the two nurses, oblivious to her distorted expression, the series of unintelligible low grunts and solitary dribble of saliva that had escaped from her lop-sided mouth.

'It's such a relief to be able to talk and move again. I don't think I'm too bad actually. I'm a tough old bird, you know.'

The male nurse smiled a compassionate acknowledgement as Daisy uttered disjointed, incoherent sounds and attempted to give him a cheeky wink.

She checked the mechanics of tentative movement in her hands and fingers. She could feel her fingertips moving over the textured bedcover and was relieved to have some sensation again.

The two nurses closed the curtains around Daisy's bed and left the ward, brushing past the waiting visitors without acknowledging them.

Daisy shut her eyes and turned on her side, feeling pleased with herself as her body seemed to respond to the instructions from her brain. She wasn't in any pain, but a feeling of extreme exhaustion washed over her, disguised as gentle undulating waves in a warm ocean, and she soon fell asleep as she floated, young and free, in the comforting turquoise water.

The ward gradually became busier. Ancillary staff arrived, chatting and laughing as a noisy, battered tea trolley rattled over the slight imperfections in the floor. The sun rose higher in the sky and filtered through the window blinds as it gained in strength. A porter's witticisms drifted through the air as he joked with another patient, cheerful dialogue mingling with the aroma of coffee and toast wafting through the ward.

In the office, the male nurse was discussing Daisy's condition with the ward sister. There was no hope. Everyone knew Daisy was going to die. For two months they had cared for her as, day-by-day she appeared to sink deeper and deeper into the bed, losing vast amounts of weight. The male nurse felt despondent as he shook his head.

'I don't know what's keeping her alive. It's incredible. I've never known anyone to hang on for this length of time.'

'Love,' the sister said, with a wise nod of the head. 'You can almost touch it when her family visit.'

'She must have been an incredible person,' said the male nurse. 'I wish I could have known her properly. She regained consciousness a few minutes ago, just for a moment. I think she tried to speak to me.'

The ward sister touched his arm. He was an excellent nurse and she knew he had grown fond of Daisy. They all had. It was as if she radiated an unseen energy that beckoned people to her bedside, even though she was unable to communicate with them.

A subconscious perception of normality penetrated Daisy's senses as she slept and she began to stir, her eyelids flickering. Through a slight gap in the curtains around her cubicle, and through unspectacled, tired eyes, she noticed the blurred images of two men and a child waiting at the door. She squinted, wondering who they were and which patient they were visiting.

With a sudden flash of memory she remembered what had happened to her. Was it yesterday or the day before? Or was it some days ago? Or even a week or more? Time seemed to spin a cocoon around her, twisting its silken strands through her senses and folding in on itself in endless ripples. She was confused and disorientated. What day was it? What week was it? What year was it?

Just a few heartbeats later, Daisy was startled by an unexpected but clear memory of the panic she had felt seconds before everything had gone black with a blinding pain in her head. She rolled over in bed to grasp her emergency buzzer. With a sinking heart she recalled the risk she had been about to take that awful afternoon as thunder rumbled in the distance and lightning flickered through her kitchen, filling the muggy air with ozone as she had prepared a meal for Naomi.

Had she come? Was it Naomi who had discovered her, unconscious on the kitchen floor? Or had she rang the doorbell and, getting no reply, merely gone home to set in motion the terrible chain of events that Daisy had been so desperate to avert?

Agitated, and with a feeling of increasing dismay at her failure to intervene, Daisy called out for help, her hand connecting with the emergency buzzer as she made a last, anguished, attempt to halt destiny.

Curiousness tinged with trepidation drew her into its embrace as she realised she had not reached for the buzzer at all. Her body had not responded and, although she could feel her finger stabbing repeatedly at the button, with a tumbling feeling of dread she realised it wasn't.

A shadow fell across her face. Relieved, she felt a smooth, cool hand cover hers. She looked up and her astonished expression melted into one of joyous recognition when she saw who had come to her aid, and the familiar but long forgotten features of his face.

'Hello, Daisy,' said the man. 'It's been such a long time.'

Daisy gasped in astonishment as she sat bolt upright in her hospital bed. It was not at all difficult to sit up, as she had expected. She glanced around the ward, which had taken on an ethereal and ghostly appearance, as if she was looking through a fog. Her eyes fell on her bed, where a few minutes before she had been struggling to reach the buzzer with an unyielding hand. With a sudden calmness and clarity of mind she realised that she had somehow passed out of her physical body. Her lifeless form lay motionless like a frozen statue on the bed, her facial features mask-like and waxy. It was surprisingly of no consequence to Daisy and she felt no attachment to the body on the bed whatsoever.

She turned her attention to the two men and child who stood, unblemished, healthy and crystal clear before her eyes. She wanted to cry out with joy, but a feeling of love and happiness such as she had never known before was consuming her and she felt humbled and small. Daisy gratefully and willingly relinquished control and let herself almost glide into their embrace as the world around her dimmed and a shimmering light took its place. She realised that words, at that moment, would be superfluous – belonging in the world she had just left. The silence seemed somehow very sacred and precious.

She touched Bill's face first. It felt warm, smooth and incredibly very much alive. He kissed her palm, just as he used to do in life. She then turned her attention to Stuart and reached out, holding his hand tightly. He was smiling at her and she heard him lightly whisper the word *"mum."* Lastly, she held out her arms for Oliver and felt the familiar weight of him as she held him close and buried her face in his fragrant soft golden-red baby hair. She felt his little hands grasp against what felt like her bare skin. She breathed, 'I was always meant to be your mother, little Oliver. It didn't matter that someone else gave birth to you.'

She handed Oliver back to Stuart as Bill took her hand and led her through busy corridors to the hospital garden. She looked back at the hospital and watched the hustle and bustle of comings and goings. People hurrying to appointments walked towards them and then, with unseeing eyes, straight through them. Sounds were distorted as if being heard through water and the only smell that pervaded her senses was that of the flowers in the garden, which was much more inviting than the antiseptic aroma of the cold, stark hospital building. Pure white stone statues glowed in the morning sunshine and rustic seats had been placed in strategic places so as to invite the many people who passed through to stay for a short while and enjoy its peace and solitude before they went on their way.

Beyond the garden was a meadow, dappled with millions of dots of yellow and white buttercups and daisies. The meadow stretched as far as the horizon, where the idyllic landscape gave way to a busy road bordering a kaleidoscope of variously sized and coloured buildings in the distance.

For the first time since she had passed over into this strange and yet welcoming world Daisy heard a clear, sharp voice.

'Let's sit for a while, love.' Bill motioned his hand towards a garden bench. The wooden seat was smooth and warm in the summer sunlight and Daisy gratefully sat down.

Stuart looked back at them, holding Oliver by the hand. He waved and walked towards the meadow beyond the garden, where he helped Oliver to gather handfuls of daisies, which they then began to make into a daisy chain.

'What happens now?' Daisy questioned.

Bill put his finger to his lips and shook his head. He took her in his arms and kissed her. They sat, arms around each other for a while. Daisy thought she had never seen such a beautiful place. The intensity of the fragrances – lavender, honeysuckle, roses and sweet peas – were stronger than she had ever smelled in life, and the birds sang clearly and tunefully as if serenading her soul in its brand new plane of existence. As Daisy and Bill sat, basking in the warmth and enjoying the peace and solitude they saw some more people, like them, leave the hospital and walk happily towards the garden.

Daisy gazed out across the meadow, where Stuart and Oliver were crouched down picking flowers. She shaded her eyes. 'What's that town over there? I don't recognise this landscape at all.'

'That, my love, is where we are going. There are lots of people waiting for you – your mam and dad, Rose, George, Elsie, Bert. Everyone. Some have been waiting a long time.'

'Well, I *was* ninety-two.' Daisy said proudly. She almost laughed out loud that death had really been nothing to worry about at all. In fact, she had hardly realised that it had happened, the transition had been so smooth. She wished she could go back and tell people not to worry about it.

'Can we ever go back?' Daisy's voice mirrored her thoughts.

Bill nodded. 'Of course. We can go back whenever we like. We can watch and learn how to put comfort and thoughts into their dreams and daydreams – but they will never see us again – that is not until we fetch them when it's their time to join us.'

'I suppose you know about Naomi and Neil, if you've been watching them?'

Bill nodded. 'Yes. I know everything.'

'I tried to stop it, Bill, but couldn't. It was too late. There was nothing I could do. That was when I had my stroke. I suppose you were there then, too?'

Bill nodded again. 'I caught you as you fell, but you were such a tough cookie, and so determined to do what you thought was right, you clung on to life like a limpet to a rock and I had to let you go again.' He smiled ruefully at Daisy. 'If you hadn't been so stubborn, I would have taken you then, and saved you all that indignity in the hospital.'

'I *had* to try and stop them, Bill. I suppose it's what drove me on. They want a baby – and Naomi might be Stuart's child.' She gazed in the direction of the two figures in the meadow. 'She will be marrying her uncle and that's illegal.'

'Daisy. You have to let it all go now. You absolutely must – or else you won't be able to move on. Did you know that around one in ten people on earth are not biologically fathered by the man who brings them up?' He placed his hand over his heart. 'It's what people *feel* in here, in their souls, that matters. That's what makes someone a parent.'

'But what will happen?'

Bill smiled. 'They've done nothing wrong. Can't you see, Daisy? There is nothing more to be done. Destiny can't be changed. It was time, Daisy. Time to leave everything behind. If you were meant to intervene then you would have done. Soon we'll pay them a visit and you'll see what I mean.'

'So what happens now – what happens to *us*. Do we just wait for Eileen, Trevor and Neil to join us? Just live our lives in that town over there as we did on earth – waiting?' Daisy was confused and yet hungry for more information of the strange perpetual existence which seemed so similar and yet so different from that she had just left. 'Then they'll have to wait for their children, and so on, into eternity?'

Bill laughed. 'It's all brand new to you Daisy. You'll learn how it all works, just like I did. Everyone does. The thing you will learn first of all, is that there is no escaping from the truth. It will come out – it is impossible to conceal, no matter how ashamed you are of what you did in life.'

'Will I see my mam and dad?'

'If you want to.'

Daisy was suddenly fearful for Tom's soul. 'Is Dad here, in heaven?'

Bill shook his head. 'No, Daisy, this is not heaven. We have to *earn* heaven.'

'Is there a hell?'

Bill nodded.

'Dad's not there, is he?' Daisy grimaced, thinking of Tom's many wrongdoings throughout his life.

Bill laughed. 'No, no, of course he's not. Hell is reserved for cold, unfeeling souls with no remorse or love. Tom wasn't like that. He just made mistakes, and all human beings make mistakes. Tom's genuine remorse during his life was his saving grace, together with his love for his children, grandchildren and great-grandchildren. He had a physical disorder in life that distorted his behaviour and made ordinary decisions difficult for him.'

Bill took Daisy's hand in his. 'It was even more painful for him when he came here – to face the people he cared about and have to tell the truth and talk about his feelings. Now, Daisy, he will have to face you – he's been waiting so long for you to come.'

Bill hesitated and then went on. 'I have been really proud of you Daisy. You have been so brave. So strong. So honest. I saw your silent tears in the dead of night and tried to give you some comfort, I sat by your bedside, night after night, as you slept and wove little thoughts into your sub-consciousness so that you would wake in the morning and I could see the smile on your face as you remembered them.'

Daisy shut her eyes and smiled, recalling her dreams.

Bill stood up. The time had come for them to move on and make their way through the meadow to the distant town. He held out his hand to Daisy.

She took one last glance over her shoulder at the hospital, which now seemed even more distant and hazy. Gazing out towards their destination she felt the sun on her face and an intense feeling of love and happiness in her heart as she waved to Stuart and Oliver. Bill and Daisy held hands as they walked through the gate, reminiscent of a similar walk, hand in hand, step for step, when, as fifteen year-olds, they had escaped from Tom after hiding in a wardrobe. She realised she felt exactly as she did then – full of hope for the future.

'What about Aunt Doris?' Daisy hardly dare ask the question, remembering Doris's suicide at Wicksteed Park, taking Oliver with her.

'She's with the rest of the family, waiting for you. Now you are here, everything depends on you, Daisy.'

'What depends on me?'

'You have to tell this family's life story.'
'How am I going to do that?'
'Don't worry. You'll find a way.'

THE END

THE EPILOGUE

Hello. I'm the author of Daisy's life story.

I make no apology for bending and tweaking the past in a way that has made this family saga work for my readers. Everything you have read so far in this trilogy of novels is crafted in the mind of a writer of fiction: a carefully calculated and planned series of events, ideas, characters and plots. Although based on true stories, it is merely a series of words on a page that are arranged for your enjoyment.

I have tried my very best to tell this unusual family saga sensitively and with due respect to the characters, both real and imaginary. However, to end the trilogy here would be like dropping a stone into a pond and then trying to stop the ripples.

I think I always knew I would have to continue writing, even though I have typed "THE END". You see, some of the characters have lived real lives and death is a destination we all arrive at eventually. If you don't want to read about real-life people arriving at this destination, then please do stop here, put down this book and, like Naomi in the story, let the truth whisper its way up into the stratosphere.

However, if you do decide to continue and read this lengthy epilogue, from this point onwards, you are about to read about something so true, precious and pure it will make you forever look up into the vast night sky and know, without any doubt, there is something much more to this microscopic world, and our briefest of existence upon it, than mere human beings can ever hope to understand.

This part of the story is not about religion. It is not about science. It is not supernatural, either, although many aspects of this final episode in the tale have made me think about the ultimate question of life, the universe and everything, as computed in the legendary novel *The Hitchhiker's Guide to the Galaxy*.

Simply put, it just "*is*".

Part One

9th August 2001

The inscription in Kettering's Book of Remembrance is embellished with a huge, hand-painted red rose.

I can't help the words bursting forth: 'Oh look – it's Gramp!'

My mother-in-law gives me a look that conveys intense irritation. I'm supposed to be quiet and reverent, looking at an inscription on the opposite page in memory of my father-in-law, Michael Ireson, who passed away a year ago today. My heart thumps in my chest as I jab my forefinger at the glass case. 'This is my great-grandfather's entry. He must have died on the same day of the year.'

Gramp's inscription is one of the biggest, most extravagant entries on the page. My mother-in-law frowns and looks down her nose. 'He must have been a popular man to have all those lines and that rose in his memory. Was he well off?'

'No,' I say. 'And nor was my grandma or any of her sisters. They must have clubbed together to pay for it. I'm sure Mum doesn't know about this, or she'd have mentioned it.'

After we have placed a memorial card on the table in the Chapel of Rest and paid our respects, we head off home. Later, I ring my mum, Margaret.

'You'll never believe what I discovered at the crematorium. Gramp must have died on the same day of the year as Rob's dad, and there's a huge inscription in the Book of Remembrance.'

'Are you sure?' Mum says after a moment of hesitation. 'It's just that I can remember when Gramp died, and the family decided not to have any sort of memorial.'

'Did he die in August?'

'It was the summer, definitely,' Mum says. 'But I can't remember the exact date. I'll ask Aunt Daisy when I see her.

She'll remember when it was'.

'Why did you decide not have a memorial for him?' I ask, suddenly curious. Mum's tone of voice has alerted me to the dark underbelly of something I obviously have never known about. 'That doesn't sound like Grandma or Aunt Daisy ...'

'Because of how things were,' Mum cuts in, clearly not wanting to go into any detail.

'Did he specify in his will that he didn't want an inscription?'

'No, nothing like that. It was because of how he'd treated people when he was alive.'

'He wasn't that bad, was he?'

There's a brief silence and rattling noise down the handset and I know mum is adjusting her hearing aid. I sigh. I might be in for a long phone call if her batteries are dying.

'He was a tyrant, Anne. Everyone was scared of him. He tried to make amends later in his life, and he'd mellowed by the time you were born. You wouldn't believe some of the awful things he did, but ...'

Mum's voice fades into nothing and I can tell she is changing her mind about revealing Gramp's sinister and secret side. 'Oh, I don't know. Let's talk about something else. I can't see any point in raking it all up now. And there's things even I don't know. It's not up to me to let the family's skeletons out of the cupboard to dance their way down the street.'

I grin at Mum's choice of words, but ignore her request. 'Go on. Tell me. You can't just say something like that about a dead person and then not explain.'

Mum sighs on the other end of the phone. 'It's best just to leave the past where it belongs. It will only bring back bad memories.'

'Oh well,' I concede. 'Just mention it to Aunt Daisy for me when you see her. She might remember someone putting it in. It's a big entry and Rob's mum said it must have cost the earth.'

After a few more minutes of general chit-chat, I ring off.

For some reason, I can't get Tom Jeffson out of my head, curious about all the "bad memories". I tentatively edge my way down a very narrow and misty memory lane. I was only fourteen when he died, but I can remember exactly how he looked and how his voice sounded, and even recall the distinctive smell of the tobacco he used in his pipe. However, all I can remember about his life is that he worked in the boot and shoe industry, like so many people who lived in Kettering in the early part of the twentieth century. He could be grumpy and irritable at times, but, by the time I was born, he was an old man. One of the nicest things about him was his generosity with the odd change in an old tea tin which he kept in a cupboard in the living room. He was always sending us to the corner shop for sweets, pop, crisps or ice-cream as a treat – usually before tea, which got him into trouble with my grandma, Rose.

I wish I'd paid more attention to him, but don't beat myself up about it. He was just the very old man who happened to live with my grandparents, and my childhood memories naturally gravitate towards them, not him.

Over the next few days, Mum's thinly-cloaked revelations play around in my head like an old 78 rpm record with the needle stuck. I remember a funny phrase being said several times when I was a child: "Tom by name and Tom by nature." There are other peculiar memories, too. Inexplicable things, like Grandad George always pulling me away when I'd sit on the fireside rug at Gramp's feet and then, if Grandad had to pop out of the room for a minute he'd say: "go and see if your grandma wants any help in the kitchen." As a child, I'd quickly cottoned-on that my younger brother and I were not allowed to be alone in the living room with Gramp and I'd always thought it was because he didn't like us being noisy when he was trying to concentrate on the television. Now, after the phone call with my mother about the inscription in the Book of Remembrance, I sense something so much darker. A fleeting hazy memory drifts its icy tendrils through my mind. I push it quickly away. Even now, I can't bear to put this down on paper.

A few days later, the phone rings. It's my Aunt Daisy. Her voice is carefully measured and hesitant, as if she's about to apologise to me for something.

'It's about the Book of Remembrance, Anne,' she says.

'You've spoken to Mum about Gramp, then?'

'Yes, when she called in yesterday. She told me what you'd found, but we definitely didn't have an inscription. We decided not to. It must be someone else.'

'That's what Mum said. But I know what I saw. Can you remember the exact date Gramp died?'

'No, I can't without looking for his death certificate, but it was in August. It's not that I don't believe you about this inscription, but I just can't understand it. The only people who could have signed the order for it to be done would have been next of kin – your Grandma, Aunt Lily or me. And we all agreed not to do it.'

'Why?'

Aunt Daisy hesitates for a second. 'It was because we said we would feel like hypocrites. All of us suffered in one way or another at his hands, and my mother probably the most. He pushed her down the stairs once. Did you know that? He was nothing but a violent bully.'

I begin to wish I hadn't said anything about the inscription. Aunt Daisy sounds as if she might be a bit upset about the whole thing, and I could have got it wrong, after all.

I twist the telephone cable around my fingers and bite my lip. 'Okay. Let's wait until next year when the book is open again, shall we? And then we'll go to the Crematorium and have a look. But we'll forget about it until then because I probably have got the wrong person anyway.'

'All right,' Aunt Daisy says. 'You'll have to remind me nearer the time. I should think it will be someone else with a similar name and not Gramp at all. But I do admit it's very strange there is a red rose by the inscription. Red roses were our Dad's favourite flowers. You painted one for him once and he had it framed. Do you remember?'

I do remember. I'd been given some oil paints for my birthday when I was about twelve or thirteen and had painted everyone pictures. The framed red rose had been hung proudly on the chimney breast in Grandma's front room – the room where Gramp had slept during his last years, turned into a bedroom because he could no longer climb the stairs. He'd loved that painting and had often told me he looked at it as he went to sleep.

'What happened to that painting when Grandma went into Northam House?' I say, wanting to see it again.

'I don't know. I haven't got it. Have you asked your mum?'

'I don't think she has it, otherwise she'd have given it to me when they moved to St Dunstan's Close.'

After the telephone conversation with Aunt Daisy, everyone quickly forgets about the mysterious inscription. Little do I know, though, that the rusty cog in the vast mechanism of a family's history which causes a shift in its future has moved slightly, and started to turn again with the coincidence of my father-in-law dying on the same day of the year as my great-grandfather.

September - December 2001

The unexpected discovery of the inscription in the Book of Remembrance excites my imagination, but I don't (can't) say anything to Mum or Aunt Daisy for fear of upsetting them. The memories they have of my great-grandfather are definitely not happy ones, but for the next three months it feels as if my long-forgotten great-grandfather is constantly trying to elbow his way back into my life with random reminders constantly cropping up.

Just days after I've discovered the inscription, we are sorting out our cupboard under the stairs and I find my great-grandma, Liz's, Bible, which reminds me of him. Then, the day after I find the Bible, I bump into a distant relative in the street, who randomly begins talking about the Jeffson family in bygone days and mentions him. I discover that he was, apparently, a founder member of the Kettering Pensioners' Parliament. A conversation with a friend at work who is researching her family tree prompts me to comment that I know my great-grandfather originated from Broughton in the late nineteenth century. Then I can't stop thinking about him for the rest of that day, wondering what his early life was like and exactly where in Broughton he had been born.

Soon, though, two more noteworthy examples occur. They are so extraordinary, they take my breath away. Only weeks after we have talked about red roses being Gramp's favourite flowers and talking about the lost painting, Aunt Daisy is surprised to find the framed, crudely-painted red rose, squirreled away in a long-forgotten box of memorabilia, along with a painting of some yellow roses I had painted for her. The next time I visit her she holds up the two paintings like trophies and tells me she wasn't even looking for them and didn't realise she had them.

Has something like this ever happened to you? You talk about someone, and then that person is walking towards you in the street when you haven't seen them for years. Or, like me, someone jogs your memory about a physical object you thought you had forgotten about and then it mysteriously turns up out of the blue?

But it's just coincidence.

Or is it?

Aunt Daisy offers me the paintings, but I decline. The timely discovery of the rose painting has spooked me, and I make up my mind I'm not going to dabble with Gramp's murky past any longer, because he is somehow trying to get inside my head, and the fact he wasn't a nice man when he was alive only makes matters worse.

Soon afterwards there is another eerie moment I can't ignore. If Gramp had borrowed St Peter's loud hailer and shouted my name from the heavens, I couldn't have been more startled.

I have an old dictionary in my desk drawer at work that

used to belong to my grandma, Rose. It has been there for years and I hardly ever refer to it. However, one day, I come across a word in a report I'm checking and need to look it up. I can still, to this day, remember the infrequently-used word. Because it's not listed in my tiny, pocket dictionary, I search for the word in the old dictionary in my drawer. As I open it, I remember that there is a leaf pressed between the pages. I smile to myself when I find it. My daughter picked it from a lilac tree in Grandma Rose's garden when she was about seven months old and Grandma pressed it as a keepsake. I'd known it was in the dictionary, but as I flick through more yellowy pages, looking for the word that I'd thought was incorrectly spelled in the report, I find something else I hadn't noticed before. It's a tiny, brown, almost disintegrated four-leafed clover. Something stirs in the darkest regions of my soul and a memory as thin and fragile as the four, fragmented leaves drifts to the surface. I had found this on Grandma's lawn one sunny summer's day when I was very small. And guess who always helped me search for four-leafed clovers, leaning forwards on his garden chair using a huge magnifying glass because his eyesight was failing? Yes, it was none other than Gramp.

The mysterious connectivity we occasionally experience with people, places, timing of events, music, art, nature and such things; the eerie presence that lingers when we think we are completely alone; the certainty of the knowing of some ephemeral fact that is just beyond our comprehension, all these things are attracted to each other like magnets. Then, before we know it is happening, the synchronicity of the here and now fits together with the distant past as neatly and perfectly as a machine-cut joint.

Part Two

7th December 2001

The second incident in a chronology of three events crucial to the writing of my Great Aunt Daisy's life story happens four months after I had discovered Tom Jeffson's inscription in the Book of Remembrance.

My father died. It wasn't sudden in the sense that one minute he was alive and the next dead, as happens in a heart attack or stroke, but it was pretty quick, nonetheless. He became ill one Saturday with a flu virus and by the following Friday night it had taken his life. He was only seventy-one.

Losing one of your parents catapults you forwards so brutally and violently it makes you feel as if your body and mind has instantly aged by twenty years. Your safety net disappears beneath you and the secure boundaries that have surrounded you disintegrate and crash down. At the same time, your remaining parent, your children and, it seems, everyone you know turn their enquiring faces towards you. Instantly, you are in the spotlight; the main character in a psychological suspense drama, expected to arrange a funeral and have all the answers to all the questions at a time you feel as if you have just been thrown from a spinning roundabout and crashed painfully to your knees.

Dad was a popular man. The phone rings constantly with his friends, ex-colleagues, distant relatives, old neighbours and people who remember him from school, all expressing their condolences and shock at his sudden departure from this world. Everyone is demanding the answer to one question: what on earth happened to him to cause his death in only a week? I don't know, do I? It was just the flu. How do I explain that to people? Folks are kind, and say they are sorry for my loss, but, to me, it makes me sound as if I've been careless in some way and lost my dad on the way to the shops.

Dads don't just die without any warning, do they? Not *my* dad, anyway. It has always been someone else's dad who dies suddenly.

Almost-deaf mothers don't suddenly turn into toddlers, do they? They are not supposed to just sit there in silence refusing to put their hearing aids in, covering their eyes with their hands like an obstinate child when you ask them if they'd like watch *Doctors* on the telly while they eat the ham sandwich you've just prepared for them.

Two sturdy rocks rise out of the huge, fatherless ocean where I am drowning under icy waves of family squabbles, funerals, hymns, bank accounts and what should be done with his commemorative decimal coins and gold cufflinks. I swim towards the rocks gratefully, towing my limp mother behind me. My Aunt Daisy and her daughter, Eileen, rescue Mum and give her some sanctuary. It briefly enables me to refocus on my own three children, who are devastated to lose their much-loved grandad so suddenly. Nicky, at thirteen, desperately needs me. He suffered the loss of one grandad last year, and now the other one has just died: the grandad with whom he watched and played endless games of snooker, supported rival football teams and thus learned the courtesy of good sportsmanship and humour. The grandad who played air guitar with him to Metallica at family barbecues and used to slip him a half of lager-shandy, whilst patiently explaining the old-fashioned rules of growing up, so that he would, hopefully, become a "thoroughly nice chap".

I try to be a good mother to my children and give them the love and reassurance they need on the death of their grandad, but I can't. I must constantly refocus on Mum, but I'm not even doing that very well. She doesn't seem to want me around. I think I irritate her by saying all the wrong things at the wrong time and putting things away in the wrong places.

My daughter, Emily, at twenty-one, expertly assumes the role of Nicky's mother and she does it so much better than me. My sister-in-law, Julie, steps in quickly after Dad's death and somehow takes my place as Mum's daughter. At the same time I realise that Aunt Daisy has turned into my mum's mother and Eileen (Mum's cousin) understands her in the way only a sister can. The only thing is, Mum doesn't have a sister.

Neither do I.

I'm so lonely.

I ache for Dad. It feels like someone has ripped a hole out of my chest where my heart is, and it's sore and raw all the time. If only I could feel his hands squeezing my shoulders, helping me through this awful time, giving me advice, telling me funny stories, making me cups of strong tea with too much sugar in it and calling me *"Fanny Annie" or "Annie Laurie."* I long to sit down with him and take some time out to complete a cryptic crossword, or go into the garden with him and prick out seedlings in the greenhouse in quiet companionship. I have a sudden urge to knit him a jumper for the winter, as if knitting him a jumper will make him come back so that he can wear it.

Someone at work calls me *Annie* on the phone, and I want to rip their head off, screaming: *"nobody but my dad calls me Annie."* Instead, after the phone call, I sit in my car in the car park and wait for the tears to come. They don't. I can't cry. Crying would be a luxury.

My husband, Rob, is the practical one. He sorts stuff out. Gets things done. He speaks clumsy words of comfort that I can't (or don't want to) hear. I am horrible to him. I tell him he doesn't know how it feels and he doesn't know what he's talking about, even though his own father died only last year. He is my husband: not my dad.

I want my dad.

My oldest son, Garry, at nineteen, is typically strong and silent, but he always seems to know how I feel and the exact moment I need to be hugged. He gives me long, crushing bear hugs without saying a word. I know he is missing his grandad, too, but I can't comfort him. Without me even asking, he pops in to see Mum every day to make sure she is all right. He is being such a good son, but I still want my dad.

I somehow keep on going, despite my new position in the family as a useless wife, bad mother and uncaring daughter.

I thank goodness for Emily for all the motherly things she is doing – making the boys' packed lunches every morning; cooking our family's dinners; grabbing my debit card and getting the shopping in; helping Nicky with his homework and making sure he has a clean, ironed shirt for school. She is a much better daughter than I am.

On the evening before Dad's funeral, my future son-in-law, Lee, is helping Emily wash up.

'Are you okay?' he says, when I hover around aimlessly in the kitchen, getting in the way, feeling as if I no longer have a place in my family as a wife, mum and daughter.

I nod. 'I'm fine. I'll be all right after tomorrow, once it's all over.'

'You don't look okay,' he says, flicking me with the tea towel.

'That's because I'm useless,' I say.

'You're not useless. You've just lost your dad.'

Then, and only then, do I disappear upstairs to cry.

Back on solid ground after the earthquake of Dad's untimely death and funeral, I find myself left with a strange, alien Mum-child. Aunt Daisy promises to help me coax her back into some sort of life. But we both know there's a big chasm to cross between her cosy, companionable retirement with Dad to a new life that she will forever refer to as *"Life A-B"* (Life After Brian).

Mum had been close to Aunt Daisy all her life. Aunt Daisy had been there when Mum was born on 5th June 1932, holding her older sister's hand when she was in labour. When my Grandma Rose died, Aunt Daisy had taken Mum under her wing then, too. Aunt Daisy was like that – a proper Earth mother. She understood perfectly how bereft Mum was feeling, because she was a widow, too.

Years ago, when Mum was a child and had reached the age when she was old enough to walk from Cornwall Road to Aunt Daisy's house in Windmill Avenue on her own, she naturally gravitated towards her aunt and her family and by all accounts was a constant visitor. I can appreciate how she felt. It must have been very hard for a young girl growing up as an only child living in a house with her parents and grandparents, especially now I know that Gramp had not been a nice person in those days.

I had been close to my Grandma Rose. She once confided in me, as an adult, that she had always felt the mother-daughter relationship with Mum was stolen away from her by her younger sister because of the difficult household circumstances she lived in. The glue of family solidarity had always held strong though, and Aunt Daisy and Grandma Rose had never fallen out over the situation of Mum preferring to be with Aunt Daisy when she was growing up.

After a traumatic six months, in one way or another, Mum's seventieth birthday in June 2002 is looming large on the horizon. It's another one of the "firsts" she is experiencing in her new life A-B.

'Do you think we can make my birthday meal into a forty-nine and a quarter year anniversary?' Mum says, raising her unplucked, bushy eyebrows under her straggly, grey hair, which needs a perm and a good cut. 'I'm not bothered about being seventy, but I am proud to have been married to your dad for forty-nine and a quarter years'.

I'm taken aback by the simple logic of mum's request. I can see what statement she is trying to make by ignoring her big-0 birthday in favour of celebrating a long and happy marriage, and I admire her for it.

'If you like,' I say. 'But don't ask me to track down balloons with 49 emblazoned all over them.'

'Oh, I don't want balloons, or any fuss. I just want everyone to celebrate mine and Brian's years of happy marriage together because we were denied our golden wedding anniversary party.'

Tears threaten. Mum seems so small and vulnerable without Dad. When he passed away they had already booked the venue for their golden wedding anniversary celebration in August 2002 and were really looking forward to it.

'I just want to celebrate our marriage in some way,' she continues, 'even though he's not here. I'd rather have been married to Brian for forty-nine years than plenty of other men I can think of for fifty or more years.'

We then have an enlightening conversation about men we know and their various shenanigans throughout the years. Mum laughs out loud and I realise that this is the first time she has laughed all the way up to her eyes since Dad died.

The next week she makes an appointment at the hairdressers. The following week I notice she is wearing a smudge of eye shadow and lipstick when I pick her up to take her and a friend to their regular "New Horizons" meeting. (New Horizons was formerly Kettering Mothers' Club, back in the nineteen-sixties. It was renamed when its members started to become grandmothers.)

I begin to sense that she is gradually adjusting to her new life A-B and, as if in confirmation of this feeling, Mum's seventieth birthday and forty-nine year anniversary celebration goes well. It's just a family meal out, but we all have fun and nobody cries, which is something of a first.

The following Sunday I know for certain she is gradually coming back to me. Mum and I had long since stopped speaking about Dad in case we upset each other. Instead, our conversations were interspersed with periods of silence where we would share a look – a moment of connectivity when the crudeness of words has no place, incongruous as they are with the silent empathy of the shared loss of a loved one.

Until that day, the underlying sadness in Mum had been so intense it had daily torn me to shreds with its cruel, sharp claws. People would say to me: *"your Mum is coping well, isn't she?"* I'd smile and agree with them, each time hearing Mum's by now robotic phrases when she talked about her plans for a shopping trip or the holiday she was planning with Aunt Daisy: *"I've got to make a new life, now,"* or *"I've got to make myself carry on."*

'My life A-B is like a series of stepping stones,' Mum says as we sit opposite each other at my dining table that Sunday evening, picking at left-overs from a family meal while she does a crossword.

She lifts her glasses and perches them on the end of her nose while she looks at me over the top of the frames. 'I've actually drawn a diagram of a river with stepping stones and labelled them all. I tick them off, one at a time. It gives me something to do.'

I chuckle. She's definitely loads better than she was. 'It seems a logical thing to do,' I say. 'It's a visual reminder that you're making progress.'

'I wouldn't call it progress,' she grimaces. 'It's just something to stop me turning to drink.'

I burst out laughing. My mum is more or less a lifetime teetotaller, her only tipple being a single brandy and Babycham on special occasions, a tiny amount of Snowball at Christmas and a Pernod and lemonade on holiday.

'You might well laugh,' she says with an old, familiar twinkle in her eyes. 'I didn't tell you I tried some of your dad's Scotch, did I? I was going to tip it all down the sink, but then I had second thoughts because I thought it would help me sleep. But it's a slippery slope. I don't want to become an alcoholic.'

I can't stop laughing. I wipe my eyes with a forefinger.

'So these stepping stones stop you having a drink?'

Mum nods enthusiastically.

'*Did* it help you sleep, though?'

'Oh no. I daren't drink it. It was only enough to cover the bottom of the glass, but the fact I'd even poured it out scared me to death. I was up all night drawing and plotting out the stepping stones to stop me drinking it. Then I decided to start keeping a diary and wrote out all the previous week's entries. I couldn't remember anything further back than a week, though. Do you think that could be an early sign of Alzheimer's?'

'No,' I giggle. 'If it is, then most of the population has it.'

'I've always been frightened of becoming an alcoholic,' Mum says, pushing herself back from the table slightly, whilst shaking her head and grimacing in mock fear. 'It's a bit like being drawn to water. You know, when you are standing on top of a high cliff and something about the swirling sea below makes you want to jump into it, just to see what it feels like?'

By this time I have collapsed onto the dining table on my crossed forearms, laughing so much I can hardly get my breath. My mum is back. My lovely, gentle mum, who is so funny without knowing it.

'What?' she says. 'What have I said that's so funny?'

Emily joins us, curious to find out why we are laughing.

'Grandma thinks she'll become an alcoholic if she drinks a whisky to help her sleep,' I explain. 'So she's been drawing stepping stones, making lists and has started a diary instead.'

Mum tuts and shakes her head knowingly. 'You'd be scared of being an alcoholic if you'd lived with a grandfather who got drunk all the time, like I did. It was horrible.'

I feel a little shudder inside me. Since finding my great-grandfather's inscription in the Book of Remembrance last August, I've purposely shoved Tom Jeffson and all his dark family secrets to the back of my mind. I think I was just a little possessed by him at the time, and the eerie coincidences and strange feelings that he was watching and stalking me from a shadowy, mysterious afterlife still scare me.

Mum continues. 'I wonder who put his memorial in The Book of Remembrance?'

'Oh, so you think it *is* Gramp's entry, then?' I say.

'It's got to be, although Aunt Daisy doesn't think so. We'll find out for definite soon, though, won't we? I'll put the date in my new diary to make sure we don't miss going to the crematorium. It can be another stepping stone to draw on my master-plan.'

After I have agreed to book the day off work for the crematorium visit, the conversation turns to Emily's wedding, which is only a couple of weeks away. Mum and Emily are discussing wedding presents, seating plans, the long-range weather forecast and what Emily can wear for *something old.*

'I know you've having money for a present,' Mum says to her, 'but I am going to give you another wedding present, too. Something very old and precious.'

I wonder what it is Mum is going to give her. I hope that whatever it is, she's given it some thought and it's not just a spur of the moment decision.

'You don't have to give us anything else, Grandma. You've given us enough already,' Emily says.

'I'm going to give you some old jewellery. It's a solid gold gate bracelet and it belonged to my mother. You don't have to wear it on your wedding day if you don't want to, but it *could* be your something old.'

I pull myself up ramrod straight at the table, indignant. I've loved that bracelet all my life. When I was younger, my Grandma Rose had shown it to me and told me that, one day, it would be mine. Now Mum has gone and promised it to Emily!

'That bracelet is supposed to be mine.'

I regret saying it immediately. I sound like a sulky child.

'No it isn't,' Mum says as calmly as if she is disputing one of my answers to the crossword in front of her. 'I inherited it when your grandma died. Anyway, what does it matter? You never wear jewellery anyway, and if you did have it, you'd only break it. What better way is there for Emily to begin her future than with something so lovely from the past?'

Mum is right. I've never been a lover of jewellery. I probably wouldn't wear it if it was mine because I would be too scared of losing something so valuable.

'Aw,' I say. 'I don't mind really. That's a lovely thing to do, Mum.'

Mum explains to me the reasoning behind her decision. 'I've been thinking about it for a while. I know I have three other grand-daughters, but it would have gone to you and then to Emily anyway – I'm just cutting out the middle-man.'

Emily speaks for the first time – hesitantly – I can tell she feels awkward about the bracelet. 'Are you sure, Grandma? Thank you so much. I promise you I'll always look after it, and Mum can wear it if she has a special occasion, can't you Mum?'

She looks enquiringly at me. I shrug my shoulders and smile. 'You are a very lucky bride. I'd have been proud to wear that bracelet on my wedding day.'

'There's another reason I'd like Emily to wear it when she gets married,' Mum continues, taking a deep breath as if she is about to reveal something I don't already know.

'Why?' Emily asks.

'Because Grandma Rose should have worn it on *her* wedding day. It was an engagement present from her fiancé, Bert. He died of tuberculosis just before their wedding. It just feels right to me. Like we are fulfilling the bracelet's destiny to be worn by a bride.'

I nod slowly, remembering the time years ago when Grandma had told me about her first love. She had even shown me her engagement ring, nestled in the same blue leather box as the gold bracelet. I knew without saying that the beautiful art deco engagement ring would be mine, one day.

I feel a tug of love for my mum that is so strong, I reach out for her across the table and grasp her hands, stroking them with my thumbs.

'Everything is going to be all right now, Mum. I just know it is. I'll always look after you. I don't mind about the bracelet – it's a lovely gesture.'

Mum gives a wry chuckle. 'I'd take that back if I were you. I might lose my marbles and, even worse, control of my bodily functions.'

I wrinkle my nose. 'I'd do my best if that happened.'

Mum winks at Emily. The mischievous twinkle is back and it makes my heart soar as high as summer's first swallow after a long hard winter. 'Then God help me, our Anne,' she says. 'You'd give me all the wrong tablets, drop me in the bath so I'd nearly drown and if you had to lift me up, I'd be like a sack of potatoes thrown across your shoulder. No, I think I'll go into a care home to be looked after properly. Then you can both visit me every day to make me laugh and we'll eat Mr Kipling cakes, drink strong tea in china teacups and do Sudoku puzzles and crosswords to stop my brain turning to mush.'

Emily is laughing out loud and agrees with Mum's comment about my clumsiness, adding a comment of her own. 'She can't even do someone's hair properly,' she says. 'I was a laughing stock at school with my uneven pigtails and unravelling plaits.'

They are making fun of me, but I don't care. I laugh with them, and then tease Mum about my pudding bowl haircut when I was a child. I am conscious that the future is edging slowly forwards for all three of us. Out of focus and stagnant since Dad died, things are now becoming fresher and clearer, but relationships have, somehow, turned turtle in the meantime. Has my mother now become another child for me to worry about and care for? Until Dad's death, my lovely parents had always been the pivot around which everyone else orbited. It's only now I realise that, up until he died, Dad was the most stable and solid influence in my life. Now he's gone, so is my momentum in life. The gravity that always drew me back onto my straight and narrow life path; the force that drove me on to achieve the absolute best I could; the deep-rooted need for my dad to be proud of me – all now dissolved into the primal swamp. A man's love for his daughter makes her feel special every day of her life, no matter how clumsy and unladylike she turns out to be. Dad always used to tease me by saying that a man was not a real man until he had conceived a daughter: even one like me, he used to add with an affectionate chuckle as he ruffled my hair.

Now, as I gaze upwards, not only is the pedestal occupied by Dad empty, but it stretches way, way up into the sky – so high I know I'll never be able to climb it. I'm not a perfect daughter. I'm not a perfect mother, either. But in the here and now, I know without any doubt that it is actually all right for me not to be perfect. I am who I am. I might have lost my life's compass, but there is no one luckier than me, because I am a gloriously imperfect mum and daughter to these two lovely women. A little voice whispers inside my head: *"neither was your dad a perfect father, nor a perfect husband, but he always did his best and that's all that matters."*

I cut myself some slack. I don't have to be perfect for everyone to love me. Why did I ever think I had to be?

The sun shines and fluffy white clouds scurry across the blue sky on the day Emily marries her husband, Lee, at St Botolph's Church in Barton Seagrave. The air is thick with the heady fragrance of honeysuckle and roses and the intermittent sound of buzzing insects adds to the bright, summery ambience of the day. Mum is the proudest of grandmothers in her cerise two-piece suit with matching shoes and handbag. She doesn't look seventy. Everyone marvels at Aunt Daisy, too. In three years' time she will be ninety years old. As they stand together, watching everyone throw confetti over the bride and groom, they seem more like sisters than aunt and niece.

I can't help constantly thinking about my dad today. He would have been so proud to see his precious grand-daughter married. In the year or so before he passed away, Emily and Lee had met up with Mum and Dad on a weekly basis in a local pub. They had often asked us to join them, but Rob and I had always felt that we didn't want to intrude on their inter-generational Thursday nights. We couldn't have known, then, just how precious these memories would become to them, the shared time with my parents being short-lived because of Dad's untimely death.

The golden bracelet sparkles in the sunlight on Emily's wrist. Is it my imagination or is there a high-pitched humming in the air? I blink, my vision suddenly blurring.

'Come on – we are needed for a photo,' Rob says.

I feel strange. Not exactly dizzy or faint, but even though there is a breeze the day is warm and my face feels hot. I look across at Aunt Daisy, who is walking up the pathway back into the church with her son. Mum is nowhere to be seen.

Something feels dreamlike and slightly magical. I can only describe it as feeling I am watching a scene in a film through disconnected eyes. As quickly as the feeling envelops me, it dissipates and everything feels normal again. I didn't have time for breakfast. Perhaps that's why I feel so strange.

Later, at the wedding reception Mum says spontaneously: 'What's next then?'

'Strawberry cheesecake and cream,' I reply.

'I don't mean what's for afters, I mean what's my next stepping stone?'

'Your holiday with Aunt Daisy?'

'That's a bit far away,' she muses. 'I need another stepping stone or two in between.'

'You could come to Cromer with us in August,' I say. 'But you'll have to sleep in the awning.'

Mum shudders. 'I had enough of caravan holidays in the sixties when we had to wee in a bucket. Now I'm an old lady I want a proper toilet and a proper bed.'

'We have a proper toilet in the caravan. You won't have to wee in a bucket, and I'll sleep in the awning so that you can have a proper bed if you want to come,' Rob says generously.

Mum wrinkles her nose. 'I don't like caravanning. I don't know what you see in it.'

'Come abroad with us next year, then.'

'Two holidays abroad? I don't think so. What do you

think I am? A millionaire. Mind you, I might meet one if I go somewhere expensive and exotic.'

Aunt Daisy has been listening to the conversation.

'In the absence of a millionaire, what you need is a complete change,' she says firmly. 'Otherwise all these holidays and days out will cost you a fortune.'

Part Three

August 2002

The change my Aunt Daisy has suggested to Mum turns into a tentative idea that the two of them could live together. Both families feel it's a great idea and over the next few weeks we look into it. Mum lives in a bungalow, so it seems logical that with Aunt Daisy's advancing years they should both live there.

Bureaucracy has a lot to answer for. The sticky red tape is whipped out and a strip torn off in readiness as soon as the first enquiry is made. Mum's bungalow is rented through a Housing Association and she had exercised her tenancy rights to continue to live there when Dad died. Now, it seems, that there is no way the Housing Association will allow Aunt Daisy to stay in the bungalow in the very remote eventuality that Mum dies before her. She simply won't have any tenancy rights at all. Why can't anyone in authority see that Mum and Aunt Daisy living together in Mum's bungalow will release a Council house suitable for a family to live in?

'It's all right,' Aunt Daisy says when we hear the news. 'What's the chance of Margaret popping-off before me? She's only seventy and I'm nearly ninety. It's only a little risk?'

Our two families eventually decide that we definitely *can't* take the risk, however small, but that we should look into the scenario of Mum moving in with Aunt Daisy instead. Aunt Daisy lives in a house owned by the Council and had a stair-lift installed a couple of years ago. To our utter disbelief, the same rule applies to Aunt Daisy. When she was widowed, tenancy rights passed to her and they can't be passed on again.

Basically, their brilliant idea is scuppered by unmoveable rules that don't take into account people's individual circumstances. So, Mum and Aunt Daisy come up with a plan, which unfortunately doesn't release any much-needed social housing. They will live half the week at Aunt Daisy's house in Windmill Avenue and the other half in Mum's bungalow, a short distance away in St Dunstan's Close.

Clunk. The three parts of the mechanics that will eventually provide the time to write the story of the Jeffson family are now locked irrevocably in place: the finding of the inscription in the Book of Remembrance; the death of my father and now Mum and Aunt Daisy's decision to live together.

These two grand ladies, like mother hens, declare that if I join them for lunch on Tuesdays I can have whatever I like, cooked especially for me, served up on a tray at 12.30 pm on the dot. What busy, full-time working mum would turn down such an offer?

On the second or third Tuesday lunchtime spent in the company of Aunt Daisy and Mum, our attention is focused on Emily and Lee's official photograph album.

'I once had a relation who lived in Barton Seagrave,' says Aunt Daisy as she peruses the photographs. 'In a cottage right near to the church.'

I remember that I had noticed Aunt Daisy re-entering the church while the photographs were being taken. 'Why did you go back into the church at the wedding? I saw you disappear and wondered if you were all right.'

'Actually, I had a bit of a funny turn. I went for a sit down in the shade. I didn't want to mention it at the time and I was fine afterwards.'

I nod in agreement. 'It *was* very hot. I felt a bit strange, too. I thought it was because I hadn't had time for breakfast.'

Aunt Daisy falls uncharacteristically quiet.

'What's up? Are you okay,' I say to Aunt Daisy after a few minutes' interlude where Mum and I have been chatting about the wedding and she hasn't joined in. I sense that she is silently reminiscing, remembering her relatives who lived in the cottage near to the church. I shiver, and sudden goose-bumps on my arm make my hairs stand on end.

Aunt Daisy speaks without looking up. She's subconsciously fiddling with the wedding ring on her finger. (It's probably all the talk of weddings and looking at the photographs.) She swivels round to face Mum. 'If I tell you something, Margaret, promise me you won't laugh at me? Do you remember at the wedding, when I said to you that Rose's bracelet looked so pretty on Emily, and that her grandma would be proud of her?'

'Eh?' Mum says. She's adjusting her hearing aid and without it she can't hear a thing. Mum needs her hearing aid plus clear sight of someone's lips to know what they are saying.

Aunt Daisy shouts her question again, spacing out the words and looking directly at Mum so that she can read her lips. Mum grimaces. I smile in amusement. They make a brilliant double act.

'Emily's. Wedding. Day. Rose's Bracelet. It. Looked. So. Pretty.'

'Yes, it did. I'm so glad I gave it to her. It was her *something old*,' Mum replies whilst re-inserting her hearing aid into her ear.

Aunt Daisy continues, still trying to make her lips move clearly so mum can read them. 'And I said that to you on the day, didn't I? When the photographs were being taken?'

Mum nods thoughtfully. 'Yes, you did. Then I got carted off to the reception like a lost sheep and had to be rounded-up to come back to the church when everyone realised I'd not been in the family photo and it had to be taken again.' She sighs and rolls her eyes. 'I was in so much trouble ...'

Aunt Daisy begins to speak normally as she interrupts. 'Well, I'm going to tell you something now – as long as you both don't repeat it to anyone. I don't want people thinking I'm losing my marbles.'

Aunt Daisy leans forwards with purpose and pans her eyes around to me. She can be such a diva at times.

'The reason I had a funny turn was because I'm sure I

saw our Rose, just as she was at the age of eighteen. She was in the crowd of people outside the church when people were throwing confetti. She was wearing her blue dress – the one she made herself for Easter in nineteen twenty-two when Bert proposed to her and gave her the bracelet.'

I don't say anything. Aunt Daisy has now turned to Mum, so I don't have to respond. Anyway, I don't want to interrupt this interesting conversation.

'One of Emily's friends was wearing blue,' Mum says. 'Perhaps you saw her and thought she looked like Rose.'

'Well, that's as may be. I did a double-take in shock. I came across all giddy and that's why had to go back in the church for a bit of a sit down.'

'I think it was the heat and your mind playing tricks on you,' Mum says. 'You saw Emily wearing the bracelet and were near to the cottage you remembered visiting in your childhood and someone reminded you of your sister as she looked in the olden days. I don't think it was a ghost.'

'Well, I think ... no I *know* ... it *was* our Rose. And it's not the first time ...'

Aunt Daisy suddenly stops, mid-sentence, and swivels back round to face me.

'What do you think, our Anne? Do you believe in ghosts?'

I mutter a reply. 'Er ... I'm not sure. I don't know.'

I am now rubbing at my arms to make the goose-bumps go away. I remember how I, too, had felt strange at the precise moment Aunt Daisy had just described. I had sensed a buzzing in the air and the fragrance of honeysuckle and roses had been so strong, I'd looked all around me to see where the flowers were. But there hadn't been any nearby. I had almost forgotten the peculiar moment.

'Tell her!' Aunt Daisy orders Mum, with a note of authority in her voice. 'Tell her about the time you saw Brian.'

It's time for me to go back to work. I glance at the clock on the mantelpiece. If I don't go right now, I'll be late back. I have a meeting at two o'clock and I haven't yet printed off the paperwork, which will take at least fifteen minutes.

Mum sees me look at the clock, lets out a relieved sigh and puffs out her cheeks. 'You need to get a wiggle on, or else you'll be late,' she says.

'*Did* you really see Dad?' I ask, ignoring the obvious body language that she doesn't want to talk about it.

'Yes. No. Not exactly. I don't know. You need to go back to work ...'

'When?'

'... or you'll be late and get into trouble. It was the Tuesday morning after my seventieth birthday at 7.32 am, but ...'

The precision about the time is not typical of my mother, who is always late for everything. I glance at the clock again. I can snatch another few minutes. 'Why didn't you tell me?'

'I told Aunt Daisy,' Mum says defensively. 'She was there, weren't you?'

Aunt Daisy nods. 'I've been reading up on the internet about visitations from deceased loved ones. It's a classic case. She was definitely visited by Brian.'

Aunt Daisy hasn't got a computer, but both her and Mum have learned how to use the internet at my house. I suspect they've made a furtive visit to the library to log on, or have been secretly accessing paranormal websites on my computer when they visit for tea and ask me if they can log on to look up some information about fuchsia diseases, or how to successfully propagate African Violets. Or, like the other day, be caught staring at a photograph on the screen of Clark Gable with his shirt off.

I glance at the clock again. If a colleague will print out the paperwork for the meeting for me, I'll have another twenty minutes or so before I need to head back to work. I whip out my mobile phone and send a quick text while Aunt Daisy explains all the things she has learned on the internet about visitations from dead loved ones.

'It's happened to me lots of times,' she says. 'White

feathers seem to be the most common sign.'

'White feathers come from fighting pigeons,' I argue. 'You see them all the time, wherever you are.'

Aunt Daisy ignores my scepticism. 'And there's butterflies and birds. Especially birds on a windowsill, tapping at the window with their beaks.'

'I've never seen that before,' I laugh. 'We once had a thrush commit suicide flying into our conservatory window. I don't suppose that counts, though, does it?'

'You might well take the Mickey,' Aunt Daisy sniffs. 'But if it happens to you, you'll change your mind, I can guarantee it.'

Mum's gone quiet and is chewing at her bottom lip. I think she is hoping I'll just go back to work now, and she won't have to tell me about her ghostly goings-on.

'Come on then, Mum.' I say to her as my mobile phone bleeps with a favourable reply from my colleague. 'What happened?'

Mum's twiddles her fingers as she speaks in a soft voice, not looking at me. 'You know that time when you are not quite awake and yet not fully asleep? I remember clearly knowing I wasn't dreaming as it was happening: it was too real to be a dream. I could see the colours of the flowers on the windowsill and even smell your dad's Old Spice aftershave.'

'Where were you when it happened?' I say, completely intrigued by Mum's story.

'It was time to get up. 7.32 am. The alarm had just gone and I'd switched it off. I really thought I had got out of bed and gone into the kitchen. I put the kettle on and started washing up the supper things from the night before. Aunt Daisy was still asleep in the bedroom, so I was trying not to make too much noise and wake her up.'

'So you were definitely in the kitchen, then? Not still in bed and dreaming?'

'Yes. I felt someone touch my shoulder and jumped. I turned around and there was Brian, dressed normally in his awful, old gardening jumper, holding out a clean, folded, white hanky to me. He was laughing and said: *"here you are – your nose always runs when you do the washing up."* '

'And does it?'

'Yes. The smell of washing-up liquid always gives me a runny nose. We used to laugh about it all the time, and he used to fetch me a tissue or a hanky and even wipe my nose for me because I'd have my hands in the soap suds.'

'I didn't know that,' I say, shaking my head in wonder.

'It didn't feel strange or anything. I'd completely forgotten he was supposed to be dead. Anyway, I took the hanky out of his hand and blew my nose, laughing with him. Then he said: *"you'd better make that cup of tea before the kettle goes cold. It's dry as a desert round here. I'm parched."*

'I put the hanky down on the draining board, dried my hands on a tea towel and reached into the cupboard to get the mugs out. I still hadn't remembered he'd died. When I turned around to say something to him, he wasn't there. Then I remembered he was dead, and with a big shudder I knew I had seen his ghost.'

'What happened then?'

'I woke up,' Aunt Daisy says, taking up the story. 'Margaret was just turning over in her bed beside me when I opened my eyes.'

'Was it all just a dream, then?' I say to Mum.

'I really don't know,' Mum replies, shaking her head. 'When I got up again and went into the kitchen, I felt the kettle and it was cold, so I thought I must have been dreaming and hadn't got up at all when the alarm went off. Then I went to the sink and there were washing up bubbles in the bowl and the water was warm. Then I saw two clean mugs with teabags in them, waiting to be filled up with hot water, and there was a white hanky on the draining board. So I'm really not sure. Perhaps I'd got up, only half-awake, and then gone back to bed.'

'Do you believe it now?' Aunt Daisy says to me, raising her eyebrows.

'I don't know ...' I begin to say, but Mum's eyes are shining, she's smiling to herself with the memory and I know instantly that she really believes she has been visited by Dad. She speaks quietly and looks upwards towards the ceiling, her face serene.

'I felt so peaceful afterwards, and that was the day I finally turned the corner. I felt much so much better after that morning. I know he's around now, even though I still don't know if I was dreaming that day or if it was real.'

I shrug my shoulders, looking at the clock. 'Thanks for the dinner,' I say abruptly as I realise I have just a few minutes to make it back to work in time for my meeting. I grab my mobile phone and punch out a text to let my colleague know I'll go straight to the meeting and ask if they could take the papers over to the meeting room.

I've cut it so fine, staying to listen to Mum's story. The car journey back to work takes only about four or five minutes. The Parish Church clock nearby is just striking two o'clock as I enter the meeting room. I can feel everyone's eyes on me as I circulate the still-warm paperwork, telling myself that I was stupid to risk being late.

Little do I know that this will not be the first time I only just make it back to work in time for an afternoon meeting on a Tuesday because of listening to Mum's or Aunt Daisy's stories.

The following Saturday afternoon, I arrive at Aunt Daisy's house to take them both to Mum's bungalow in St Dunstan's Close until Wednesday lunchtime, when Trevor, Aunt Daisy's son, will collect them and take them back to Windmill Avenue. So far, the arrangements are working well and both Mum and Aunt Daisy are enjoying the enhanced social life brought about by living in two houses and having two sets of friends and neighbours.

I have hardly had a chance to enter the room before Aunt Daisy stands up, a huge, youthful grin splitting her face. If she was a child she would be jigging up and down in excitement.

'I've been thinking, our Anne – and I've talked about it to

your mum – I've come up with a really big stepping stone for her to get her teeth into?'

She is holding in her hand a few sheets of blue Basildon Bond notepaper filled with her small, neat handwriting. They are flapping and fluttering around, mirroring her enthusiasm. She swirls around and scoops up some photographs from the occasional table beside her armchair. 'I've made a few notes to get us going, and I've found some old photographs so you know who I'm talking about.'

'Hang on ... get going on what?' I laugh.

'My life story.'

'And your grandma's,' says Mum as she enters the room from the kitchen, carrying a tray containing three mugs of tea and some home-made jam tarts.

Aunt Daisy plonks herself down, grabs a jam tart and offers the plate to me. 'Since the wedding, I just can't stop thinking about our Rose and her poor Bert. I know how much you love writing stories. I thought Rose's happy ending might make a nice story for a women's magazine. Remember how she sent off your little stories years ago and they got published by The People's Friend? Well, we could do it again, couldn't we?'

'I ... I ... don't know,' I stutter. I've always been embarrassed by my secret hobby. The short stories that were published years ago were sent off by Grandma without my knowledge. I was grateful to her at the time, because they earned me some money when Rob and I were new parents and hard-up, but after initial beginner's luck, my next two stories were rejected, and so I'd chucked my writing pen into the metaphoric bin and given up.

'Not many people know about my writing ...' I begin to say.

'That doesn't matter. We don't have to tell anyone.'

'I don't know what people will think of me if they know I'm a writer,' I go on.

'Since when have you ever worried about what people think of you!' Mum interjects forcefully with a reproachful chuckle. She's right – I've never cared what other people think. But her statement doesn't apply to my writing. Even my children don't know how much I enjoy writing and it is something I do when alone.

'It's not like you're a secret alcoholic or anything – not like some I could mention. I don't know why you're so ashamed of it. You've always been good with words.' Mum is speaking with her mouth full of jam tart. I want to tell her not to speak with her mouth full. Anything but talk about writing.

'Your Mum desperately needs another stepping stone,' Aunt Daisy pleads, 'don't you, Margaret? Go on, Anne. Say you'll do it. We don't have to try to get it published if you don't want to.'

Aunt Daisy holds out the sheets of notepaper and photographs again. She might be pushing ninety but she reminds me of a little girl pleading for a pair of shiny new shoes. I fleetingly wonder if she really wants me to do this for herself and is using Mum's stepping stones as an excuse.

'All right. I'll have a think about it.' I say, taking the bundle from her hand.

Aunt Daisy nods. 'It can be just for the family. A memoir of our lives for the next generation. You might feel differently about trying to get it published when it's finished, though.'

A memoir of our lives ...

'Hang on.' I protest. 'I thought it was just a story or two.'

'It could turn into a serial,' Aunt Daisy pleads, stretching boundaries to their limits. 'A collection of stories that tells our life story.'

'I'm not using my real name.'

'Well, use mine then. I don't care,' Aunt Daisy retorts, pursing her lips. 'Or use our Rose's name, like you did before.'

We discuss the life story project for the rest of the afternoon. The conversation reminds me to tell Mum and Aunt Daisy that I have booked the day off work a week on Friday, which is the day we have planned to visit Kettering Crematorium to view the Book of Remembrance, because it is exactly one year since I discovered Gramp's inscription.

The trouble with stepping stones is that sometimes they take you in a different direction to that you have planned for yourself. You have no choice but to tread on them, because they are the only ones available. I know Aunt Daisy is right. Mum *does* need a long-term focus after Dad's death. And since my Grandma Rose passed away a few years ago, Mum has struggled with deep regrets and made some profound statements about her relationship with her mother. I know she hasn't properly come to terms with losing Grandma, and telling this story will probably help.

Now, with the death of my dad, Mum needs me more than she has ever done in her life. I am her only daughter. I have no option but to follow her onto this stepping stone, but I have an uneasy premonition I am about to become stranded, sucked into the swirling waters of my secret hobby, committing my Tuesday lunchtimes, Saturday afternoons and goodness knows how many of my evenings to writing a memoir that might never see the light of day.

'Just let them tell their little tales of the past, type it all up in chronological order and then give them each a copy,' Rob says when I tell him that Aunt Daisy wants to tell her and Grandma Rose's life stories, helped by Mum. 'They can do what they like with it then.'

'I want to do a proper job, though. If I'm putting my name to it, I want to be able to write it on my own terms,' I whine, feeling torn in two directions.

Rob is getting tired of the conversation. I can tell by the tone in his voice and the way he edges his way out of the room while he is talking. 'I thought you just said you didn't want your name on it?'

'I don't. But I *do* want to take the credit for it if it turns out to be good enough to publish.'

Rob is losing patience with me. 'Look. Do you really want to get to your Aunt Daisy's age and regret not writing that book you've been going on about for the last thirty years? It seems to me to be as good a basis as any, and if your great grandfather was a bit of a lad in his younger days, wouldn't finding out all those secrets your mum talks about be good material? What do you think your grandma would want if she was alive?'

'Oh, that's easy. She'd be up for it.'

I realise, for the first time, that writing this life story about Aunt Daisy and Grandma will involve their memories of their father, and I had previously promised myself that I wouldn't delve into his turbulent, murky life because of all the weird, coincidental things that had happened to me after I'd discovered his inscription in the Book of Remembrance. I might never have seen a ghost, but I didn't want to risk scaring myself witless again.

Over the next few days, everyone in the family says that writing the story is a good idea and tells me I'll never know what I can achieve if I don't try.

By Tuesday lunchtime, I've made up my mind. I *shall* write Aunt Daisy and Grandma's life story, beginning with the tragedy of the loss of Grandma's first love and their brother, Arthur, within the space of just a few weeks. I've even fitted in a visit to the library at lunchtime the day before and taken out some local history books and chronicles of life in the 1920s. But I will try at all costs to avoid bringing Gramp into the story because he won't be a sympathetic character.

When I arrive at Mum's bungalow, Aunt Daisy is dishing up my favourite dinner, buoyant and chirpy. She hustles me into the living room.

'Sit down,' she says. 'I've got something to run by you. I've been thinking – we need to write this story as a proper book, not a serial for a magazine. There's lots of things I've never told a living soul about.'

Mum appears, carrying my dinner on a tray. 'We've talked about nothing else since Saturday,' she says.

As we eat our dinner together I can feel myself becoming more and more excited by the project. I am finally going to take the leap and become a proper writer. I might not be any good, but if I don't try then I'll never know. Rob is right. I don't want to get to Aunt Daisy's age and regret not even giving my writing a chance.

Despite my silent pledge to ignore Tom Jeffson's part in the story, long-forgotten memories unfurl inside me like butterflies emerging from cocoons, their wings moist and wrinkled. I can picture him, almost blind, watching the cricket on a small TV at his side, his nose only inches from the screen. I remember feeling indignant when he told me that girls wouldn't understand the rules of cricket. I recall all the old ladies, sitting around Grandma's living room on crammed-in high backed chairs, knitting, sewing, drinking tea out of floral china tea cups, reading The Woman's Weekly, gossiping about the neighbours.

I remember one lady in particular. 'Who was the lady who couldn't stop nodding?' I ask Aunt Daisy.

She knows instantly who I mean. 'Mrs Summerley. She used to live at the end of Cornwall Road. They owned the chip shop in Rockingham Road.'

'Oh, right. Did she have Parkinson's Disease?'

'Yes, I think she must have done,' Aunt Daisy replies. 'She was a friend of our mam's. She didn't like our dad, though. They used to gripe at each other all the time.'

'Was she there *every* day?'

Mum interrupts. 'It sometimes seemed like it,' she laughs. 'She was usually there on Sunday afternoons. We always used to visit on a Sunday afternoon until you got old enough to protest and want to stay at home. I suppose that's why you think she was there every day.'

That evening, I open up a brand new notepad and begin to write down my own memories of life at my grandma's house in Cornwall Road. I need to set the scene and, fortunately, it's one I can visualise and remember in some detail. I've not even completed half a page before I tear out the first page and start again. This is repeated a few times. I sigh in exasperation and give up. I put down the notepad and pen and lean back in my chair, closing my eyes. I'm not going to be able to do this. I don't know how or where to start.

In the dark place behind my closed eyelids I see a shapes that look like tiny, comma-shaped embryos in a vast, black space and try to conjure up the characters in the story I have been tasked to write, but am now wondering if I have the ability to do so.

From the moment we are conceived, we inherit some static attributes – such as our place in the world, our hair and skin colour, attractiveness, intelligence and whether we will be a passive introvert or a loud, gregarious type of person. There are then many ways our life stories can be told. Nature versus nurture. Add into the mix disappointments, embarrassments, tragedies and celebrations and a character's own, individual story begins to emerge, interacting with other characters in numerous ways. When these stories are decorated with scars such as terror, life-destroying feelings of inadequacy or shame about something we have done, or, conversely, jewels of good fortune, determination and brutal doggedness to achieve a goal, there are then infinite ways someone's individual life story can unfold.

'Are you asleep?' Rob says, waving his hand in front of my face. I open my eyes.

'No. I'm just trying to work out how to write this book.'

In my heart, I now know what I have to do. Aunt Daisy's memories of the past will be faded. Not only will they have lost their lustre with her advancing years, they will be restricted and bound by a single point of view. Mum's memories will be from another perspective and will be useful: it's always good to hear the same story from another's viewpoint, but even so, Mum's memories will not be enough to turn these stories and anecdotes from a two-dimensional, linear memoir into a book people will want to read.

Another factor we can't ignore is that Grandma is no longer with us and her input is going to be second-hand at worst and conjecture at best. There will be no way of knowing how she, or any of the other characters in the story who are no longer alive, actually *felt*. I realise that Mum and Aunt Daisy can only provide the embryos of the majority of the characters with their memories and stories, but I must give them life with my imagination. It's the only way to tell this story in a way that will make people want to read it. For some inexplicable reason I remember the word "triumvirate" – the word I was looking up in Grandma's old dictionary at work on the day I found the four-leafed clover. Aunt Daisy, Mum and I have, without realising, formed ourselves into a triumvirate. We all have a role to play. I might be the writer of the book, but each of us has an equal part in the telling of the story.

Part Four

Throughout the course of my life so far, I have often lamented, in the way writers are naturally inclined to do, over the many ways you can write a story about one of the simplest and most used words in the English Language.

Love.

It is a concept that is detached from anything tangible, and yet it is a word everyone says, often inappropriately, all the time. Love, and the absence of it, is an experience few of us can avoid. In all its forms, across all cultures, it consumes huge chunks of our lives. You could fill a library with the number of books written about love: philosophical and theoretical; works of fiction and poetry to name just a few. Philosophers have put forward their own unique understanding on its meaning throughout ancient and modern times, and there are thousands of different definitions of all the many types of love human beings are capable of experiencing.

As I begin to shape and form an outline of the story in my mind, time and time again my train of thought returns to the symbolic red rose in the Book of Remembrance which triggered the chain of events leading to our decision to write this book. Robert Burns compared love to a red, red rose and I feel that its discovery beside the inscription in the Book of Remembrance, together with the painting I did for Gramp when I was thirteen, has urged me to craft this story around love. Although love in all its forms will be the central, most significant aspect of the Jeffson family saga, I know it will be a long and difficult path to navigate.

I can't ignore Tom Jeffson in this story any longer. For his daughters to agree not to remember him in any way after his death, he must have done some dreadful things to them during his life, but was this just because of tough love or was there more to it?

It doesn't take a genius to work out that Tom Jeffson is going to be a very difficult character for me to create, and the hard fact that I knew him as a child is only going to cause more complications. I didn't hate Gramp: I didn't love him, either, even though he was always kind to me and took a great interest in my hobbies and various childhood quests (for example my obsession to find a four-leaved clover on his back lawn).

Aunt Daisy lifts her glasses from the bridge of her nose with her thumb and forefinger and nods her head wisely in my direction.

'I know our Rose wouldn't have been happy with Bert,' she says in dramatic conclusion to the tale of my grandma's doomed first romance.

'How can you know that?' Mum asks. 'You were just a little girl.'

'It was all too intense and – I've got to say it – superficial.' Aunt Daisy holds up her hand and counts off on her fingers the reasons she feels Bert and Rose wouldn't have been happy in their marriage.

'For one, his family was rich and we weren't. Two, he was a handsome man and our Rose was just a plain-looking girl. And thirdly, his parents bought their first house for them as a wedding present without even consulting Rose. He had even told her she wasn't allowed to take her chest of drawers into the new house because it was too old and scratched.'

Aunt Daisy shakes her head in a theatrical diatribe of misgivings. 'It wasn't an equal match. I know our mam had her reservations, too, even though outwardly she was thrilled Rose was going to marry into money.'

I rub at my chin thoughtfully. 'We can't know how Grandma actually *felt* about him, though, can we? After all, she's not here to tell us.'

Aunt Daisy concedes. 'Yes, you're right, but I *was* there throughout their courtship, even though I was only a little girl.'

'What was Grandma like as an eighteen year-old,' I ask. 'Describe her to me. Not her appearance. Her personality.

Her beliefs, likes and dislikes.'

'Well, as I just said, Rose wasn't what you'd call pretty, but she was independent and had her own mind. She was insistent she was going to carry on working after her marriage; and that was in the olden days when women gave up work when they got married.'

'What did Gramp think about that?'

'He was furious. And so was Bert. He said he wasn't going to have a wife of his working in a shoe factory.'

'How did Grandma react to that?'

'She and Bert had a row about it, but she wouldn't give in to him. I remember it well. We were walking through the park one day to catch the bus to go and see Arthur in Rushden Sanatorium. I'd found a huge, shiny conker and I gave it to Arthur when I got there. There's another story about that conker, but I'll tell you that another day.'

I write the words "conker story" in my notebook and underline them twice as a reminder to ask Aunt Daisy about the story at a later date. 'What was Bert like – not in appearance, but his character?'

Aunt Daisy scratches her head. 'He was a handsome, very traditional man, but when he let his hair down he could be great fun. I think he was secretly proud of Rose for voicing her opinions and being a little bit different to other girls, but at the end of the day, once they were engaged, he wanted her to be like everyone else and conform. Oh – and he daren't say a word out of place to his mother. She had him and his father right under her thumb and they daren't say or do anything without her say-so. She even chose our Rose's bridesmaids for her. To be honest, Bert was a bit of a wimp, I thought. Always did what people expected of him. A little bit boring after a while. Now, when I think of my Bill ...'

I'm scribbling away in my notepad, the characters of my grandma at eighteen and Bert forming in my mind. Aunt Daisy and Mum are laughing about some crazy thing Aunt Daisy did with Uncle Bill when they were young, but then something Mum says about George, my grandad, captures my attention again.

'Our Dad wasn't physically strong,' Mum sighs. 'He was so thin and small, and with his shaky hands and bad chest I always felt he was a bit pathetic compared to what our mam had told me Bert was like.'

'Huh,' Aunt Daisy retorts. 'George might not have been Mister Universe, but he was the strongest person in that household when I was growing up. He kept our mam on the right side of the nut-house door, I can tell you.'

I smile with fond memories of my grandad, George. He would sit in a corner of a room, inconspicuous, quiet, but observing everything. If someone said something silly, or it looked as if an argument was brewing, he'd make a witty comment and then close one eye in my direction in a conspiratorial wink, aimed just at me. My grandad had also been a hero in World War I. He had been very brave and had saved lives, even though it was hard to believe he would have ever been strong enough.

'Mum,' I say. 'Tell me more about Grandad in the war. I know he would never talk about it, but it can't hurt him now.'

'There's not much to tell,' Mum replies. 'Even I didn't know any specific details – nor did our mam. He got a medal for bravery. One of the men he saved kept in touch with him, right up until he died. He was sixteen when he joined up and only nineteen when he came home with shell shock and a bad chest, but with all his arms and legs intact, unlike so many men who'd served with him.'

'What did he do when he came back from the war?'

'Worked in a shoe factory.'

I remember Grandma telling me once never, ever to mention war to Grandad, because just speaking about it would make him get the shakes so badly he wouldn't even be able to fill his own pipe or hold a cup of tea without it spilling.

Mum continues. 'His bad chest was from the effects of mustard gas. It permanently damaged his lungs. And his shakes were because of the shell shock. He had the trembles in his hands for the rest of his life.'

'He wouldn't take part in Remembrance Sunday,' Aunt Daisy says. 'He couldn't bear to watch it on the telly or go to the war memorial for the service. He used to go to the allotment or busy himself in the garden instead.'

Mum blinks back moisture in her eyes. 'He *did* always remember the fallen in his own way,' she says. 'He used to take himself off on his own and our mam used to say he cried like a baby. He just couldn't bear to break down in public, that was all.'

I gulp. Poor Grandad. There must have been so many survivors like him; unable to come to terms with the terrible sights and loss of life they had witnessed. 'He was a hero, Mum,' I say as she wipes a tear from the corner of her eye. 'You don't have to be big and muscular to be a hero.'

'I owe my whole life to George,' Aunt Daisy says to me, her palms upturned.

'Why?'

She sighs, fishes a hanky out from up her sleeve and blows her nose. I look at Mum, who shrugs her shoulders. She obviously doesn't know what Aunt Daisy means.

'It doesn't matter,' Aunt Daisy says. 'It's all in the past now. We shouldn't rake it all up.'

'If you are telling your life story, isn't this what it's all about?' Mum says. 'The past?'

Aunt Daisy retaliates, quite forcefully. 'Not this bit of the past. I've never told a living soul about how George saved me, and I never shall.'

'You can't just leave us in suspense,' I wail. 'We are either telling this story or we aren't.'

'Well – this is not going in the story, and I don't think your grandad's past in the war should either,' she says. 'Even our Eileen and Trevor don't know.'

I close my notebook and place it on the coffee table in front of me, along with my pen. 'All right then. It's your story.'

Aunt Daisy stuffs her hanky back up her sleeve and levers herself off the sofa. 'Wait here,' she orders, as if Mum and I are about to take off and fly around the room like released balloons while she is gone.

She shuffles over to the sideboard and rootles around for a while. Then, sighing in exasperation because she can't find what she is looking for, she turns her attention to another cupboard.

'What are you looking for?' Mum asks.

'That photo. The one taken when I was May Queen,' Aunt Daisy says.

'What's that got to do with George?' I say.

'It was being May Queen that made it happen,' she mumbles. 'What's it called – you know, something that makes something else happen?'

'A catalyst?' I reply.

'Yes, I think that's the word.'

She finds the photo and hands it to Mum. I slide across the sofa to look at it.

Aunt Daisy smiles. 'This was taken on the happiest day of my life. I was twelve years-old and the dress I was wearing was the best money could buy. I had fresh flowers in my hair, too. I could hardly believe that I'd been chosen to be May Queen of Kettering.'

Aunt Daisy looks stunning and so happy in the photograph. She passes it over to me. 'The girl chosen had to be nominated for lots of different things. It was more than just being pretty. You had to be doing well at school, for example, and you had to tell the committee about a time you'd been brave, and kind to others, that sort of thing.'

'That must have been hard.' I speculate out loud. 'Did you have to stand up in front of the committee and be interviewed?'

'Yes, it was made up of school headmasters, the girl guides leader and the Mayor. It was the proudest moment of my life to be chosen out of lots of other girls.'

'What happened afterwards, then? Did it all go wrong?'

'Oh no. It was a perfect day. The sun shone and the whole family turned out in their Sunday best to see me crowned. People threw rose petals high into the air all around me. It was wonderful.'

Aunt Daisy's happy smile slides incrementally from her face, and she looks down at her hands.

'Well?' Mum says expectantly. 'What happened that day that involved my dad saving your life? Our mam never said anything to me.'

The air becomes heavy with dark energy from the past. The silence pounds in my ears, and because Aunt Daisy is becoming distressed, I look out of the window at the traffic in the distance, feeling uncomfortable.

Aunt Daisy sighs. Her voice is thick and nasal. 'I'm sorry. I don't think I should say any more. I still can't bring myself to talk about it. I never have been able to.'

She isn't crying, but the unshed tears inside her can't be concealed, despite her closing her eyelids, as if she is trying to exorcise the memory from her mind.

'It might help to talk about it,' Mum says gently. 'If you've not told a living soul about it since you were twelve, now might be a good time to tell us. We will keep it to ourselves if you want us to, and it doesn't have to go in your life story.'

'Mum's right,' I say, standing up to walk over to where Aunt Daisy is sitting. I put my hand her shoulder. 'We are in control of what goes in the story and it's perfectly all right to leave things out. I'm not going to use Grandad's war story, either. If he couldn't bear to talk about his time in the trenches for the whole of his life, I'm certainly not going to try and second guess what it was like and write about it.'

Aunt Daisy has now taken off her glasses and put them in her lap: her fingertips are pressed tightly into her eye sockets and she is shaking her head slowly. What on earth happened to her? It must have been terrible for not to be able to talk about it. And just how *did* my grandad save her life?

This story is about Aunt Daisy and Grandma Rose, not about me - the author. However, something then happens in my life that gives Aunt Daisy a brief hiatus in the telling of her life story and time to think about events in her past.

Rob and I go on holiday to Cromer in our caravan, as planned.

One day, Rob is stretched out in his camping chair in the sun and I notice that one side of his neck is slightly bigger than the other.

'You've got a bit of a lump in your neck,' I say. 'Did you know?'

Rob rubs at his neck, finding the lump with his fingers for the first time. 'No, I didn't. And I can't even feel it unless I tip my head back.'

He's worried. I know he is. Although we speculate over the next day or so what could be causing it, and eventually settle on a salivary gland infection, I ring the doctor's surgery from the campsite and make him an appointment for the following week.

Two weeks later, we are sitting in a Consultant's office at the hospital.

'It will have to be removed,' the Consultant says. 'And it's best to do it sooner rather than later.'

'Is it cancerous?' Rob says. My heart thumps painfully at the sound of the word.

'Well,' the consultant replies, 'the cells removed in the biopsy aren't normal, but on the grand scale of nastiness of one to a hundred, with one being the most nasty and a hundred the least – thyroid gland cancer is about a ninety-nine. If we leave this lump where it is, and don't remove it, it *could* turn into cancer.'

'What will the operation entail?' I ask. 'Does he have to have his thyroid gland removed completely?'

'Ah. This is the clever bit,' the consultant says to Rob with a smile. 'If I remove the half with the lump – or nodule as it's called – and leave the other side intact, radioactive medicine will see off any remaining nasty cells in one go without the need for further treatment. And the half of your thyroid that's left should continue to work perfectly well.'

'Will there be any side effects?' Rob asks, his voice surprisingly normal.

'No, you'll just be mildly radioactive for a couple of days after the treatment and will have to be careful with other people around you. That's all.'

Rob's operation is a success and he makes a complete recovery. The consultant says he is lucky that we noticed the lump so early and I thank God that I saw it that day in Cromer when he had his head back, sunbathing.

Aunt Daisy, Mum and I forget about her life story for a few weeks while I go through my mini-crisis, our Tuesdays and Saturdays passing by with talk of knitting patterns, recipes and speculating on what is happening next in Coronation Street, Doctors and Emmerdale. We don't even mention Aunt Daisy's life story project and, after her getting so upset over the May Queen photograph, I don't think either Mum or I want to be the first to mention it.

Since they decided to live together, it's not often Mum and Aunt Daisy are apart, but, on this particular Tuesday, Mum is out with her friends, Joyce and Eric. Aunt Daisy has stayed at home in the bungalow and she is cooking my lunch for me, as usual. When I arrive it seems strange to see Aunt Daisy in her pinny, bustling about in Mum's kitchen on her own.

She serves up my dinner on a tray. 'I'm really glad you still came even though Margaret's not here. I want to talk to you about something while she's out of the way.'

'Oh. What's that, then?'

'My life story.'

This sounds ominous and I can't stop my face wrinkling into a cringe. 'Okay,' I say hesitantly as Aunt Daisy puts the telly on and then fetches her own tray. 'But why can't you tell me in front of Mum?'

'Because I can't. It'll only upset her and she'll think badly of me if she knows what happened after I was May Queen.'

We chat about trivial things during lunch. I know that once we have finished eating, she is going tell me about the time Grandad saved her life.

After lunch, I stand up to take my tray out into the kitchen. 'Shall we chat while we wash up?' I say, wanting to reassure her, without actually saying it, that I won't be writing anything down.

Aunt Daisy plucks a clean tea towel from a drawer. 'Good idea. I'll dry. You wash.'

There's a minute or two's silence while I fill the washing-up bowl with soapy water.

'It's about George. You remember I said he saved my life?' she begins.

'Yes. It was somehow tied up with you being May Queen, wasn't it? That's why you got upset when you showed us the photograph.'

'I'll start at the beginning,' she says. 'The day after I was May Queen, the General Strike of nineteen twenty-six was declared. Our Rose and George both worked at the same factory as our dad. He was a foreman and Rose and George both worked on the factory floor. He didn't support the politics of the General Strike, but Rose and George both did; so much so, they went and signed up to join the picket lines.'

'Even Grandma?' I say, surprised.

'Yes. That was what put Tom into such a bad temper. He was furious and forbade Rose to go out on the picket line, but our Rose always did know her own mind. She wasn't about to be dictated to by our dad. She argued the toss with him all through that week. Oh, he said some terrible things to her, but she wouldn't be told what to do. He told her to concentrate on women's things, such as the recipes and knitting patterns in the *Woman's Weekly* magazine, and keep her nose out of business that was a man's concern. She told him to stuff the *Woman's Weekly* up his arse.'

I burst out laughing, full of pride for my feisty Grandma. I can just imagine how incensed my great-grandad must have been, knowing that this was in the nineteen-twenties when women were supposed to be lady-like, subservient to men and do as they were told.

'On the following Sunday lunchtime, Tom went to the

Club as usual. Because of the General Strike he was in a bad mood, and whenever he was in a bad mood he would come home absolutely paralytic.'

Aunt Daisy leans on the draining board, the tea towel slung over her shoulder. She gives a deep sigh and shakes her head. 'It was all my fault, what happened then; my mam said so.'

Aunt Daisy then covers her eyes with one hand. She clutches tightly at the draining board edge with the other. She is breathing so fast, she is almost panting. This memory of hers must be absolutely dreadful.

'Cross your heart you'll never tell anyone else?' she pleads.

'I promise.'

'And you won't write it in my life story?'

'No, not if you don't want me to.'

There is a long silence while I continue to wash up, the crockery and saucepans piling up on the draining board. I empty the soapy water down the sink, hoping the action will act as a trigger for her to unburden the secret that has remained buried deep within her for all these years.

'I was in our back yard with Billy Potter,' she mumbles. 'He was an older lad who lived a few doors away. He was a bit slow-witted – a late developer, I suppose you'd say nowadays. Anyway, our dad came home, absolutely blind drunk. He saw me with Billy and came up to the top of the garden, yelling his head off. He hated me having anything to do with Billy Potter. Then it happened.'

'What?'

Aunt Daisy's voice is now a throaty whisper. 'He touched me, Anne. He thrust his dirty hand up inside my knickers and touched me.'

'Who? Billy Potter?'

'No, our dad. But it was my own fault. You see, I was showing off in the May Queen dress. I'd put it on to show my friends in the street, and then Billy and I went into my garden to look at his book of garden birds and I didn't go back inside to take it off and change into my playing clothes.

When Dad came up the entry I was showing off again – to Billy. I was pulling the dress up and doing *Knees Up Mother Brown*. When I saw Dad coming, shouting the odds, I jumped up on the wall quickly, making out I was just looking at the book, but he'd already seen me prancing about and was furious.

'When he got within a few yards of me, he yelled out to Billy to bugger off home and called him a half-wit. Billy jumped over the wall, scared, and garden-hopped to his own back yard.

'Dad then grabbed me round the waist and yanked me off the wall, but his hand was up between my legs. I didn't know what was happening for a start. He was crushing me into him so hard I couldn't breathe. Then I felt his hand inside my knickers and he thrust his fingers inside me so hard I squealed out in pain.'

I realise my heart is pounding and I'm holding my breath in shock. I prise the tea towel out of Aunt Daisy's hand and dry my own hands. 'The bastard,' I say. 'The absolute bastard. He was nothing but a dirty pervert.'

Aunt Daisy's shoulders feel thin and bony beneath my arms as I hug her. The years between us fall away. At that moment, we are as close as sisters, even though our ages are separated by two generations.

'Did he ... did he ever... you know?' I am spluttering with rage. I can't get the words out.

'No, but he would have done if it hadn't been for George. He saved me, Anne. I've always known it.'

'Did Grandma know about this?'

'Yes. But it was kept in the family. I was lucky that Billy came to my rescue and Dad eventually had to let me go because Billy was in next door's garden, shouting his head off for help, and one of the neighbours came out to see what all the fuss was about. A few days later, Billy told our Rose that Dad had put his hand up my dress, and then Rose told my mother. Our mam was furious. She hit our dad over the head and nearly killed him, but he managed to worm his way back into her affections. It didn't matter what he ever did, she always forgave him. Then, they blamed *me* for showing off in my May Queen dress. Our Mam said I was a little hussy and would get what I deserved one day. She forbade me to ever speak about it again and ordered me to say it was Billy that had interfered with me if any of the neighbours mentioned anything.'

I shout out, much too loudly. 'It wasn't *your* fault, Aunt Daisy. You were just a twelve year-old child who wanted to wear a pretty dress and dance around in it!'

'Oh, it *was* my fault. I should have been sharper – more careful. It was stupid of me to show off in front of Billy.'

'Aunt Daisy ...' I release her from my hug and hold her shoulders firmly. 'This was never, ever, your fault. Are you telling me that, when I was twelve, if my dad had done this to me, *you* would say it was my fault?'

'No,' she splutters. 'Of course not. Your dad would never have done anything like that ...'

'But if he did – had done?'

She shakes her head helplessly. I tear off a couple of sheets of kitchen roll and hand them to her. She is blinking furiously, trying to clear the tears from her eyes. She lifts her glasses and rubs away at her eyes and cheeks, and then blows her nose.

'Being May Queen was such a special day. It was magical,' she says in a throaty whisper. 'The best day of my life. Even knowing what came afterwards doesn't change anything about that day. I loved every second of it.'

'I'm so glad you've told me, Aunt Daisy. You might start to feel a bit better about it now you've actually told someone. I can't believe you've carried this guilt with you all these years.'

Aunt Daisy shakes her head, holding the tissue to her nose. 'Afterwards, when your grandma and George got married, they wouldn't move out into their own home. They lived right there in Cornwall Road to watch over me as I grew up. George never let me out of his sight. He lay down the law to Rose and our mam and said I mustn't be left alone with Tom even for one second. He made me promise I would tell him if Tom ever tried anything again. He might have been small in stature, but to me George was a mountain of a man. I felt safe because I always sensed Dad would try something again if he was drunk. George promised me he would never, ever leave me alone in that house with a father who had interfered with me and a mother who blamed me for what had happened.'

'So is that why Rose and George never moved out, then?'

Aunt Daisy nods, holding the tissue over her nose. 'Rose desperately wanted her own house, but George was adamant they had to stay put until I left home. He had concerns about leaving our mam, too. You see, Tom was a tyrant in those days, Anne. He was such a dangerous man. That's why I don't know if I can bring myself to go to the Crematorium on Friday to look at the Book of Remembrance.'

I make us both a mug of tea and we retreat into the living room. Aunt Daisy is small and pale and she is shaking so much, she can't hold her mug without steadying it with both hands.

'Please don't tell anyone, will you?' she whispers. 'It makes me feel so dirty.'

I shake my head, disgusted that Aunt Daisy has been made to feel like this for almost her entire life. 'I promise I won't tell anyone if you don't want me to. Do you think he ever abused anyone else in the family?'

'I don't think so, apart from our mam. He was a filthy bastard, though. Our mam used to call his fancy women "red-lipped strumpets"; she should have left him, but she wouldn't because of the fear of scandal. She put up with so much.'

'What do you mean "apart from our mam?" '

'He used to force himself on her. Night after night, Rose and I used to hear it. It's a wonder it didn't put both of us off men for the rest of our lives. Once, Rose saw what he'd done to the tops of her legs – they were black and blue with bruises.'

I begin to feel sick. My great-grandma, Liz, was as much

378

a victim as Aunt Daisy. 'I really think you need to tell Auntie Eileen about this,' I plead.

She shakes her head. 'I'm too ashamed.'

'Well you've no need to be ashamed.'

'What do you think about it all?' she asks, her eighty-seven year old eyes so full of childish innocence it makes a lump form in my throat.

'I think you've been incredibly brave all these years. For you to have gone through something as awful as that, and reached your age without ever telling a single soul, spells out the word COURAGE in great big letters to me.'

Aunt Daisy's throws a wonky smile when I say the word *courage*. 'It's like I've got poison inside me,' she says.

'Guilt is like that. Your mum was wrong and you weren't to blame in any way, but, because you were just a child, for your whole life you have believed what she said was true. I think Grandma Liz was terrified of what would happen if it all came out in public. It would have been such a stigma if her husband had been exposed as a paedophile, especially in those days.'

'It would have been a stigma for me, too,' Aunt Daisy says, rubbing at her forehead. 'Everyone talked about girls who had been *interfered with*. It was as if you were shop-soiled goods. I can remember one girl at school; she never did get married.'

I can remember my great-grandma, Liz. She was such a lovely, gentle person. I can imagine the turmoil she found herself in after her husband had done such a terrible thing to her daughter. Perhaps she was only trying to protect her daughter, knowing that if it all came out in public, her little girl would be vilified and people would talk about her for many years to come. But then again, this was the nineteen-twenties. Perhaps divorce wasn't such an easy option as nowadays.

I can't leave Aunt Daisy on her own. I find my bag and extract my mobile phone and go out into the garden. Having explained to my boss that my great-aunt is unwell, I manage to book a half-day annual leave.

That night I have such a vivid dream, I feel compelled to write it all down when I wake up in the morning. It must be because Aunt Daisy's terrible experience is playing constantly on my mind.

In this dream, I was taken by the hand and led into a massive marble temple, where, on a huge chair at one end, sat my great-grandfather, Tom Jeffson. He was distressed and upset, blubbering like a baby, sobbing and pleading with me to let him tell his side of the story.

The dream leaves me feeling disturbed and exhausted. We are scheduled to visit the crematorium on Friday to view the Book of Remembrance and now I don't even want to look at the inscription, knowing now what a horrible man my great-grandfather had been.

In my head, all I can hear is Tom's voice repeating: *"I'm sorry, so, so sorry."* As I make breakfast, I put the radio on full blast in my kitchen to try and re-programme my brain, shut him out and forget about the horrible dream. I really don't like having to think about, or even talk about, Tom Jeffson.

I ring Mum's number before I go to work, firstly to ask her about her day out yesterday and secondly to check if Aunt Daisy is okay.

Aunt Daisy answers the telephone. She is surprisingly chirpy. 'I've told Margaret what happened to me,' she says. 'And you were right, it's done me the world of good to talk about it. And I've decided – you can put it in the story, after all.'

'Are you going to tell Auntie Eileen and Trevor?'

'I've been thinking about that, and no – not just yet. I don't want to upset them. I feel much better now I've told you and Margaret. I should have got it off my chest years ago. And when you said that I'd had courage to carry that secret all those years, you were right. Bringing this out into the open in the story is what I have to do to help people who might have gone through the same sort of thing. At least some good might come of it now. But I still feel dirty inside, I don't want Eileen and Trevor to know. Not just yet, anyway.'

I then tell Aunt Daisy I've been so worried about her, I can't get it out of my head. I tell her about my dream where Gramp is crying in the marble temple and repeating over and over again that he is sorry.

'I think it's a sign,' she says. 'We need to get my story written down, warts and all, before I pop off.' (She's always looking for "signs", and she makes dying sound like just popping out to the shops for a pint of milk.)

I chuckle at her. 'I've been thinking, too, Aunt Daisy. I don't want to write this story as a memoir. I want to write it as a novel. What do you think?'

'Oh. What a good idea! Will I be able to get my photograph taken for the cover?'

'Oh yes,' I laugh down the telephone. 'We will have to go shopping for a special outfit.'

We then make arrangements for our visit to the crematorium on Friday. Aunt Daisy has decided to face up to her demons and come along, despite her earlier misgivings. We decide to invite my mother-in-law along, too, because after all, my father-in-law's inscription is on the opposite page in the Book of Remembrance. I still feel apprehensive about the visit, though. I don't know if I can bear to even look at the inscription after knowing what Tom did to my lovely Aunt Daisy when she was twelve.

Soon, it's Friday and the second anniversary of the death of my father-in-law when the Book of Remembrance is open at the designated page.

Aunt Daisy is buoyant and talkative on the journey to the crematorium. She's still not convinced the inscription is her father's, because she can't think of anyone who could have signed the order for it to be placed there. My mother-in-law, who is sitting in the back of my car with Mum, explains the procedure she had to go through two years ago when my father-in-law died.

Aunt Daisy turns to face me from the passenger seat. She

prods me in the arm. 'See – I told you so. You have to be the next of kin, and it wasn't me, it wasn't our Rose, and I know it wasn't Lily. If the old sod has somehow got his name in the Book of Remembrance, someone's done it under false pretences.'

'We'll find out in a minute, once and for all,' Mum says. 'I just hope you're ready for it.'

'We mustn't forget about Michael. It's his day of remembrance, too.' my mother-in-law chirps up from the back.

After parking up in the crematorium car park, we make our way to the Chapel of Rest. Fortunately, there is no one else there. It's a tiny room and the four of us crowd round the book, open at today's date in its glass cabinet.

'Well, I'll be ...,' Aunt Daisy says, her hand flying up to her mouth to stop herself swearing. 'You're right. It *is* him. But I don't know who would have put it in. That red rose must have cost a fortune!'

My mother-in-law reads my father-in-law's inscription out loud and then steps over to the Bible reading in a cabinet on the opposite side of the room. I can tell she's not happy about Aunt Daisy's outburst and her almost swearing in the Chapel of Rest. I begin to wonder if perhaps I should have made two journeys today – one with her and another with Mum and Aunt Daisy.

Aunt Daisy is still standing with her hand clamped over her mouth, shaking her head at Mum. I'm torn between the two – should I stand with my mother-in-law or comfort Aunt Daisy?

Aunt Daisy sits down heavily on a chair in the corner of the room. She's flabbergasted. Mum has another look, just to make sure. She then whips a piece of paper out of her handbag and carefully copies out the inscription.

'I need to ring our Eileen,' Aunt Daisy says.

I hand her my mobile phone, having already found Auntie Eileen's number for her. She stares at the small green screen with the black numbers. 'How do I ring it?'

I tell her to just press the green button.

From the one-sided conversation, I can tell Eileen is as surprised as Aunt Daisy. When Aunt Daisy gives me back my phone, she purses her lips, as much in anger as surprise. I cancel the call for her.

'I'm going to get to the bottom of this,' she says, 'if it's the last thing I do.'

'Perhaps it was one of his *floozies*,' I say a short while later when we are speculating on who could have placed the order for the inscription. 'Perhaps she pretended to be you or one of your sisters. We'll have to do a bit of detective work and try to find out who it was.'

We are sitting at a table in Telford Lodge, having decided to go for a bite of lunch after our visit to the crematorium. Aunt Daisy, after the initial shock, is chatty and bubbly again, excited about writing her life story as a novel.

'I shall pose like this for my photograph,' she says, flinging back her arm and placing her hand delicately behind her cocked head, like Rose in the film *Titanic*. 'Then I'll hold a glass of wine in one hand and a long-stemmed cigarette holder in the other and give a sexy smile for the photographer when he takes my photograph.'

'What will you be wearing?' Mum asks with a grin. 'You'll have to go to Marks and Sparks for something posher than those tartan slacks and a hand-knitted jumper.'

I start to giggle. Aunt Daisy doesn't look her age, even in tartan trousers. 'It will have to be either black for a tragedy or something bright, such as yellow, for a happy ending.'

'Oh no. Nothing so boring as black. I shall wear bright pink like Barbara Cartland. And I'll have a pink feather boa. And I might even have my hair dyed pink when I next have a perm.'

I want to capture this moment. Me, Mum and Aunt Daisy, having lunch together, laughing, joking, happy because Aunt Daisy seems to be free, at last, from the corrosion of guilt that has blighted her for years. It's clearly done her the world of good to finally get this awful revelation about her father off her chest.

Mum, too, is happier than she has been since Dad died nine months ago. I wish I had a camera to take a photograph of them both as they are right now – a permanent physical record of my eighty-seven year old great aunt pretending to be Barbara Cartland and my mum howling with laughter, a glass of lemon and lime juice in her hand. I can't wait to write this novel. I'm as excited as a six year-old on Christmas morning. I now know exactly where I'm going with it.

'Sorry, Tom,' I say out loud with a laugh, raising my glass of Coke into the air. 'I'm afraid your sordid secrets are about to be told to the world.'

Aunt Daisy raises up her tea cup. 'Cheers, Dad,' she chuckles. 'You might have thought you got away with everything, but every dog has his day, and now we are going to have ours and there's not a thing you can do about it.'

I am in a permanent state of wonder, staggering through everyday life in a daze. Aunt Daisy and Grandma Rose's stories are as tightly intertwined and tangled as an ancient Virginia creeper. Rose and Daisy. Daisy and Rose. Sometimes it's difficult to tell the difference between the two of them.

I begin to realise that the common denominator in every single tale, anecdote and memory is their father, Tom. There are shocking stories. Deeply personal, I don't see how I can put them in the novel, and wonder if they are best left at the bottom of the box file that contains all my notes, never to again see the light of day. I laugh until I cry with tales of Aunt Daisy as a child and teenager. She must have been a handful and was downright naughty sometimes. Then I am told stories about attempted suicides; child abandonment; acrimonious breakdowns in relationships; my Grandma being trapped in a situation with no way of escape; extra-marital affairs and the birth of a baby with a terrible deformation. Then Mum and Aunt Daisy have a conversation and speculate about someone who was – publicly – their cousin and who Aunt Daisy always suspected was really their half-sister. Then there is a distant cousin who is biologically someone's mother but the baby was secretly given away to another woman, and tales of distant uncles marrying someone who might have been their niece – the list of secrets and family crises goes on and on, some of it going back to the nineteenth century. Some of it I shall use in the novel, and some of it, Aunt Daisy says, I must leave out because of the ructions her revelations will cause.

Life in the Jeffson family for the last hundred years has been like an iceberg, the respectable ten per cent above the water with the dirty ninety per cent hidden away, but lurking nonetheless, ready to tear a fatal hole, not in the hull of a ship but in lives stretching out way into the future.

At the end of that day, when I sit at my computer typing up my notes, I know there is some true story I can't ever write about. But, as I use up a whole pack of post-it notes and piece together all the elements to map-out a novel based on Aunt Daisy's tales of the past, I find there is very little I need to leave out, because, by writing the story as a novel with some made-up characters alongside real-life characters, the material I have is as rich as a table laden with exotic ingredients.

I do, however, have a big problem. How can I write about all this stuff when people's roots have been based on huge lies? These people are still alive and living in Kettering and the surrounding area, with their false histories and genes painstakingly researched. It will feel as if I am replacing their cherished family trees with plastic daffodils if I churn up some of these secrets and lies out of the earth.

After taking some legal advice, we find out it would be best if we change the names of characters still living, as well as the family name, unless people expressly give their permission to use their real names. Over the course of the next few weeks we ask all the living characters what they want to be called in the novel (and also if they want to appear at all). Mum says she wants me to use her real name. Aunt Daisy picks "Daisy" because Uncle Bill used to whistle and sing *Bicycle Made For Two* to her when they were courting. Auntie Eileen picks the name "Eileen" because she had named her favourite doll Eileen when she was a child.

'The emotions won't change,' I reassure Aunt Daisy. 'Because even with fictitious characters, it will be yours and Mum's memories and emotions that write this novel. All we are doing is tapping into them using my imagination.'

At this point, we decide that one of our characters – someone very, very special to Aunt Daisy – will be given life. Her baby son, Neil, died tragically of meningitis as a toddler. 'Use his real name,' Aunt Daisy says. 'It's important to me that you do.'

We then talk about what sort of life to give him. 'I don't really mind what he does with his life so much as *who* he is. I want him to be a good person, Anne. To be there, in the background of my story, alive and real. I want him to have a place because he never got a chance to make his own place in the world.'

However, there is one terrible event in Aunt Daisy's life she doesn't want me to write about. I agree whole-heartedly and we talk about how we might change the story to accommodate her wishes and yet include the character as he was in real life, because to leave him out would be unthinkable to her. We decide that the best way to do this is to invent a character to run alongside him as we tell his story in such a way that it is, in parts, based on the truth, but with a fictitious outcome.

Part Five

July 2006

Almost four years have passed since Aunt Daisy, Mum and I decided to write the novel.

As I stand in my office, chatting to my boss about an agenda for a Council meeting, I hear a dog barking, tied up in the car park below. In three days' time we are flying out to Ibiza for a holiday and I'm a bit miffed because the temperature in England this week is hotter than in the Mediterranean.

I peer out of the window to check on the dog's welfare and see Mum hurrying across the car park in the burning sunshine. She is heading towards the library, carrying a Burberry shopping bag, obviously off to choose her books to take on holiday. I know this because yesterday she told me that was the last thing she had to pack in her suitcase. As if she is telepathic, she stops and looks around. (She knows which window is my office.) I wave. She waves back.

Twenty minutes later I just happen to see her returning across the car park. She might now be seventy-four years old, but she has walked for half an hour in the heat to get this far and is now heading off back home. She is so fit, she puts me to shame.

I wave and she looks up. I gesture for her to come into the Council offices and run downstairs into the foyer to meet her.

'Phew,' she says. 'It's a bit hot today.'

'I'll be finishing for lunch in about fifteen minutes. I'll run you home if you like. It's too much for you to walk back home in this heat.'

A colleague, Jean, joins us in the foyer. She knows Mum and says: 'It's not long until your holiday now, Margaret. I bet you are really looking forward to it.'

'Oh, I am,' Mum replies with a smile. 'I might even meet a millionaire and just stay there to live a life of luxury.'

Eighteen months ago, Mum had become a great-grandma for the first time. 'You'd never do that,' I tease. 'You love Tyler too much to ever leave him behind.'

'That's true,' she says. 'He's the light of my life. I can't wait to play with him for two whole weeks.'

I go back up into the office to fetch my bag and Mum stays in the foyer, chatting to Jean for a few minutes.

Once we are in the car Mum tells me how much she is looking forward to our family holiday. 'I never thought I'd come to terms with life after Brian,' she says. 'But I think I have. Thank you so much for inviting me on holiday with you all.'

'You can come away with us whenever you like,' I say. 'You know that.'

As I drive Mum home from the library that lunchtime, we talk about the novel, which is almost complete. We agree to suggest the title "Twisted Garlands" to Aunt Daisy, having decided a few weeks ago that, once it is edited, we are going to try and secure an agent with a view to seeking publication.

We pull into the driveway of Mum's bungalow. Her front garden is crammed with colourful summer bedding plants. Mum sighs. 'I hope my neighbour keeps my garden well-watered while we are away, especially if the weather carries on like this. I've been having to do it all twice a day and it's really tedious filling up watering cans.'

'You need a hose pipe,' I say. 'I'll get one for you when we get back from Ibiza.'

The following day, Mum rings me before I go to work.

'I've hurt my back,' she says. 'I tried lifting two watering cans at once last night and felt something go pop. I've just rang the doctor's and got an appointment late this afternoon. Do you think you can leave off a bit early and take me? I don't think I shall be able to walk.'

I'm alarmed and annoyed at her. I can hardly believe she has tried to lift two heavy watering cans and has hurt her back so badly she can't even walk only two days before we are due to fly out on holiday.

Later, armed with strong painkillers and the advice to return to the surgery when we get back from holiday if her back hasn't improved, Mum is apologetic.

'I'm sorry,' she says. 'It was such a silly thing to do. I didn't think.'

Three weeks later, our holiday in Ibiza now just a memory, Mum and I are back in the doctor's surgery.

She can hardly lever herself out of the waiting room chair when her name is called and I have to help her up. She can't walk without holding on to me, either. The pain has etched itself into the lines on her face and she looks so much older than only a few weeks ago.

'I think it must be a slipped disc,' Mum says to the doctor during her consultation. 'I'm in terrible pain, and I spent most of my holiday in my room, reading, because I could hardly even walk along the corridor to the lift.'

She turns to me. 'Anne's holiday was completely ruined, wasn't it?'

'No it wasn't,' I argue. 'I just felt so helpless and sorry for you because you couldn't get out and about and enjoy yourself.'

I explain that Mum saw a doctor in Ibiza, because she had some other health problems, too, as well as the pain in her back. I show him the pills he had prescribed for her.

The doctor says he is going to order an X-ray and gives us a form to take to the hospital. The next day, I can't take Mum to the hospital for her X-ray because I'm at work, but Auntie Eileen takes her instead. Just two days later, Mum receives a call from the doctor's surgery receptionist. She has to go for a blood test, too.

Again, Auntie Eileen takes her. The next morning, my telephone rings at work.

'Can you come round right now?' Aunt Daisy says, her voice high and panicky. 'Your Mum's in a right pickle. She's in so much pain with her back she can't move out of the chair. And she seems hot and delirious – not making any sense at all. I think we need to take her to A & E.'

I'm shocked when I get to Mum's bungalow. Every tiny movement causes her to cry out in pain. I ring the doctor's surgery and the receptionist tells me the doctor will call me back very soon.

Within a few minutes the doctor rings back. He says he will visit her at home in an hour or so.

I ring work and book the rest of the day off as annual leave. Mum is obviously very ill, and I wonder if it is something else other than her back that is causing it.

The doctor arrives after lunch and examines Mum. It's clear she is not going to be able to get herself into my car and the doctor proclaims that we will need to call an ambulance if she has to go to A & E. He asks if he can use the telephone and rings someone at the hospital.

After the phone call, the doctor gestures with his head for me to join him in the hallway while Aunt Daisy busies herself packing a few essential items in a bag for Mum to take with her. 'The blood test results came back as urgent this morning,' he says. 'They show that Margaret's back problem could be a symptom of something else which needs further investigation. She might need to stay in for a few days.'

'Is it osteoporosis?' I ask.

The doctor doesn't answer my question. He reminds me of a politician, skirting the issue. Instead, he says: 'The X-ray and blood test results indicate she will probably need a bone biopsy and some other tests. How long has she had this pain in her back?'

'Since the middle of July. She did it when she tried to lift two watering cans of water at once. Why does she need a bone biopsy?'

Again, the doctor doesn't directly respond to my query. 'I've referred her to a consultant – they will be able to fill you in with the details at the hospital. Can you go in the ambulance with her?'

'Of course,' I say, my heart thumping behind my breastbone. The doctor obviously doesn't want to give me any more information. 'And I'll stay with her as long as I have to.'

The ambulance arrives. Aunt Daisy wants to come to the hospital, too, but only one person is allowed to accompany Mum in the ambulance.

When we arrive, Mum is wheeled straight into a cubicle in A & E. She squeals out in pain when the paramedics transfer her onto an examination couch. A nurse fetches her some pillows to make her more comfortable.

It seems like hours before she is seen by anyone, other than the nurse who has taken her details. She needs to go to the toilet and when I ask someone, a friendly nurse brings her a commode. She pulls the curtains round the cubicle and, with my help, the nurse and I assist Mum to slide off the couch onto the commode. I'm clumsy and don't know how to move someone who is in so much pain and helpless. The movement takes her breath away and she cries out.

If it was me in Mum's place I would be embarrassed to use the commode with someone else in the cubicle, even if it was only my daughter, so I ask her if she wants me to go and wait in the corridor. She shakes her head. 'I don't really care,' she says, her chin falling on her chest. Alarmed, I decide to stay but turn my back in deference to giving her some privacy and pretend to read a notice on the wall.

After a minute or two, a Registrar turns up and slides around the curtain. He has Mum's notes in his hand. She is still sitting on the commode with her knickers round her ankles.

'My mum needed the toilet. I'll just help her get off this commode,' I explain.

As I take mum's arm to help her get up, the doctor disappears back round the curtain, only to reappear just seconds later. I can't get mum up on my own and I don't know the best way to lift her. I stand behind her and try clumsily to heave her up, but she squeals in pain.

'It doesn't matter. Leave her there,' the doctor says irritably as he perches on the couch, mum's notes by his side. He leafs through the pages and finds the blood test results. While he is doing this, I am deeply shocked by the lack of privacy and dignity afforded my mum but don't say anything. For all I know, it's quite normal for a doctor to be asking a patient questions while she is sitting on a commode.

'How long have you had this back pain?' he asks mum.

Mum frowns, 'I'm sorry ... I didn't quite catch ...' Her voice fades and she looks towards me for help, bewildered.

I explain to the doctor that Mum is deaf, and ask if I can answer his questions on her behalf.

'Does she have a hearing aid?'

'Yes,' I reply. 'But she can't hear properly without lip-reading, even with her hearing aid in.'

I'm embarrassed and don't want to say to the doctor that she won't be able to read his lips because he has a foreign accent. He bends right down almost double to look Mum in the face, as her chin is by now resting on her chest. Apart from the obvious pain she is in, I'm so worried about her. Her forehead is red and shiny and when I take her hand to reassure her, it is cold, but clammy. I wonder if she is in some sort of shock because of the intensity of the pain.

'Can you turn up your hearing aid,' he shouts in Mum's face. 'I need to ask you some questions.'

Mum looks up in panic. I know she hasn't heard him properly and doesn't understand what he has just said. I feel angry, but don't say anything else.

The medical interview with Mum doesn't go well and the doctor quickly becomes frustrated. Mum is trying her hardest to read his lips but I know that his foreign accent isn't helping matters.

'Perhaps I can help?' I venture again, trying to ignore the elephant in the room that is the sight of my Mum, trying constantly to pull her knickers up over her knees whilst sitting on a commode and being interviewed by a doctor.

'Does she have dementia?'

'No!' I retort, quite forcefully. 'She's just deaf – she usually manages perfectly well, but she's in such a lot of pain, and feels so ill ...'

I wait for Mum's usual spirited comment of: *"I'm deaf, not daft."* But it doesn't come. Her head slumps forwards again and she gives up with the knickers.

'Can I have something for the pain?' she mumbles. 'Please?'

The doctor sighs and reluctantly allows me answer the remainder of his questions. Why do they treat people like this? People like my lovely Mum, who has always been so respectable and proper, and I know will be feeling horrified that she is sitting on a commode, her knickers round her knees, being interviewed by a doctor. I can't see her eyes, but I know she is crying because a dew drop forms on the end of her nose. I get up off my chair – mid-sentence – to pull a tissue from a box on the other side of the cubicle. 'Excuse me for a minute,' I say.

The doctor gives me a look that says: *how dare you have the audacity to interrupt my questions.*

I pass the tissue to Mum, who takes it from me without looking up. Her knickers slide down around her ankles again – along with her shattered dignity.

After seeing the doctor in A & E, Mum is transferred to a ward which is clearly full of very ill people because most of the curtains are drawn around their beds.

After a while, my sister-in-law arrives, bringing Mum some clean nighties, her dressing gown and further supplies of underwear having heard that she is going to have to stay in hospital. We chat for a while, our voices low. Mum seems comfortable, for the moment, having been given some strong medicine for the pain and has fallen asleep when a different doctor arrives to explain that she has been booked in for a bone biopsy the next day.

He gently wakes Mum up and explains to her that she will have a short general anaesthetic, which will be better for her, but that she may be in a bit of pain afterwards. Then he patiently answers my questions about the procedure. The biopsy has apparently to be taken from her pelvis, not her back where the pain is.

Mum nods. 'Thank you, Doctor,' she says in a way that tells me she hasn't heard a word he's said. Never mind, I'll fill her in when the doctor's gone. It's not worth the rigmarole of explaining that she's deaf.

'If the pain is in her back, why do you need to take the biopsy from her pelvis?' I ask.

'Because it is the best place to obtain a bone marrow sample,' he says with a smile and then, before I can ask any more questions, he disappears through the curtains.

Once I've explained about the biopsy to Mum, I go in search of a nurse to explain her deafness and need for people to face her and speak clearly when they talk to her, so that she can read their lips.

The two nurses at the other end of the ward are rushing around. They are so busy, I feel terrible for even thinking about interrupting them. There is a lady on the opposite side of the ward to Mum who is obviously very poorly because the curtains are flapping and moving constantly with a hive of health care workers buzzing around her bed. With a thumping heart I realise there is some sort of medical emergency going on, because I can hear the doctor's voice too, followed by an anguished, long drawn out *"Noooo"*.

A frail, elderly man and a woman of about my age are ejected from the cubicle. The man is distressed and looks as if he is crying, the woman white-faced, trying to comfort him.

I spin around to find a spare chair for the elderly man and take it over to them.

'Thank you,' the woman says. 'They won't let us stay. It's my mother, she's ...'

'If there's anything I can do or fetch for you,' I say helplessly and shrug my shoulders, 'I'm sitting with my mum over there.'

I give them some privacy – well, as much as I can as they are plonked in the middle of the ward while goodness knows what terrible procedure is being done to the poor woman behind the curtains.

'What's going on?' Mum asks when I return.

'Someone's really poorly. An emergency. All the nurses and the doctor are behind the curtains with her, and her husband and daughter have been sent out. I fetched him a chair.'

'Oh dear. Poor soul. You're a good girl, even if you did nearly kill me this afternoon in A & E trying to lift me off that commode. Did you manage to find someone to explain that I'm deaf and need to be able to lip-read? I'm really worried I won't be able to hear people when they speak to me if you're not here.'

I shake my head. 'No, sorry. They're all too busy. If I can't speak to someone before I have to go, I'll write a note and leave it on your bedside cabinet.'

Mum nods. 'All right. I don't know how many times today I've told people I'm deaf. I'm used to being treated as if I'm half-witted, but when you're ill it seems to get elevated to senile dementia!'

'You heard that doctor back in A & E, then?' I say with a grimace.

'Not really. I read his lips as much as I was able to. I might not have been able to understand him, but I did make out the word *dementia*.'

Mum raises her eyebrows and laughs out loud. 'I feel ever so much better now. I don't know what they've given me, but whatever it is, it's hit the spot. I feel like giggling all the time.'

'Probably morphine. You were spark out for an hour, snoring and slobbering like a bulldog.'

'Well, I feel much better now I've had a sleep. And if it *is* morphine, they can give me as much of that as they like. I'm not scared of becoming a junkie if it makes me feel like this.'

Soon, Aunt Daisy arrives with Eileen. She's carrying an armful of magazines, a newspaper, Mum's current library book and her enormous, clunky mobile phone. There is a rule that only two people are allowed at the bedside, so I take the opportunity to slide off home, promising Mum that

I'll be back tomorrow as soon as it's visiting time.

The day after the biopsy is taken we have to see the Consultant, who is expected to visit the ward that evening. Mum is continuing to be given very strong painkiller medicine, which sends her to sleep for long periods and then makes her laugh like a hyena when she's awake, but now she is up and sitting in a chair, a drip attached to her arm. It's progress from how ill she was when she first arrived on the ward.

Just after eight o'clock, the Consultant arrives. She asks for a wheelchair to be brought for Mum to sit in while she talks to us in her office. Mum transfers into it with difficulty, and somehow we manage to make our way to the Consultant's office, together with my sister-in-law, who has just popped in to visit Mum.

The female Consultant's bedside manner is impeccable, in sharp contrast to the registrar we saw in A & E who had attempted to get Mum's medical history while she was sitting on a commode. After I've explained that Mum is deaf, she sits directly opposite her, so that Mum can read her lips. She takes her hand and says she mustn't worry about being deaf, and to interrupt her at any time if she hasn't heard or understood anything she is saying. She can't, however, sugar the pill she is about to deliver.

'I'm afraid you have a condition called Multiple Myeloma, Margaret. It's a disease that causes weakness in the bones.' She draws a little diagram of a bone on a pad of paper, peppering the drawing with a few dots. 'These dots represent little holes in the bone, caused by a type of cancerous cell in the bone marrow. It causes the holes to be punched out of the bone from the inside.'

'Cancer?' my sister-in-law and I say in shocked unison.

'Yes. It is what is causing Margaret so much pain. The vertebra in her lower back are affected.'

'Is it curable?' Mum asks, her bottom lip giving a little wobble.

'At your age, I'm so sorry, but you should consider it to be a terminal illness,' the Consultant says. 'Younger patients can sometimes go into remission with bone marrow transplants, but the older you are, the less likely transplants are to work.'

Although reeling with shock, I'm glad the Consultant is being truthful. Whatever we are faced with, we need the truth. I grab Mum's hand and squeeze it. She squeezes it back, and I get the feeling she is comforting me, rather than the other way round.

Mum's voice is unbelievably calm and rational when she eventually speaks. 'Can you treat it, then?'

'Oh yes, we can treat it with chemotherapy and other drugs to help with your bones. We have lots of options to relieve the symptoms.'

Mum dives straight in with the big question. 'How long have I got, do you think?'

'Well, it's difficult to say, but I've had Multiple Myeloma patients live for up to ten years with the condition. There are lots of drugs we can try until we get the right combination for you.'

'Will these drugs get rid of this awful pain?'

'I promise you will we do everything we can to manage the pain.'

'Will I be disabled? In a wheelchair?'

The consultant looks at me and then back at Mum. 'How mobile are you now?'

'I walk everywhere,' Mum says at the same time as I say: 'She's really fit for her age usually.'

The Consultant smiles. She's relieved Mum is taking the news so well. 'Once we've got things under control, I would say that you should be able to get around just fine, but you might need to take a bus or taxi instead of walking, and if you do walk anywhere you might need the help of a walking stick.'

'That's all right then,' Mum says. 'If I have to, I'll use a mobility scooter to get to the library and back, and I don't mind using a walking stick.'

Mum squeezes my hand again. 'Cheer up, Anne,' she says. 'Ten years makes me eighty-four before I die. It's a good old innings – it's not the end of the world, is it? It could be a lot worse.'

Fifteen, long, tortuous weeks later, Mum is unrecognisable from the apple-cheeked, cheerful grandmother who put her back out watering her garden. She sighs. Her breath smells of ketones, which the nurse has explained is as a result of her body processes being out of kilter because she's not eating. I feel a slight increase in the pressure of her fingers around mine. When she speaks, her voice is flat and breathy and her eyes are closed, but from the hand squeeze I know she is aware I'm there beside her.

'I've been on a diet all my life,' she whispers, 'and now look where it's got me. I'm still fat. I wish I hadn't bothered.'

Mum doesn't realise how much weight she has lost since August, but I don't tell her.

It's almost midnight and Mum is exhausted. She hasn't been out of her bed since Sunday afternoon. Yesterday, I rang round Mum's closest friends and asked them to come and visit her in Cransley Hospice today, if they were able. While her friends sat with her this afternoon, Aunt Daisy and I took the opportunity to go home, have a bath and put on some clean clothes. It was the first time I had been home since Monday night.

I want Mum to die now, right this minute. I can't bear to see her suffering any longer. I wouldn't let my dog suffer like this. Then panic kicks in and I feel a terrible guilt for wanting her to die. I have to cherish every single second I have left with my wonderful mother, who is so intelligent (but always denies it), so funny (without knowing it) and who has fought this sneaky, unpredictable form of cancer with magnificent spirit and dignity for the last fifteen weeks (but who keeps insisting she is a pathetic wimp).

Chemotherapy hasn't worked. Her kidneys are now failing and her heart is weak. On Sunday, we were told that she didn't have much longer, but, somehow, she's still here – in her wakeful spells sharing profound statements about living and loving and making funny observations like the one she has just made. Since Sunday, several times she has been insistent she can see Dad waiting for her and has reassured me that she isn't frightened of dying. She can't understand why everyone else can't see him, sitting patiently on the end of her bed, or by her bedside reading the Daily Mirror. Aunt Daisy is the only one who believes her. (Surprisingly, her Consultant assures me that it is very common in patients who are approaching death, and that she now believes it herself.) It creeps me out, to tell the truth, especially when her eyes light up and she points towards him, and even describes what he is doing, or what he is wearing, when I'm on my own with her in the middle of the night.

I'm so tired, I can't function properly. After my bath this afternoon, I drifted off to sleep on the sofa at home. Whenever I'm tired or stressed, and go to sleep in the daytime, I suffer from sleep paralysis and sometimes it is accompanied by hallucinations. Once, a few years ago, the television was on and, as I watched the screen, unable to move a single muscle or cry out to alert my husband to the fact I was having an "episode", the actor on the screen began speaking to me personally. Then, another time, my grandma Rose was on her hands and knees searching on my living room floor for a lost button from her cardigan. Paralysed, able only to blink and move my eyes, I lay on the sofa, watching my husband reading a Shooting Times magazine while my dead Grandma crawled around on the floor at his feet. I remember being unreasonably cross with him afterwards for not realising I was suffering from sleep paralysis.

Having a sleep paralysis episode is terrifying. Some sufferers actually feel and see imaginary clowns or alien-like creatures jumping up and down on their chests, trying to hurt them. They feel as if they are about to suffocate. Thankfully, I've never experienced that terror. My hallucinations have never been of the malevolent kind.

It happened to me again today. I'm not surprised. I'm right in the middle of one of the most stressful times in my life. I had woken up on the sofa after my bath this afternoon and couldn't move, no matter how much I tried to wave my hand in front of my face. I could feel my hand and arm going up and down, and my fingers wiggling frantically, but there was nothing in front of my eyes. I knew that if I kept my eyes open there would probably soon be a hallucination – and there was. Dad was sitting in one of my armchairs drinking a mug of tea and watching the television. He was wearing his old green gardening jumper, sitting forwards with his elbows on his knees, cradling his tea in his hands, concentrating hard on the programme that was on at the time. Thankfully, he didn't look at me. If he had looked my way, or spoken to me, I think I might just have died with fright. It was the cruellest of hallucinations, but, even as it was happening, I knew it was just that – a product of my imagination. Why couldn't it have consisted of a laughing, dancing life-size Peter Rabbit, like the last time I had sleep paralysis?

I don't know how much longer I can keep going. I just want it all to be over.

Mum has drifted into a deep sleep again and so I gently slide my hand from under hers and stand up. I might as well grab a coffee while she is asleep. When I open the door to Mum's room, I see my brother at the end of the corridor, holding the swing doors open for Aunt Daisy. I can't believe she's come back to the hospice again after being here nearly all day. If I feel exhausted at the age of fifty, how tired must she be at the age of ninety-one?

'Eileen is picking me up at nine o'clock,' Aunt Daisy explains, 'and then I'll come back again early tomorrow so that you can have a bit of a break again.'

'She's gone back to sleep now,' I say.

My brother suggests that Aunt Daisy and I go into the day room, while he takes over and sits with Mum. Aunt Daisy produces a packet of chocolate chip cookies and an angel cake from her bag as a contribution to the day room's store of goodies. I don't need asking twice!

When in the day room, I tell Aunt Daisy about the sleep paralysis episode I'd experienced that afternoon. She already knows I suffer from it, because she occasionally does, too. So did my grandma, Rose. When I'd mentioned it to my doctor years ago, he said it was quite often hereditary.

Her hand flies up to her mouth in shock when I say that I saw my dad sitting in an armchair. 'It was just a hallucination, like the Peter Rabbit I saw last time,' I say with a sigh. 'But how cruel is life that it happened to be a hallucination of Dad in his green gardening jumper, looking normal, drinking tea while he watched the telly. I'm just glad he didn't look at me, or speak to me. If he had done, I would have died of fright.'

'He was wearing his gardening jumper?' Aunt Daisy asks.

'Yes. Do you remember it? It was really scruffy and unravelling around the neck. Mum used to try and throw it out, but he always used to retrieve it, saying it had plenty of wear left in it.'

'Oh Anne. I really think he *has* paid you a visit. Remember just after he died, Margaret was making tea in the kitchen and he came to her and gave her a hanky to wipe her runny nose?'

'Oh yeah,' I say. 'I remember.'

'Well, it's *tea,* isn't it? If he was drinking tea in your hallucination, then he was trying to tell you, without frightening you, that it was really him because your mum was making tea when he visited her just after he died.'

'It's just all in my imagination, Aunt Daisy,' I argue, but the huge amount of doubt creeping into my mind is making my heart thud so fast, it hurts.

I'm dreading the long night before me. I know that I will only have to say the word and Aunt Daisy will stay with me, but I can't ask her. She's far too old to stay up all night. When my brother walks into the day room, his daughter is with him. They say they will both stay with me throughout the night and we can take shifts. My brother raises his eyebrows when I say I'm scared to be alone with Mum in the middle of the night, but I sense he knows what I mean.

We have a decision to make on Mum's behalf. The nurses have taken out her hearing aid. I try to imagine whether it would be a blessing in your last hours on earth to be completely isolated from the world around you, or whether you would want to want to be part of every moment. We decide we will have the television on, very low, and will put Mum's hearing aid in for her. Mum might have been deaf for most of her life, but she was always well able to shut herself off from her surroundings if it was too noisy or confusing to her, even with her hearing aid in. She used to panic if the batteries ran out, or if she had temporarily mislaid it. We agree that, without it, Mum will feel isolated and alone, and it's important that we make every effort to ensure she feels loved and cherished in her last hours.

It's a long, long night. There are times when Mum is constantly restless, but not awake. A nurse arrives with a syringe driver and places in a line in her neck. She explains that it will be much easier to manage Mum's medication and keep her comfortable.

In the morning, my brother and his daughter leave the hospice and there is a short period when I'm alone with Mum. I'm willing her to wake up. I desperately want to talk to her, alone, because I want to tell her that I think I've seen Dad, too.

When Aunt Daisy arrives during the morning, Mum still hasn't woken up. I suspect the medication she is being given through the line in her neck is keeping her asleep. She looks settled and peaceful. Aunt Daisy is obviously here for the rest of the day, because her shopping bag is like Doctor Who's Tardis and she pulls out her knitting, three packets of biscuits, fruit, enough sandwiches to feed a football team, magazines and a crossword book.

'Did you manage to get some sleep?' she asks me. The look of love in her eyes is so transparent and pure, I know the transition from being my great-aunt and godmother to taking up the baton as my surrogate mother is now beginning.

'A couple of hours. I'll have to nip home at some point today to have a bath and get changed,' I say with a yawn. 'But I'm not going to have forty winks on the sofa again after yesterday's episode.'

I tell her that my brother and I have decided to put Mum's hearing aid back in for her. She agrees with our decision, saying that she knows Mum would want it, if we could ask her. Aunt Daisy gently takes Mum's hand and leans in close to her ear, whispering, 'Margaret. I'm here. I'm going to stay with you all day so that Anne can go home for a couple of hours.'

There's no response. Not even a flicker. Aunt Daisy leans over to the bedside table, extracts a tissue from a box and wipes a tear from the corner of her eye.

She then tells me the story of when Mum was born. I've heard it all before, but she tells it with such love and passion, I'm spellbound. The bond between my mother and her aunt was forged at the very moment of her birth and has endured for the entire seventy-four years of her life.

'Do you think you are soul-mates?' I say.

'I've always known we are,' Aunt Daisy replies. 'Babies bring their own love with them when they are born. Loving your mum has never taken away any of the love I feel for my own children, the same as it didn't take away Margaret's love for Rose. It's something very special, Anne. Soul-mates can be anything to each other, not just husbands and wives. In our case it is aunt and niece.'

There's a tightly-wound ball of emotion in my throat and I gulp. I can't allow myself the luxury of crying just yet. I've got to keep a grip on myself because today might be the day my mother dies. If Aunt Daisy is here when it happens, she will have been there when mum was born and there when she dies, too.

'I'm so glad you two have lived together for the last five years,' I say.

'I just want her back,' Aunt Daisy whispers as she strokes Mum's hand. She leans in close to Mum's ear to speak to her again. 'Don't worry about Anne and me, Margaret. We are going to look after each other.' She looks up at me. I place my hand over both hers and Mum's so that the three of us can make a silent pact, even though Mum probably isn't aware of it.

Thursday is a peaceful day, full of grace and love. When I go into the day room to make coffee, a nurse follows me in and tells me some of the signs that indicate death is imminent. Sometimes, though, people just slip away with little or no sign. She says it often seems as if someone waits until their loved ones pop out to the toilet, or to the day room for a few minutes, and then choose their own moment of death, leaving behind a relative who feels guilty they weren't there.

It feels surreal to be discussing my mother's imminent death, but the care she has had in this lovely hospice has been magnificent. It's not just the patient the staff look after, but their families, too. The nurse gives me a hug, and it somehow makes me feel strong enough to face what is to come.

The day passes by with a steady stream of visitors. We tell everyone that Mum has her hearing aid in, and so we must assume she can hear something of what is being said in the room. Everyone puts their mouth close to her ear, speak their words of comfort and hold her hand. Most give her a gentle kiss on the cheek or forehead. Some people cry when they leave, saying that a lovely person like my mum doesn't deserve this to happen to her. I think everyone senses that this is her last day. We talk a lot, mostly about happy times but sometimes we laugh with each other about amusing incidents, too. All day, the atmosphere in Mum's room is not one of solemn reverence, as perhaps it should be, but instead everyone who visits tries to remain cheerful and, without being morbid or too sad, pay their last respects.

There is no mention at all by staff about how many people Mum has at her bedside, and some of her visitors linger in the hospice, sitting with each other in the day room for a while, catching up with either my brother or me over a cup of tea and a biscuit. Before we know it, it's nine o'clock again and Eileen has arrived to collect Aunt Daisy to take her home. She doesn't want to go and protests with the energy of a two-year old, but we are all worried about her, and so she reluctantly capitulates, making Eileen promise to be at her house early the next morning to bring her back here.

'Aunt Daisy's going now,' I say in Mum's ear. Just then, the door to Mum's room opens and my daughter, Emily, walks in with twenty-two month old Tyler in her arms.

'Tyler's just come to say a quick goodnight to his grandma,' Emily announces, sitting on the foot of the bed.

Now, Mum hasn't, as far as we have been aware, been conscious since yesterday evening when she spoke what may become her famous last words. But then it seems to me as if she is making a massive effort to open her eyes. Her hand twitches as if she is trying to reach something. Emily places her hand over Mum's and leans in, close to her ear to let her know she is here. Tyler is telling it like it is, in the loud voice of a typical toddler. He points at Mum, shouts 'Mam-ma' over and over again and bounces up and down on the end of the bed in his pyjamas to get her attention.

Mum's face brightens and she opens her eyes, very briefly.

Aunt Daisy is still sitting right beside her. The two of them share a fleeting look before Mum's eyelids close again. She has been conscious for less than half a minute, but we are all astounded. My heart pounds. I go out to tell a nurse that Mum has woken up, albeit very briefly. When everyone has gone home, the nurse returns with a small tray containing more medication, saying it's important now that she is kept pain-free. Together, the nurse and I give Mum a head-to-toe wash as best we can and change her nightie. Without any words being spoken, I know that she is making sure Mum is clean and fresh so that she can slip away in dignity. Two days previously, I had gone into town and tracked down two new nighties with long sleeves because

Mum's arms had felt cold to the touch. We put her in one of these new nighties and I comb her hair.

'There,' I say patting her hand. 'All nice and clean and looking very glamorous in that new nightie.' I fancy Mum's face brightens again. I instinctively know she is pleased with me. Telepathically, she laughs and tells me she is proud because I've managed to look after her without dropping her on her head or breaking one of her limbs.

Well, I like to imagine that's what she was thinking, anyway.

My brother and his daughter are back for the night shift. At midnight, I retreat to the day room and cover myself with a blanket in a recliner armchair. I manage to sleep for a couple of hours before I wake up and want to be with Mum.

I take over and tell them to try and get some sleep themselves.

'I thought you were scared to be on your own,' my brother says.

'Not any more,' I reply. 'I'm all right now.'

There is no change. Mum is peaceful and calm, but because she had woken up briefly a few hours ago, I'm constantly looking for signs she might regain consciousness again.

I'm grateful for the television and the background noise, even if it is on the lowest setting. At five-thirty I have an overwhelming urge to go out into the hospice garden for some air and so I open the patio door in the room and step outside. There is a seat about twenty feet away and I sink down onto it. The cool air washes over my face and arms like a refreshing shower and the feeling of peace is overwhelming and memorable. I glance back at Mum's room and realise I've left the door ajar. It's not a cold night, but today *is* 1st December and Mum might be in a draught, so I jump up and go back into her room, shutting the door behind me.

Countdown is on the telly. Countdown is Mum's

favourite television programme, and it was Dad's too. She is very good at it. I grab a piece of paper and a pen and whisper each of the letters in turn, into her ear, so that Mum can hear me if she is able to.

She doesn't respond throughout the next twenty minutes or so while the programme is on, but then, suddenly. I detect a change in her. Her breathing has slowed, but it isn't just that. I get the overwhelming feeling that she is peacefully drifting away. I press the buzzer and grab my mobile phone to ring my brother in the day room. A nurse arrives within seconds.

'Her breathing. It's changed,' I mumble.

My brother and his daughter appear. Standing behind me, my brother squeezes my shoulders with his hands, just like Dad used to do. He'd creep up behind me, say *boo* to make me jump and then squeeze my shoulders.

I haven't seen Mum take a breath since the nurse arrived. The music for the conundrum starts on Countdown and plays for the full thirty seconds before the nurse steps over to the other side of the bed and takes mum's wrist.

'That's it,' she says after a few seconds. 'She's passed.'

I look over my shoulder, expecting to see my brother, but he isn't there, directly behind me, but he is standing in the doorway to the en-suite bathroom rubbing his forehead in anguish, the sound of the toilet flushing behind him. I realise the pressure has lifted from my shoulders. My niece is crying on the other side of the bed, holding her grandma's hand.

The nurse says a few words in sympathy and then steps out of the room, leaving us. 'I'll be just outside the door when you need me,' she says. 'But take your time, there's no rush.'

Later that day, when my brother and I are talking about Mum's last words (about being on a diet all her life) and the wonderful realisation that Aunt Daisy was the first person Mum saw when she was born, and the last person she saw before she died, I ask him if he put his arm around me or squeezed my shoulders at the moment of her death.

'No,' he said. 'I went straight into the toilet after you rang me, and then, when I came out, Mum wasn't breathing and I was gutted because I'd missed it. There was nobody behind you. You must have imagined it.'

I tell him I didn't imagine it

Then I'm jolted by an unexpected frisson of elation through the fog of exhaustion and grief and feel like shouting with joy.

How can I ever feel sad for Mum when I know for certain that she is reunited with her beloved Brian again?

Part Six

Saturday, 23rd June 2007

This morning, I type the final full stop and straight away begin printing out the last chapters of the thick, unwieldy manuscript Aunt Daisy, Mum and I have created over the last five years. "Twisted Garlands" is finally ready for Aunt Daisy to read in its entirety. Of course, she has read most of it before, but only in discrete chapters. The manuscript is just short of 190,000 words, which is something I am a little worried about. It is twice as long as the average novel.

'Bring it over this afternoon – come early if you can,' Aunt Daisy says excitedly when I ring to tell her the manuscript is finished. 'I can't wait to get started on it.'

'I've got Tyler this afternoon,' I say.

'Lovely. I'll measure him for the new jumper I'm about to start knitting for him and he can watch that new Bob the Builder DVD I got for him.'

Over the last six months, Aunt Daisy and I have become even closer than before. No one can take the place of your mother, but Aunt Daisy has now become my surrogate grandmother. She's had a tough six months: first losing Mum, then she suffered a fall back in March while she was hanging out washing and hurt herself quite badly. Now, she's up and running again, firing on all cylinders as we say.

We've both worked very hard on the novel since Mum passed away. We have exercised an impressive amount of poetic licence, though. We have invented two more female characters – Lydia and Naomi – to get round some of the difficulties associated with writing a novel based on a true story, and we have both come to love them. They almost seem like real people to us, and we talk about them as if they are.

We have discussed some parts of the novel with family members who are still alive, explaining the reasons we have changed names and created additional characters, and even changed outcomes to make the story work for our readers.

I'm immensely proud of what I have created from Aunt Daisy's memories. Whatever the future holds for "Twisted Garlands", I know I could not possibly have worked harder or been more dedicated to its creation over the past five years.

After lunch, I assemble the manuscript to take round to Aunt Daisy's. En-route, I stop off at my daughter's house to collect Tyler for the afternoon. The charcoal sky overhead rattles and rumbles like a heavy old steam train and the large plops of rain splatter on the road in giant, inky spots. We make a quick pit-stop at the Co-op in St John's Road to buy a Milky Bar for Tyler and pick up some cakes for Aunt Daisy and me to enjoy later. When I strap him back into his car seat, the storm lets everyone know it means business, and there's a deafening thunderclap overhead.

'Dunder,' Tyler says pointing up into the sky. He doesn't seem frightened and leans forwards in his car seat to get a better view of the sky when there's another flash of lightning. I'm alarmed to see it's forked lightning, and even more startled when the lightning is accompanied by another, louder, clap of thunder almost immediately.

I'm not scared of storms. Well, not unless they are directly overhead, as this one is. I scuttle quickly around the car like a frightened mouse and slide into the relative safety of the driver's seat.

It's just a short drive to Aunt Daisy's house in Windmill Avenue, but the driving rain on the windscreen is beginning to sound like it is full of hard gravel and the car's windscreen wipers are barely coping. When we pull up, I look around at the two precious cargoes on the back seat: my grandson and my manuscript. I don't want either of them to get wet.

I decide to ring Aunt Daisy's house number from my mobile phone to ask her to open the front door ready to dash inside with Tyler. There's no reply. I then try her mobile phone. There's still no reply.

'Be a good boy and wait here,' I say to Tyler. 'Granny's just going to get Aunt Daisy to open the door for us, and then I'll come back and get you.'

'Dunder in the sky,' Tyler says pointing upwards, still fascinated by the thunderstorm raging around us.

I dash to Aunt Daisy's front door and ring the bell. After a few seconds I peer through the venetian blinds into her front room as my soaked hair trickles rainwater down my neck. The television is on, so she must be there. Perhaps she's upstairs? I can see through the living room to the kitchen and beyond because the kitchen door is open; so is the back door that leads into a lean-to where she keeps her collection of gardening tools and her mobile scooter.

I decide to shout through the letter-box. A waft of food cooking greets me.

'Aunt Daisy? It's only me. Don't worry. Take your time. I'll go and wait in the car out of the rain.'

I jump back in the car. My hair is hanging in dripping rats' tails around my head. 'Granny get wet,' Tyler says with a giggle.

After a minute or two, the front door still hasn't opened. I decide to ring her again, but again there is no reply. A horrible feeling begins in the pit of my stomach. With a shaky hand, I scroll down the numbers on my phone's contact list and dial Auntie Eileen.

'I don't want to worry you,' I say. 'But I can't get hold of your mum. I'm here – outside. She knows I'm coming this afternoon, and I can smell her dinner cooking through the letterbox, so I know she's there.'

'I'll come now,' Auntie Eileen says, ringing off quickly.

I decide to venture out into the rain again. There is a clap of thunder so loud it rings in my ears and deafens me for a few seconds. 'Dunder,' Tyler shouts as I open the car door. He is attempting to free himself from the car seat straps. He's obviously not frightened, so I can risk another trip to Aunt Daisy's front door, leaving him safely in the car.

I shout through the letter box again. Then, when there's no response I run round the side of the house and clamber up onto a black wheelie bin to look over the fence into the back garden. Not only is her back door open, but the outside door to the lean-to is open, too. The aroma of food cooking now smells of burning, and the horrible feeling inside my chest turns into an involuntary sob.

'Aunt Daisy!' I scream.

Eileen pulls up in her car. She runs down the garden path brandishing a front door key. We burst into the living room and the sight of Aunt Daisy's slippered feet in the kitchen greets us. She's fallen over and isn't moving.

'Mum?' Auntie Eileen yells.

We hurry through to the kitchen. Aunt Daisy's face lights up in a ghoulish yellow-grey colour as another flash of lightning outside lights up the dimly lit kitchen. I dial 999 on my phone. Just as the operator answers, there's a terrific clap of thunder.

The operator asks me lots of questions.

'We need an ambulance,' I keep saying, frustrated at the operator's questions. I've already told her Aunt Daisy is not moving or responsive. She says the ambulance is on its way and she needs me to concentrate and follow her instructions.

'My two year-old grandson is in the back of my car,' I say in a panic. 'And there's a terrible storm.'

'Is he strapped in?'

'Yes.'

'Then he'll be fine. Just leave him there. I need you to stay with your Aunt and do what I say.'

'Her daughter is here, too ...'

'Okay, pass the phone over to her, can you?'

I give my phone to Auntie Eileen and dash to the front door, worried about Tyler. The ambulance has just pulled up outside, its blue light flashing. I leave the door open for the paramedics while I run to my car to fetch Tyler, shouting to them that Aunt Daisy is in the kitchen.

When I return with Tyler in my arms, he is beyond excited at seeing the ambulance with its flashing blue light outside, shouting *"nee naw, nee naw"* at the top of his voice and trying to twist himself out of my arms. I don't know what to do with him. Am I about to create a sad memory in his innocent little mind of his Aunt Daisy being carried out on a stretcher?'

I bend down, find the new Bob the Builder DVD and shove it into the DVD player.

'Bob Builder,' he says excitedly as I plonk him in an armchair and spin it round, right in front of the TV screen so he can't see what's going on in the kitchen.

I unwrap the Milky Bar, shove the whole thing in his hand and just leave him there. I edge my way into the kitchen, trying not to get in the way.

'Is she ...?' I begin to say to Eileen.

'... breathing,' Auntie Eileen finishes. 'Yes. Just about.'

I go over to the oven and turn it off. Inside, there is an almost burnt chicken portion. A saucepan of peeled potatoes, thankfully with the gas unlit, sits on the top of the cooker.

A paramedic tell me it was lucky I was visiting Aunt Daisy that afternoon. Auntie Eileen tells him that, if I hadn't been visiting, she could easily have lay there, on the kitchen floor, until tomorrow because she had already spoken to her that day. The paramedics estimate that she probably fell around an hour ago, judging by the state of the shrivelled chicken portion I have just extracted from the oven.

Auntie Eileen goes off with Aunt Daisy in the ambulance. I stay in the house and wash up in the kitchen and tidy the living room before collecting together a small wash bag for her. I go upstairs and find a clean towel, a nightie and some underwear and busy myself until the Bob the Builder DVD finishes.

When I return to my car to strap Tyler back into his car seat, the first thing I see is the manuscript on the back seat. It's lit up in a golden ray of sunshine that is just peeping its way out of the dark clouds tumbling overhead. The rain has almost stopped now; the storm is over.

It's a good few minutes before I can compose myself enough to drive to the hospital to take Aunt Daisy's bag, not knowing whether she is going to survive. When I arrive at the hospital, a receptionist locates Aunt Daisy and directs me to where she is being treated. I have to leave her bag with the staff because they won't let me in to see her with Tyler and I can't find Eileen.

The next time I see Aunt Daisy she is in bed in a ward, hooked up to a drip. She's conscious, but the massive stroke she has suffered means she can't speak or move one side of her body. I hold her good hand and she squeezes it in acknowledgement. A nurse tells me she understands everything that is said to her and will blink once for yes and twice for no, even though she can't make a sound in response because her voice box is paralysed.

My eyes water and my lip trembles. Aunt Daisy blinks at me furiously.

'Look at the pickle you've got yourself into now,' I say, pulling myself together because I sense she is telling me not to be upset. 'It's a good job I was coming round on Saturday, wasn't it?'

She blinks once and squeezes my hand again.

'I hope you're going to be able to read that flaming manuscript after all this,' I say, trying to be upbeat. 'Or I suppose I'll have to read it to you, here, won't I?'

She blinks once, and I tell her that I'll read her a chapter at a time, and come in to see her after work for an hour each day until she is well enough to sit up and read it for herself.

A nurse appears and asks me who I am. I tell her that she is my grandma's sister, and that I am her Goddaughter. Then, with my eyes swimming with sentimental tears, I add that she is very special to me. The nurse says that she has never known a lady as old as Aunt Daisy have so many visitors. It's been two days since her stroke, but I can tell the staff are already very fond of her. Even though the stroke has badly affected her body, it can't take away her zest for life or her strong spirit, and it shines out like a beacon in the bay of the six-bedded room she now occupies.

The next day, I call into the hospital after work with Chapters One and Two of the manuscript in my bag. Quietly, I read them to her, holding her hand. She squeezes it periodically and I can tell she is pleased with it.

Over the next few days we make progress. Sometimes, Aunt Daisy is so tired she can't keep awake for more than a few pages, but Eileen rings me and says she is so grateful that I'm visiting every day at tea-time. It means that she can go home for a few hours, knowing that she isn't being left alone until Trevor arrives during the evening. Some of the nurses have told her they are sneaking in and listening, too. They want to know when they can read it.

'If and when it's published,' I tell Auntie Eileen. 'And definitely not until Aunt Daisy has read it all.'

One day, Aunt Daisy has an unexpected visitor while I am there. Her eyes well-up with surprised, happy tears as he slides into the seat I had been occupying whilst I read quietly to her.

I don't know him well. He is a distant relative and lives in Lincolnshire. He tells me he has recently been ill and looks old and tired since the last time I saw him. He does, though, have quite a major part in Aunt Daisy's life story because he was such an important part of her life in his younger days.

He's been driving for nearly two hours. I offer to fetch him a cup of tea and a sandwich and he accepts my offer gratefully. When I leave the ward, I look back over my shoulder and the love radiating between the two of them is obvious.

When I return, Aunt Daisy has drifted off to sleep again.

Oliver and I talk while he drinks his tea and eats his sandwiches. After asking about each other's families, our conversation drifts to the manuscript and his place in Aunt Daisy's life story.

'She loved you from the second she saw you packed into a cardboard box when she picked you up from the train station,' I say.

'And I've *always* loved her,' Oliver says, gazing at Aunt

Daisy as she sleeps. 'She should have been my mother. She always says she would have adopted me, if she'd been allowed to. And I know my life would have been very different with her as my mother. I had a terrible upbringing, as you know from the story.'

'Your story is one of the central plots in the book,' I say. 'There's not many people can say they were packed into a cardboard box during the war and put on the early morning goods train to travel, unaccompanied, to Kettering, to live out the rest of their life in a huge lie. I can't let you read it yet, though, because I promised Aunt Daisy she would be the first person to read the entire manuscript and I'm only about half way through reading it to her.'

We then chat about writing. It turns out that he has dabbled a little over the years and is really keen to write his own memoir, once he feels well enough.

After a while he says, 'I know it's a big thing to ask because I've already given my blessing to you including my story. But, as you've already said, you have written this book as a novel, not a memoir, so do you think you could possibly change it and kill me off as a baby so that I can write my own memoir? I'm really sorry if it's going to make a lot of work for you.'

My heart sinks. It's going to take a huge amount of re-writing to edit Oliver out of the story. We notice, then, that Aunt Daisy has woken up and has obviously been listening.

'What do you think, Aunt Daisy?' I ask her.

She blinks. Once. Then squeezes Oliver's hand.

Each day, I carry on with the reading of the manuscript, despite knowing I am going to have to re-write it to take account of Oliver's wishes. Despite his terrible upbringing (at the hands of the woman who was really his grandmother and, right up until he found out the truth in his late-fifties, believed was his mother), he is one of the world's nicest people, and his life story is, indeed, very special. I can understand why he wants to tell it for himself.

416

By now, Aunt Daisy is becoming much weaker. She can't swallow; so she can't eat. It's not possible to fit a feeding tube, either, and the only nourishment she is getting is through the drip in her arm. Her lips are very cracked, despite everyone's efforts to keep them moist, and she is still unable to make more than a very basic grunt or two. Despite this, I don't think she is in pain, and she can't possibly be bored because she has so many visitors.

'Oh, Aunt Daisy. What on earth do you want me to do with Oliver's story? I think I'll have to come up with some suggestions and then you can tell me yes or no. Do you think there is any other way, rather than killing him off?'

She blinks once. Then, a few seconds later, she blinks twice. I understand – she doesn't know the best way to do it, either.

I eventually finish reading the manuscript to her at her bedside. The ending was written about three months ago. It is pure fiction because we had both agreed that it wasn't possible to write an ending based on the true story and have used the fictitious characters of Lydia and Naomi in the last few chapters.

'Well, that's it then,' I say brightly. 'The End. This last part of the story has gone off course a bit, but our readers will sympathise with the modern day characters. I think the ending works pretty well and demonstrates the danger of keeping secrets about parentage, which is what we wanted to achieve.'

Aunt Daisy grunts and is clearly trying to tell me something.

'Do you think it's ready to send off to agents – once I've edited Oliver out?' I ask her.

She blinks twice. So no, she doesn't think it's ready for submission. Now I have to try and guess which part she's not happy with.

'Is it the ending we need to change?'

She blinks once, grunts again and raises her good hand slightly from the bed.

I then make a few suggestions for changes to the ending,

417

all of which result in two blinks. She must be getting so frustrated with me because I can't understand what she wants me to change.

'But we can't have another ending, can we? The last part of the book is about fictitious characters. We can't suddenly start going backwards halfway through the novel.'

Aunt Daisy's eyes are shut. She opens them briefly and then there is a definite solitary blink.

'Why are you saying *yes?*' I whisper.

She blinks again. Once.

'Okay,' I say, with a thump in my throat. 'I think I get it. Do you want the ending to mirror what is happening now?'

She shuts her eyes for a few seconds, opens them, blinks once and then shuts them again.

'As long as you're sure ...'

She grunts, without opening her eyes. She's exhausted. I need to let her sleep.

***

Aunt Daisy passed away in hospital one Sunday afternoon in early August, very peacefully, with her family by her side.

I've tried several times at this point to write a paragraph that describes accurately how bereft I felt once Aunt Daisy had gone, but writing about her in the same sentence as the word *death* just doesn't seem appropriate. She was the strongest, most *alive* woman I have ever known. You don't have to be wealthy or an academic genius to possess natural wisdom and emotional intelligence. She was, I think, one of this world's ordinary people who possess something very noble and rare – heroic virtue.

Perhaps Aunt Daisy, Mum and I shouldn't have written the novel that became the Jefson family trilogy. Maybe Aunt Daisy's wisdom would have been better channelled into writing another book completely.

A *"How To"* book on life.

Postscript

The family's real name was Jeffcoat.

My Great Aunt Daisy's real name was Rita Crick, but it is of no consequence whether other characters bore their own name or a pseudonym in the novels.

On 11th November 2016, Barbara Harris (Eileen in the novels) passed away in her sleep, aged 83 – just five weeks before *Ashes on Fallen Snow* was due to be published. It is a fitting tribute that I dedicate this book to her, in recognition of her valuable input and support in the writing and re-writing of the trilogy, which has, incredibly, now taken almost fourteen years.

The novel was originally entitled *Twisted Garlands*. After coming within a cat's whisker of being traditionally published, and on the recommendation of a literary agent, the novel was split into the trilogy that became *Sunlight on Broken Glass, Melody of Raindrops* and *Ashes on Fallen Snow*. Sadly, the trilogy didn't quite make it by traditional means, and so I took the difficult decision to publish independently instead.

It has never been possible to discover the identity of the person who placed an inscription in memory of Tom Frisby Jeffcoat in Kettering's Book of Remembrance, but this memorial, accompanied by a red rose, bears testimony to the fact that, despite his multi-faceted and colourful life, he was loved. Had it not been for this inscription, the trilogy would never have been conceived, of that I am sure.

The inscription is from the 23rd Psalm.

My Grandma, Rose Foster (real name), had an iron will, an independent mind and a big heart and I hope you, as a reader, have grown to know and love her through her character in the novels. She always believed in God and led her life accordingly. She was generous, kind and, above all, forgiving. She was forever helping other people and for many years attended Carey Baptist Church in King Street whenever she was able. If anyone was able to forgive Tom, it would have been Rose. If anyone who knew Tom Jeffcoat can enlighten me, I shall be eternally grateful. Otherwise, I shall let the tale rest here and assume it must have been his daughter, Rose, who had second thoughts about placing the inscription and did so in secret, without telling anyone else in the family.

Rest in Peace, Tom. On behalf of your family, I forgive you, too.